The Prisoner
of Eldaron

Crimson Worlds
Successors II

Jay Allan

Crimson Worlds Series

Marines (Crimson Worlds I)
The Cost of Victory (Crimson Worlds II)
A Little Rebellion (Crimson Worlds III)
The First Imperium (Crimson Worlds IV)
The Line Must Hold (Crimson Worlds V)
To Hell's Heart (Crimson Worlds VI)
The Shadow Legions(Crimson Worlds VII)
Even Legends Die (Crimson Worlds VIII)
The Fall (Crimson Worlds IX)
War Stories (Crimson World Prequels)

Also By Jay Allan

Gehenna Dawn (Portal Worlds I)
The Ten Thousand (Portal Worlds II)
Into the Darkness (Refugees I)
The Prisoner of Eldaron (Successors II)
The Dragon's Banner

Coming Soon

Shadow of Empire (Far Stars I)
Shadow of the Gods (Refugees II)
Homefront (Portal Wars II)
The Black Flag (Successors III)

www.crimsonworlds.com

The Prisoner of Eldaron

The Prisoner of Eldaron is a work of fiction. All names, characters, incidents, and locations are fictitious. Any resemblance to actual persons, living or dead, events or places is entirely coincidental.

ISBN: 978-0692514023

Chapter 1

Freighter Carlyle
Epsilon-14 System
100,000 kilometers from Atlantia Warp Gate
Earthdate: June, 2319 AD (34 Years After the Fall)

"All systems fully operational, Skipper." Cal Durham looked across *Carlyle*'s tiny bridge toward the freighter's captain. "We can execute the burn whenever you are ready."

Jackson Marne nodded. "Enter the course into the navcom, Cal. Acceleration at 3g." Three gravities of thrust was a lot for a freighter, and he knew he'd get some grumbling from the crew. But Marne was a navy vet, and he didn't have a sympathetic ear for pointless whining. Before the Fall he'd served in Augustus Garret's fleet, where he'd become accustomed to stretches of five or six gravities sitting at his workstation—and thirty or more crammed into the acceleration tanks. And *no one* bitched to Augustus Garret about his orders, however uncomfortable they were.

These powder puffs have never been in a tank. They have no idea what real spacers deal with.

Marne had been hauling cargo since the days just after the Fall, almost from the moment he'd mustered out of the fleet. He'd been born on Earth, and with the home world in ruins after the final war between the Superpowers, he'd chosen Atlantia as a place to settle, a decision made on data no more comprehensive than a few photos of the planet's magnificent rocky coasts. Atlantia had lived up to its reputation as an achingly beautiful world and a fine place to live, but Marne was a spacer at heart, and perfect weather and beautiful coastlines were pleasures relegated to brief periods between voyages. He'd gone to the naval academy at eighteen, and the merchant services almost immediately after he mustered out, which meant he had spent most of his adult life within the confines of a ship in space.

He'd been an executive officer on his first freighter, but for the last twenty-five years he'd served as a captain. The job had become routine to him, even with the increased threat of piracy in recent years. But the veteran skipper was nervous about this run. *Maybe it's the secrecy*, he thought, trying to brush aside the tense feeling in his gut. The public manifest stated that *Carlyle* was carrying pharmaceuticals, some medicinal, some recreational—and all derived from the sea life teeming in Atlantia's bountiful oceans. For decades, indeed, ever since the planet had been colonized, its only exports of significant value had been an assortment of products derived from the oceans that covered 90% of its surface.

But that's not what we're really carrying. Our actual cargo is far more valuable, almost beyond price.

Carlyle didn't have a load of drugs or a stasis-preserved hold full of delicacies from the sea, not on this run. Her bays instead carried very special ores, raw material rich in stable trans-uranium elements, the first shipment since production on Glaciem had been restored, after a still-unexplained attack on that world that had left dozens of mine workers dead.

Cavenaugh Freight was the oldest and largest shipping firm on Atlantia, the only one even marginally comparable to the great transport combines that had developed on the wealthier worlds since the Fall. Marne hadn't been at all surprised when the government entrusted the very special cargo to Cavenaugh, but he'd been more than a little startled when Elsworth Cavenaugh told him he and *Carlyle* had been selected for the run. Marne was a senior captain, and he'd been reasonably close to old man Cavenaugh back when the company had been smaller and its operations more informal. But the firm was much larger now than it had been years before, and the former CEO was well over one hundred years old and long retired. Elsworth IV was now in charge, and Marne had never had a close relationship with the old man's arrogant offspring. He was among the most experienced of Cavenaugh's captains, but he'd never played the social and political games it took to obtain high profile voyages.

Whatever the reasoning that had put him in command, Marne knew the significance of the run. Atlantia, though one of the older colonies, had never been a particularly wealthy world. Its pharmaceutical products enjoyed heavy demand, but they were expensive to manufacture, and that kept profit margins fairly low. And the planet needed many imports—electronics, software, vehicles. Its general lack of industrialization created a trade deficit that had plagued its economy since the Fall. The final war between the Superpowers had freed all the worlds of Occupied Space, but Atlantia, for all its natural beauty, had been more prosperous under Alliance control than as a truly independent planet.

But now that will all change. All because of Glaciem.

The frigid world on the outskirts of Atlantia's solar system had barely been explored for most of the 130 years since the first colonization party transited in to the Epsilon Indi system. Indeed, men had lived on Atlantia for half a century before they'd even bothered to name it. It was far from the warp gates and so distant from the primary there was little reason to even think about it...just another lifeless rock of little value. That was until one of the rare scientific expeditions to the frigid planet discovered something extraordinary. Glaciem was one of the eleven places in Occupied Space where STUs had been found to exist in naturally-occurring deposits.

Stable trans-uranic elements were super-heavy metals, materials ensconced on the period table north of uranium, far north in the case of the very special isotopes in *Carlyle's* hold. Many such elements had been synthesized in laboratories over the years, but most were extremely radioactive, with half-lives too short to allow the creation of meaningful quantities. However, the ore Marne's ship was carrying was rich with a very special element, number 164 on the periodic table, dead center in a still poorly understood phenomenon known as the second island of stability.

For reasons human science had not yet fully explained, there were two small segments of elements on the periodic table that produced isotopes far more stable than those around them. The first island existed in the low-120s, and the elements in that range had half-lives of days and weeks, while those just before and after decayed in microseconds. But it was the second island that produced truly useful elements, with half-lives in the millions of years. These materials were still radioactive, though far less so than those outside the island. There was a plethora of uses for such heavy metals, but the most important was in spaceship drives, where even minute quantities could easily be converted to less-stable super-heavy elements and achieve critical mass almost instantaneously, with the release of enormous energies.

The elements in the second island had been known for over a century, but they had been produced only in the lab by particle accelerators. The process was almost incalculably expensive, at least when producing quantities useful for anything but research. It had been widely believed that no such element would be found in a naturally-occurring state, but that assertion had been proven profoundly wrong when a party of explorers discovered the first veins of the material on a frozen moon in the Beta Cariolis system.

No one had developed a credible hypothesis to explain why the material was found on a few rare—and in nine cases out of eleven—frigid worlds, but that didn't stop the gold rush mentality every time a new source was found. And now Atlantia had its own priceless resource, one that promised to expand and invigorate the planet's economy for generations to come.

That's the future down in my hold, the promise of prosperity for millions of Atlantians.

If it gets through.

Carlyle was a strong ship, one of the best-armed in the Cavenaugh fleet. She was a match for most pirates, one of the reasons Marne had only been attacked once in the almost sixty trips he'd made as her captain. And the true nature of her cargo was a closely-guarded secret. When *Carlyle* returned, Marne knew he and his people would be fifteen minute celebrities, the guardians of the first delivery from the mines of Glaciem. Their single cargo run would double the value of Atlantia's exports by itself, and the potential wealth from fully exploiting that frozen planet's treasure was almost incalculable. Atlantians had long enjoyed their planet's magnificent climate and almost unimaginable natural beauty, but soon they would feel the effects of an influx of real wealth, something none of them could have imagined just a few years before.

But fame, however fleeting, still lay ahead. For now, only a handful of people outside of the crew had any idea what the ship was carrying. *Carlyle*'s launch had been unexciting in appearance, just another run of routine pharmaceuticals to the eyes of anyone interested enough to pay attention.

Still, Marne had a bad feeling. *Carlyle* was bound for Arcadia, a four jump run from Atlantia, and one that didn't involve passing through any high risk areas. But he couldn't shake the discomfort that had plagued him since his ship's launch. His cargo was classified, but he didn't think much of peoples' ability to keep secrets. All it would take was one bout of bragging by the pompous Elsworth IV or a politician's loose lips in bed with his mistress, and the word would be out. And every pirate in Occupied Space would salivate at the chance to bag a cargo of STUs.

"How's the scope?" Marne had been asking the question every half hour since he'd been on the bridge. It was a waste of time, he knew. The AI would warn them immediately of any contact. But it made him feel better to check. Epsilon-14 was a useless system, its three planets so utterly without value no one had ever maintained so much as an outpost there. It's only use was as part of the quickest trade route between Atlantia and Arcadia…and Marne knew for a fact there were no Arcadian vessels scheduled for a run to Atlantia right now.

"Clear, Skipper. No contacts." Durham didn't sound bored

or irritated as Marne knew he'd be if their roles were reversed. *Your paranoia has probably rubbed off on him. He's been glancing down at the scope every few minutes for the past six hours, even when you haven't asked.*

Cal Durham was a great executive officer, and Marne knew he was lucky to have him. He'd have sworn Durham was ex-navy, but he wasn't. He was just one of those rare people who seemed born to spend their lives blasting through the depths of space, and he was an odds on favorite to secure a captain's berth before long. Perhaps he'd even take over *Carlyle* one day soon.

Marne himself was close to retirement, perhaps another trip or two, and he'd be done. He'd spent a life in space, and as much as it so often seemed like home, he knew it wasn't. In recent years his thoughts had focused more on the cost of a career like his. He was ready to hang up his captain's uniform and try to repair some of the devastation his decades in space had wreaked on his personal life.

He had an estranged wife, one who'd tried for years to deal with the endless separations until she'd finally decided she just didn't care anymore. And a son and a daughter he hardly knew, both grown now and harboring their own resentments for childhoods spent mostly without a father. He'd told himself there was still time, but he wasn't sure he really believed it. They didn't hate him, he was fairly certain of that. He hadn't been an abusive monster, and his career had supported them all, including expensive educations for both children. They just didn't know him, not really. He was like nothing to them, someone who should have been part of their lives, but for the most part, wasn't. He suspected that might be harder to overcome than if he'd done something truly awful.

Forgiveness is one thing, difficult perhaps, but attainable. But how does one overcome irrelevance?

"Skipper, I'm getting energy readings from the Wolf-441 warp gate."

Marne snapped his head toward Durham, feeling his stomach clench as he did. "Full power to scanners, Cal. It's probably nothing to worry about, but let's make sure." Marne didn't believe that. He didn't believe it for a second.

*   *   *   *   *

"Scanning report complete, Captain. It appears to be an Atlantian freighter—a fairly large one, approximately 150,000 tons displacement." Lars Treven's tone was mundane, professional, but it was lacking enthusiasm. Atlantian ships tended to be poor prizes. Other than an occasional shipment of some of the more sought-after of its pharmaceutical exports, the planet's freighters were barely worth attacking.

"All hands to battlestations, Mister Treven. We have ourselves a target." Ivan Yurich held back a smile at Treven's lackluster tone. He knew his first mate was expecting a mundane cargo from the Atlantian ship, one that would barely cover the expedition's costs. But Marne knew better.

He had been *Black Viper's* captain for ten years, the first six as an independent pirate, and the last four as a member of the Black Flag Syndicate. He'd enjoyed being answerable to no one, but finally the Black Flag had made him an offer he couldn't refuse—stunning upgrades for his ship at no cost and an ongoing intel feed leading him to the richest targets in Occupied Space. His recruitment hadn't been all carrot, though. Significant stick had been in evidence as well, especially when his contact assured him, without any detectable emotion, that he'd walk out of their meeting a member of the syndicate...or with a bounty on his head so large, every pirate and adventurer in Occupied Space would be after him.

His ship's name had simply been *Viper* then, becoming *Black Viper* when she bowed to the nomenclature of the shadowy organization. His new allies—masters?—had been true to their words, and the value of his ship's prizes had increased dramatically. The Black Flag organization had provided access to better venues to sell booty as well, and even after kicking 40% of the take upstairs, his profitability was way up, more than double what it had been in his days as an independent.

The massive increase in prize money had other advantages as well, not the least of which was recruiting quality crew members. He'd managed to ease out some of his less capable people over the last few years, and now he had more veterans of the various navies than ever before. That made his crew old—anyone who had served in a Superpower's navy was at least in his mid-fifties—but he found it to be a worthwhile trade. Younger crews were harder to control and more likely to do stupid things, while his combat veterans had lived long enough to appreciate a good situation. *Black Viper* ran much like a naval vessel, and that discipline showed in its extraordinary record of bagging major prizes.

Here was another example of the perks of being part of the Black Flag. Yurich didn't think much more of Atlantian prizes than his first mate, but he'd been assured there would be a freighter in Epsilon-14, one carrying a cargo of enormous value. Stable trans-uranium elements, a treasure beyond gold, beyond jewels. It didn't seem likely that an Atlantian ship would be carrying such a load, but four years of flawless intel had made a believer out of him. And it dovetailed with the vague rumors he'd heard that the Atlantians had discovered a source of the precious material somewhere in their solar system.

"The contact is sending us a message, Captain. They are identifying themselves as the Atlantian freighter *Carlyle* and requesting our ID."

Yurich allowed a little of the repressed smile slip onto his lips. He loved the chase, enjoyed watching his prey slowly figure out the danger…and then try to flee. He hadn't been particularly bloodthirsty as pirates go—it was more the excitement of the hunt that appealed to him, and he'd often allowed the crews of his targets to flee in whatever lifeboats or escape pods they had. But that was the past. The Black Flag had a few rules that were sacrosanct, and one of them was that no one got away. A valuable hostage might be taken here and there, but otherwise everyone got a bullet in the head or went out the airlock. Yurich had been uncomfortable with it at first, but he shocked himself with how quickly he'd adapted to being a cold blooded killer.

"Let her wonder who we are, Mister Treven. Bring us closer. Not a direct route, nothing that will make her bolt immediately." He knew the freighter's captain would be edgy to begin with, and the lack of a response to his communique would only make that worse. Pirates weren't common in Epsilon-14, but neither was commercial traffic. It was only a matter of time—and not much of it—before his target blasted its engines and made a run for it. But that was of no account. *Black Viper* had thrust capacity no freighter could match. If she ran, Yulich's ship would catch her. But it would be an easier raid if he could get closer before his prey took off.

Yurich looked down at his screen, calculating a course that would get his ship nearer without looking like it was closing to attack. "Three gees thrust, coordinates 076.098.223," he said.

"Three gees, 076.098.223," Treven snapped back. "Commencing now."

Yurich heard the roar of *Black Viper's* engines and felt the pressure pushing against him as his ship accelerated. "Activate needle guns."

"All needlers report ready, Captain." *Black Viper* had two laser cannons, but they were strictly for use in emergencies, when the ship found itself facing a dangerous opponent. The heavy weapons were too powerful, too indiscriminant for disabling potential prizes. Yurich's ship had its needle guns for that. The needlers were a pirate's weapon, thin, tightly focused beams designed to disable a ship without damaging its cargo.

Yurich stared at his display, watching the thrust slowly alter his ship's vector. If the Atlantian vessel hesitated another few minutes, *Black Viper* would be on her before she could do anything about it.

"Reading thrust from the enemy ship, Captain. I'd estimate somewhere between 3g and 4g." Treven lowered his face to his scope, and he paused for a few seconds. "It looks like they're blasting almost directly away from us…back toward the Atlantia warp gate."

Damn. This captain is good. And that's a lot of thrust for a freighter.

"Change course to directly pursue. Increase thrust to 5g."
Five gees would make everyone on *Black Viper* profoundly miserable—and it would degrade their performance too. But he
didn't have any intention of letting that ship escape back to the
Atlantia system. Not with the cargo he knew she had on board.
This prize was worth a dozen normal raids, and Yurich was
determined to get her.

*   *   *   *   *

"The vessel is changing its thrust vector, Captain. They
are blasting directly toward us." Durham looked up from his
workstation toward Marne. "They're accelerating at five gees,
Captain."

A cold feeling gripped Jackson Marne's gut. *Carlyle* was
maxed out just above 3g, and that meant she wasn't going to
make it back through the warp gate before the pirate caught
her. And Marne didn't have a doubt in his mind it was a pirate
chasing them.

"Arm all weapons, prepare to engage." His naval instincts
took over, and he felt the exhilaration he'd experienced years
before, when he'd served on one of the Alliance's cruisers. But
he'd been a junior officer then, with little responsibility beyond
following orders. Now he was in command...and *Carlyle* was
no Alliance warship. A pirate ship that could pull five gees was
probably strong enough to defeat any freighter, even one as
well-armed as *Carlyle*.

"Weapons armed, Captain." Durham's voice was shaky.
Unlike Marne, *Carlyle's* first mate had never served on a naval
vessel, never encountered a pirate in his years on various freighters. Marne could see his number two was trying to muster his
strength, just as he imagined the rest of the crew was doing. He
knew one or two of his people had survived a pirate encounter before, but to his knowledge, he was the only naval veteran
aboard.

Which is bad…because we're likely to get boarded. And that means combat at close quarters.

"Cut thrust, and bring us about." There was no point in running…they weren't going to get away. And if it came down to a fight, Marne preferred his people focused, not half out of it from carrying three times their weight around. Besides, he knew the enemy would try and target *Carlyle's* engines, and with no thrust he could try to protect them, keeping the front of his ship toward the pirate. Maybe his people could score a lucky shot, damage the enemy enough to give them a chance to make a run for it.

Maybe, but probably not…

"Engines disengaged," Durham said, struggling to sound confident. "Positioning adjustment complete. The ship's bow is vectored toward the approaching vessel, Captain."

"Range?" Marne damned well knew the range…it was on his own display. But he wanted to keep Durham focused on his duties, with as little time as possible to ponder their scant chances of success in the conflict now unfolding.

"Eighty thousand meters, Captain. Enemy approaching at approximately one thousand meters per second."

Marne took a deep breath. That was close range for military vessels, and one thousand meters per second was a crawl to the ships the Superpowers had used to fight their wars. But it was fast for pirates and the freighters upon whom they preyed, and eighty thousand meters was extreme range for *Carlyle's* two double-turreted laser batteries.

"We open fire at 60,000 kilometers." Marne knew he had one advantage, and one only. The pirate had to take his ship whole, and that meant he had to disable *Carlyle's* engines and weapons with their needle guns. Marne was under no such restrictions. He would be just as happy to blow the pirates to hell, which meant he could fire his heavier laser turrets at least 20,000 kilometers farther out. *Carlyle's* guns weren't warship turrets, but they were heavy weapons for a freighter.

"Seventy thousand kilometers. The enemy is still on a direct course. Decelerating now."

Of course. Zipping past us won't serve them. They need to board or their attack is a wasted effort.

He flipped his com unit. "Rand, are you and Jager ready?" *Carlyle's* two gunners were jacks of all trades, men from the regular crew who'd been trained to fire the defensive batteries. It was far from ideal in a battle situation, but it was all a freighter could afford.

Still, they're coming right at us. Rand and Jager should be able to rely on the AI for plotting. This pirate probably doesn't expect that we've got two double turrets. Get ready for a surprise...

"Yes, Captain," Rand replied. "We're ready." His tone implied anything but.

"Stay focused, both of you. I know you can do it." A lie, but a useful one. His two makeshift gunners needed every bit of confidence they could get.

"We are, Captain."

Still shaky, but maybe a bit better...

"Sixty thousand kilometers, Captain." Durham turned and looked toward Marne's chair.

Marne met his gaze and uttered a single word.

"Fire."

Chapter 2

Martian Council Chamber
Beneath the Ruins of the Ares Metroplex
Planet Mars, Sol IV
Earthdate: 2319 AD (34 Years After the Fall)

"My family has served the Confederation as long as there has been a Confederation. My great-great grandfather, Preston Vance, came here on the first colony ship. A Vance has served on this council as long as it has existed…and today, I stand here before you, and for the first time in my life, I am ashamed of that legacy. I never thought I would live to see the day this council would allow itself to be led by cowardice."

Roderick Vance stared around the room. The faces had different expressions, mostly variations on shock and surprise, though a couple were straight outrage. He knew his words had been direct, provocative. He'd been trying to get somewhere with his colleagues for months now, and his time and patience were at an end. This was his last attempt, to shock them into action…before he took far more drastic steps.

Katarina Berchtold was the only one who'd managed to maintain her poker face. Either she wasn't angry at Vance's harsh words, or she was hiding it well. Vance hadn't though much of Berchtold years before, during the crises preceding and in the aftermath of the Fall, but he had to admit she'd gotten wiser as she'd aged, and she was quite capable now. He imagined she understood his theatrics were intended to force some kind of meaningful response, and she had decided not to tip her hand. He had no idea where she stood on the issue, and that alone showed him how formidable she had become.

She looked like she was about to say something, but another voice intruded. "Your words are outrageous, Mr. Vance, and I for one have no intention of tolerating your abuse. This is the ruling council of the Martian Confederation, not some room full of peasants and supplicants...and you will treat us with the respect we deserve."

Vance didn't know what Berchtold was thinking, but he could read Boris Vallen like a book. Sebastien Vallen had been a longtime ally of the Vances, both Roderick and his father before him—and one of the few people Roderick had truly trusted, something that did not remotely extend to Sebastien's difficult and egotistical son.

I give you all the respect you deserve, Boris. None at all. Your father's death was a terrible loss, and all the more so because he left such a pathetic creature to fill his enormous shoes...

"We are past hurt feelings, *Mister* Vallen. I have no time to indulge your delusions of self-worth, nor to fence with you over etiquette."

Be careful...don't make this a fight between you and Boris. That won't help...

"We are facing a crisis that I believe is the most dangerous to threaten us since the Fall itself." Vance stared coldly at Vallen. "I'm sure you all remember the price Mars paid in that terrible event...and the horrors endured by the scattered survivors on Earth. Even now, three decades later, we remain deep underground, living in the tunnels our ancestors scratched out of the Martian landscape more than a century ago. The magnificent cities of the Confederation? The wondrous domes and the soaring architecture that spoke proudly of a Martian future? Gone, shattered...half buried under the encroaching red sands."

Vance's voice was deep, determined. He had secrets, plans and more plans, but his words were nothing but the truth. No Martian over forty years of age could help but recall the beauty of the surface cities, the great buildings that were now aban-

doned ruins under the broken domes. Vance had been the head
of Martian Intelligence, then as now, and he'd failed to stop the
disaster. He'd tried, fought as hard as he thought he could, but
it hadn't been enough. This time he had sworn to himself he
would not fail, whatever he had to do.

Whatever I have to do.

"Mr. Vance," Vallen said, his voice quivering with rage, "I,
for one, am tired of your dire warnings, of your endless lectur-
ing on what actions we must take. You offer no evidence, other
than a destroyed base on Eris. Perhaps you have uncovered
nothing more than a slaving ring, a common criminal enterprise.
Odious, a horror that stuns the sensibilities? Yes, certainly. A
crisis that threatens the Confederation? Doubtful."

Vallen paused, glancing around the table, clearly trying to
gauge the sentiment of the others. "May I remind you," he
said, "it was on your watch that the enemy ship was allowed to
approach Mars thirty years ago. It was you who sent our space
fleet into battle in the outer system, exposing us to the nuclear
attack that collapsed the domes…and drove us underground to
live the best way we could in these dark and depressing tunnels.
Now you…"

"The tunnels are well-lit, Mr. Vallen…and I believe your
estate, underground as it is, has some forty rooms. Decorated,
I might add, with half a dozen Old Master paintings imported
from Earth by your great grandfather and somehow saved from
the surface destruction…a fate all the more noteworthy since at
least a dozen of your family's servants were not so fortunate."

It was wildly off-topic, but he had to discredit Vallen any
way he could. The servants comment was particularly below
the belt. Sebastien Vallen had been the family patriarch then,
and Vance knew perfectly well he had ordered all of the family's
staff underground before the bombs landed. It was the major
domo, a man who had served the Vallens for almost sixty years,
who had sent them back to retrieve the family treasures. He also
knew the elder Vallen had felt guilt and regret about what had
happened until the day he died, and he'd ordered the precious
artworks stored away so he never had to look at them again.

Vance doubted the great man's son felt the same way...Boris Vallen had returned the paintings to the walls two days after his father's death.

"You can attempt to divert the discussion with lies about my family, Mr. Vance, but the fact remains. Your intelligence operation failed to warn us of the impending attack. You had dispatched our fleet to the outer system, laying us bare to the enemy. And we have paid the price for your failure for thirty years."

Vance didn't usually pay attention to Vallen's comments, but his adversary was hitting close to his weak spots. He might argue with Vallen's accusations—indeed, he knew the situation had been extremely complex three decades earlier, when the fateful events had occurred. He had not left Mars defenseless. Gavin Stark had managed his attack only because his forces had developed a virtually undetectable class of stealth vessels...and he had used one to sneak into orbit and launch the surprise attack. Still, Vance blamed himself, and he'd regretted that day for three decades. Indeed, it was one of the things driving him now, pushing him to desperately make his case. Roderick Vance might carry his regrets to his grave, but he'd be damned if he would allow another disaster...not while he still lived.

Vance took a deep breath, willing himself to remain calm. He and Vallen were trying to goad each other, and the one who lost his temper first would make his adversary seem more reasonable by comparison. "I will not spar with you endlessly, Mr. Vallen. Your father understood facts, he listened to reason. You do not. You may hurl your accusations at me as long as you wish. Indeed, I still carry my regrets of those fateful days so long ago. I still remember staring up at the domes, at the jagged remnants still standing and the lifeless streets and broken buildings that had been Ares City hours before. I recall the tumult, the desperate efforts to get our people underground, to minimize the losses from the devastation. We saved 97% of the population that day...saved our people. I was there, in the middle of it all."

Vance stared at the others in turn, focusing a few seconds

on each before moving his gaze to the next. "And yet much died that day, beyond the thousands who failed to reach safety in time. Decades of work, the struggles of millions to build our world…vanished in an instant." He slapped his hand down on the table. "I do not seek absolution for my efforts that day, nor will I argue who was at fault. That would be pointless, and it would do no good for anyone. But we cannot allow such a disaster to befall us again. Not ever. We must act and act now… and not allow the threat to grow."

He paused again, gathering himself, sucking in a deep breath. "Stand with me, my colleagues. Let us mobilize our forces. Vote with me to send troops to Earth, to aid the survivors there and to hunt down and destroy whatever force is kidnapping men and women to make slaves of them. Authorize our fleet to leave the solar system, to ally with the Black Eagles and the forces on Armstrong…and to scour space for signs of the enemy. Join with me, and let us take action. Before it is too late. Before we are once again staring into the abyss…"

He sat down, his eyes moving around the room, gauging the thoughts of the other council members. He'd given an impassioned plea, and he knew he had some friends in the room…or at least political allies. But he realized as he heard Vallen giving his own closing argument, he was going to lose the vote. He was sure he had made his point, won the debate in objective terms. But objectivity wasn't going to rule here, and neither was judgment. Fear was in control, and the men and women surrounding him were too afraid to commit to anything. Drawing inward, devoting all the Confederation's forces to its own close-in defenses felt safer to them. Vance knew their logic was flawed, that allowing an enemy to gain strength ultimately placed them all in greater danger. But the council couldn't see past their immediate fears to realize that, and they voted accordingly.

In the end, Roderick Vance was almost alone, only one of his colleagues switching sides and voting with him. To his surprise, it was Katarina Berchtold.

"Are you sure about this, Roderick?" General Astor sat in one of the massive wood chairs facing Vance's desk. The library was a beautiful room, paneled with cherry wood imported from Earth a century earlier and painstakingly cleansed of radiation when Vance had moved them from the ruins of his surface estate to the underground cluster of rooms that had been his home for more than thirty years. It had been breathtakingly expensive when his grandfather had imported it, all the more so for the costs of transporting the boards to Mars. Now, with Earth's cherry trees extinct, its value was beyond calculation, a luxury that literally could not be replaced at any price.

"Yes, Arch. I'm sure." Vance's tone was deadpan, without emotion. "I failed to act quickly enough once, and we've spent thirty years living in tunnels as a result. I won't let that happen again. Whatever I have to do."

"You are talking about treason, Roderick. About destroying the Confederation and making yourself a dictator." The general's voice lacked judgment or condemnation; he was merely stating facts.

"You know me, Arch, as well or better than anyone. Do you really think I want to do this? That it is lust for power that drives me?"

Astor shook his head. "Of course not. If I believed that, I'd have a company of commandoes on the way down here to arrest you." The officer sat motionless, his uniform as spare and unadorned as the commander of the Martian ground forces could make it. He shook his head slowly. "There is no other way?"

"I have been trying for months, Arch. I tried again this morning. They won't listen. They are committed to remaining isolationist, no matter what is happening in Occupied Space. I might be able to convince Kat Berchtold, but the rest of them won't even consider the possibility that the danger afflicting the survivors on Earth and the former colonies in space will eventually reach us as well. And we can't wait, Arch. I don't know what is happening, but I know in my gut it's bad, the worst crisis we have faced since the Fall. People are still disappearing from

Earth, despite the destruction of the base on Eris. And now I'm getting reports from some of the other systems...increasing piracy, crime waves, new regimes taking power. Something is going on, something coordinated. And whatever it is, we know almost nothing about it."

Vance's voice trailed off. It had been more than thirty years since the tragic events mankind now referred to as "the Fall," but he still bore the self-inflicted guilt, the feeling that he had failed to protect Mars, that if he had been more competent, if he had moved faster, he might have saved his world's great cit-ies...and the billions on Earth who had perished in the nuclear fires.

"They'll shoot you if you fail, Roderick. You and everybody who supports you." Astor's voice remained calm, despite the subject matter of their conversation. "And Boris Vallen will barely manage to restrain his glee as he gives the order."

"That's a pleasant thought," Vance replied sourly. "But it's a risk I have to take. And I'm afraid I've put you on the spot, old friend. If you don't turn me in, they'll consider you a part of it...even if you run back to your quarters and hide under the bed until it's over."

The general moved his hand back over his head, brushing his thick gray hair away from his eyes. "Well, Roderick, the way I see it, there are damned few people in this world you can trust... and even fewer with reliable judgment. And you fit in both camps for me. I'm in...with whatever you think is necessary." He nodded solemnly, and then his non-committal look gave way to a tentative smile. "I guess if I was too worried about getting shot I'd have picked a different career. I'm too old a soldier to let fear guide me now...and certainly not over loyalty to an old friend."

"Thank you, Arch. It means a lot." Roderick Vance had a reputation as a cold fish, but he couldn't keep the emotion out of his voice. He didn't think much of people, not most of them at least. But he was constantly surprised at the quality a scant few could exhibit.

"I have one condition though." The smile slipped from

the soldier's face. "When the crisis is over, we give back the power...we reconstitute the ruling council." He paused for a few seconds before continuing. "We both know Mars has never been a democracy, not really. I'm okay with that. We've both seen what people do with their votes, both on Earth and now out in the colonies. But the Confederation has never been a totalitarian regime either. And I'm not about to let it become one now. Not permanently, at least." Astor stared across the table at his friend. He'd laid down his condition, and he had a nervous look on his face as he waited for the reply.

"That's an easy one, Arch. Agreed...with all my heart. I don't want to rule Mars, my old friend, not even during the crisis. But I can't let disaster strike again, not when I can do something to make sure we're ready this time."

Astor nodded slowly. "But after we've come through the crisis, defeated whatever enemy or enemies are behind it all... you will restore the council?"

Vance smiled. "How is your Earth history, Arch?"

Astor looked confused. "Not too bad. Probably not what it should be. Why?"

"Are you familiar with the story of Cincinnatus?"

"Ancient Rome?"

"Yes. Cincinnatus was one of the most revered of the early Romans. He was appointed dictator not once but twice in times of crisis. He led his people to victory both times...and after each crisis abated, he immediately surrendered his powers at once and returned to his farm."

"You have no farm, my friend." The smile returned to Astor's face. "Yet I believe that you will be the Cincinnatus of the Martian Confederation."

"No, Arch, I will not. For Cincinnatus was granted his power by the Senate, and I will seize mine by force. I can hope only to be a pale reflection of the Roman legend. But I swear to you now, as a friend, as a member of the council, as a descendant of one of the earliest settlers of our world...whatever power I take, as soon as the enemy is defeated and the danger past, I shall give it up without question or delay, and I will retire to private life."

Astor stood up slowly and extended his hand. "Your word is all I have ever needed, old friend."

Vance leapt to his feet and took his ally's hand. "Thank you, Arch." He paused, and inside he pushed hard against the sadness that threatened to overcome him. He was gratified for Astor's support, but he knew he was being driven to do something he'd considered anathema his entire life. He had visions of himself, of the hell he would have unleashed on anyone else who'd tried to seize control of the Confederation. He knew it was different now, that he didn't have a choice, that the true evil would be to do nothing and perhaps allow millions to die. And despite the shadowy nature of the enemy, he had no doubt inaction would lead to disaster. But he still felt somehow...unclean.

He forced his doubts into the depths of his mind. There was no time for them now. "We'll need troops ready, Arch, ones we can count on to stand with us no matter what."

"I'll take care of it. I may need to shuffle a few units around, but I'll have them ready when you need them." He paused. "By the way, when will that be?"

Vance sighed hard. "Soon, Arch. Ten days...two weeks tops. I'm sure Vallen's people at least are watching me. And the sooner we devote all resources to unmasking our enemy the better our chance of success."

Astor shook his head. "Two weeks? That's not much time to plan a revolution." He turned and moved toward the door. "I'd better get going, Roderick. If you want those troops ready, I've got my work cut out for me."

Vance nodded. "Good luck, Arch."

"Good luck, Roderick...I think we're both going to need our share of it in the next few days."

Chapter 3

Freighter Carlyle
Epsilon-14 System
100,000 kilometers from Atlantia Warp Gate
Earthdate: 2319 AD (34 Years After the Fall)

Black Viper shook hard. The hit from the freighter had torn a gash in the hull, and air and liquids had spewed out into space, freezing instantly in the frigid vacuum. The force of the explosion threw the ship into a nasty spin, knocking the thrusters out of alignment and forcing Yulich to cut off the main engines.

"Fire positioning jets now," he roared, angry at the unexpected accuracy of the freighter's weapons. The hit itself wasn't too serious, but he had to get the ship's roll under control so he could reengage the engines and bring his needle guns to bear.

"Engaging now, Captain." Treven had his headset on, and he was getting reports from the engine room. Negating the ship's uncontrolled spin required firing a sequence of perfectly timed bursts from the ship's positioning engines. The small jets weren't powerful enough to build any meaningful thrust. They were intended to change a ship's physical bearing, not its thrust vector.

Yulich could feel the spinning begin to slow as the tiny jets fired. His eyes were fixed on his display, and he saw that another enemy shot had just missed.

That blast that hit us had to be from a 20 gigawatt turret at least. That's a heavy gun for a freighter.

"Arm the forward laser cannon," he said suddenly, the words

slipping out almost before he'd even thought about them. It was instinct, his naval experience manifesting itself. This was a well-armed freighter, and he was willing to bet she had a skilled captain too, probably also ex-navy. He scolded himself for expecting anything less on such an important shipment.

"Yes, Captain." Treven's tone was odd, a combination of resignation and relief.

Yulich understood, but he knew the first mate was misinterpreting his intentions. He wasn't giving up on taking the prize, he was just planning to soften it up a bit before moving in closer and taking it apart with the needlers. One blast, maybe two. The ship's cargo was metal ores, valuable but not fragile like a load of delicate electronics or pharmaceuticals. As long as they managed not to hit the hold itself, shaking up the ship a little shouldn't hurt the booty.

He flipped on the intraship com, connecting to the gunnery control room. "Listen carefully down there. I want one solid hit, two tops...just to soften up that ship. Anybody gets carried away and destroys the target, I'll throw him out the airlock myself. You understand me?"

"Yes," came the nervous reply.

Lintner, Yulich thought. *Good. He's the best man down there.*

Yulich hesitated. *Maybe I should wait it out...hold fire until the needlers are in range.* But then *Black Viper* shook again. Another hit, this one amidships.

Fuck, who the hell is at the targeting controls on that freighter?

"Fire!" he shouted. "Now!"

*   *   *   *   *

"Second hit, Captain! I think this one is more serious than that first. We're losing air from their midsection." There was fear in Durham's voice, but excitement too. His blood was up, and he was focused on the battle *Carlyle* and her crew were fighting for survival.

"Maintain fire." Marne knew that was easier said than done. *Carlyle* didn't have a warship's reactor, and that meant it took a long time to recharge the lasers. He wasn't sure if it was Rand or Jager that had tagged the pirate ship twice, but he was ready to put them both in for a bonus when they got back. If they got back. The fight was far from over.

He glanced down at his screen. The laser turret was charging, but the small bar was less than half colored in. The small number next to the graph read 39%. *Come on*, Marne thought, as if he could will the lasers to charge faster. Unfortunately, the laws of physics proved immune to his impatience. They'd get one more shot before the pirate's needle guns were in range, just one. By the time they charged up after that, the pirate's needlers would have blasted *Carlyle's* guns to slag.

Better make that shot count, boys...

Suddenly, the ship shook hard, and the lights blinked out for a few seconds. Marne grabbed ahold of his chair, but Durham slipped off his and fell hard to the deck. Marne hadn't expected the pirate to start shooting until he was in needle gun range, but apparently his gunners' success had provoked a harsh response.

"Damage rep..." Marne's voice trailed off when he realized his first mate was on the deck. He punched at the controls on his workstation, his eyes focused on his screen as he pulled up the report himself.

That was no needle gun. That was a laser cannon...and a damned bigger one than we've got.

The numbers scrolling past his eyes told a grim tale. That shot had knocked out a whole series of conduits, interrupting power flow to the lasers. The big guns were still getting power, but their recharge time was measured now in minutes, not seconds. That meant they were out of the fight...and *Carlyle's* chance of beating the pirate had gone down with them.

"You okay?" he asked, glancing over briefly as his second in command struggled to get back to his feet.

"I'm fine," Durham answered. But it was clear from his tone that 'fine' was an overstatement. He staggered back to his chair and sat down, his face a mask of pain, his left arm cradled gently in his lap. The lasers won't be ready to fire for four minutes, Captain," he said, telling Marne what he already knew. "Should we make a run for it?"

Marne sighed. Most captains would do just that—engage the engines and make a dash for the warp gate—but he was too old a veteran to kid himself. Their chances of making it were exactly zero. And with the power conduit damaged they had no hope in a laser duel. That left one thing, one last chance to avoid captivity or death.

"All hands are to prepare to repel boarders. I want everyone fully armed and ready in five minutes." Any pirate worth his salt had a large crew of skilled fighters for a boarding party. But it was *Carlyle's* last hope, however grim, and he was determined to take it.

He leapt up and walked to a small locker on the side of the bridge. He punched in a six digit code, and the door slid open, revealing an assortment of weapons and body armor. He reached in and grabbed a heavy vest, sliding his arm through one side and wiggling into it.

"I don't know what you can do with that arm, Cal, but try to get into one of these vests." He reached in and grabbed a belt and holster and strapped it on, slamming an auto-pistol into place. Then he took a heavy sub-machine gun, short-ranged but hard hitting. Perfect for fighting boarders.

He pulled out a heavy survival knife and snapped the sheath onto his belt. He was ready. As ready as he was going to be, at least.

*   *   *   *   *

Lars Treven stood in the breaching tube, waiting for the word to board the freighter. He had a simple survival suit under his body armor, nothing suitable for an extended EVA, but enough to keep him alive if he ended up in an area that lost life support...or even in deep space for a brief period. He was wearing a hyperfiber vest over it, with an ammo belt strapped across his chest. He held a compact carbine in his hand, and there was a sawed-off shotgun with a pistol grip jammed into a makeshift holster on one thigh. A sheathed blade hung on the other side, just in case it came to knife work.

Some of the crew complained about his insistence they wear survival gear under their body armor. The tight, heavily insulated suits were hot and almost torturously uncomfortable, but Treven had led a dozen boarding actions as *Black Viper's* first mate, and he believed in being prepared. He wasn't about to see one hull breach take out half his boarding party.

Once *Black Viper* had taken out the enemy's laser cannons, the rest of the space battle had been straightforward. As soon as they came in range, the needle guns made short work of the target's weapons and engines. The Atlantian ship was a floating wreck now, with life support and a full cargo hold...but not much else. *Except armed men*, he reminded himself. Not that he expected any real trouble securing the prize. *Black Viper's* crew were tough fighters, veterans of a dozens of boarding actions. They were more than a match for a freighter's complement.

But that doesn't mean some crewman from a transport ship can't put a bullet between your eyes.

"Alright, boys, let's stay sharp. These people managed to beat up the *Viper* pretty badly...don't let them do the same to you. And remember, we need prisoners, at least until we've confirmed the cargo."

"Boarding teams ready. Breaching enemy hull in ten seconds. Good luck, boys." The captain's voice was loud on Treven's helmet com. The first mate knew *Viper's* commander was restless sitting on the bridge while his people boarded the target. Yulich had always accompanied his men when they swarmed aboard an enemy ship, at least until another of the Black Flag's rules had changed his policy. The captain didn't leave the ship, period. Not unless there was a true emergency.

The Black Flag was strange for a criminal outfit, tightly organized and utterly intolerant of disobedience in some ways, yet very hands off in others. Treven had never served in a military organization, but he and Yulich had discussed it many times. The syndicate seemed in many ways to function more like a military organization than a loose confederation of pirates. Its ships went on assigned campaigns, chasing intel-derived targets; they didn't prowl the transit lanes hoping to sight a prize. Its captains followed orders…or they got so large a bounty placed on their heads, their own crews climbed over each other to get to them first. Yet the pirates filling its ranks enjoyed significant freedom. If something wasn't covered under the Black Flag codes, pretty much anything was allowed.

Treven slipped to the side as the tube shook hard, and he grabbed onto one of the handholds. "Alright, boys, we're breaching now."

The tube was designed to bore through the hull of a disabled freighter, providing a route for boarders to move in and seize the ship. Once the diamond-edged iridium cutting blades had penetrated the hull, a series of jets released a foam substance that quickly expanded and hardened around the new connection, maintaining or restoring atmospheric integrity.

Treven checked his carbine, making sure the cartridge was firmly in place. It was the third time he'd done it, but he didn't intend to end up dead because he'd been careless before a fight.

The tube shook again as it pushed forward. A few seconds later the red warning light flashed. Then the hatch dropped and the first two rows of pirates swarmed onboard the freighter. An instant later Treven heard gunfire. He saw one of his people drop to the deck…then another. Then a dozen of his pirates opened up in response, riddling the three shooters with automatic fire.

Treven sighed. There were two types of freighter crews. The first type—which accounted for about ninety percent of them—panicked at the thought of battle, thinking of nothing but surrendering or fleeing to an escape pod. Then there was the other kind, the ones with a good captain and a lot of esprit de corps, and probably more than one naval vet scattered around.

Now he knew which kind he was facing.

*   *   *   *   *

Marne slipped down the corridor, moving quickly but carefully, paying attention to every sound. Deep down, he knew his ship was taken, that his crew didn't have a chance to fight off the invaders. Freighters ran on a far different business model than pirates, one that required keeping costs down. No cargo run paid as well as piracy, and no transport vessel could support a pirate's armament and crew size.

Carlyle was strong as freighters went, powerful enough to chase off most small raiders. But this attacker was tougher than most, a big ship that almost certainly carried three or four times the crew *Carlyle* did. The laser cannons had been *Carlyle's* best chance to repel the attacker, but the enemy ship had fired back with her own larger turrets, knocking out Marne's big guns before finishing off *Carlyle's* engines and defenses with her needlers. Marne would never surrender, but once the laser cannons went down, he knew the fight was hopeless.

"Let's go. Down to the cargo hold. We'll have solid cover in there, and a good field of fire as they approach." He gestured forward, turning for an instant, as if to confirm the five crewmembers he'd been leading were still with him. They didn't have anywhere else to go, not really, but Marne knew fear worked in bizarre ways sometimes. He half expected them all to bolt for the escape pods.

If they do, they'll just get gunned down by the pirates. No one attacking this shipment is going to let anybody escape, and they all know that. But that doesn't mean they won't run for it anyway.

He stopped abruptly at an intersection, peering cautiously around the corner. Then he pulled a small 'pad from his belt. The main AI was tracking the invaders using the scanners and cameras situated around the ship.

Good, he thought. *They haven't gotten this far yet. We'll have time to set up a strong position.*

Good job, Cal. His first mate had taken command of the forward defenses. Durham wasn't military, but Marne was sure his exec would fight to the end.

Which will be soon. The men defending the boarding point will be the first to die. He sighed. Most of them are probably dead already. He knew he could check, his 'pad would have updated data available. But he slipped it back in the pouch on his belt. He didn't want to know.

He turned toward his men and nodded. Then he swung around the corner—if he'd missed any enemies down the hall, he'd be the first one to find out—and raced toward the entrance to the cargo hold. "Open hatch 216," he snapped into his com, directing the ship's AI to allow entry to the storage area. He stood outside the door as it opened, and then he waved for his people to run inside. He took one last look down the hall after they'd all passed him…then he ducked in himself, ordering the AI to close and bolt the hatch as he did.

"Let's get ready." He looked around the hold. It was only partially full, three long rows of large canisters, each filled with ore rich in the super-heavy transuranic element that was number 164 on the periodic table. The material represented six months of production from the mines on Glaciem, and when fully-refined—a process requiring equipment not yet possessed by Atlantia—it would produce in excess of five thousand kilograms of the precious metal.

"Houk, Zabon…you two over there." He pointed toward one of the large canisters. "One on each side, where you can get a good line of sight. He turned, waving toward another container on the other side of the entry. "Bliss, Wantague…behind that one, same thing. Whatever comes through that hatch, we need to take it down immediately. If they get in here, we're done."

We're done anyway…even if we beat them back, they'd blast the ship before they left the system. Still, better to die on our feet, fighting…

"Sampson, you're with me." He walked up to the first canister directly in front of the hatch. "I'll take the left, you take the right." He moved around to the side of the three meter tall container and crouched down, just far enough back to give himself cover.

"This ore is dense as hell...stay behind these canisters, and you'll be fine. I doubt they've got anything that can blast through this stuff.

He knelt down, leaning against the container and bringing his rifle to bear. One glance to each side confirmed his people had done the same thing. They were ready. Or whatever passed for ready right now...

*   *   *   *   *

"Fucking hell, it's just a few freighter jockeys hiding in the hold! Clear them the hell out and let's be done with this." Yulich was usually calm, uncommonly so for men of his profession. But it was clear *Black Viper's* captain was frustrated, all the more so because he was stuck on the bridge while his people were being gunned down in one attack after another on the enemy cargo hold.

"I know, Captain, but their fire has been accurate as hell... and whatever cargo they've got in those containers, it makes for great cover. I hope there's nothing fragile in there, because we must have put five thousand rounds in those canisters." Treven twitched as he spoke, wincing from the pain in his arm. He'd caught a round during the last firefight. He'd packed it with sterile foam and resealed his survival suit with the patch kit, but it still hurt like hell. Treven had been in over a dozen boarding actions, but this was the first time he'd been wounded, and he was finding it difficult to ignore the pain and focus on the battle.

"Don't worry about that, Lars, it's fine. Just finish off those bastards holed up in there so we can load up this cargo and get the hell out of here." A pause then: "And tell the boys... everybody's bounty on this one is doubled if we get away with that cargo."

"Yes, sir," Treven snapped back. Double bounty…that would be helpful at breathing some life into a crew that was quickly becoming demoralized. *But what the hell could an Atlantian ship be carrying that was so valuable? What does the captain know that I don't?*

"Alright, men, let's get it together. These freighter jockeys have chased us back three times. I don't want to see a fucking fourth, so I'm gonna shoot the first one of you who runs. You hear me?"

He paused, listening to the ominous silence on the com line. He realized the threat had been a bit heavy handed considering the losses they had suffered. *All it would take is one bullet in your back…*

"And listen to this. If you pull your heads out of your asses and get your jobs done, the captain just told me…double boun-ties for everyone." *That* elicited a loud cheer over the main com line, and he saw the difference in the bearing of the men stand-ing before him. Double bounty was a battle cry to *Black Viper's* pirates, like an officer in some ancient army waving a tattered flag.

He held up his assault rifle and popped out the almost-empty cartridge, quickly replacing it with a full one. He only had two left, but he was going in at the head of the men this time, and he knew the first few seconds would decide the fight. Either they'd follow him in quickly, getting past the enemy cover and wip-ing out the few holdouts still remaining, or he'd find himself in there alone…and get blown away almost immediately. In which case, none of this was his problem anymore.

He had less than half the men he'd started with. They'd had a dozen casualties already, and he'd detached at least another ten men to ferry the wounded back to *Black Viper*. Pirates had a bloodthirsty reputation, but they were a brotherhood of sorts. He served with those men every day…they fought side by side. Besides, it did nothing for the morale of those still in the fight to see their wounded comrades ill-treated. Treven wasn't a military veteran, but he knew that much of the motivations that made men fight.

"Alright, boys…follow me." He jumped off and ran down the short corridor, toward the blasted door of the cargo hold.

Follow me…such powerful words. Why is it so much harder to lead, to be first and so comparatively easy to go on the heels of someone else?

He scolded himself for letting his thoughts wander. It wasn't the time. He could already hear his enemies firing as he approached the twisted wreckage of the door, and he leveled his rifle and opened up on full auto as he leapt through.

*   *   *   *   *

Marne propped himself up on the heavy canister…the farthest one from the door the enemy had used to force their way into the hold. He was alone, at least he thought so…though it was possible there were still survivors somewhere on *Carlyle*. Wherever they were, though, it wasn't the hold. He'd seen each of his five comrades go down, the last two under the brutal blasts of the pirate leader's shotgun. He was covered in blood, mostly Sampson's. The last blast of that damned shotgun had blown off the crewman's head and most of his chest. Marne knew he was damned lucky he wasn't dead himself. He'd reacted quickly and managed to plant his survival knife in the pirate's thigh before falling back to his current position. The last position. He glanced over his shoulder at the heavy plasti-steel doors of the cargo hatch. They were ten meters across and four high. But *Carlyle* was in deep space, not the hospitable confines of a loading dock. There was no escape that way, nowhere to go. Unless…

What the hell does escape mean anyway? You're dead where you sit…as soon as they get their wounded out of here and scour the hold they'll find you. And you're fresh out of ammo. You even left your knife behind, ten centimeters into that pirate's thigh. But that doesn't mean you have to let them win…

He reached down to his belt, feeling a wave of pain as he

moved his arm. He'd landed hard, and now he realized he'd injured himself worse than he'd thought. It was probably a break, but he put it out of his mind. It hurt like hell, but considering his situation it didn't seem very important. He gritted his teeth and pulled the small 'pad from its pocket, lifting it up where he could see it.

He moved his finger across the screen, bringing up a login page. He didn't see any way he could escape—and with his entire crew dead and his ship taken, he wasn't even sure he should want to. But he wasn't dead yet. He could deny the enemy the precious cargo *Carlyle* was carrying. One last bit of spite, the only vengeance he could exact for his slain crew.

He punched in the access code, the one that identified him to *Carlyle's* AI as the ship's captain, empowered to issue any order. The screen went blank, and a single line appeared. *Identification acknowledged, awaiting command-level order.* There was a row of icons below the sentence, each one representing an order only *Carlyle's* commander was authorized to issue. He blinked, running his eyes over the 'pad before taking another look around, checking for any enemy activity. *Nothing yet...*

He moved his hand, slowly, painfully, across the pad, his gloved finger settling on one of the icons. "Prepare to launch all escape pods," he said into his com as he pressed the glowing button on the 'pad. His com was still connected to the AI, and the pirates had not destroyed *Carlyle's* main computer yet. *They will regret that bit of carelessness...*

"Ready to launch upon command," came the reply.

He punched another icon on the 'pad. "I want the cargo doors opened simultaneously with the launch of the escape pods." Between the confusion of the pods and trying to retrieve their men who would be blasted out into space, he doubted the pirates would have time to try to recover the cargo...at least not before the fine ore was hopelessly scattered through space. It wouldn't save him...it wouldn't save his ship. But it was the only way he had to strike back. He could at least deny his murderers the riches his ship held.

"The ship is currently in a vacuum environment. Opening

doors will cause immediate decompression in the cargo hold, and in the adjoining corridors, as the cargo hold door is no longer an airtight seal."

Damned right it's not airtight.

The enemy had blown their way into the hold, and the door was a twisted heap of wreckage. "Acknowledged. My orders are to be obeyed nevertheless. And detach all magnetic cargo cradles five seconds before opening doors."

"Acknowledged. Awaiting order to commence."

Marne took a deep breath. He found himself shaking, fighting off a wave of panic. It was one thing to plan a suicidal action, but quite another to actually do it. He knew intellectually he had no chance…and after the losses his people had inflicted on the pirates, he was damned sure he didn't want to be taken alive. But still, he found it difficult to proceed, and the order stuck in his throat for a few seconds. Finally, he balled his hands into fists, feeling a wave of pain shoot up the injured arm as he did.

"Execute," he said softly, coldly.

He heard a loud crash. Then another. Ore bins tipping over as their magnetic locks disengaged. He heard shouting too, the surprised yells of the pirates on the other side of the hold, taken by surprise as the massive canisters tipped over in *Carlyle's* 1g of simulated gravity.

Five seconds, he thought. *Such a short time, yet it can seem like so long…*

His thought hung there for a time that seemed almost indeterminate. Then the doors opened, and he felt himself being sucked out into space. There were canisters, and clouds of loose ore flying out of the hold as well, drifting into space, dispersing, just as he'd hoped.

They'll never manage to collect all that, he thought as he turned his head and looked at the mass of his ship, slowing receding behind him. He felt a sudden pang of sadness. Not because he was going to die, but because he knew he'd never set foot on *Carlyle* again. She was badly damaged, and the pirates would almost certainly blow her to atoms before they left. But even if they didn't, he was moving away from her at 40 meters per second, and his survival suit had ten minutes of life support.

Will I suffocate or freeze first? The thought was odd, strangely detached emotionally, as if how he would die was an academic question of no particular consequence. Neither way sounded particularly pleasant, and he found himself wishing he'd saved his pistol and one last round. But he hadn't, so he just leaned back and looked out at the stars.

Chapter 4

"The Nest" – Black Eagles Base
Second Moon of Eos, Eta Cassiopeiae VII
Earthdate: 2318 AD (34 Years After the Fall)

"Nice!" Darius Cain kept his eyes focused on his opponent, even as he rolled to dodge the savage swing of the pugil stick. He'd never been truly convinced the primitive weapons had any real place in modern training programs, but the Marines had used them—his father had used them—and that was enough for him. Besides, even without any direct correlation to modern fighting techniques, a bout with the sticks was damned fine physical training.

Cain snapped back to his feet, his own stick out in front of him, waiting for an opening. He'd been holding back in the fight, as he had been since he'd begun training his newest student. But his protégé was getting better, and each time Cain had been obliged to expend a bit more effort to fend off the increasingly well-aimed attacks.

Axe was older than Cain, by more than twenty years, and he hadn't had the course of rejuv treatments the leader of the Black Eagles had enjoyed. But he acquitted himself well, and Cain was proud of his trainee. Axe didn't look much like the average new recruit that made it to the Nest, but Darius saw through age and infirmity to an inner quality, one he felt was strong and clear.

Despite his years and the lack of a chemical age-fighting regimen, Axe looked great. The former gang leader turned village elder had been a wreck when Roderick Vance's spy had taken him to Mars from the post-Fall ruins of Earth. Axe was in his mid-fifties, and he'd been suffering from several aggressive cancers, the result of severe radiation exposure, both during the Fall and in the years that followed. He was malnourished, plagued by a dozen nutritional deficiencies and hobbled by a leg that had been twice broken and poorly set both times. He'd had less than a year to live if he'd remained on Earth, and probably substantially less.

The Martian doctors had treated the cancers, saving Axe's life and restoring him to moderately good health. But when he'd gotten to the Nest, the Black Eagles' medical staff practically rebuilt him. He was too old to start rejuv therapies, but they'd rebroken and fused his leg and pumped him full of vitamins, micro-nutrients, and supplements. They'd induced selective internal regeneration to restore his internal organs to perfect condition. When he walked out of the infirmary, he felt twenty years younger. But that had just been the start.

The Eagles had outstanding doctors by any standard, but their training staff was without equal. They put Axe through an intense regimen, six hours a day of running, lifting, and combat simulations. Within two months he was 85 kilos of pure muscle. He'd pushed himself brutally, tirelessly taking advantage of any training the Eagles offered.

Cain understood his new friend's determination. He'd been the founder and leader of a settlement called Jericho, one of the largest villages on post-Fall Earth, and he'd been left for dead by the slavers who had destroyed the town and taken his people off-planet, destined for a life of bondage. Including Ellie, his wife.

Left behind, wounded and sick, he'd had no prospect to save any of them, but then fate intervened, first in the form of a Martian agent sent to investigate the destruction of Jericho and later by an unlikely confederation of powers, including the Black Eagles. Cain's mercenaries had attacked and destroyed the slavers' base on the planetoid of Eris, but they'd gotten there too late to save Ellie and the others. Axe's beloved wife and the rest of his people were out there somewhere, probably living and working under appalling conditions. And despite the apparent hopelessness of ever finding them somewhere in the vastness of man's dominion in space, he was determined to try.

Thanks to Darius Cain's sponsorship, he was stronger than he had been in decades...and he had the resources to mount a credible search. Darius knew Axe realized he was looking for a needle in a haystack, but he was just as sure his guest didn't care. The sequence of events that had taken him from a sick old man prowling around the outskirts of Jericho to a strong and capable warrior had been equally unlikely, surely. Darius didn't expect Axe would give up easily. Or at all.

Hope doesn't die...not until you surrender. And that will never happen. Not while there is breath in his lungs.

Suddenly, Darius saw his chance, and he lunged, smacking his pugil stick against Axe's face. The Earther went down hard.

"You've got to pay attention, Axe," Darius said, keeping most of the scolding tone from his voice. "I know you've got a lot to think about, but against an enemy less friendly than me, one of those zone outs of yours will cost you your life." He reached down, offering his opponent an assist. "And if you get yourself killed, you've got no chance to find any of them. Take care of yourself first and foremost. For them as much as you. Remember that."

Axe grabbed onto Cain's hand and hopped up to his feet. "I know you're right, Darius. It's just hard. I saved her life just before the Fall, and we've been together ever since." A sad look came over his face. "Were together."

Cain nodded. "I understand what you are feeling." He paused. "No, perhaps I don't, at least not completely. But if you will take a bit of advice, I would give you some."

"Of course, Darius."

"You need to think clearly. I know you're planning to go running off in search of Ellie...and the rest of your people. But I think that is poor thinking...cloudy, driven by emotion and not rationality. Yes, you want to find them, but I think you should wait." Cain paused, seeing the uncertainty in Axe's eyes. "Listen to me...I know it feels unnatural to delay. Every emotion inside you is screaming to go now, berating you for not going yesterday. But feelings do not design sound tactics, and you have to ask this question...do you just want to make yourself feel better by running off—and probably getting killed—just to act like you are doing something? Or do you want the best chance of finding and rescuing them?"

Axe took a deep breath and hesitated, wiping the sweat from his forehead. "To find them, of course," he finally said.

"Are you sure? Because if that's the case, you need to use your head and not your heart. If you leave now, alone, you know you're not going to find them. And even if you do, you don't have the power to rescue them. But there is something far vaster going on out there, some enemy that has not yet revealed itself. We fight the same war, my friend, and patience will serve your goal better than zealotry. If you rush forward, if you get yourself killed needlessly, the search is over. Your friends— Ellie—they will die in some hellhole, an iridium mine on a frigid asteroid or working sixteen hour days in a factory on a remote moon."

Cain could see his words cut at Axe, but he knew his friend needed to hear the truth, or at least some of it. Darius was a realist, and he realized Axe's chances of finding his wife and friends were almost non-existent, no matter what he did. But he was a leader of soldiers too, and he knew sometimes illusion could be important, that a lie told to oneself could bolster morale...and in turn contribute to ultimate victory. Some losses were best absorbed gradually, and he knew Axe's self-delusion would give him time to adjust, to become accustomed to the losses he had suffered. Then, after time had passed, after he had exerted all his efforts in the search, perhaps he would be able to make peace with the loss of his people.

Besides, war was coming. Darius didn't doubt that for an instant. Every military instinct he had was twitching, warning him that the fight on Eris was just the beginning of what was to come. He was a veteran, and his Black Eagles were the best soldiers in Occupied Space, but they had never faced a struggle like the one he could feel gathering. The Eagles had fought contained conflicts, disputes between worlds, and they were almost always far superior to their adversaries. But his gut was telling him this new war would be different—widespread, cataclysmic, a true fight for survival. The kind of war his father had fought...and his mother.

He didn't have much information about this new enemy, but he was sure they were out there somewhere. And the fact that they almost certainly knew more about him—and the Eagles and Roderick Vance and the rest of the forces that would stand against them—was deeply troubling. Darius knew it was a massive strategic advantage, one he intended to do something about. He knew he had to learn more, and he had already dispatched some of his most trusted people to track down the few vague leads he had. He was asking a lot of them, to turn the scraps he'd given them into solid information, but they were Black Eagles... which meant he never expected anything less than excellence.

He intended to try to keep Axe at the Nest, at least until his agents returned with whatever intelligence they could collect. Whatever meager possibility there was to rescue Ellie and the rest of Axe's people, it would be much stronger when they knew more about the enemy. And if Axe was going to risk his life chasing after a phantom, Darius was determined to give him at least some chance of success.

Axe had been standing silently, clearly considering Darius' words. Cain smiled and reached out, slapping his friend lightly on the shoulder. "Come on, let's grab a shower and get something to eat. We'll talk more over dinner."

*   *   *   *   *

"Mmmmm." Darius was lying face down on the bed, his eyes closed. Ana was hovering over him, her hands working their way across his back...creating something he was sure had to be magic. Darius Cain had always been tightly wound, even as a child, and the tragic cost of the Second Incursion had only made things worse. He'd been overcome with grief when word arrived that his father had died on his way back from the victorious war against the First Imperium, and he'd withdrawn even more completely from normal relationships with the people around him. He'd grown more and more insular, standing up to the authorities on Atlantia, stubbornly refusing to do as he was told until he'd been compelled to leave his home world one step ahead of the police.

His military career had been about focus and the drive for excellence. Wounded in battle several times, he'd felt pain, the loss of friends, the joy of victory. He lived like a king, the master of an invincible army, showered with riches by those who would enjoy its favor. He'd had mistresses from a dozen worlds, some of the most beautiful and exotic women in Occupied Space. But he couldn't recall ever feeling true relaxation, not like this at least. Ana Bazarov had magic fingers. It was the only explanation.

"You really need to get more rest, maybe get away for a while. I'd swear this back of yours is so knotted up it's harder than your armor." Ana had been his guest, a refugee he'd plucked from the fighting on Karelia two years earlier...just as a pack of Raschiddan soldiers had been ready to assault her. She'd caught his eye right away, and for reasons he still didn't understand, the thought of her being hurt enraged him, so much so he'd had the offending troops summarily executed. Then he'd brought her with him, feeling guilty about not giving her a choice, but absolutely refusing to leave her behind on a Karelia now under the control of the Raschiddan government.

"There's a lot going on right now. I'm a little tense." He twisted his head as he spoke, and his neck cracked loudly.

"A little?" she asked, trying and failing to suppress a chuckle as she did. "You think?" She managed to hold back some of the laugh, but none of the sarcasm.

He pushed her playfully to the side and rolled over, his eyes finding hers. "My, aren't we the sarcastic one today? Is that where we've ended up?" He leaned in and kissed her, putting a hand on her cheek as he did. Things were indeed tense, and he'd been under a lot of stress, even by the standards of his life as a mercenary...and as one of the most feared men in Occupied Space. Cain didn't care much what people thought of him, beyond his soldiers and his few true friends. Still, he had to admit Ana had upset that near-invulnerability. He was still trying to convince himself she was just another mistress, a pleasant diversion he would tire of eventually, but his mind was too logical to accept what it could tell was nonsense.

But it wasn't the recent developments in his love life that had him so stressed. Darius Cain hated unanswered questions, despised the notion that he had an enemy he didn't understand. It was anathema to how he conducted his affairs. He always had the best intelligence, the most detailed and carefully-crafted plans. Now he was feeling around in the dark, ceding the initiative, waiting to see what his adversaries would do, where they would strike. It was driving him mad, pushing him to take action, any action, just to feel like he was doing something. His logic had held him back so far, and his discipline. But he couldn't wait forever, and if he didn't get some decent intel soon, he knew he was going to have to start shooting blindly. And that sequence of thoughts was taking him around in a circle, one that cranked up the tension with every frustrating lap.

Ana's touch was the one thing that gave him relief, and his time with her was the only bit of true relaxation he got. He'd wondered more than once if he would have been able to maintain his judgment without the brief periods of calm she gave him.

Would you have mobilized the Eagles and headed off half-cocked, following an emotional need to strike anywhere rather than to stay here idle? He didn't know the answer.

She had been with him almost two years now. She'd hated him at first, an understandable reaction since the Eagles had just invaded her world, a lightning assault that had crushed the native army and ended thirty years of Karelian independence in less than one of the planet's twenty-two hour days. But he'd surprised her, first by finding her thirteen year old sister, who'd been lost and wandering through the burning city, and then by respecting her wishes…in everything except his refusal to leave her and her sister behind on Karelia, alone and at the mercy of the new Raschiddan overlords. He hadn't forced himself on her nor required her to do anything…nothing except accompanying him and his soldiers when they departed. She'd been treated like an honored guest, and it had only been months later the two had shared anything more than a brief conversation.

Things had gone well beyond that now. Darius had always tried to avoid emotional attachments, feeling they tended to overrule logic—and he'd always considered rationality to be his master. He was different than most of the people he'd met, and he prided himself on being free of the need most had to believe blindly in people and causes. That was their weakness, emotional need overruling realism, and it had no place in his life.

He'd always felt that relationships caused needless pain too…the heartache of his father's death, for example. Still, he'd found it wasn't always possible to avoid them. He was close friends with Erik Teller, his second-in-command and a companion since childhood, and he knew the pain he would experience if his exec ever fell in one of the Eagles' battles. And he loved his mother deeply, though he rarely saw her. It stirred up too many confusing emotions…guilt, regret, the pain of his father's loss. He knew she disapproved of him, of the choices he'd made—it was clear to him, though she generally held her tongue about it. Of course, staying away just created more guilt, making the whole swirling brew that much more complicated…and reinforcing his view that emotions were best strictly controlled.

He told himself he avoided his mother to spare her the difficulties a close relationship would cause, but he knew that explanation was incomplete—and that it let him off the hook far more easily than he deserved. Still, though he made no apologies for his life's choices, he knew many people considered him little more than a butcher, a brutal killer. The less he allowed his mother into his life, the more he insulated her from the hatred people felt toward him.

Then there was his brother…he wasn't sure what he thought of Elias. They'd gotten along well enough as children, but they'd dealt with their father's disappearance in wildly different ways, and that had driven a wedge between them. Darius would have described his feelings for Elias as casual hatred, and he hadn't seen his twin for years before they'd been thrown together by Roderick Vance's summons. Now, he found his feelings to be far more muddled than he'd thought before. He still had a healthy measure of anger and disdain for the man who shared his DNA, but he was more confused now. And that interfered with clear thought, crisp decision-making. It reinforced his desire to avoid emotional entanglements even as it caused him more.

Now he had yet another confusing set of impulses to deal with, the strange cocktail of irrationality surrounding his feelings for Ana. He'd always kept his sexual relationships tight, focused. He'd treated his mistresses kindly and with great generosity, but he'd always been clear about the ground rules. There had been emotion involved, certainly. He wasn't a cyborg. But there was no place in his life for the distracting foolishness that so often accompanied dating rituals between men and women. He had affection for the women he bedded, but he'd never let one of them really get through his emotional defenses. At least until Ana Bazarov found her way into his life.

His most recent group of mistresses still resided in the Nest, in conditions of considerable comfort and luxury, but he hadn't seen any of them in months. They didn't realize they'd all been discarded, cast aside in favor of another, though he imagined they wondered what had changed. Indeed, Darius didn't understand it yet either. He and Ana had not discussed their relationship. She had not asked him where she stood in his life, if she was just another of his women or something more. She hadn't even asked for any assurances the way the others had, no guarantees she wouldn't be cast aside with nothing if he tired of her. But he'd moved her into his own quarters, a thing he'd never done before. And he spent his nights with her, all of them. He'd never done that before either.

He leaned back on the bed, reaching behind his head and

propping up a stack of pillows as he did. He sighed softly and looked around the room. His quarters were Spartan but comfortable, far more mundane than one would have expected for a man of his wealth and power. But he was a soldier first and foremost, and he was uncomfortable with excess frill. His mistresses all had far plusher suites. Indeed, the guest quarters Ana had occupied before moving into his were considerably more luxurious. But she'd never once said anything about the sparse and simple rooms. He found it refreshing.

"Have you heard back from any of the scouts?" Ana had been sleeping with Darius a long time before she'd first asked any questions about Black Eagle business, and she still sounded uncomfortable when she did.

"No, nothing yet. I had so little to give them, I wouldn't be surprised if they all came back empty handed." He sighed again. "I don't know what we're facing, Ana. I've never been in this position before."

"Do you really think there is some massive enemy out there? I know the slaving ring on Eris was a large operation, but perhaps it was just that, a big criminal organization that is now destroyed."

He leaned back on the small stack of pillows and sighed. "It's tempting to think that. It would make things simpler. Most people would let themselves accept that, go back to life as usual without the stress and worry."

"But not you." It was almost a question but not quite. Ana had come to know and understand him well, far more quickly than anyone else ever had. "You're usually right, aren't you?"

"Yes," he said, his voice deadpan, not a trace of ego in the response. "About things like this. The truth is almost always worse than people allow themselves to believe. I'm sure there is something bigger going on. When we fought the Gold Spears on Lysandria, there were troops there we've never encountered before, thousands of them…well trained and equipped. I know all the major merc companies, Ana. I have no idea where they came from."

"What do you think it is?" There was something in her

voice, not fear exactly, but unease.

"You think the same thing I do, don't you?" he asked, ignoring her question.

"I really don't know, Darius. I'd never been off of Karelia before you came there. Never farther than thirty kilometers from the capital. I really have no idea what's out there, not even the things you know about already."

He reached out and took her hand. "But you're afraid, aren't you? You're shaking."

"Because I know you. I know the kind of man you are."

Darius felt a twinge. Usually when the conversation turned to what kind of man he was things tended to get ugly. "What do you mean?" he asked, a touch of defensiveness in his tone. He didn't care what most people thought, but he'd come to realize his usual defense mechanisms didn't work with Ana.

"Nothing bad." She forced a smile, clearly understanding she had inadvertently touched a nerve. "You're smart. You don't let fear or neediness interfere with your judgment. I can tell how worried you are, and it scares me. Anything that has you so tense, so concerned…it has to be catastrophic."

He moved his hand to her cheek, slowly brushing back her hair. "You don't have to worry, Ana. The Nest is the most heavily defended place in Occupied Space." He looked as her, trying to decide if he'd allayed her fears. He wasn't sure…she tended to see through him, to understand exactly what he was thinking, in a way no one ever had before. And what he was feeling was fear. He didn't know much about the enemy, or what they were planning. But he was sure that no place was safe…not even the Nest.

Maybe especially not the Nest.

Chapter 5

Elias Cain was losing patience. He'd been on to something, he was sure of it, but now the trail had gone cold. It had started simply enough, with the bust of two men selling illegal goods, banned imports from Malagar. The Malagari government was hardly a government at all, more of a loose framework of local rulers. The planet had few real laws, and none at all regulating its trade with other worlds. So along with exotic foodstuffs and rare hardwoods from its great forests, its ships carried potent hallucinogenic liquors and pleasure-inducing drugs from its jungle zones. On Atlantia, a world where recreational drugs were banned, along with all alcoholic beverages stronger than table wine, such commerce was unwelcome. After a few years of trying to police Malagari freighters, the government simply redlined Malagar, barring access to the Atlantia—and the entire Epsilon Indi system—to its traders.

Nevertheless, Malagari goods still found their way onto Atlantia's black markets, the government prohibitions proving no more effective than similar policies on other worlds. But the illegal imports weren't Cain's primary concern. He'd become quite interested in the apparent level of organization behind businesses like smuggling and illegal importation. He'd always viewed criminals as just that, lawless adventurers seeking to build their fortunes flouting a planet's laws. But after learning how large the slaving ring had been on Earth and how strong a base they had built in secrecy on Eris, he began to wonder if there was a relationship between different criminal groups. Was routine crime on Atlantia all homegrown and organic? Or was there something—someone—else behind much of it? Human history had seen many versions of organized crime. Could such a thing exist in an interstellar scale?

Pellas Spaceport was the main hub of freight moving to and from Atlantia, and the landing bays of the main complex were surrounded by clusters of dive bars, the type of establishment frequented by career spacers and transients who traveled the warp gates of Occupied Space. Half of them had hidden brothels on their upper levels, just the kind of place Elias would have busted without a second thought a few months earlier. But he didn't have time for that now. His mind was on something bigger…and much more disturbing.

He'd been thinking differently about many things recently, actively questioning much of what he saw going on around him. He didn't have any newfound sympathy for criminals, for those who sought to profit from breaking the rules but, though he'd never admit it, his brother had gotten to him. He felt like he was paying closer attention to things he had always taken on faith, and he was starting to come to different conclusions that he had before. Very uncomfortable ones. Starting with the fact that he realized there was as much crime and immorality in the centers of power as in the sleazy bars around the spaceport. Perhaps more.

He'd spent many sleepless nights deep in thought since he'd returned, wondering what he needed to do, how to proceed. It was one thing to see the corruption around him more clearly, and quite another to determine a way to deal with it. The politicians had exempted themselves from many of the rules they had imposed on the public, creating a legal shield that allowed them to avoid prosecution, even when their actions were discovered. Elias was finding it difficult to devise a way to clean up the government without violating many of the very laws he'd sworn to uphold. He knew that would mean nothing to Darius, that his brother would take whatever action suited him and damned the laws and the corrupt politicians who'd written them. But that was against everything Elias had believed his entire adult life. He detested the dishonestly of those in power, but would he be any better than they if he ignored the laws himself, pursuing what he judged to be right and not what was legal? What authority did he have to set himself up as sole arbiter of right and wrong?

He found the whole thing upsetting, all the more so because of his new suspicions that much of the crime on Atlantia had its origin someplace offworld. The Black Eagles had destroyed the slavers' base on Eris, leaving nothing behind but radioactive slag. Still, whoever had built that base, and supported such a vast operation, clearly had enormous resources. He doubted the destruction of one base had finished them off...and that meant they were still out there, plotting their next move.

He had no proof, nor any real specifics about what he was looking for, but he'd come to believe the slavers were just one part of a massive criminal organization that operated throughout occupied space. Including Atlantia.

Your imagination is running wild. You don't know any of this, you're just speculating wildly. But it does explain a lot of things. At the very least, they were sending those people somewhere...

Now he began to wonder, to ask the question he'd tried to hold at bay, the inquiry that threatened his very belief system. Did the crime on Atlantia exist under the noses of the government and the politicians...or were they part of it? And what would he do if he found proof, evidence that his world had become controlled by evil and dishonest men and women? He'd never thought of himself as a potential rebel. Indeed, he'd have gladly crushed any who rose up against their legal government. But now he was deep in confusion, unsure what to do or even whether he should try to learn more.

"Captain Cain..."

He turned abruptly, his tension increasing the suddenness

and apparent hostility of his move. His hand had moved toward his gun, but then he snapped his arm away. The man standing in front of him was one of his own, not an enemy.

"Yes, Lieutenant?" Anson Haviland was a decorated officer, and his second-in-command...and a man who had wielded his badge of office in as heavy-handed a manner as Elias himself. *As much a martinet as me*, he thought, echoing what he imagined Darius would have said.

"Sir, there is news. A distress drone transited through the Epsilon-14 warp gate. We've been ordered back to headquarters immediately."

"Epsilon-14? There's nothing even there. Except..."

Carlyle. The first shipment of STUs. Has she left yet? The departure of the first STU shipment was a closely-guarded secret, one above his own pay grade.

"Let's go." Cain had a cold feeling in his gut. He'd been nervous about sending the freighter unescorted, but Atlantia didn't have a navy, not really. Just a small fleet of patrol boats. And the Ministry of Trade had decided secrecy was better protection for the inaugural STU shipment than a meager show of arms. Cain hadn't agreed, but he'd bowed to the orders of his superiors.

He knew what his brother would say about that too.

*   *   *   *   *

"Captain Cain, I don't have to remind you again how disturbing we found your trip to the Sol system. Atlantia is not Earth's old Wild West. We have laws here, and as—until recently at least—one of our most promising enforcement officers, you are expected to set the example. Atlantia is an orderly society, and its citizens are not allowed to simply pick up and leave—and travel wherever they may choose. They must be granted a travel permit. This policy is for their own safety as well as the good of the state.

"Sir, I apologize if I may have inadvertently violated any

policy, but as you know, I did have a travel permit." Elias felt something inside, something new. An anger, a growing resentment, not just at the Chief, but at the excessive regulation he suddenly saw so much more clearly than he had before. He had been nothing but a loyal Atlantian, and now that he found himself under the harsh light he'd placed on so many others, he found himself confused, questioning all he had believed. He controlled himself; he was still an Atlantian officer of the law, and his discipline was as strong as it had been. But underneath the iron façade, he was deeply troubled, questioning many things he had always accepted.

The Chief sighed. "You do not help your cause, Elias, with verbal gymnastics. You had a travel permit to Mars for recreational purposes, a document you were able to obtain easily and quickly because of your record to that point. You did not receive such deference to allow you to engage in a meeting with representatives of foreign governments…much less mercenary companies like the Black Eagles. I know Darius Cain is your brother, but must I remind you he is a wanted criminal on Atlantia? You saw him. Did you attempt to apprehend him?"

"No, sir. That would have been…difficult. He was accompanied by a regiment of his soldiers." Elias knew he was being evasive. He had many issues with Darius, but he couldn't imagine ever turning his brother in, even if it had been remotely feasible. Beyond simple loyalty to his twin, he shuddered to think of how the Black Eagles would react if an Atlantian enforcement officer arrested their commander and dragged him back for trial. The Atlantian defense forces were reasonably well trained and equipped, but he didn't try to fool himself that they were a match for the Eagles. And the thought of those mercenaries, enraged as they would be at the abduction of their leader, was enough to turn his blood cold.

"I will be honest with you, Elias. You have damaged your career. Badly. Indeed, there is still an investigation underway, and the possibility remains that you will be brought up on charges. Of course, that would mean the end of your service… and a substantial prison term as well." The Chief paused, allowing his words to hang briefly in the air. "But if you complete this mission with the competence you have displayed so often in the past, I am assured that you will be granted a full pardon for your transgressions…and returned to the advancement track within the agency. And you and I shall never speak of your unfortunate conduct again. Not many men get an opportunity to wash away their sins."

Elias fought back another wave of anger, a stronger one. He resented his actions being characterized as transgressions, much less sins. He had met with Roderick Vance, that was true—and with his brother and mother as well…but the matter hadn't had anything to do with Atlantia or its foreign policy. He'd divulged no secrets, made no representations on behalf of Atlantia or its government. And he hadn't even joined in the attack on Eris. He'd been back on Mars, recovering from an assassination attempt that had come close—very close—to finishing him off.

"Yes, sir. I will do my best." He tried to speak naturally, to make his answer sound appreciative and not resentful, but he found it difficult. "Thank you for the opportunity." He spat out the last words like something that tasted bad.

He stood up, struggling to hide the tension he felt in every muscle. "With your permission, sir, I will go prepare for the mission. The sooner we lift off the better."

"I couldn't agree more, Captain Cain." A short pause. "Don't let me down, Elias. You are getting a second chance. I wouldn't expect a third…"

*   *   *   *   *

Armando DeSilva leaned back in his almost absurdly plush chair. The seat was made from Arcadian leather, hand stitched and buttery soft to the touch. It was a perk of DeSilva's office, one of many the taxpayers of Atlantia funded for their president.

Atlantia's highest-ranking politician had come from nothing. Indeed, he had arrived as a teenager along with his parents, refugees from Earth, just after the Fall. Not many people had escaped Earth's final agony, but DeSilva's father had been an engineer, and his skills were badly needed on a planet struggling to adjust to full independence after the Alliance's destruction.

DeSilva had built a political machine the likes of which Atlantia's unsophisticated citizen-politicians had never seen, and in just six years the ambitious young politico had built a 60% majority in the Planetary Assembly and gotten himself elected president in a landslide. There had been rumors of intimidation at the polls and widespread voter fraud, but they didn't last long. Not once he'd gotten into office and gained control over the courts and law enforcement agencies. He sent his most zealous enforcers after his political opponents, and he filled the prisons with those he deemed as a threat, all in the name of law and order, of course. He'd been reelected twice, the last time unopposed, and he'd occupied the office for ten years now.

"I am concerned," he said, his voice a slow drawl, very unlike the fast speech typical among Atlantians. "Captain Cain is, by all accounts, a true believer...and a gifted officer. What if he is able to uncover something...inconvenient while he is in Epsilon-14?"

"Elias Cain will find nothing in his quest. He will return empty handed, having found neither the *Carlyle* nor any trace of her attacker. We have made certain of this. And the Black Flag will return you half the value of *Carlyle's* cargo, a king's ransom. And a treasure that will be utterly secret. Yours to do with as you please. To enhance your grip on power, perhaps..."

DeSilva stared across his desk at the woman sitting in one of his guest chairs. She was attractive, there was no question about that, slim, classy, professional. But there was something else too, something he couldn't quite place. A darkness? To look at her, she could have been the representative of a trading house or a large bank, but when she spoke he felt odd. Like a shiver going down his spine.

"I appreciate your confidence, Asha, but I still feel we must have a contingency plan in place, just in case Elias Cain does uncover some evidence of the...interception...of *Carlyle*." The mysterious emissary had been on Atlantia for two years, and she'd kept every promise she had made. But he was still uncomfortable. He knew little about her, other than the fact that she had powerful friends. She'd aided him in fairly innocuous ways at first, but things had rapidly escalated in recent months. Now he had conspired with her to see an Atlantian ship taken by pirates, its crew murdered and its priceless cargo lost...at least as far as anyone outside his inner circle knew.

"In that extremely unlikely circumstance," she replied, her tone cool and professional, but having the usual effect on DeSilva nevertheless, "I would propose that we simply eliminate Captain Cain."

"That is easier said than done." Greg Moore had been sitting quietly in the second guest chair, but now he spoke up. "The Cain family is still revered by the public. Erik Cain is a hero, loved by the people, and his death defending Occupied Space during the Second Incursion only increased his legend. And unlike his brother, Elias Cain has been a loyal Atlantia, widely regarded as an exemplary citizen. There will be considerable backlash if we attempt to sanction him...and certainly if he is condemned and executed."

DeSilva sighed. "Public heroes are an inconvenience, but I fear my chief of staff is correct. Elias is the only Cain remaining on Atlantia at present. I'd love to be rid of him, but I am very concerned about potential fallout."

Asha looked over at Moore then back to DeSilva. "There are deaths, gentlemen...and there are deaths." Her intonation changed considerably in the second half of her statement. "If you decide Elias Cain must die, we will have to devise something suitable...an appropriately disreputable death." She stared across the table at Atlantia's president. "If he were to be arrested and executed, or even shot by the police, there would be a backlash. But, were he to be found dead of an overdose of some illegal substance, alongside a whore perhaps, I suspect the public reaction would be quite different."

Moore had a stunned expression on his face. He looked like he was going to say something, but DeSilva beat him to it. "And if we were to decide such a measure was necessary, are your... friends...in a positon to assist us? We couldn't risk using any of our personnel. Elias Cain is too well-liked among our operatives. If the truth ever came out..." He let his voice trail off slowly. There was no point in taking 'what ifs' like that too far.

"Of course, Mr. President. If you wish to take that step, my associates would be pleased to handle it for you." She smiled sweetly, as if she'd just promised to help him plan a party.

"Thank you, Asha. As always, your assistance is greatly appreciated." He paused for a few seconds, an uncomfortable look on his face. Finally, he said, "Would you excuse us for a few moments? Greg and I have some government business to discuss. Privately."

"Of course," she said, standing up and smiling. "As always, I am at your disposal if you need me." She turned and walked across the room, closing the door behind her as she left.

"Sir, I don't think..."

"I know, Greg," DeSilva interrupted. "But we may have no choice. We took a risk on this whole *Carlyle* affair, but we had good reasons. We're halfway through our third term. Atlantia has never even had a president run for reelection after a single term, much less contemplate a fourth. We've moved ahead as quickly as we could, secured control of the media and most of the agencies. But we have to be ready when the inevitable reaction comes. We control the polling places, so we can deliver ourselves any percent of the vote we want. But I don't think our dear Atlantians are as passive as we assume they are. They are naïve, not interested in politics, and they have been more accepting of restrictive laws than I'd expected. But pressure is building, and when it blows, we're going to have to be ready. Our stated poll numbers and the actual ones are two very different things."

"I understand, sir, but I don't trust Asha, and I have even less faith in these mysterious friends of hers. Who is she really... and where did she come from?"

"I've asked the same questions myself, but she's come through on everything she has promised. And we need her help. We can win another election, hang on to power for a while longer, but sooner or later we're going end up with a revolution on our hands. The time is coming when we need to secure our power more...forcefully. I've been president for ten years, Greg, and I don't intend to retire and retreat to some seaside manor and write my memoirs. We've allowed the Atlantians to hang on to democratic pretensions, meaningless though they might have been. But the day is coming when we must dispense with all of it...and rule these people as their true masters. And to do that, we need Asha's help. And we need the funding from our share of *Carlyle's* cargo."

Moore sighed. "You may be right, sir, but it still makes me nervous."

"Me too, Greg. But we have to be ready to seize what is ours. Do you see yourself retiring to private life? Getting a dog, hanging up a shingle in some sleepy seaside town and practicing law for the rest of your life, writing wills and handling petty lawsuits?"

Moore smiled. "No, thank you. I like my position...and the power."

"The Political Class on Earth had the right idea...but they became complacent, and they let themselves get dragged into pointless conflicts with the other Superpowers. We won't make that mistake, Greg."

The smile slipped from Moore's face. "Still, we need to be careful."

"We will, Greg. But you know as well as I do, we'll have to get rid of Elias Cain eventually. Could you imagine if he chose to run against me? It's going to take a long time to wear down the Cain name on Atlantia. But for now, let's say I'll be happy when the only Cain on this planet is that statue down in Founders' Square." He stared across the desk, his eyes blazing. "Until the day we pull that thing down too..."

*   *   *   *   *

"We leave in twenty minutes, and we're going to be moving at full thrust all the way, so let your people know, Commander. I don't want to hear any complaining once we're underway." Elias had changed from his uniform into a set of unmarked fatigues. He had a suit of body armor and an assortment of heavy weapons already stowed aboard *Zephyr*. When he suited up, he'd look a lot more like military than police. But he was chasing pirates now and, he suspected, heavily armed ones. If it came to a fight, he and his people would be ready.

"Yes, Captain Cain. We'll be ready." *Zephyr's* commanding officer sounded edgy. Jamie Wheaton's job had been to patrol the space around Atlantia and the overall Epsilon Indi system. That hadn't entailed much combat with pirates. Atlantia had never been a major target for raids. Its exports simply weren't valuable enough to cover the enormous costs of operating in space and still produce a profit for the raiders. They tended to focus on richer worlds like Arcadia and Columbia…though Jarrod Tyler's aggressive countermeasures had significantly cut down on raiding activity on Columbian shipping.

Tyler's policy of having captured pirates crucified during planetwide broadcasts had exerted somewhat of an intimidating influence on the raiders. Columbia's dictator was not a man to be trifled with, and he certainly had no hesitation about making that clear to would-be pirates. And none of the buccaneers dared to go near the outer system either. Darius Cain's Black Eagles had built their Nest on a moon orbiting Eta Cassiopeiae VII. The pirates were afraid of Jarrod Tyler, but they were utterly terrified of Darius Cain and his Black Eagles. The rumored fates of the few who had dared to approach the Eagles' domain made crucifixion at Tyler's hands seem like a merciful end.

"We're just going on a search mission, Commander." Elias was trying to sound soothing, but he missed the mark, and he could see Wheaton was unconvinced. The trunks of arms his people had already loaded onto the small ship spoke volumes about what he really expected.

"Whatever the mission, sir," Wheaton said, clearly trying to hide her concern, "*Zephyr* is at your disposal."

Cain just nodded. He turned and panned his eyes over the small cluster of his people, twenty of the agency's best. He'd have preferred a larger force, but he couldn't squeeze any more in *Zephyr's* small hull. The trip would be miserable as it was. But Wheaton's ship was the only one in port, and Cain knew every day's delay lowered his already shaky chances of finding out what had happened to *Carlyle*.

"Alright," he barked, looking back toward his people. "Let's get onboard. All of you in line, now. And don't get in the way of Commander Wheaton and her crew."

Cain was determined to get to the bottom of this mystery, and not for the promised pardon. He'd listened to the Chief's words with outward respect, but he didn't believe any of it. If the powers that be wanted him gone, his success on this mission wouldn't change a thing. Elias Cain had come to a conclusion, one that ran counter to all he'd believed for years. Atlantia's government was corrupt, and its laws had gone well beyond maintaining an orderly society. He'd put off considering the true implications of his realization. He wasn't ready to consider that he'd allowed himself to become a tool of oppression…and even less so to imagine what he would do in the future, how his current disillusionment would steer him in the days and years to come.

For now, he would find out what happened to *Carlyle*, not for a pardon, not even because there were Atlantian citizens on that ship. He would do it to get to the bottom of a mystery he could see was far deeper and more complex than he'd originally imagined. He was convinced there was more to *Carlyle's* disappearance than met the eye…and if there was an interstellar crime ring operating throughout Occupied Space, he *had* to know about it.

Chapter 6

Marine Hospital
Planet Armstrong, Gamma Pavonis III
Earthdate: 2319 AD (34 Years After the Fall)

Sarah Cain sat at her desk, her fingers moving along her display, scrolling through long lines of text she wasn't really reading. She had plenty of work to do, but her thoughts were elsewhere, and she found it difficult to focus. The whole affair on Eris had been upsetting for her, beyond of course the normal trauma of battle and death. She and Erik had battled for many years, alongside Augustus Garret and Roderick Vance—and thousands of others—to defeat Gavin Stark and his Shadow Legions. The thought that mankind was once again about to face some dark and secretive enemy was too much for her to contemplate, like some nightmare from the past manifesting itself anew. But she was older now, and sadder. Weaker. She had fought her wars with all the strength she could muster, but she didn't think she had the strength to face another. Especially without Erik.

She also realized that whatever was coming—and despite her best efforts, she couldn't convince herself it was anything less than a catastrophe unfolding around them all—her sons would likely be at the forefront. Darius certainly. His Black Eagles were mercenaries who fought for pay. But she knew him well enough to realize he would not stay out of the fight to come. He wasn't as cold-blooded as he liked to believe, and she was certain he would rise to fight any enemy that threatened all mankind. And his Eagles would follow him. She had seen how they behaved around him, and she recognized true loyalty when she saw it. Darius' soldiers idolized him. He might not realize it himself, but she knew they would follow him, to hell if he led them there.

If the enemy didn't come after them first. No competent adversary could leave the Black Eagles alone. They were far too strong. No, whether he chose it or not, Darius would end up at the center of any major conflict that occurred.

Elias would get drawn in too. He'd allowed himself to become a martinet of sorts, seeking moral justification from enforcing the laws of Atlantia without question, but she was sure he had too much of his father in him to ever follow anyone blindly for long. He would realize the corruption of those he served, and then he would face a true crisis of faith. Would he become cold and cynical as his brother had? Angry and vengeful? Would he internalize the stress and guilt and pain, as his father had done for so many years? Or would he find another way? She didn't know, but she was sure he'd end up at the forefront of the fight that was coming one way or another. She was beginning to believe it was a Cain family curse.

Will none of us ever be allowed to live quietly, in peace?

The thought of her boys enduring the kind of war that she and Erik had fought all their lives terrified her. Like any parents, the two of them had hoped for a better life for their children… or at least a safer one. Erik Cain had been a survivor, a man who had fought countless battles and lived through all of them— until the last one finally claimed him. The thought of her sons dying, as Erik finally had, made her mad with worry. She knew there was nothing she could do, nothing she could say, to prevent it. But it terrified her nevertheless.

She'd returned from Mars and plunged into her work at the hospital, seeking distraction in duty. The administrative tasks had piled up in her absence, and she had plenty to do. But she just couldn't concentrate. Every few minutes her mind would drift…to worry about Darius and Elias, or to fall into wild speculations about what enemy was lurking somewhere in the darkness, a foe that had ruthlessly preyed upon the helpless survivors on Earth, kidnapping them and shipping them off to a life somewhere as slaves. The frigid amorality of such a scheme reminded her of Gavin Stark...and that awoke terrible memories she had long suppressed.

The war against Stark and his Shadow Legions remained in her memories as the worst she had fought.   The First Imperium had been a terrifying enemy, the soulless machines a horror out of some primal nightmare. But an external adversary was something she could understand, and the victory, even with its terrible cost, had been all of mankind's. But the war with the Shadow Legions was a bitter, dirty struggle, a fight against one man's bid for power...and a horror she still struggled to comprehend. Over 90% of the human race had died before Stark was defeated, and Earth, man's birthplace, was reduced to a radioactive nightmare.

This feels like Stark, she thought again, imagining who could be behind such a plot. She knew Stark was dead...killed by Erik in a final desperate struggle. *Could humanity have bred another monster like Gavin Stark?* History was full of similar creatures, but none had been so relentless and capable as Stark, nor had any come close to doing the damage he had. A history full of world wars and mass genocide couldn't come close to matching Gavin Stark's death toll. She couldn't even imagine how mankind would deal with another conflict like the Shadow Wars. Indeed, if fate had decreed that man would again face a monster like Stark, perhaps it would be the final battle, one that would end this time not in a costly victory, but in defeat...and slavery. She wondered if humanity had the strength to somehow come together once again to face a waking nightmare. She found herself hoping, tapping into the inner strength that had sustained her though her endless wars, but in her heart she knew she didn't believe it.

She looked across the room, her eyes catching a spray of light on the wall, hundreds of shades of brilliant blue. A smile slipped onto her lips, and she reached out and picked up the source of the display, a large chunk of crystalline rock sitting on her desk. The lights danced across the wall as she scooped it up and brought it closer to her face. It had been a gift, given to her years before by someone who'd come into her life as an enemy but became a close friend before he died.

Anderson-45 had been one of the Shadow Legion soldiers, a clone created for a single purpose...to fight to subjugate all humanity under Gavin Stark's rule. He had been captured, the first Shadow Legion warrior to be taken alive. When Sarah had initially seen him, he was heavily conditioned, and lacking utterly in knowledge about anything other than obedience and war. She had worked with him tirelessly, unraveling his conditioning, helping him grasp for his own humanity...and she'd watched as the man inside the former slave-soldier blossomed.

Anderson-45 had spent the rest of his short life carrying on the work Sarah had begun, helping the thousands of Shadow Legion troopers who had survived the war adapt to normal lives. It had been a difficult task, and Stark's former soldiers had faced considerable prejudice and lack of acceptance. She knew Anderson-45 and his cohorts had fought because they hadn't had a choice, because they were conditioned to follow orders. But the costs of the Shadow War had been so horrendous, few of the survivors had been in the mood to understand and accept the warriors who had served Stark. Indeed, there had been an active movement, even in the Corps, to terminate all of Stark's creations.

Despite how he had come into existence, Sarah had seen Anderson-45 blossom into as much of a human being as any she'd ever known. He'd become a voracious reader, especially of history. He'd had a ravenous sweet tooth. He'd even developed a sense of humor, becoming quite the good-natured practical joker. And he'd spent hours one day picking out the crystal she held in her hands. The stone wasn't particularly valuable. They were quite common on Armstrong, though ones that refracted only blue light were relatively rare. And Anderson-45 knew that blue was Sarah's favorite color.

She moved her hand across her eyes, wiping away a tear. Anderson-45 had been a good friend, but he was gone now too, like so many people in Sarah's life. Erik, of course, and Elias Holm, Darius Jax…so many others. She had outlived them all. She was alone, save only for her children. And though she loved them with all her heart, they had always been a challenge as well. Erik Cain had been her lover and closest companion for almost forty years, and she'd cherished every moment they'd had together, but he had always been a stubborn man, hard and resistant to change. And if anything, his sons were even more resolute than their father had been. She knew her two boys loved her, but she knew they didn't *need* her. And that had been a painful realization, one that had finally sent her packing from the home she and Erik had shared. Sarah Cain had always felt useful…a combat surgeon, one who had saved countless lives, the matriarch of her little family. She'd be damned if she could spend the rest of her days staring out at the ocean and thinking of everything that was gone. At least on Armstrong she had a hospital to run, the largest in Occupied Space. She could do good there…save lives.

And now you're sitting at your desk in that hospital thinking about all the same things. No, I will not lose myself in the past. I have work to do…I serve a purpose here and now…

She looked down at the screen, rolling back half a dozen pages she'd barely even skimmed. It was time to get to work. Whatever crisis was unfolding, she would face it when it came. Darius was trying to investigate, and she was sure Elias was too, in his own way. And no doubt Roderick Vance would convince the Confederation to take things seriously in the wake of events on Eris. But for now, her work was here…in the hospital.

"There is a visitor to see you, General Cain." Her AI interrupted just as she started to focus on the first report on her screen.

"Who is it?" She wasn't in the mood for guests.

"He claims to have a delivery for you, General. He says he must give it to you personally. Both he and the package have been scanned for weapons and harmful substances."

"She sighed. She wasn't expecting anything, and she really didn't want to be interrupted just when she'd forced herself to focus on her work. She was about to tell the AI to send him away when it occurred to her it could be something from Roderick or Darius. Both of them were prone to secrecy and a bit of the cloak and dagger.

"Send him in."

"Yes, General."

She turned and looked up as her door slid open, and a tall, slim man walked in…followed by a less than subtle-looking Marine guard. The Corps was a vastly shrunken shadow of its former self, but it still took care of its own. And Sarah Cain was a legend, a veteran of the twenty-five years of almost non-stop warfare that had ended with the Fall. Hundreds of thousands of Marines had served during that time, but few had lived through it all, and those who did were revered by the tiny cadre that had followed them.

"Please, come in and have a seat." She suppressed a smile as she looked up at the Marine, standing half a meter behind the visitor, his hand on the holstered pistol at his waist. "That will be all, Corporal." Then, a few seconds later, in response to the Marine's uncomfortable hesitation, "I'll be fine…really."

"Yes, General." The corporal snapped off a salute and turned to leave, clearly unhappy with Sarah's order.

"So, how can I help you, Mister…?" she asked, her eyes moving slowly, taking stock of her visitor.

"Hallis, General Cain. Jan Hallis." The man paused for a few seconds before reaching down into a small bag at his side. "I was hired to bring this to you, General." He pulled out a small box and set it down on the desk.

Sarah looked down, but she made no move to take the package. "What is that?"

"I don't know. The box was given to me as is. As I said, I was simply hired to deliver it to you."

"Hired? By Whom?"

"I'm afraid I can't say, General Cain. I was instructed to bring this to you, but to provide no further information." He paused for a moment, and added, "Which is not to say I know anything further. I do not."

Sarah stared at the visitor for a few seconds, trying to analyze what was going on. Something didn't feel quite right, but she couldn't place it.

But the package has been scanned already...several times, I'd bet, knowing how my Marines think.

She picked up the box and slowly opened it and looked inside. For an instant, she wasn't sure what it was, but then she pulled back a small bit of packing material and gasped. It was a ring...a Marine Corps Academy ring. The numbers 2260 were stamped into the platinum on each side. She stared at it for a few seconds...2260, that was the year Erik had graduated. Then she flipped it around and looked inside...and her heart fluttered when she saw the inscription. 'Captain Erik Daniel Cain.'

She felt a pang of sadness, but an instant later that was swept aside by a wave of fiery rage. "What is this?" she yelled, leaping up from her desk. "Some sick joke? Where did you get this?"

The man shied away. He was ten centimeters taller, but there was something about her, the anger, almost a primal rage, that intimidated him. Sarah Cain was a doctor, a mother...she was a lot of things. But standing in her office at that moment, she was all Marine. And one look at her face suggested her visitor would be lucky to leave the room alive.

Then she saw it, out of the corner of her eye...the scratch. It was small, almost unnoticeable, but it was right where it was supposed to be. She remembered when Erik had done it, one year when he'd gotten a bug to have a vegetable garden. He'd forgotten to take the ring off before he went out to tend the plants, and he scraped it along one of the metal rods he'd set to hold his tomatoes.

She felt her stomach doing flips. How? How was this possible? "What is the meaning of this?" she asked, her tone one of menace itself, leaving no question about what she would do to this man if he was perpetrating some kind of trick.

"General, I was just hired to deliver it to you. I really don't know anything else." His voice was one of utter surprise. He was either a superb actor, or he'd had no warning that the package might provoke a hostile reaction.

She glared at him and then looked back at the ring.

Who could have known about that scratch, about exactly where it was? But if this isn't a fake…

"Where did you get this?" Her words were like a hammer on an anvil. "Where?" she repeated, her tone one of naked intimidation.

The man stood in front of her, clearly shaken. "I was hired to bring it to you, General Cain," he repeated, his voice tentative. "That is all I know."

"Who hired you?" Her tone was like ice.

"Just a man. He didn't give me a name. He told me it had been taken from a prisoner…and that I should bring it here and give it to General Cain."

"Where?" she asked, her voice like death itself. Her eyes were on fire, locked on the man standing in front of her. She was one of the most noted surgeons in Occupied Space, but she had been a Marine even longer than a doctor, and she knew a hundred ways to hurt a man. If this visitor didn't tell her what she wanted to know, she was going to start at number one and work her way through them all.

"I wasn't supposed to say," he stammered out pathetically. "I was warned not to say…"

"I wouldn't worry about what you were warned about if I was you. Because, if you don't tell me right now, you will never leave this room." She stood up and stared across the desk at him. "And it will neither pleasant, nor quick…I assure you of that." Her hand reached under her desk, and she pressed a small button. And instant later, the Marine corporal came rushing back into the room, weapon drawn this time.

"So what will it be, Mr. Hallis?"

The man squirmed miserably, as if caught between two threats, two people who scared him to his core. Finally, he took a breath and tried, only partially successfully, to return Sarah's stare.

"Eldaron," he said. It was on Eldaron."

Chapter 7

Vance Estate
Beneath the Ruins of the Ares Metroplex
Planet Mars, Sol IV
Earthdate: 2319 AD (34 Years After the Fall)

Roderick Vance sat behind his desk, eyes closed, head resting in his hands. He'd been planning the operation almost nonstop for two weeks, and finally the preparations were in place. Now it was time. Time to make history…as the first man to attempt to seize control of the Martian Confederation. Whatever happened, he realized, future generations would learn about this moment, discuss the justifications, or lack thereof. Would he be regarded as a hero? Or the basest traitor in Martian history? Only time would tell.

He tried to clear his head, to focus on the present. There were concerns far more pressing than history's judgment. In a few hours he would be the absolute dictator of the Martian Confederation. Or he'd be dead, killed in his failed coup. Or sitting in a cell, awaiting disgrace and execution.

He'd gotten up this morning—from a sleepless and uncomfortable night—and he'd walked into his bathroom. Then he retched and emptied the contents of his stomach. His thoughts were a toxic brew of tension and uncertainty. But he controlled it all. He'd considered things from every possible angle before he decided he had no choice. He was doing what had to be done, and nothing more.

Better to take the risk of being branded traitor than to be the man who stood by and did nothing while disaster unfolded...

He looked over at the chronometer. It read five past five. If things were going according to plan, Astor's troops were on the move. Vance had made it clear to the soldiers...they were to use delay force only if they were assaulted. He wanted no casualties. The coup was to be bloodless, perfectly executed, and completed before anyone could put up meaningful resistance. By the time most Martians awoke, they would have a new government.

But that was wishful thinking, and Vance knew it. It was almost impossible to carry out an operation so large and complex with no screw-ups. There was a long list of arrests, mostly powerful people with their own household staffs. All it would take was one dedicated retainer trying to interfere with his master's arrest, and there would be violence. And once it started, it would spread easily. Word that there were soldiers arresting people would quickly turn to cries that they were shooting civilians. It wouldn't matter if the shots were fired in self-defense... a coup Vance hoped to complete in a few hours would turn into a bloody rebellion, and any hope of his rallying public support would be lost. He'd still be able to rule, but he'd have to do it with guns and stun rods.

Vance sighed. There was nothing to be done now except wait. He'd intended to join the soldiers out in the underground pavilions, to speak directly to the people, but Astor had convinced him to remain in his quarters, protected by a company of soldiers. If he went out, a single shot could end the coup in its tracks...and Astor and the others who had sworn loyalty to him would be in a very dangerous position. Vance, at least, was already a member of the civilian government. If Astor or Admiral Campbell stepped into the shoes of a dead Roderick Vance, it would become a military takeover. That was something almost certain to cause increased resistance, giving the new would-be dictator a choice between massive escalation and defeat and execution for treason.

Vance was restless, but he was accustomed to acting behind

the scenes. He tried to imagine some of his old friends—Erik Cain, Elias Holm, Augustus Garret—sitting quietly in their quarters while a battle they had planned raged. But those men had been warriors, and Vance's service had always been behind the scenes, in shadowy halls and secret meetings. He'd always been the spy the soldier's trusted, the one who'd had their backs. But he'd never been one of them, not really.

Still, he'd always gotten along with the military. He respected them, understood the things that were important to them in ways most government functionaries didn't. And now, he found many of them were willing to stand with him. General Astor, for one...and all the officers he'd brought onboard. And Duncan Campbell, the retired former commander of Mars' fleet. He hadn't even found it difficult to convince them. None of them were comfortable with the plan, but they all understood the threat, and they were old enough to remember the bombings and the Fall...and they realized something like that could easily happen again. And to a man, they trusted his motives, and they were willing to believe his assurances that when the crisis had passed, he would restore the council.

He was scheduled to address the people at 9AM, and his operatives had already secured the broadcast center. With any luck everything else would be nailed down by then. It would be far better to announce a fait accompli than to tell his Martian countrymen there was an active revolution going on outside their doors. But he'd have to wait and see. He'd done all he could, read and reread every detail of the plan. It was as perfect as he could make it. Now he would find out if fortune was with him...or if it would make a mess of his carefully planned grab for power.

*   *   *   *   *

The girl's shriek ripped through the air, awakening Boris Vallen from a sound sleep. There was a shaft of light cutting through the darkness, illuminating the large and plush bed. He turned instinctively toward her, but she was already moving, shadowy arms grabbing her, pulling her off the bed. He could see the sheets slip off, as the gloved hands pulled her roughly to the side. She stood next to the bed, naked, crying, and behind her, Vallen could see the soldiers, five of them, all clad in body armor and armed with assault rifles.

"Mr. Vallen," one of the soldiers said, "you are under arrest. Please get dressed, sir. You will be coming with us." The man stood slightly in front of the others, and he wore a captain's insignia on his collar.

Vallen felt a surge of rage, an intense desire to spring off the bed, attack these impudent creatures. Didn't they know who he was? A member of the council. Head of the Valen family. His mind raced with images of what he would do, how he would see these fools punished. But he didn't move. Fear was a far stronger motivation for Boris Vallen, and one look at the soldiers with their guns at the ready was enough to dissuade any real resistance.

"What is this about? I demand to know." He still hadn't moved.

"I'm sorry, Mr. Vallen. You are under arrest. That is all I can say at this time."

The soldier behind the captain pulled a blanket from the bed and draped it over the girl's shoulders. She was shaking, clearly terrified, but she was beginning to calm down a bit. She slipped a hand out from under the covering, wiping tears from her face.

"This is an outrage!" Vallen roared, his anger momentarily overcoming his fear. "I am a member of the council. You have no right to arrest me, not under any circumstances!"

The captain maintained his composure, showing not the slightest emotion. "As I said, Mr. Vallen, you are under arrest. I am sorry for the abrupt nature of our visit, and I can assure you that we have no desire to cause you injury. But you are coming with us." His voice changed on the last six words, the ominous timbre of a veteran combat commander overshadowing the polite, almost apologetic tone he'd been using.

The officer took a step toward the bed. "Now, we must go, Mr. Vallen. These two gentlemen will accompany you while you get dressed."

Vallen paused for a few seconds, but he didn't have the courage to push the captain any further. He moved to the side of the bed and stood up, wrapping a sheet around himself as he did.

"What about me?"

It was the girl. Vallen stared over at her with a blistering expression on his face. He was too scared to challenge the Marines standing in his room, but he had no such hesitation in dealing with his recent bedmate. She was the daughter of one of his retainers, sharing his bed half out of awe at snaring Vallen's interest and half out of intimidation, about the fear of what a refusal would have meant to her family's position.

"Shut up," Vallen snapped at her, his voice dripping with venom. He'd enjoyed the lopsided nature of their relationship. Boris Vallen was a bully at heart, and now that he was standing here and submitting to these Marines, his anger had to come out somewhere.

"That is not necessary, Mr. Vallen," the Captain said sharply. He turned toward the girl. "You will be released as soon as we leave. You are to return to your quarters and remain there until you receive other instructions." His tone was softer, not quite soothing, but close enough for a Marine in full combat gear.

He turned and stared at Vallen, momentarily allowing his true feelings to slip onto his face. "Hardesty, Jamis...please help Mr. Vallen get to his feet and assist him in getting dressed. We are on a timetable." He stood there and watched as the two burly Marines grabbed Vallen's shoulders and half-walked, half-pushed the whimpering man toward the closet.

"You can go," he said softly to the still-sobbing girl. "Go home...and stay there for the rest of the day."

*   *   *   *   *

"Admiral Campbell, sir…" The sentry was clearly surprised when Campbell emerged from the shuttle's hatch, but he quickly snapped to attention. "It is quite a surprise to see you, sir." Duncan Campbell was a legend in the Martian navy, but he had been retired for several years, and now he was standing in *John Carter's* shuttle bay, clad in his full dress uniform.

Duncan Campbell nodded and smiled. "As you were, crewman. I'm just here to pay a visit with Admiral Melander."

"Yes, sir…welcome aboard. I will advise Admiral Melander that you have arrived."

Campbell nodded, struggling to keep his face from betraying the tension he felt. He knew Xavier Melander well. Indeed the top Martian admiral had been his protégé, and his self-chosen replacement when he'd finally stepped down from the top job. But friendship only went so far, and Campbell wasn't sure how Melander would react to what he had to say.

"That will be fine, crewman."

Tell him his old friend is here to lure him into a treasonous plot…

The sentry turned toward the com unit and announced Campbell's arrival. A few seconds later he turned toward the admiral and said, "Admiral Melander will see you immediately, sir. I will arrange an escort for…"

"I think I remember my way to the admiral's quarters well enough, crewman." Those rooms had been Duncan Campbell's home for many years.

"Very well, sir. As you wish." The sentry seemed uncomfortable letting so august a personality as the Confederation's legendary fighting admiral walk alone through the corridors, but he simply stepped out of the way and stood at attention. Arguing with flag officers wasn't in his job description.

Campbell walked down the corridor toward the central lifts. He knew he could take one of the intraship cars, but he preferred to walk. *To procrastinate. You're in no rush to see if your friend of thirty years has you clapped in irons.*

The corridor was long. It was almost half a kilometer from *Carter's* shuttle bay to the main lift. The Martian behemoth, and her sister ship *Sword of Ares* were the largest and most powerful vessels ever built by man, eclipsing even the Alliance's vaunted Yorktown class battlewagons. But the Yorktowns were all gone, the last of them during the Second Incursion, along with *Sword of Ares*. *John Carter* was a vestige of a lost time, before the Fall, when mankind's industry and military might was vastly superior to what it had become. *Carter* was a symbol, a statement to any who looked upon her awesome presence that the Martian Confederation alone retained the power to field such a ship. It was an image that required one to forget the vessel was a fortunate remnant, a freak survivor, forty years old and patched together with a hodgepodge of different systems. Still, even in her weakened state, she was the strongest thing in space. By far.

Campbell slipped into one of the lift cars. "Deck ten," he said softly, feeling the acid in his stomach as he got closer to his old friend.

"Deck ten," the AI said as the doors opened.

Campbell stepped out into familiar territory. Deck ten, officers' country. He walked down the hall, back toward the ship's outer hull. *John Carter's* flag bridge was deep within the center of her two million tons, as protected as a space could be. But the ship's designers, no doubt assuming the admiral would be at his station on the bridge in battle, had put the fleet commander's quarters right up against the ship's hull, allowing them to provide such an august personage with a panoramic view of the majesty of space through a pair of expansive hyper-polycarbonate windows.

Campbell had scoffed at the idea the day he'd moved in so many years ago, wondering why anyone would worry about such things on a warship. But he'd come to truly appreciate that view, the relief from staring at cold metal walls…especially on long voyages. He knew Xavier Melander well enough to suspect he felt the same.

He walked down to the end of the hall, stopping at a door with a Marine guard standing in front of it. It was tradition to post a sentry outside the admiral's quarters, one Campbell had always thought unnecessary. But now he wondered if this Marine would be the one who'd end up arresting him when

Melander heard what he had to say.

"Admiral Campbell!" The Marine snapped to attention. "Admiral Melander is waiting for you, sir."

Campbell nodded as the guard stepped aside, pressing the button to open the door. The steel hatch slipped open, and Campbell stepped inside.

"Duncan!" Xavier Melander was slightly disheveled, his tangled hair hastily combed and his off-duty uniform a bit rumpled. He was a tall man, and slender. He stood a good five centimeters over Campbell's own considerable height, but the Scot outweighed his taller friend by ten kilos. Most of that was his large build…and a bit the slight paunch that had been a side effect of retirement.

"How are you, old friend?" Campbell stepped forward and extended his hand. "It's been a long time."

"Far too long." Melander paused, his smile morphing into a concerned expression. "But I don't think this is a social call." He ran his eyes up and down over Campbell's uniform. "Dress reds? At least you still fit in them." He stared at his old comrade for a few seconds. "Barely," he added, with the sort of slightly mocking humor common between old friends.

Campbell knew he wore his tension on his face, but he couldn't stifle a small laugh at Melander's friendly jab. "Yes, I had to wiggle around a bit to get into the pants, but you know these damned things are uncomfortable no matter what."

"That I do…that I do." Melander paused. "I'd offer you a Scotch if it wasn't so indecently early."

"Maybe you'd better…" Campbell's voice was tight. It was time to tell his friend what was going on…and see what the commander of the Confederation's navy did about it.

"So it's that kind of visit, is it?" Melander took a few steps over toward a small counter, reaching up and pulling two small glasses out of a small rack. He leaned over, and a few seconds later he pulled out a bottle, about half full. "From Earth…my last, I'm afraid."

The Fall had effectively destroyed all Earth industry, leaving little behind but radioactive debris and tiny villages of survivors scratching out sustenance-level existences on a terribly wounded planet. There had been an active market for Earth products, wines and liquors and various foodstuffs, but that had long ago petered out. Thirty-four years later there was little left, save the odd bottle stashed somewhere…and generally not for sale at any price.

Campbell felt a twinge of guilt. Melander was a good friend…and he was about to put him on the spot in an incredibly difficult way. Still, he needed a drink first. "You are too generous, old friend. My own stash is long gone." He walked toward the small bar as Melander poured two drinks, and offered him one. He took it gratefully and held it up. "To friends," he said softly.

"To friends," Melander repeated.

Campbell gulped the Scotch, savoring the smoky liquid as it slid down his throat. He nodded and set the glass on the bar. Melander followed suit. Then he looked right at his friend, his eyes wide. "So tell me why you're here, Duncan. The thought of something having *you* so nervous is unnerving."

Campbell nodded and took a deep breath. "You are familiar with the episode with the slave ring on Earth and their base on Eris, aren't you?"

Melander nodded. "Of course. Bad business all around. There was a lot of grumbling about it. Some people in the fleet didn't like the Black Eagles coming in and cleaning up what should have been our mess to deal with. There was even talk about chasing them out of the system if they come back."

"Well, you'd be well advised to quash that kind of nonsense. The Eagles are better than us, Xavier. The last thing Mars needs is a conflict with them."

Melander was silent for a few seconds. Campbell knew his friend didn't like being told the Martian forces were anything less than the best in Occupied Space. Campbell wasn't any happier about it than Melander. But he was too old an officer to ignore fact. And the fact was, Darius Cain's warriors were the toughest outfit that currently existed, possibly that had ever existed.

"I know you're right." Melander's voice was soft, with the

slightest hint of defeat for having to acknowledge the Black Eagles' superiority. "But it still hurts to admit it."

"Well, fortunately the Eagles are more likely to be on our side than lined up against us." He looked right at Melander. It was time to get to the point. "But the Eagles had to do it, Xavier…because we couldn't. Because the council wouldn't let us. Roderick Vance tried his best, but they are dead set on worrying about Mars and Mars only…as if what happens in the rest of Occupied Space—and even the solar system—doesn't affect us."

Melander nodded. "So we get to the heart of it. Roderick Vance is planning something…so why don't you tell me what it is? I know General Astor has been moving troops around, positioning his most loyal units around the Metroplex. So tell me…is this a power play, some kind of bear hug to influence the council?" He paused, staring straight into Campbell's eyes. "Or is it a full-blown coup?"

"How do you know all this?" Campbell stood there with a stunned look on his face.

"You didn't think you left the fleet in the hands of a fool, did you Duncan? A large base on Eris? Slaving parties on Earth, right under our nose? The council may be full of fools, my old friend, but I knew Roderick Vance would do something." A pause. "Though if it is a coup, I must say, I am surprised he chose such an audacious path. And you're here to secure my participation…are you not?"

"I am impressed, Xavier. And yes, that is why I am here." Campbell felt his stomach twist into knots. He'd imagined dozens of times how he was going to break the news to Melander, but he'd never imagined an exchange like this."

"Is there no other way?" Melander's voice was deadly serious.

"No. Roderick has tried repeatedly to sway the council. They'd rather bury their heads than deal with the fact that we likely face a new threat."

Melander stood unmoving, taking a deep breath…then another. Finally, he said, "I wouldn't do this, Duncan, not for anyone but Roderick Vance. He's the only one I'd trust, myself included, not to abuse the power he seizes."

Campbell felt a wave of relief. "You know, all the way up here I was imagining myself getting dragged off to the brig…"

"You underestimated me, my friend. But I will forgive you."

"No. I'd never underestimate you. But you are a patriot… and I had a difficult time with this myself. We live our lives, and we rarely imagine moments like this, where we must look past what we believe in, take actions we might have condemned in normal circumstances."

"Duncan…I've never told you much about my past, before we became friends." Melander's voice was soft, a heavy sadness clinging to his words. "I was a young officer when the bombs fell…I was with you when we fought the Shadow fleet. On *Ranger*."

"I know." Campbell's voice was sympathetic. *Ranger* had lost over 60% of its crew in that fateful battle…and she returned when the rest of the fleet limped back to find Mars' great cities destroyed, their magnificent domes shattered.

"But you don't know I was married then…"

Campbell's eyes widened. He hadn't known. Few naval officers married, especially back then, before the Fall. It was just too difficult to balance family and a career that took one away for years at a time. And he'd never known Xavier Melander to have a wife…

"Yes," Melander continued. "Julia. And a daughter…Maria." He paused, taking a quick breath and fighting back emotions that still clearly plagued him even after so many years. "Whatever you say about Roderick Vance and whether he should have been able to prevent the attack, he did a remarkable job of evacuating the people that day. To save ninety-seven percent of the population in such circumstances was extraordinary."

Campbell felt his stomach tense up again. He knew where this was going…

"But three percent was still a lot of people, Duncan. About six hundred thousand." He was looking right at Campbell, but his friend knew he was seeing something else. "They died, Duncan. They died in that rubble, both of them. I know billions were killed on Earth during the Fall, and my pain is no different than anyone else's. But they were *my* family."

Campbell took a step toward Melander, and put his hand on his friend's shoulder. He wanted to say something, anything, but the words wouldn't come, so he just stood there.

"That's why you can count me in, Duncan. I don't know whether Roderick Vance made a mistake back then, if Stark tricked him, if he could have prevented the bombing if he'd done something different. But that doesn't matter. If we are facing another enemy, something like the Shadow Legions, there is no one else I'd rather have in charge than Vance...no one I am sure will be more ready to stand against whatever is out there, to do what has to be done." He looked up at his old mentor. "And that's what matters, Duncan. All that matters..."

Chapter 8

He could see her, a shimmering image in front of him, just as she had been that day so long ago. Her dress of Arcadian silk, her hair twisted into a series of looped braids, held in place with half a dozen jeweled clasps. Ingrid, his wife. Not as she was now, years older with that sadness in her eyes, but young and happy at their wedding, looking toward the future with no thought of the loneliness and disappointment that lay ahead.

He reached out, longing to touch her again, to feel her warmth, even on his palm for just a moment. But she was just beyond his reach, and his arm moved through the empty air. Then she was gone, and he saw only the solid gray metal of the hull. He was alone again.

Jackson Marne lay on the cold hard deck of the escape pod, weak, barely moving. The pod was a nightmare, a foul refuge reeking of weeks of sweat and shit and vomit. And dried blood. *Carlyle's* captain lay in the middle of all of it, too weak now to stand or even to do much more than futilely reach out an arm, trying to touch an image that existed only in his hallucinating mind.

It had been weeks now since his improbable escape from *Carlyle*, and now he lay once again, out of supplies and waiting for death. Had he managed to survive his ship's destruction only to live for a few more weeks, trapped alone in an escape pod? Could the unlikely streak of luck that had led him to his lifeboat have been for nothing, only to see him die now instead of then?

He'd been sure he was finished when he had overridden *Carlyle's* control systems and opened the cargo hold to space. He'd disengaged the magnetic cradles too, and when the atmosphere of the pressurized hull rushed out into the vacuum, an emperor's treasure in STUs went with it, cast out into the blackness. *Carlyle* had been carrying not refined ingots of the precious metal that could be gathered up, even in space, but vats of ores in need of processing. The granular material was blasted out of the hold and hopelessly scattered in seconds, denying the pirates who had attacked Marne's ship the booty they had sought.

He'd known he would be blasted into space along with *Carlyle's* cargo, but even slowly suffocating as his suit exhausted its scant oxygen supply was a merciful end compared to what the pirates would have done to a captain who'd inflicted heavy casualties and denied them a priceless treasure. But Marne's naval training—and a huge amount of luck—had saved him.

He'd jettisoned *Carlyle's* escape pods as well as her cargo, and by pure chance, one of them had drifted close to where he was floating in space. Then the old lessons kicked in, the emergency survival training he'd never had to use during his naval service. He maintained his calm, pushed back against the fear, and he focused on the nearby pod. He pulled his small oxygen canister from his back, sucking in one last deep breath before yanking the hose out and sliding his finger over the valve. He stared at the pod, his eyes fixed on it as he moved his gloved finger aside and allowed a burst of precious oxygen to blast out.

The escaping gas altered his vector, bringing him closer to a collision course with the pod. Closer, but not on target. His chest ached, his lungs screamed for more air. But the die was cast, he'd torn the suit's hose from the canister. He would either reach the pod, or he would die in the next two minutes. He kept his eyes locked on the pod and angled the oxygen bottle, moving his finger, allowing more gas to escape. His vector changed again, but he was still off. It was going to be close, but he was going to sail by. And he wouldn't have enough time to bring himself about for another run. Not before he suffocated.

This was always a longshot. You only had fifteen more minutes anyway. It was worth it…better to die trying to survive than to sit and wait…

His lungs felt like they were about to explode, and he could feel his consciousness beginning to slip away. Thoughts of his wife and his daughters drifted into his mind, the realization that he'd never see them again. But the navy training was still there, pushing everything aside, demanding he keep trying. He stared right at the pod, blurry as his vision beginning to fail, and he moved the air bottle. He knew it was his last chance. Part of him was already resigned to death, but there was still a spark, a last bit of strength that wouldn't yield. He slipped his finger to the side, letting out a short burst of air.

He couldn't see what his last effort had done. He closed his eyes, ready at last to let go. Then he slammed hard into something. The pod.

A flood of adrenalin gave him a last burst of clarity, and he reached out and grabbed onto one of the handholds. His momentum almost caused him to bounce off and sail past, but he held on firmly. He reached over, hitting the outside controls. He punched at the keys once, twice…finally, on the third try the control shifted to the side, and the outside hatch slid open.

He pulled himself inside, slapping at the inner lever as he did. His first effort hit this time, and the outside door snapped shut. His chest was in agony, his mind screaming for air. He could see the display next to the controls, the blue light of the bar moving slowly to the right as the airlock pressurized and filled with oxygen. He was almost gone, the last shreds of his consciousness slipping away. He had one last thought, to pop his helmet, and his hand pawed weakly at the latch.

He heard something, a loud click, just before the blackness took him. Then he awoke with a start. He was still on his back in the middle of the airlock, but each breath filled his lungs with cool, oxygen-rich air. His clarity returned, and he lay there for a few minutes, gathering his strength. He'd done it...somehow, he'd actually done it. He'd managed to get into the pod.

Don't get excited. The pirates will be blowing you away any second.

Even if this group of raiders was less bloodthirsty than most, they weren't likely to be merciful after the losses they had suffered. Still, he was grateful for the air, and he breathed deeply.

He slid over to the side, putting his hand out to help himself up. But he pushed too hard in the weightlessness of the pod, and he slammed into the ceiling. He felt a wave of pain. His chest on fire, and now he remembered how hard he had hit the hull. Movement in space was a strange experience, and he hadn't exactly had pinpoint control with the oxygen bottle. He figured he'd broken some ribs, three at least, maybe four or five. But that didn't matter. Pain or not, he knew he had to get inside the main cabin. The pirates would probably destroy the pod any minute, but until then he knew he couldn't give up. He gritted his teeth and reached out, grabbing the handhold next to the inner door. He pulled himself up and punched at the control. The door slid aside, and he manhandled his way into the main cabin.

The pod was small, designed to hold two people. But it had three days of food and supplies...and an air recycler that could keep him breathing almost indefinitely. Marne made his way across the tiny deck, pulling himself down to the floor, reaching his arm into the loop of one of the harnesses. He lay there, waiting for the pirates to blow his tiny sanctuary to bits. He felt the seconds go by, then the minutes. Then he fell asleep.

When he woke up and glanced at the chronometer, he realized that hours had gone by. And he was still there. Had the pirates missed him somehow? Had luck intervened on his behalf again?

He moved slowly, and every millimeter of it hurt. His ribs were definitely broken, and the rest of his body was banged up as well. But he forced himself upright, toward the pod's tiny control panel. There was a sensor display, but the screen was full of interference. As far as he could see, *Carlyle* was gone. So was the pirate vessel. But he couldn't get a good reading. There was interference all around the pod.

Of course. The STUs. He remembered from his navy days. Transuranic elements wreaked havoc on scanning systems. *Did that save me? Did it hide me from the pirates?*

He'd spent the first few days waiting for the raiders to return, but nothing appeared on his scanner. Eventually, the pod drifted clear of the greatest concentrations of granular ore, but even then the scope was clear. There were some trace elements, some residual energy readings…enough to suggest that *Carlyle* had been blasted to atoms. He couldn't be sure, but it made sense. The raiders had lost their booty, but they wouldn't have left any evidence behind of their attack.

He'd eaten half rations, extending the three day, two person food supply to twelve days…and then he went hungry. He did what he could to treat his injuries, but that proved to be very little, and every day, the pain became worse. He knew he had internal bleeding, but there was nothing he could do about it. By the twenty-third day, he'd become too weak to move, to even drag himself to the water recycler for a drink.

It seemed odd to him, a strange sequence of events that had saved him only to let him die lying on the deck of the pod. His ship was gone, his crew dead. He was ready to face his end, save for one thing. His family. He longed to have on last chance, just to speak to them, to tell Ingrid how much he'd loved her, how sorry he was for the endless hours she'd spent alone. And his girls…adults now, though he still thought of them as the young children who had always been excited at his return…even after Ingrid had slipped into melancholy. He knew they had grown angry with them as they'd aged, and as they'd seen what his absences had done to their mother. And to them as well… the brief, passing moments he'd given his girls, a poor substitute for a life with their father.

They would never know. They would hear he had died, and they would feel a touch of sadness, and ache perhaps that they didn't fully understand. And then they would forget. They would adjust quickly to his being gone, for that had always been their lives.

"Scanner contact." The pod's AI brought him out of his daydreams.

"What?" he said, drifting in and out of clarity. "Confirm contact."

"Confirmed. Preliminary analysis suggests an Atlantia patrol ship, *Tradewinds* class."

He could hear the AI's words, but they seemed unreal. An Atlantian ship? Was he being rescued...was that possible? Might he see his girls again? Have a last chance to make things right with Ingrid?

No, he thought. I am hallucinating again. I am lost, and soon it will all be over. He could hear the sound of the AI speaking again, but he couldn't make out the words. It seemed distant...and slipped further away. And then the darkness took him.

*   *   *   *   *

"Can you hear me?"

The voice was distant, strange...almost like an echo. A hallucination, like before. He ignored it, but then he heard it again.

"Captain Marne...can you hear me?" It was clearer this time, closer. Then he felt something. A hand on his shoulder?

His eyelids felt heavy, but he forced them open. Light... much brighter than on the pod. And shadowy forms, moving around, hovering over him.

"He has four broken ribs, and he is dehydrated and severely malnourished, but he should be fine. It's a good thing we got here when we did."

He heard the words, but the meaning came slowly. He wasn't dead. Had he been rescued?

"Where..." He tried to speak, but his throat was parched, and he barely got out one word. He becoming more aware. His chest...pain. Every breath was a small agony. And there was something on his arm. He tried to turn to see, but as soon as he twisted his midsection, a wave of pain forced him back.

An IV? Then I was rescued. Is it really possible? Pirates? No, they wouldn't try to help me.

He realized he was lying in a bed...in some kind of sickbay. He had been rescued!

"Don't try to speak yet. You were extremely dehydrated, and we are giving you fluids and nutritional supplements. Just nod if you understand me."

He moved his head slowly, first downward then back up in a serviceable nod.

"Very good. You are on the Atlantian Patrol ship *Zephyr*. Are you Captain Marne?"

He nodded again, moving too aggressively at first and feeling another sharp pain. But his mind was clearing, and despite the pain and weakness, he was beginning to feel better.

"Pirates," he rasped.

"*Carlyle* was destroyed?"

"Yes," Marne answered, nodding as he did.

"So the cargo was taken."

It was another voice, from the cluster of men surrounding his bed. He didn't think it was directed at him, but he answered anyway. "No...they...didn't...get...cargo." It was still difficult to speak, but it was getting a bit easier. Still, his throat was so dry. "Water," he said softly.

"Okay, Captain, but just a little for now." It was the first voice again. An instant later he felt something against his lips, a small glass. "Slowly now..."

The hand tipped the glass, and Marne felt the cool water hit his parched tongue. It was miraculous...he'd never imagined a sip of water could be so wonderful. He hunched forward into the glass, gulping at the water pouring into his mouth.

"Slowly," the voice repeated. "You will just make yourself sick and throw it all up if you drink too quickly."

Marne obeyed, though it took all the will he could muster not to drink it all in a single swallow. "More," he said as the last drops slid down his throat.

"Not yet, Captain. In a few minutes you can have another glass. You'll be feeling better very soon…and even more so when I can fuse those broken ribs."

"Captain, what did you mean they didn't get the cargo?" The second voice again.

"I opened the bay doors…the ore scattered."

"That would explain the scanning problems we've had, Captain Cain." A third voice, female this time, coming from the back of the group. "Clouds of STU-rich ores would scramble things up, even after they'd spread out some. I'd imagine the pirate's sensor suite had been downright crippled when *Carlyle* dumped the cargo."

"That would explain how the pod escaped."

"Captain Marne, allow us to introduce ourselves. I am Captain Elias Cain." The speaker turned and gestured toward a man standing next to him. "This is Dr. Calth. He has been tending to you for the past twelve hours since we brought you onboard. And this…" He waved toward a woman standing behind him. "…is Commander Wheaton. *Zephyr* is her ship." The speaker paused for a few seconds. "You're safe with u, Captain. We've come to investigate the fate of your vessel, and anything else you can tell us would be extremely helpful."

*   *   *   *   *

"Are you sure?" Elias sat at the tiny table, staring across at *Zephyr's* commander. Jamie Wheaton was a petite woman, but Cain had sensed a toughness in her during his days on *Zephyr*, one that had surprised him and turned his first impression on its head. He'd done some checking after their first meeting, and he'd discovered she had served with the tiny expeditionary force Atlantia had contributed to the War of the Second Incursion. He'd been surprised to find that she was eight years older than he was…she had a very young look to her. But that didn't matter…anyone who had spent their early-20s fighting the First

Imperium was a veteran and deserved to be treated as one.

"Absolutely not," she said, with considerable firmness. "It's a wild guess, Captain. But we did pick up some energy readings… and a few trails of particle debris. Pirates are generally good at hiding where they went, but according to Captain Marne, *Carlyle* managed to hit her attacker. If that's the case, what we found is consistent with some types of battle damage."

"So you believe they went through the Gamma Hydra warp gate?"

"I believe it's possible, Captain." She paused, clearly thinking for a few seconds. "Probable."

Elias leaned back in the chair. He was thinking about the situation with his usual ruthless intensity, but there was something else in the back of his mind, something that had nothing to do with duty. He was impressed with Jamie Wheaton, and now he was beginning to realize his thoughts went beyond professional respect. He admired her. Liked her. She was interesting, and strong too…disciplined. It wasn't something he intended to act on, but he couldn't help but realize there was something there. He wasn't sure, but he guessed she felt the same thing.

"If we pursued them through the Gamma Hydra gate—assuming that's where they went—could you pick up a similar trail in that system?" Whatever proto-flirtation was developing in his mind, he pushed it aside. There was work to do, and that came first.

She twitched uncomfortably. "This is all theoretical, of course, since we do not have authority to pursue beyond this system…but the answer to your question is, 'I don't know.'" It depends on how damaged they are, and how much they managed to repair quickly. And time is not on our side. Every day that passes reduces the chance to pick up any kind of trail at all."

Cain leaned back in his chair, bumping his head on the wall behind. *Zephyr* was no battleship with a plush briefing room. Cramped quarters were the order of the day everywhere within her spare hull, especially with twenty of his agents crammed onboard.

"If we transit to Atlantia and request permission to pursue…" He had a doubtful expression on his face as he spoke.

"There is no point. By the time we could maneuver back to the Atlantia gate and then transit back again, there's virtually no chance we'd still be able to pick up a trail. We're already late."

Cain sighed. His hands were tied. Their orders were clear… transit to Epsilon-14 and investigate what had happened to *Carlyle*. They had done that, at least as far as their orders allowed. There was nothing to do but return to base.

But if these pirates are connected in some way to whoever was behind the slaving ring on Earth, hunting this ship down could be the best lead we've got…

"I know what you're thinking, Captain Cain. But even if we had authorization, there is no guarantee we could track them. We might transit into Gamma Hydra only to find nothing."

"I don't believe that, Commander. I understand your caution, but I am confident you can track this ship. If we don't waste any more time."

She smiled briefly, but it slipped off her lips almost as soon as it appeared. "Thank you, Captain. I appreciate your faith in my abilities, but it doesn't really matter, does it? Even if we both believe we can track these people, we don't have authorization to do it."

"No," Elias said. "We don't." He could feel his stomach tighten. He was treading new ground here. He knew what Darius would do in his place…probably after a flurry of expletives about what the Atlantia high command could do to itself. But it wasn't that easy for him. And even if he decided to take matters into his own hands, he would need Wheaton's support to do it.

She sat across the table, staring back at him with a strange look on her face. He wasn't sure, but he thought she might be waiting for him to suggest exactly what was going through his mind. But he knew the second the words escaped his lips he'd put her in a difficult position. Regulations would require her to refuse his request…and to turn him in as soon as they got back to Atlantia.

And that would be the end, all they'd need to throw me in a cell for decades.

But if he passed up a chance to learn more about the mysterious enemy he believed existed out there somewhere, his adherence to regulations could cost millions of lives. He knew the terrible struggles his parents had lived through. He and his brother had been named for friends of theirs, Marines who had not survived those wars. Images of his father passed in front of his eyes, standing out on the patio late at night, staring out into the inky darkness. Elias had never experienced anything like what Erik and Sarah Cain had, the terrible battles, the constant struggle to hold off final defeat. He hadn't carried the psychic scars that had so clearly plagued his father.

What if something like that was coming again, a new enemy, one as terrible as Stark's Shadow Legions? What if humanity was about to face another test like those it had a generation before? The sooner he could identify that enemy, the more time the worlds of Occupied Space would have to prepare. If he allowed mindless adherence to regulations to prevent them from following this pirate, he would give up the best lead he had. He'd always equated ethics and morality with following the rules, but now he wondered if he'd been too simplistic. What if the rules were written by corrupt men and women? What if he could save lives by breaking them?

"Jamie," he said softly, "I am going to ask for your help in something…something difficult and dangerous…"

Chapter 9

Inner Sanctum of the Triumvirate
Planet Vali, Draconia Terminii IV
Earthdate: 2319 AD (34 Years After the Fall)

"I am sure you have both read Agent Mazeri's most recent report. I am at a loss to understand why *Black Viper* was so incapable of securing the target vessel's cargo. Indeed, I recall that this council was quite specific in its directive that an adequately armed and led vessel be detached on this mission. Yet *Black Viper's* crew suffered 40% casualties taking control of a freighter...and they still allowed the target to dump its holds to space. Now, a valuable cargo is lost, and the funds intended to finance the coup on Atlantia are gone."

One paused, rasping to catch his breath before continuing. He sat on a motorized chair or, more accurately, in it. The lower half of his body was encased in a shroud of metal, and the back of the chair extended upward as far as his head. Three separate sections of tubing ran from an IV in his left arm to a large mechanism on the back of the apparatus. Two of the clear hoses were red with blood flowing to and from the hemocleansing unit built into the chair. The other was clear, providing fluids and pharmaceuticals to One's frail body.

The entire setup represented the best leading edge science could do to keep a very old man alive a bit longer, and the chair's occupant indeed appeared ancient to any who laid eyes upon him. But though his weakness and frailty were undeniable, the impression of great age was an illusion. One was three years shy of his fortieth birthday, though he hadn't been born, not in any conventional sense, at least, and his *birthday* was actually the day he'd been removed from the artificial support crèche. He was a clone, just like the other two men in the room, created from the DNA of Gavin Stark, arch-spy and would be conqueror...and the man most directly responsible for the Fall and the deaths of billions of human beings. And like all the Shadow Legion clones, he suffered from accelerated aging.

"We must make a determination," One continued. Do we replace the lost funding from other sources? Or do we delay the timetable on Atlantia?" He looked across the great triangular table at his two companions...and identical clones.

"Resources are quite stretched at the present time," Three said, "but before he discuss alternate plans, I believe we must also look to accountability. Does the fault for this failure lie with Captain Yulich and his crew? With Agent Mazeri and her planning of the operation? Or is it elsewhere within our organization? Must we look more closely at the senior command levels of the Black Flag?" Three wheezed as he spoke, and he leaned against the back of his own powered medical support chair. His head remained motionless, held in a small bracket, but his eyes moved back and forth between his two companions. There was menace in his tone, and anger, clear even through the weakness of his voice.

Two was leaning forward, one shriveled arm resting on the table. The other was missing, and his sleeve was pinned neatly to his tunic. He wasn't strong enough for regeneration, and his shoulder was too weak and withered to support a prosthesis. There was a large bandage around his neck too, with a small speaker situated in the center. "I share your frustration, Three. Indeed, your anger as well. But I must caution against too strong an emphasis on establishing blame." His voice was different than the others, mechanical. The voice synthesizer that had replaced his vocal apparatus was clearly artificial, but it was stronger than the natural speech his associates managed.

"But we must enforce discipline," One said. "We do not tol-

erate failure. It is a cornerstone of our philosophy. Our operatives and allies must fear us more than they do the enemy. If
we allow something like this to go unpunished, what message
does that send? Despite three decades of research, we have
been unable to replicate the cloning technology that created us,
the process by which our sire produced an entire army. We are
relegated to using far more conventional recruiting techniques,
which places a premium on maintaining order."

"I agree," Three responded. "Terror must be maintained,
along with rewards for success. There is no other system that
will work for us. Fear and greed are the two great human moti-
vators." He rushed the last few words out before he fell into a
coughing spasm.

Two sat quietly, waiting for his associate to gather himself.
Then he said, "I am not repudiating our operational doctrine.
Rather, I am simply stating that this is a particularly crucial
period for us. Our respective physical conditions have continued to deteriorate. We cannot now long delay the transfer of
our intellects into the Intelligence, and while we have researched
the subject extensively, considerable uncertainty remains as to
how our thought processes will function as part of that great
machine. We cannot know if efficiency will be compromised…
or indeed, enhanced by the superior computational capability of
being part of something like the Intelligence. I do not council against discipline, but I do urge you both to consider our
primary objectives and the importance of focusing our efforts
right now. We have spent decades building to this moment, but
now we stand on the verge of at last launching our invasion of
Occupied Space.

"The Eldaron operation is about to commence, and its success is vital to our long term plans. We have committed substantial forces and other resources to that world, and nothing
must be allowed to interfere with the successful completion of
our goals." He paused. Even with the synthesizer, speaking
was tiring for him. "Darius Cain and the Black Eagles are the
greatest threat to our plans. More than any other force, they
have the potential to form a cadre around which a unified resis-

tance can develop. And if they join with the remnants of the Marine Corps, they will become an even stronger army. We have risked much on Eldaron to ensure that Darius Cain's warriors go to that world...and that they do not leave it. No distraction is acceptable now. The forces are in position; the Tyrant understands both the rewards for success and the penalty for failure. All is ready. The Black Eagles will fight their last battle on Eldaron."

"We are rambling," One said, putting as much volume as he could into his voice, "and Two is correct. We must focus. Clearly, Eldaron is our primary operation at present. Darius Cain and the Black Eagles must be destroyed before we launch the final campaign. I trust we are all in agreement on this?"

"Yes," answered Three.

"We are," replied Two.

"Very well," One continued. "Now, let us discuss Atlantia. We had planned to provide the proceeds from the sale of the now-lost STUs to the existing government as a secret resource, intended to fund their assumption of total power. "We must decide now. Do we indefinitely delay that operation...or do we find the funding for it in our already over-stretched budgets?"

"I would say delay it," replied Two. "After all, Atlantia is but a single world, and not one of the most powerful. But Elias Cain is on Atlantia. Our operation there would not only secure our control of that world through a proxy government, but it would give us the chance to eliminate a Cain. Elias is not in the position to threaten us as directly as his brother, but I strongly counsel that we do not underestimate any member of that family. Our latest reports suggest that Elias was involved in some way in the debacle in the Sol system that resulted in the loss of our base on Eris and a sixty percent reduction in the number of slave shipments from Earth. I need not repeat the impact this has had on projected troops levels and industrial output."

One moved his head slightly, the best version of a nod he could manage. "I agree with Two. Elias Cain is currently out of favor with his superiors, which limits his present capabilities. However, the most the Atlantians are likely to do under the current regime is to dismiss him from his post…or possibly to imprison him for a limited period." The malevolence in his voice grew. "However, if our proxies assume total power, Elias Cain can be easily disposed of…shot in some cellar without significant difficulty."

"So it is agreed then," Three said. We will divert resources from the strategic reserve to support the government takeover on Atlantia. I propose that we suspend any action on assessing punishment for the debacle over the Atlantian freighter. My reasoning is specific. Agent Mazeri has always been reliable, and if we are going to invest directly in the Atlantian government, I for one would be more comfortable with her in place to watch over events as they unfold. People being what they are, we do not want to allow the Atlantians to feel too independent. They must be made to understand that they are in charge on Atlantia…but also beholden to us, part of our new regime. Agent Mazeri has always been particularly skilled at…educating those in such positions."

"I concur," One said. "Indeed, Agent Mazeri should be expressly told that any guilt in the matter of the *Carlyle* will be extinguished by successful stewardship of the Atlantian transition."

"Yes," Two added. "We are agreed." He paused, a soft rattling sound coming from his voice synthesizer as he drew in a deep breath. "And now, to the most important piece of business. The package has been delivered to General Cain on Armstrong. She took the courier prisoner as we anticipated, but he knows nothing except what we wanted him to know. Undoubtedly, despite his assurances of secrecy, he passed on the source of the package to her. We know she departed from Armstrong almost immediately after, and we can only surmise her destination was the Nest. Unfortunately, between the vigilance of the Black Eagles and the paranoid quality of Jarrod Tyler's government on Columbia, our intelligence capacity in the Eta Cassiopeiae system is extremely limited.

"There is nowhere else she could have gone," Three said, his struggling voice nevertheless presenting an air of certainty.

"There was some concern she would go to General Gilson, but her departure from Armstrong suggests she is indeed going to seek out Darius Cain's assistance…just as we anticipated."

"I submit that General Cain did not even advise General Gilson as to the package's contents," One said. "The Marines would no doubt go berserk if they knew what was in that box, but they are simply not in a position to mount an attack on a target as strong as Eldaron. Sarah Cain would have known that Gilson in all probability would have nevertheless launched even a hopeless attack. And she also knows the Eagles are stronger… our prediction that she would immediately go to her son appears to be confirmed."

"Indeed," Three said, "we are down to the last variable, the reaction of Darius Cain. Everything we know about the man suggests he will attack Eldaron immediately. He will suspect a trap, of course, but his belief in the invincibility of the Black Eagles will support a rationalization that his people can prevail nevertheless. Even without knowledge of the secret forces we have stationed there, he will see a difficult target…one that will cause him to deploy his full strength. And once they have landed all their forces, we will release the secret armies. And at long last the Black Eagles will be overwhelmed and destroyed."

"And then the invasion can begin." One managed a smile, one that would have chilled the spine of anyone less reptilian than his clone partners. "And we will establish a new order that will rule all mankind for millennia to come."

Chapter 10

"The Nest" – Black Eagles Base
Second Moon of Eos, Eta Cassiopeiae VII
Earthdate: 2318 AD (34 Years After the Fall)

"We have a scanner contact, Captain. Approaching from the Delta-Vega warp gate."

"Details on my screen, Lieutenant." Captain Rolf Anders sat in the middle of the Nest's small command center, supervising the overnight watch, guarding over the Black Eagles' home base and the space around it. Time of day was a relatively meaningless concept in a place like the Nest. Eos was the seventh planet from Eta Cassiopeiae, so far from that sun that it hardly received enough illumination to justify the term daylight. And the Nest itself was mostly below ground, buried kilometers under the surface of Eos' second moon. But Darius Cain felt that humans needed to maintain some connection to natural norms, so the Nest functioned on Earth time. And Anders and his skeleton staff had pulled the graveyard shift.

"It's a small ship, sir. Approximately 4,000 tons. Decelerating at 3g on a vector almost directly toward the Nest." The lieutenant had relayed the incoming feed directly to Anders' display, but she still reported each data point as it came in.

"Warn them off, Lieutenant." There were buoys all around the outer system, advising all approaching vessels the area was off-limits. The pre-recorded messages started off polite but progressed through several stages of increasing intensity until they outright threatened the destruction of any unauthorized vessels. But the ship was still approaching. "And put *Eagle Two* on alert." The approaching vessel didn't look particularly threatening, especially to an installation as strong as the Nest. But Eagles doctrine was clear. It was far better to take excessive action than to cede the initiative to a potential enemy. In simpler terms...don't take any chances.

"Captain, we've got a response coming in. The ship requests permission to dock at the Nest."

"We're not expecting any vessels, Lieutenant. Advise them permission is denied."

The lieutenant turned back to her workstation, but an instant later she spun around, looking over at Anders, her eyes wide with surprise. "They advise that General Cain is aboard, sir."

Anders shook his head. "General Cain in on the nest, Lieutenant...in his quarters. That's..."

"General Sarah Cain, sir."

Anders opened his mouth, but he closed it again without saying a word. Sarah Cain had never visited the Nest, but every Eagle knew who she was. If it really was her in that ship. The Eagles had plenty of enemies, and any of them could pretend to be Sarah Cain. Indeed, someone could even have captured her to use her as a way to get past the Nest's defenses. He had no idea how to proceed. This had just gone way above his pay grade.

"Lieutenant, get me the general's private line." Waking Darius Cain in the middle of the night wasn't near the top of any Eagle's to do list. But failing to report something like this—whether it turned out to be genuine or a trick—was even lower.

"General Cain...this is Captain Anders in the control center, sir. We have a ship approaching, and they request permission to dock..."

*   *   *   *   *

"*Who* is aboard?" Darius was groggy, and Ander's words were still sinking in. He'd always been a poor sleeper, not as bad as his father certainly, but he'd rarely slept for more than four hours, and even then he usually woke a few times during the night. But Ana was in bed with him now, and he found her presence made him more restful. He'd even slept straight through the night a few times since she'd moved into his quarters.

"Your mother, sir. The vessel is the *Westwind*, an Armstrong-registered transport."

"My mother lives on Armstrong, Captain, but if she was planning a visit to the Nest, she would have sent me a message so advising me."

"Yes, sir. I understand. Nevertheless, there is a woman on that vessel insisting she is General Sarah Cain and requesting permission to dock." Anders paused. "I didn't know what to do, sir."

Darius sighed. "You did the right thing, Captain. I'll be right up." He slapped his hand down on the com unit, closing the line. Then he sat up and swung his legs over the edge of the bed.

"Your mother is here?" Ana's voice was soft, and he could feel her hand gently stroking his back.

"I don't know," he replied. "It's a surprise if she is. I would have expected her to send a message first. She's never been to the Nest, you know." He tried to hide the twinge in his voice, the sadness at his mother's disapproval, but it slipped out anyway. Darius had lived his life according to his own code of discipline, and that meant never showing weakness. To anyone. But he found it difficult around Ana. She saw through his defenses...right to the inner man no one else knew existed.

"I'm sure your mother would have come to visit you before... but she is busy, you're busy..."

He stood up and began to get dressed, turning back toward her as he pulled his tunic over his head. "No...." He shook his head slowly. "It is my fault. I left. After my father disappeared. I was young, angry, in pain like I'd never imagined. I just went my own way, left everything behind. She was devastated too, alone…she needed me. But I just couldn't stay there anymore. I don't like Elias' chosen path any more than he does mine, but at least he remained on Atlantia for her. I just added to her pain…"

Ana held his gaze—something few people did. To most people, General Darius Cain was a figure to be feared, a dangerous and impatient man. But it was clear that Ana Bazarov saw something different when she looked at her lover. She looked like she was about to say something, but the words didn't come. Instead, she just got up and walked around the bed, putting her arms around him for a few seconds.

"I'll be fine, Ana," he said, putting his hand on top of hers. "I don't even know if it is my mother…or just some kind of trick. It wouldn't be the first time somebody lied to try to get close to the Nest. The Eagles have many rivals and enemies, and they'd love to get inside our defenses." He returned her hug for a few seconds then he slowly pulled away. "One way or another, I've got to go deal with this."

He walked toward the door, stopping just short and turning his head back to Ana. "If it is my mother, it won't be good news she brings. If she just wanted to visit she would have sent word ahead. She is a very strong woman…whatever sent her running to the Nest has to be downright critical."

He turned back toward the door and continued walking, slapping his hand against the sensor to open the hatch. Then he slipped out into the hall without another word.

*   *   *   *   *

"This is General Darius Cain." He sat at a workstation, staring at the ship on his display. The vessel had followed all the commands Captain Anders had issued, and it sat at a dead stop, 500,000 kilometers from the Nest. "I wish to speak to General Sarah Cain." He turned toward Anders. "Get me visual on this line."

"Yes, sir," Anders replied. An instant later, the room's main screen activated. It was blank for a few seconds, as the signal passed through the kilometers of empty space and back again. Then an image appeared, a tall, slim woman, her long blonde hair, now streaked slightly with gray, tied up loosely behind her head.

"Hello, mother." Darius Cain stood in his control room, the nerve center where he'd planned and launched his many meticulous campaigns. Cain was widely considered to be fearless, pitiless, an unstoppable force. But the face on the screen unnerved him, and his voice was tentative, uncertain. He knew enough about his mother, career Marine and battlefield surgeon that she was, to understand she wouldn't have shown up on his doorstep unannounced without a good reason. And that almost certainly meant trouble.

"Hello, Darius," she replied, the words reverberating in his headset. The four second delay while signals moved back and forth made conversation annoying, but not impossible. "I must talk to you immediately…in person. It is important, not something we can discuss over the com. Please advise your people to let my ship through." Her voice was strong, direct, but Darius could hear—feel—something else there. Tension. Confusion. Her façade could fool most people, but he saw right through it.

He felt his stomach tense. *She is upset…I've never seen her so unnerved. Not since that night…*

He turned toward Anders. "Captain, *Eagle Two* is to launch immediately and dock with that vessel. I want an honor guard aboard to escort General Cain back here." He felt an odd feeling, a twinge of guilt at his caution. His mother had come all this way, clearly upset about something…and he wouldn't allow her ship to land. But the Eagles had a lot of enemies, and any of them could have captured his mother…or impersonated her somehow. Darius Cain was a suspicious man who trusted almost no one outside his inner circle, but he knew it couldn't be any other way. When he made mistakes, men and women died.

"Yes, sir," came the crisp reply.

Darius turned back to the screen. "I am sending a ship to

dock with you, mother. It will take you aboard and bring you back here. If you have any companions, they may accompany you, though I request that you limit this to personnel you trust completely. This is the quickest way to get you here. Your ship will have to submit to a full search before I can allow it to approach the Nest. The vessel may leave immediately after you transfer, or its commander may allow my inspectors aboard. Once it passes the security check, it may approach and land... and we will provide it with any required refit or resupply."

"Is that really necessary, Darius?" Sarah looked impatient, but it quickly faded. "Very well, whatever you feel is... appropriate."

He felt another pang of guilt. He was uncomfortable dealing with his mother, and that fact increased his anxiety. Feelings mingled...guilt, love, resentment, sadness. "I afraid it is, mother. It has nothing to do with you. We have security protocols that are never overridden. Under any circumstances. An occupational hazard, I'm afraid."

He watched the screen, waiting the two seconds for his words to reach her location. There it was, the flash of disapproval on her face at the mention of his occupation. She stifled it almost immediately, but he still saw it. It was almost involuntary, the impression people had, the idea that anyone who had to maintain almost paranoid security was suspect. Cain usually ignored it, being almost completely unconcerned with what most people thought. But it stung coming from his mother.

"*Eagle Two* will be there shortly, mother," he said, his voice clipped, uncomfortable. "I will see you soon." He cut the line, and he turned around and walked toward the door.

He wondered why no one considered how disciplined his soldiers were before they formed their judgments, or compared the Eagles to the packs of brigands and vandals many of the warring planets fielded as armies. He wished for an instant that they ever considered the fact that he had turned down dozens of jobs, accepting contracts only in legitimate conflicts, where war was almost certain with or without the Eagles' intervention. He'd turned away an endless parade of would-be tyrants and brutal dictators. Sadly, many worlds suffered under such kinds of leaders, but the service of the Black Eagles was off the table for them...because of an ethical decision made by the monster who commanded the great mercenary company.

Why is morality so overly simplified...even by people like my mother? Corrupt governments can imprison and kill their own citizens, often for simply disagreeing with outrageous mandates...yet they are usually spared the kind of universal condemnation the Eagles so often suffer. Such hypocrisy. They all act as judges, as arbiters of right and wrong, so ready to make determinations without facts, without analysis. They don't even realize they disapprove of us not because of what we do, as they state, but because we are the best...and because they fear us.

He paused at the edge of the control room. "I want *Eagle Two* back as quickly as possible, Captain Anders." Then he slipped through the door into the corridor. He headed first toward his quarters, but he stopped just short of the lift. Ana was there. If he went back, she would try to comfort him...and she would probably succeed, at least to an extent. But there was no time for that now. He had to stay sharp, be the ruthless monster everyone thought he was. His mother was here for a reason, and whatever it was, he suspected he would be compelled to take some kind of action. Sooner rather than later.

He turned and walked back down the hallway toward his office. He had a feeling he would soon need the Darius Cain they all feared so greatly, the cold-blooded warrior...and Ana Bazarov saw right through that mask, to the man below the invincible armor. And there was no time for that man now.

*   *   *   *   *

Sarah Cain walked through the clear umbilical connecting *Eagle Two* to the Nest's primary surface airlock. She didn't approve of many of the choices Darius had made, but she still felt a bit of awe seeing the scope of what he had built in so short a time. She'd known about the Nest, of course, and the Eagles' fleet, but actually seeing the scale of her son's power up close was a shock.

The Eagle vessels were lined up in neat rows, each one of the strongest warships still in Occupied Space. They were smaller than the old Alliance Yorktowns certainly, far smaller. But there were none of those behemoths left, and most of the worlds of Occupied Space struggled to field squadrons of frigates and other small craft. Looking out over Darius' fleet, the ships perfectly lined up in their landing cradles, made her truly realize just how superior the Black Eagles were, how much stronger and more capable than the other military forces in Occupied Space. Even the Marines had wasted away over the years through endless rounds of belt-tightening until only two regiments remained...along with the hospital and a dozen ships still left over from Augustus Garret's mighty fleets.

She knew Erik would be proud too, gratified by Darius' capabilities, despite any disapproval he might have felt for his son's mercenary activities.

If he disapproved...

Erik Cain had been a Marine. He'd fought for his comrades, not for pay, and so mankind could have a chance at a brighter future. But he'd always been an enigma, a man who didn't think much of the people he struggled to protect. He wanted to have faith they could learn from history's mistakes, build a future based on freedom and not coerced obedience. But Sarah more than anyone knew he'd never really believed it.

She was sure his doubts would have become set in stone if he'd seen how many worlds—Atlantia among them—had changed since he'd been gone, how quickly the descendants of the adventurers who'd left Earth to find freedom among the stars were prepared to surrender it, just as the people of Earth had so long before.

He might have made the same choices as Darius. Perhaps he'd be here on this moon with his son, commanding the greatest mercenary company in human space.

No, he was a Marine. If he'd fought again it would have been for the Corps.

He might have accepted Darius' choices, but she couldn't imagine Erik Cain fighting under any banner but that of the Corps'. She pushed back a wave of sadness, the pain and loneliness she'd learned to handle, but that had never really gone away. And now it was trying to flood back into her mind...

"This is the lift, General Cain." The lieutenant's voice pulled her from her daydream. His tone was respectful and courteous. She knew the Eagles were savage fighters, feared throughout Occupied Space, but since the moment she'd set foot on *Eagle Two*, she'd seen nothing but courteous professionalism from everyone she'd encountered.

Two of the soldiers of her escort were already inside the large car, standing at attention along the back wall. The lieutenant and the two other Eagles stood outside, waiting for her to step in.

She nodded and walked in, followed by the three remaining soldiers. An instant later the door slid shut, and the lift began to drop. The feeling in her stomach told her it was moving quickly, very quickly. Still, it was several minutes before it came to a stop and the doors opened.

Her eyes widened as she looked out into the large room. It was at least fifty meters square, and the ceiling was ten meters above, carved from the solid rock and polished to a glossy sheen. There were soldiers in two long lines, three meters apart, creating a path for her party to traverse. The men and women wore what had to be full dress uniforms, sleek black tunics with bright white pants and polished black boots. The tunics were covered with platinum lace and insignia, and the soldiers held assault rifles at their sides.

Sarah had been part of the Corps since she was seventeen, and she was no stranger to military ceremony. But she couldn't recall seeing a more perfect assembly of troops before. Again, it ran counter to her expectations of the Eagles, her imaginings of a bloodthirsty group of brigands, coarse men and women, clad in torn fatigues with bloodstained bandanas tied around their heads. This force was as disciplined as any she'd ever looked upon...as perfect as any group of Marines she'd seen.

Her first two guards stepped out of the elevator car, falling in next to each other in perfect formation. The lieutenant gestured for her to follow, and walked next to her when she stepped out, followed closely by the last two troopers. The second she set foot outside the lift, a band she hadn't noticed began playing the Marine Corps Hymn.

She walked slowly forward, still shocked at the rigid perfection of the ranks of soldiers around her. Whatever Darius had inherited from his parents, there wasn't a doubt in her mind all of Erik's military aptitude had passed to his son.

She looked straight ahead as she walked, trying to see over the shoulders of the two hulking guards in front of her. But then they stopped abruptly and stepped to the side, revealing Darius standing there in his own dress uniform. He had a serious expression on his face, but when he saw her, he smiled.

"Hello, mother." He leaned forward and embraced her. "Welcome to the Nest. Your visit is long overdue, and I hope you will find the time to come more often in the future." She could hear the emotion in his statement, though she realized it would not be obvious to most listeners.

"Darius, I can't tell you how happy it makes me to see you." She returned his hug, and she extended herself up on her toes and kissed her son on the cheek. She held onto his shoulders as she pulled her lips away slowly, and she whispered into his ear.

"I have to speak with you alone, Darius. It's important."

*   *   *   *   *

"If this is true, I will destroy them! I will raze their cities, and kill them all. What Rome did to Carthage will seem like a love tap." Darius was furious, and the anger pulsated through every nerve in his body. The room seemed to shake from the cold energy of his voice, and his stare was like death. His right hand was clasped in a tight fist...around a small chunk of metal. His father's Marine Corps ring.

"I don't know anything for sure, Darius. But I can't think of any way someone could have gotten that ring unless…" He voice tailed off as she tried to choke back tears. "Unless your father did not die on that ship. His ring would have been with him, and if the ship lost containment it would have been vaporized…along…" She paused again briefly. "…along with everything else onboard."

"If father survived the attack on that ship…it means he was taken prisoner. That the ship was disabled and boarded. But who?" He looked at his mother, his gaze a mix of fury and almost childlike confusion. "Who would have attacked that ship and taken prisoners before destroying it?" His mind was already answering his question, but he wasn't ready to face the possibility that whatever force his people had faced on Lysandria and Eris had been in existence all those years ago. Was it possible that an organized powerful enemy had been operating in total secrecy for decades, gathering strength as the worlds of Occupied Space became weaker and ever more disunited?

Sarah's eyes were locked on her son's. "I came right here. I wanted to tell Cat Gilson, but the Marines aren't strong enough to do anything. If we even knew what to do."

"I know what I am going to do. I am going to Eldaron…and I am going to tear apart every millimeter of that world, search every room, every cave, question every leader. If he is there, I will find him. If the people of Eldaron know anything about this, they will tell me." His tone on the last few words was like ice.

"But we don't have any proof, Darius. Just this ring." Sarah's voice was uncertain, shaky. If there was the slightest chance Erik Cain was alive somewhere, she knew she had to do something, anything, to try to find and rescue him. But she couldn't condemn an entire world to the apocalypse that would follow an invasion by the Black Eagles.

She turned and looked into Darius' eyes. She saw nothing there but rage…and determination so resolute she realized in an instant no force in Occupied Space would stand in his way. Her son did not share her ethical doubts about invading a planet on such thin evidence, and if they found that the Eldari had kept Erik Cain prisoner for so many years...she shuddered to think of what he would do to them. His rage would run as hot as the core of a star, and millions—whether they'd had any involvement in the scheme or not—would die.

Perhaps I shouldn't have told him, she thought, feeling a flush of doubts. But they quickly subsided. If there was any chance Erik was still alive, she had to see everything possible done. Sarah had always been disciplined, and her Marine training and years of service had only increased her capacity to control herself, even if difficult situations. But it was taking everything she had to stay focused now. A thousand questions bombarded her mind from the nether land at the fringe of her thoughts.

Was it really possible that Erik was actually alive? Or had he been captured and died in the interim? And perhaps the worst of all...how badly had he suffered? Fifteen years of captivity... what kind of hell had he had to endure for so long? She, more than anyone else, understood how helplessness would be the worst torture Erik Cain could experience. If by some miracle he was still alive, what had the years of captivity done to him?

Then there was the other thing that had been plaguing her since she'd discovered the source of the ring. "Darius, if this is more than some kind of hoax, if Erik is a prisoner on Eldaron...then this may all be some kind of trap. Who would have sent the ring to me except someone who *wanted* us to come to Eldaron...who *wanted* the Eagles to attack there?

Darius stared back at his mother, not the slightest change in his expression.

"Of course it's a trap," he said calmly. "Whatever is waiting for us on Eldaron, we can be sure our enemies believe it is enough to destroy us. No doubt that is the purpose behind the sudden appearance of this ring."

Sarah nodded, wiping a tear from her face. "So, what do we do? We can't just ignore this, not if there's a chance your father is still alive."

Cain maintained his stare, his face rigid, like something carved from a solid block of stone. "I'm not going to ignore anything, mother. We go in, that's what we do…and we show these bastards that whatever they have planned, they underestimated the Black Eagles."

Chapter 11

Central Broadcast Center
Beneath the Ruins of the Ares Metroplex
Planet Mars, Sol IV
Earthdate: 2319 AD (34 Years After the Fall)

"We'll be ready in five minutes, Mr. Vance." The technician's voice was edgy, nervous. Vance didn't know if the man was a supporter, if he was working so diligently because he believed in the reasons for the coup...or if he was just afraid, intimidated by the armed troops who had stormed through the doors an hour before. And for the moment, he realized it didn't matter.

"That will be fine." Roderick Vance turned and looked out over the room. The black-clad soldiers were all around...as he knew they were in most of the other vital installations in the Ares Metroplex...and the other cities of Mars as well. Things had gone smoothly for the most part, though there had been some resistance. Vance had known his goal of a totally bloodless coup was unrealistic, but as the reports began to stream in of scattered resistance, and the fighting it took to overcome it, he struggled to maintain his focus. Astor's last report had brought the total to one hundred two dead. Not a lot in the context of seizing control of an entire planet, but far more than Vance had allowed himself to expect.

Xavier Melander had been a pleasant surprise, at least. The navy was with him, without a shot fired or even a threatening word reaching his ear. And control of the fleet practically guaranteed the success of the coup. Vance hadn't had the same relationship with Melander he'd had with his successor, and he hadn't been sure the admiral trusted him enough to accept his assurances he would step down as soon as the crisis was over. He'd blamed himself for so long over failing to stop the disastrous attack that had devastated the surface cities, he'd become increasingly hesitant to believe that anyone truly trusted him. But Melander...and Astor and Campbell, and a lot of others too, proved that hypothesis to be flat out wrong. He still had support, enough at least to sustain his desperate gamble.

His greatest worry had been a struggle between Duncan Campbell and Melander for control of the fleet. Campbell was a legend in the Martian navy, but Melander was its current commander. Vance imagined Martian ships dividing into factions... battling each other in an orgy of wasteful killing. That would have been a tragedy for myriad reasons, not the least of which was Vance knew he'd need the fleet—all of it—intact and united if his fears proved to be correct and mankind faced another challenge like the Shadow War.

He walked slowly across the room, a pair of soldiers falling into step on each side behind him—the same four who'd been following him since he'd left his bedroom that morning. He suspected Astor had charged them personally with protecting him, and they'd been taking their orders so seriously, he'd had to argue for privacy when he'd gone to the bathroom earlier.

There was a podium set up in front of a large white backdrop. The flag of the Martian Confederation hung just behind where he would stand in just a few moments, when he addressed the people and advised them they now lived in a dictatorship. The news would be a shock, he knew. The council had refused to release the news of the situation on Earth and the destruction of the base on Eris for fear of causing a panic, so few Martians had any idea what had instigated the morning's actions. Those who lived near crucial installations had probably seen the troops moving about all morning...or even heard gunfire from one of the places security personnel had resisted. But for the most part, what he had to say would be shocking.

"We're ready, sir." The technicians pranced nervously around Vance, uncertain how to behave or even what to call him. Was he their president now? Their prime minister? Their king?

Vance nodded and stepped up to the podium. He stood silently for a few seconds, taking a deep breath...then another. Finally, he stared straight ahead and said, "I'm ready."

A second later, one of the technicians made a thumbs up gesture. He was on the air.

"Good morning, my fellow Martians. I am addressing you this morning on matters of great importance, and I ask you, one and all, to set aside whatever you are doing and give me your undivided attention." His speech was being sent out on the priority circuit, which mean that every screen, com unit, and public address system on the planet was broadcasting his words. Virtually every inhabitant of Mars would hear what he had to say, and soon after he would know if they accepted what he had done...or if he faced a long and bloody struggle to establish his authority.

"Approximately six months ago, I became aware of a worrisome situation on Earth, and further investigation established that a large and well-supplied organization was kidnapping people and shipping them offworld...to be used someplace unknown as slave labor. Subsequently, we discovered a large and well-armed base on the dwarf planet Eris, operated by the same organization."

He paused, giving his audience a chance to absorb what he had said. He'd intended to start with the announcement of the coup, but at the last minute, he decided to provide some background information first.

"That base was attacked and destroyed by a force of Black Eagle ships and soldiers." He'd debated whether to mention the Eagles or not. Darius Cain's mercenaries inspired fear throughout Occupied Space, and he knew suggesting they were his allies—though he knew that was a considerable exaggeration of the current relationship—would be useful in intimidating any potential resistance. He'd have preferred to convince the people with logic and facts...but he had to acknowledge that fear was probably more effective in the short term.

"This information was not released at the time because the council decided it would cause needless panic. During the intervening time, nothing has been done, either by way of investigating the mysterious organization behind this terrible crime…or preparing militarily to face it." His voice was deadly serious, almost grim. It had been more than fifteen years since the Confederation had fought its last war…and that struggle, against the First Imperium, hadn't come close to Mars itself. The period before the Fall had been a quarter century of almost constant conflict, but a new generation had come of age since Confederation forces last fired their weapons against an external enemy.

"This course of action was foolhardy, and it ends now. As Martians, you all deserve to know about any threats to the Confederation, and I believe that this shadowy force represents an extreme danger to all of Occupied Space. The resources required to operate the slaving ring and build the base on Eris were enormous. This is no ordinary criminal enterprise. It is an organized entity, and one that wields great power." He gripped the podium tightly and forced himself to continue. "Those of you as old as me remember another time, another enemy. You remember the beauty of the surface cities, the grandeur of Martian civilization, all that our parents and grandparents had achieved. And you remember the day all of that ended at the hands of another enemy…a deadly threat we did not recognize until it was too late to avoid cataclysm." He stood still, staring at the camera, his own mind drifting back to that terrible day.

"I cannot—I will not—stand by and allow another catastrophe to befall us. I do not know what is out there, or how powerful this potential new enemy may be. But I must follow my instincts…and they are screaming a grave warning to me, one I cannot ignore." He pounded a fist on the podium.

"The council would not take this threat seriously, so I have been forced to disband it. The members of the council have all been detained, and the Assembly has been adjourned." A pause. He'd just told them their government had been dissolved. He tried to imagine the reactions all around the planet as people heard those words. "And I have taken temporary control of the Confederation. I have the support of both the army and the navy, the commanders of which understand the crisis and share my concerns on ensuring we are ready to face whatever new enemy is gathering in the darkness."

The army and the navy...or at least the two commanders and a few picked forces. It remains to be seen how the rank and file react. Still, that should intimidate most people nursing thoughts of resistance...

"I want to assure every Martian that this is a temporary measure, one born of necessity, and when the danger has passed, I will gladly lay down the powers I have taken, and I will retire to manage my private affairs."

Nobody believes that. Which is funny, because it's true. They can't imagine how much I just want to fade away, to manage my business interests...even sit and read a book. And for once, not know about every disaster waiting to explode. Fifty years of intelligence work...that's too much for any man...

"But for the duration of the crisis, I must insist that all Martians work together, that we refrain from any acts of civil disobedience or anything else that impairs the readiness of the Confederation to face whatever crises befall us. I respect the core of independent thought that resides inside each of us, but now that must be subordinate to our joint effort to resist and defeat whatever enemy is gathering in the darkness. We must stand as one, walk forward as one...fight as one. And we shall. For any Martian that fails to do his duty now serves the enemy...and will be treated accordingly."

There. The hammer. How many listening understand what that means? How many realize that if they do not do as you say, your soldiers will come for them, drag them from their homes in front of their bawling children? I cannot leave us helpless before another enemy. I will not. But must I become what I despise in order to resist an even greater evil?

"It is with all of this in mind that I now declare a state of martial law to exist throughout the Martian Confederation. Henceforth, all public gatherings of more than three people are prohibited. All non-citizens present on territory of the Confederation are ordered to report to the closest consulate offices within two days for review of residency status. All civil proceedings are hereby suspended for the duration of the crisis. All media is hereby placed under the control of designated government authorities…"

*   *   *   *   *

"This is an outrage. You are a traitor! I will see you executed for this!"

"You will find that a difficult task at the present time, Mr. Vallen. Your authority is rather limited at present. Indeed, I have done what had to be done, largely because your previous influence contributed to the council's failing in its obligation to act in the interests and for the protection of the Confederation and its people. I will now remedy that." He felt a wave of anger…at Vallen, at men like him who had been born into positions of power and luxury but who lived as parasites, indulging their every whims, no matter what the cost to others. *I would do Mars a favor if I had them all shot…*

Stop it. You took power to save the Confederation, not indulge old hatreds. Do not become what you despise.

"Might I suggest you take some time to consider the relative comfort of your captivity? Your own clothes, plenty to eat. A comfortable cell. I can provide you with some history texts if you care to study the conditions others in your position have been compelled to endure. Assuming they weren't just shot in the back of the head and dumped in a trench somewhere."

"I am a member of the Confederation's high council. I demand to be released at once!"

"I'm afraid the council no longer exists, Mr. Vallen, and you have no authority to demand release. However, if you are fortunate, the interim government will not have the time or resources to look more closely at your past business transactions. As in most times such as these, transgressions such as defrauding the government and misuse of influence will be punished far more severely than in normal circumstances." His voice had deepened, becoming dark and threatening. "We wouldn't want to see you stand before a firing squad or mount the scaffold, would we?"

Vance had always been a measured man, but he was capable of considerable coldness. He knew if Vallen pushed him hard enough he would send the snotty little prick to his death in a heartbeat.

Give thanks for your father, Boris...my respect for him is the only reason you're not lying on a concrete floor on the lower levels. Or more likely, crumpled next to the recycling unit with a bullet hole in your head.

"Behave, Boris, and you will survive this...and no doubt return one day to a position of power you can abuse as you have done ever since your father died. I will not kill Sebastien Vallen's son, nor seize the Vallen family assets...unless you give me no choice. Your father was a good man, one of the best I ever knew, and I owe him better. I can only imagine the disappointment he felt in you, the shame and astonishment that his son could be such a useless pile of excrement. But I will not sacrifice my mission, nor devote more time to controlling your actions. If you cause any trouble—any at all—I will forget my debt to a friend, and you will never leave this prison."

He glared at his rival for half a minute, and then he turned and walked away from the cell. Vallen had return the gaze, quivering with rage as he did, but managing to control himself. Vance was impressed. He hadn't been at all certain the damned fool had it in him.

Fear is a wonderful motivator...

*   *   *   *   *

"I want to thank you all...for coming to this meeting on such short notice, but also for your help in the recent...troubles. I want to assure you all once again that when I am certain the crisis has passed, I will lay down the power you have helped me take, and I will retire to private life."

"Roderick, I think I speak for everyone here when I say your integrity is beyond question, at least as far as we are concerned. I would not have supported you if I didn't trust you. We have done today what had to be done and nothing more. I suggest we move forward with no further doubts or hesitation...and prepare to face the dangers that prompted our actions." General Astor was sitting to Vance's right, still wearing the black combat uniform from the morning's operations. There was a tear in the jacket, and a small blood stain on the left arm, barely visible on the dark fabric. He had a holstered pistol on his belt, along with a row of extra clips. The first two cartridges were missing.

"I agree with General Astor," Duncan Campbell added simply.

Vance forced a smile. "Thank you all. With your assistance, I am confident we will be able to face and defeat whatever enemy we face...and quickly return to representative government." He wasn't remotely confident...he didn't have the slightest idea of what they faced, and his gut was telling him it would be every bit as bad as the Shadow War, and quite possibly worse. But he owed his allies a pep talk. Morale was important in any war, and he couldn't afford to have his top commanders despairing before the first battle had been fought.

"What do we do first...what should we call you?" Admiral Melander looked around the room, his gaze settling on Vance. In the rush to execute the coup, they had never discussed Vance's post-coup title.

"I suppose we will have to come up with something for public consumption," Vance said, looking and sounding as if he had tasted something bad, "but in the meetings of this advisory council, I am Roderick."

The others looked a little uncomfortable, but Vance repeated himself. "I am Roderick. I have known you all for years. We are friends, every one of us. We do what we do now for Mars, and for mankind as a whole, but nothing between us has changed."

He knew that wasn't really true, but he wanted to hold on to some informality with his closest associates, a touch of normality as he tread ground he'd never imagined he would. He'd read enough history—seen enough of it—to know how power changed men. The people in the room with him right now would be his lifeline. They would anchor him, keep him the man he had always been.

I hope.

"Very well...Roderick." Melander looked around the room, as if inviting them all to answer the question he was about to ask. "What do we do first?"

They all looked toward Vance, waiting for him to speak before offering their own thoughts.

"Well, we must prioritize our needs," Vance said, realizing even these highly-ranked men would draw their strength from him. He'd taken power, and now he had to lead. "We must rally our forces, mobilize all reserves and mothballed ships and equipment...because I believe we face one hell of a fight, all the more dangerous because we know almost nothing about what we will face."

A series of nods worked its way around the table.

"We also need allies. As in the wars against the First Imperium, I believe our new enemy will threaten all of Occupied Space. We cannot fight alone. We do not have the resources. I believe we will need to build a great alliance, to combine the strength of all the colony worlds. It is no secret that our strength is a tithe of what it was before the Fall. An enemy will not need hundreds of warships and millions of soldiers to subjugate mankind, especially if our worlds stand alone, falling one by one until what remains is too weak to mount a strong defense."

"Allies?" It was General Astor, and there was heavy doubt in his voice. "Is that likely? Few even know about this enemy yet, and we are estranged from most of the former colonies, as much as anything because of so many years of isolationist policy."

"Indeed, Arch...we will find things more difficult than they might have been. The council chose to worry about internal affairs and ignore everything else. In the years right after the Fall, we ignored the pleas for help from the colony worlds, so many of them inhospitable places, rich in resources but dependent on imported food, manufactured goods, spare parts for life support systems. We think mostly, of course, of the dead on Earth during the Fall, the billions killed in the terrible death throes of the Superpowers. But people died elsewhere too, on planets all across Occupied Space…for lack of a few crucial pieces of equipment or some basic supplies. We suffered too on Mars, but we had the old cities to retreat to, the refuges where our grandparents had lived. We lost three percent of our people in the initial attack…but almost everyone else survived. That was not the case many other places."

Vance stopped and took a deep breath. He hadn't intended to rehash the policy mistakes of the years after the Fall. Everyone in the room knew that Mars had turned inward after the Shadow Legions were defeated…and they knew there was widespread resentment of man's oldest colony on the other worlds.

"So what do we do?" Astor asked. "How do we convince these worlds to band together, to join with us?"

"We choose a few, the ones most likely to listen to what we have to say…and after we have them, momentum will be on our side. Worlds that mistrust us will see a growing coalition, and they will be more likely to listen to our arguments. And when war erupts, fear will do our work for us, and the worlds remaining unaligned will flock to our banners, as they did during the Second Incursion."

"What few, Roderick?"

"Armstrong, certainly. General Gilson and the Marines will join us. I am sure of it."

Astor nodded. "I'm sure they will, but the Corps we remember doesn't exist anymore. General Gilson has done all she could, but lack of resources—and the terrible losses during the Second Incursion—have whittled down what was once the greatest ground force in human history to a shadow of its former self."

"That is true, Arch. Gilson fields only four battalions, barely a cadre for the army we will need. And there are few surviving veterans left to recall. That pool was drained, during the Shadow War and the Second Incursion, when thousands returned to the flag and died in the devastating battles of those struggles. Given an injection of resources, I think Gilson could double, perhaps triple her ground forces. But no more. At least not without starting with raw recruits."

"So, twelve battalions of veteran Marines?" Astor nodded. "That is a significant force by any measure. A good start at least." He paused. "Am I correct that the resources you speak of would come from us?"

"Yes," Vance replied. "Mars is wealthier and more populous than any colony world. The Marines are already as large a force as Armstrong can support. We must be prepared to equip and supply the veterans returning to the colors."

"Keep in mind, Roderick, our own resources are not what they once were. Our people voted to forego rebuilding the domes so we could focus what wealth we had to maintaining the terraforming program. It is one thing to sacrifice for our children and grandchildren, but I'm not sure funding other worlds' armies is going to be very popular."

"It won't be, Xavier. That is one reason we took the action we did today. If we run this coming war based on popular opinion, we will lose."

Melander nodded, as did most of the others. "Arcadia?"

"Yes, Xavier, Arcadia for sure. We have maintained good relations with Kara Sanders. I have never met her son, but I have heard good things. I am sure they will listen to what we have to say...and the Arcadian Senate will do whatever the Sanders' propose."

"Arcadia is strong," Duncan Campbell said, "one of the toughest of the colony worlds."

"Yes. They are." Vance took a deep breath and exhaled before continuing. He knew his next suggestion would get a lot of blowback. "And I want to send an emissary to the Black Eagles."

The room was silent for a few seconds, every eye fixed on

Vance. Finally, General Astor spoke first. "The Black Eagles are mercenaries, Roderick. Killers. They fight for money, with no regard for the suffering they cause. Darius Cain is a monster…he brings shame on his great father."

"Nonsense, Arch. You know better than that. Yes, they are mercenaries, but have you ever truly studied their campaigns? They strike swiftly, inflicting as little strategic damage as possible to their targets. They do not commit atrocities. They do not plunder the worlds they attack. They accept the surrenders of their adversaries, and they release their prisoners unharmed as soon as hostilities cease."

Astor stared back at Vance. "Perhaps I overstated things, Roderick, but the Black Eagles have killed more human beings than any force since the Second Incursion. They have invaded over a dozen worlds, planets that now exist under the rule of their neighbors, those wealthy enough to pay the Eagles' blood price."

"And what would have happened in those wars if the losing worlds hadn't been quickly subdued by the Eagles? How long would the conflicts have lasted? How many invaders would have resorted to strategic bombings, destroying cities and factories in the process of winning their wars? How many more lives would have been lost in years long struggles instead of lightning conquests?" Vance was panning his gaze around the room as he spoke. They had all supported him in his coup, but they hadn't truly adjusted their minds to the reality they faced. They still nursed old impressions, stereotypes and bigotries they could no longer afford to indulge.

"As far as is known, the Black Eagles have honored every contract they've executed. You may not agree with their philosophies. You may say they are mercenaries who fight for pay. That is fine. But if you clear the stereotypes from your thoughts and look at the facts…you will see I am right." He paused, trying to gauge if he was making any progress. He ended up flipping a coin mentally. "The Black Eagles are the most capable fighting force in Occupied Space. Whether you agree with my assessment of their conduct or not, there is no choice. The

Eagles have already fought against this enemy on Eris, the only force to have done so. We need their strength. It is that simple."

"Will they join with us?" Melander said matter-of-factly. "Will they fight for a cause instead of for pay?"

"They fought on Eris, Xavier." Vance spoke softly, calmly. "We have received no bill from them for ridding the Sol system of a major enemy base. Darius Cain was extremely reasonable when he came to Mars at my request." He paused, looking around the table. "He was not the fire-breathing monster some of you seem to think he is."

"We followed you into this because we have faith in you, Roderick. We will trust your judgment. We must have allies, that much is clear. And there is no question the Black Eagles would be a powerful force in any fight we may face." Duncan Campbell's voice had a touch of doubt in it, but he just nodded.

Melander nodded first. Then Astor, followed by the others. However reluctantly, Vance's advisory council had agreed. They would send an emissary to the Nest. They would try to enlist the Black Eagles to the fight.

*   *   *   *   *

"Just listen to me before you rush to judgment." Vance was sitting at a small table, staring across at the room's sole other occupant. The chamber wasn't a cell, it was a plush hotel suite, but its occupant had been held captive nevertheless, and her anger was written clearly on her face.

"Why do you care about my judgment, Roderick?" Katarina Berchtold spoke calmly, in measured tones, not what Vance had expected.

"Because I have come to respect you, Katarina."

A short caustic laugh escaped from her lips. "You have? Forgive me if my recollections are somewhat different. You have always been dismissive of me, so utterly convinced of your own unchallengeable correctness. What miracle has won me your respect? The fact that I sided with you on the last vote? Is that why I was dragged from my bed this morning by armed men? Because you admire me so?"

Vance sighed. He'd always considered himself to be open-minded, ready to consider any argument as long as it was supported by facts. But now he was seeing himself through Berchtold's eyes, not those of an enemy but rather a colleague who had become somewhat of an ally in recent years. Her perception of him as arrogant and self-righteous stung.

"I am sorry about this morning's events, Katarina. I really am." He sucked in a deep breath, trying to keep his mind alert, focused. It had been a long and eventful day, and it was well past midnight. "I would have preferred to speak with you first... but I simply couldn't take the chance. The council's refusal to take any action put the entire future of the Confederation in jeopardy. I was at the forefront in the wars that preceded the Fall. The perception that such a conflict cannot occur again in based on folly, on the desire to see things in an appealing way. But burying one's head in the sand only invites disaster. Haven't we lived through enough? Isn't three decades crawling through underground tunnels enough to remind us our survival depends on our vigilance?"

Berchtold took a deep breath. "Roderick, you know I share some of your concerns about recent events. But if you expect me to endorse your coup..." Her voice trailed off. "It wasn't the right way. I'm not saying your concerns are invalid, but you can't save the Confederation by first destroying it."

"I don't want to destroy the Confederation. I want to save it. Would it be preserved if we fall to an enemy? Can you honestly say the council's intransigence did not invite just such a disaster?" He paused. "And do you feel the council was truly a representative government? In its early days, our leaders were infused with a spirit of civic obligation. They put their personal interests aside when it came time for them to serve on the council. They viewed such service as a duty, and they retired after a term, returning to private life. What has happened since then? How long have you been on the council? How long have I? How much have men like Boris Vallen profited from their graft and influence peddling? The council? What was that august body in recent years except an entrenched aristocracy, one far more representative of the great economic families than the people?"

"So you correct the problem of entrenched power by seizing total control, by becoming a dictator?" There was anger in her voice, but confusion as well, and Vance could tell she was conflicted. He knew she understood the danger, and he also suspected she realized the council had long ago veered from its roots, becoming corrupt and aloof.

"You have known me for almost fifty years, Katarina. You will have to judge for yourself. I have promised to step down when the crisis is over. You must decide if you believe me or not." He paused. "Because if you can trust me in this, I desperately need your help…"

Chapter 12

APS Zephyr
Gamma-Hydra System
Outer System
Earthdate: 2319 AD (34 Years After the Fall)

Elias stared out at the screen, his stomach twisted into knots. It had turned out to be easier than he'd expected to convince Jamie Wheaton to violate orders and chase after the tenuous trail left by the pirate vessel. He wasn't sure if her own sense of duty to hunt down the raiders had been at play…or if the spark he'd felt between the two of them had been mutual—and strong enough for her to risk throwing away her career to help him.

He hoped it was the former. He already felt guilty for even suggesting it…and if she was doing it solely out of affection for him, it would be that much worse. Elias hadn't considered just how intransigent Atlantia's authorities could be, not until recently. Or how often those in positions of power and favor escaped the rigid judgment that befell others. He and Wheaton were following the spirit of their orders, but not the letter. And in Atlantia's increasingly officious government, the letter was all that mattered unless you were one of the true insiders.

"Anything yet?" He'd told himself he wasn't going to ask again, that she would tell him if she picked up the trail. But it came out of his mouth anyway.

"Maybe," she said, her voice tentative.

He felt a rush of excitement. He knew he was already in

trouble back home, but if this unauthorized chase proved to be fruitful, he figured there was a good chance Wheaton would escape any fatal damage to her career. The authorities would blame him, no matter what happened, he suspected. But he had rapidly approached the point where he didn't care anymore. Indeed, he wasn't even sure he was going back to Atlantia. If they managed to find the pirates, he was planning to continue to investigate, by himself if necessary. The ship they were chasing was only a clue, he was sure of that…part of the trail leading to something much bigger. Possibly a danger to all Occupied Space, a menace that had to be stopped. If they weren't already too late.

He opened his mouth, but then he closed it again.

She will tell you when she knows…

"I think we've got it!" She looked up from the scope, and stared at him across the cramped space of *Zephyr's* bridge. "It's weak, and there's no way to be sure it's not from some other ship…but it's right where it should be for a vessel moving from the Epsilon-14 warp gate straight through to Zed-4.

He stepped across the control room, ducking twice to avoid low-hanging conduits. "That's great news." He felt a wave of relief. At least he hadn't convinced her to make the unauthorized transit for no reason. There was no guarantee they would find the pirates, but at least they were still on the trail.

"Ensign Berry, scanners on full power, thousand kilometer sweep on either side of that particle track. I want the AI crunching on it immediately."

"Yes, Commander." Megan Berry was a rookie, making her first voyage on *Zephyr*, but she sounded steady enough. Elias wondered how she would hold up if they caught the pirate… and it came to a battle.

The Atlantian Patrol Service was always short of seasoned personnel, because it tended to encourage significant turnover of its crews. The government had grown increasingly paranoid about armed forces outside its own internal security units. An army, and more recently, a navy of sorts, were essential to a growing sovereign planet, but the personnel of the Patrol spent far too long in space, away from the watchful eyes of their superiors.

The policy of turning over most crews after one or two terms had been presented as a way to ensure there were plenty of trained reserves available in an emergency, but Elias knew that was crap. Experienced reservists made sense for the army, perhaps, but if the active duty Patrol personnel were lost in some conflict, their ships would be gone too...and recalling retirees wouldn't do a thing to provide vessels for them to man. Atlantia hadn't had its own fleet for long, and they had nothing in mothball as some other worlds did.

The way the Patrol was run was just one more example of folly, of those seeking to accumulate political power putting their own needs and concerns over what was best for the planet and its people. Elias knew they would pay the price if Atlantia was ever attacked by another world, one with actual veterans manning its ships. But he was beginning to realize that those obsessed with political careers only had attention to spare for actions that furthered their own positions.

"Getting results now, Commander." Berry sounded excited. "It's a match to the trail we found in Epsilon-14. Probability ninety-six percent."

Elias felt a wave of excitement. They hadn't lost their quarry, not yet at least.

"Very well, Ensign. Continue recording...and set a course to follow the trail. Three gee acceleration." Wheaton turned toward Elias. "Well, at least we didn't come here for nothing." It hung in the air heavily between the two of them, but unspoken in front of the others: *At least we didn't violate orders and trash our careers for no reason.*

Elias just nodded.

Yes, at least we didn't do it for nothing. And maybe we can save your career, at least, when this is all over...

*   *   *   *   *

"Captain, we're picking up a contact. Too far out for meaningful data, but it is possible it is following us." Lars Treven looked like hell. His arm was in a cast, and his upper leg was wrapped with a large bandage. His face was covered in bruises where his helmet had smacked into a bulkhead when he'd almost been blown out of *Carlyle's* hold and into space. He'd been dazed and in pain, bleeding from his wounds, but somehow he'd managed to hold on...and eventually pull himself back into the corridor and close an emergency hatch behind him. Most of his boarding party, the ones still alive at that point, had been blasted out into space, where his insistence they wear survival suits under their armor had saved their lives. Most of them, at least.

"On my screen." Yulich looked down at the workstation, just as the sensor data displayed. There it was...an unidentified ship of some kind. Its course was close to a pursuit vector, but not exactly.

It could be heading for the Archenar warp gate...planning to swing around the primary for a gravity assist.

But if I was following a ship, I'd vary my approach vector too...

"Okay, let's not get too concerned," Yulich said, more for the benefit of the bridge crew than anything else. Still, despite his public nonchalance, he was concerned. *Black Viper* had taken considerable damage from *Carlyle's* laser cannons. Yulich had done everything he could on the fly to address his ship's damage, but he didn't doubt *Black Viper* was leaving a particle trail behind it, one that could have been followed.

"Lars, let's plot a course change...straight for planet three." The system's third planet was a tiny colony, settled by a group of religious fanatics or something similar...Yulich couldn't remember exactly. But it was a legitimate destination, and if that ship was following *Black Viper*, it would have to make a significant course change to maintain contact.

And then we'll know if we've got a shadow on our tail...

"Calculating navigation plan now, Captain." Treven struggled to work the controls, angling his body so his cast was in his lap, and his good arm was turned toward the keyboard. He really should have been in a sickbay, or at least resting in his quarters, but *Black Viper* wasn't a naval vessel, with multiple backups for each position, and there was no one on the ship who could replace the first mate, at least not anyone nearly as good. Especially not after the losses they'd taken in the *Carlyle* debacle.

They'd managed to recover most of the boarding party personnel who'd been blown into space from *Carlyle's* hold before they ran out of life support, but not all of them. Added to those killed in the fighting, *Black Viper* had lost over a third of her complement, and she was undermanned at every post.

"Course change locked in, Captain."

Yulich sighed. A diversion to planet three would cost time, and if this ship wasn't following them, the delay would be for no reason at all. He was half tempted to just run, take off in a completely different direction. He figured he was already going to be in trouble when they got back to base. The Black Flag didn't look kindly on failure…and he was returning with his ship and crew shot up and a vital cargo lost. The last thing he needed was to explain why he'd wasted time flitting around an irrelevant system.

"Engage," he said grimly, deciding to take things one step at a time. Whatever waited for him at base, he had to get there first to find out.

And if this is ship is military, we're in no shape to face it now…

*   *   *   *   *

"Target course change, Commander." Berry spun around, looking toward Wheaton as she spoke.

Zephyr's captain had been staring down at her own workstation, but her head snapped up, and she returned Berry's gaze.

"Report," she snapped. Berry was a rookie, but Wheaton knew her officer would never learn if she went too softly on her.

Berry looked back at her screen. "They are applying thrust at 2.94g, Commander. The new vector is 076.024.301."

Wheaton punched at her own controls, bringing up a rotating 3D display of the system. She stared for a few seconds, and then she pulled up a summary of system data.

Where the hell could they be going? There's nothing in Gamma Hydra worth a pirate's time.

Planet three was the only one occupied, and its population was less than 50,000. She read the small synopsis. Colonized by a small religious sect under charter from the old Alliance. No resources to speak of, no army or navy. No trade ships.

Just a bunch of farmers living off the land. No place a pirate would want to go. Unless they've got some kind of damage and need to land...

"Continue to monitor, Ensign, but continue on our present course. And get the AI crunching this. I need to know if they're really heading to planet three or if they're revectoring toward another exit gate."

"Yes, Commander."

Where the hell are you going? Planet three? Or are you just messing with us, trying to throw us off?

She paused for a few seconds.

Or are you trying to see if we follow you? Yes, that makes sense...

"Ensign, ask Captain Cain to come to the bridge."

"Yes, Commander."

She felt a twinge of guilt. She'd just convinced him to go back to his quarters and get some rest, and now she was calling him back less than an hour later. But she wanted his input. She'd been impressed with his tactical insights...as well as the way he looked in his uniform, though she'd forced that part out of her mind. Mostly.

Wheaton had been focused on her career for a long time, and the inevitable result of that had been a dearth of personal relationships. Atlantia's policies toward its nascent fleet tended to push all but the strongest candidates into retirement after a term or two at most. But Wheaton's combat history, and her impeccable service record had kept her in uniform for fifteen years. She was mostly fine with the cost of her career, though she still thought occasionally about what she'd been missing.

She'd heard of Elias Cain before, of course. Everyone on Atlantia knew of the planet's renowned family. Erik Cain was a bonafide hero, by far the planet's most famous former resident. There were statues of him in half the town squares...though Elias had told her that his father had *hated* that kind of attention, and he'd only put on a good face at the innumerable ceremonies he'd been compelled to attend because he considered the honors to be directed at his Marines more than himself.

Elias himself was well-known too, long-considered one of the most promising members of the Patrol. That reputation was still there for public consumption, but within the Patrol itself, word had spread that he had fallen into disfavor. He had taken a long leave of absence, gone on some mysterious trip... but that was all Wheaton knew about it. She'd been a little concerned when she'd been assigned to work with him and his team. Muck tended to spread in the tense environment that had become Atlantian politics. And she'd worked too long and hard to put it all at risk. Or so she had thought.

The Elias Cain who had come aboard her ship was not at all what she expected. He had a reputation as something of a martinet, but her impression of him now was completely different than her expectations had been. He seemed troubled—that was no surprise—but otherwise she found his company extremely pleasant. And he was smart, very smart. She still couldn't believe she'd agreed to exceed her orders, to engage in a hot pursuit of the pirate vessel. It made sense, of course... they'd been sent to find out what had happened. But the Patrol had become mired in regulation and procedure, and its officer and operatives had very little operational flexibility. She figured she'd be okay as long as they found something. If they didn't...

"You wanted to see me, Commander." Elias walked through the hatch onto the bridge.

"Yes, Captain," she said, holding back the smile that had tried to break onto her mouth. "The target vessel has changed course. I think they're heading for planet three."

Cain walked over to her workstation and looked at the screen. "That doesn't make any sense. There's nothing there of value... and I doubt they've got a base in this system. Besides, it's not the course they were on when we found them." He turned and looked right at Wheaton, pausing for an instant and pulling back slightly when he realized how close they were. "They must be baiting us, trying to confirm we're following them," he said, pulling his face back a few more centimeters from hers as he did.

"I thought that too," she replied. "But what do we do? If we change course ourselves, they'll know we're after them. But if we stay on our present heading, we'll have to transit when we reach the gate. If we don't, they'll know then...and they'll make a break for it in another direction."

Elias sighed softly. "It's a gamble either way. If we tip them off, they'll run for it, probably through the Fomalhaut gate. We might be able to catch them, but that's not what I want." His voice deepened, a cold edge slipping in. "I want them to go to their base. Those bastards didn't luck into a shipment of STUs. That's more coincidence than I can believe in. No, they knew about it. And that means they're part of something larger, an organization with far reaching tentacles. We're not after a pirate ship...we need to find where they're going, what exists out there a rung above this vessel and crew." He paused. "I say we stay on course, and go through the Zed-4 gate. That's where those pirates were heading. Unless I'm very wrong, they'll sit tight in this system a while, to give us time to move deeper into Zed-4... and then they'll come through. We'll find a dust cloud or an asteroid belt, somewhere we can shut down and hide...and wait for them to come through."

Wheaton listened, and then she thought quietly for a few seconds. Finally, she leaned closer to Elias and whispered, "I agree with your logic, Elias, and your plan. But what are we going to do if we find what you're looking for? *Zephyr* isn't a battleship...we can't handle a pirate base or a whole fleet."

He didn't say anything. He just turned and looked at her, his eyes locked on hers. He didn't need words...she knew the answer to her question. He had no idea. Not yet, at least.

Chapter 13

Central Detention Section – "The Black Cells"
Beneath the Citadel
Planet Eldaron, Denebola IV
Earthdate: 2319 AD (34 Years After the Fall)

The prisoner sat against the cold stone of the cell's wall, staring out into shadowy nothingness. His prison had a source of outside light, a tube about forty centimeters wide reaching up at least ten meters to a small skylight. But that was closed now, as it usually was, and the only illumination came from a small fixture in the ceiling. That was on most of the time, around the clock, though there had been periods when it had gone off, and he'd been plunged into total darkness for what felt like days and days.

He suspected there was some method to the madness, some purpose to how his captors provided light and took it away…or beat him relentlessly for periods of time and then left him alone for months. It had all been part of their strategy to break him, he was sure of that. And they *had* broken him, to an extent at least. He hated the thought that he had allowed them to get to him in any way, that he'd failed to stoically resist the effects of the sustained abuse. But the prisoner had lived a difficult life, one full of struggle and pain, and his will was strong. He had clung to a part of himself, despite the best efforts of his jailors to destroy him completely.

He had tried for years to escape, to assault everyone who had entered his cell, but he'd ceased those efforts years before. He knew that was one way he'd been broken. His constant efforts had been as much about embracing defiance as any realistic hope of escape. But he just didn't have the drive to do it anymore...to endure the brutal punishments that followed every futile attempt. Years of malnutrition and lack of exercise had withered his once strong body. And his bones had been broken so many times and healed haphazardly, he could barely still walk.

He'd clung to memories, of visions of the past, people important in his life. That had been a source of strength...and pain as well. He had wondered many times, was a man stronger when he had connections...loved ones, friends, home? Or were those weaknesses, did they sap the pure iron will of the man who had nothing left, nothing to lose? He'd been both of those men in his life, and he wanted to believe he was stronger for those he'd left behind. But those images had brought him as much pain as strength, and as the years passed, he'd come to realize the memories were reminders of what he'd once had, what had been taken from him. Those thoughts fueled his anger and his defiance, but his inability to do anything, even to lash out effectively at his captors turned everything to frustration.

The man he had been—and he drew a sharp distinction between that and what he had become—would never have given up. And for years he had kept that spark alive. But now it was dimming, flickering out under the onslaught of time and pain and loneliness. He'd begun to think of striking at the guards again, gathering what strength he had for one last attempt...not to escape, but to fight hard enough, to force his jailors to kill him. Then his pain would be over.

He couldn't imagine killing himself, cutting open his wrists on a jagged bit of stone or hanging himself with a bit of torn clothing. There was enough of him left to make such a surrender unthinkable. But dying on his feet in battle? Yes, that he could do that. It would be a fitting end...

*   *   *   *   *

"I want those emplacements ready in three days, General Vlad...and not an hour longer." The Tyrant sat on his throne, a great construction built of native black marble, encrusted with gold and silver...and the priceless gems mined in Eldaron's jungle belt. He'd had it built at enormous expense, though truth be told, he hated the gaudy thing. The man who had been known as Maranov relished raw power, not the pomp and frill that so often accompanied it. But the throne and things like it sent a message to all who bore witness to them, a testament to the glory and magnificence of Eldaron's Tyrant. Even the title had been designed for maximum effect...to state openly, without obfuscation or spin, that he was the absolute ruler of this world, that his merest whim was law.

"Yes, Tyrant," the general answered, his voice betraying a hint of worry. The Tyrant knew all his people were on edge. He'd never been tolerant of delay and failure, but since he'd returned from Vali, he'd driven those around him with an unstoppable fury. A dozen ministers and project managers had been executed, the most egregious by slow and extremely unpleasant means. Fear was his motivator, and he'd honed his techniques through twenty years of absolute rule. But this time, he was driven by his own fear.

The Black Eagles are coming, he thought. *You would all work harder if you knew what you would soon face.*

Darius Cain's vaunted mercenaries were indeed a fearsome force, a private army so good it had never lost a battle...never even come close to defeat. Eldaron was a strong world, one he knew could put up a powerful defense, even against an enemy as deadly as the Eagles. But Eldaron did not have to face the Black Eagles alone. The Triumvirate had supplemented his world's defenses, and thirty thousand of their frontline troops were deployed in secret bunkers, waiting for the Black Eagles to land. The Tyrant couldn't match Cain's killers one to one...he knew that. But with the Triumvirate's Omega soldiers added to his native army, he would outnumber the invaders almost ten to one. And he would have the advantage of surprise, as tens of thousands of crack troops emerged, hitting Darius Cain's mercenaries when they were fully engaged with his regular army.

Still, though he would never allow anyone to see, the Tyrant was scared. He knew what was at stake. Success would propel him near the top of the Triumvirate's organization...making him the ruler of a hundred worlds instead of just one. The reward for success had been made clear to him during his visit to Vali. But he knew well the cost of failure too, and even if Cain's Black Eagles didn't kill him in their victory, his own masters surely would. And he still had images of Vali in his mind, the massive fortifications of the Triumvirate's stronghold, the endless expanse of slave-operated factories and mines, producing an astonishing flow of weapons and equipment. The Triumvirate ruled over a truly vast organization, one that had been kept hidden from those of Occupied Space, even as it existed all around them. No, there would be no escape from failure. He would defeat the Eagles and kill Darius Cain, or he would die. It was that simple.

"Well?" he roared, staring at the officer standing in front of him. "What are you waiting for?" He waved his arm, gesturing for the general to be on his way. The Eagles were coming. There was no time to waste.

He watched the general bow and then turn and hurry for the exit. He was an amusing image, misjudging how quickly he could walk and not look like he was running away. The Eldari dress uniforms were a sight to see, as ostentatious as the throne, with lace and medals...and feathers protruding from the garish headgear. The Tyrant didn't much care for the stupid—and shockingly expensive—court uniforms any more than he did for his glittering, uncomfortable throne, but he understood the purpose they served. The need to change into foppish, and enormously uncomfortable, garb before entering the audience hall only reinforced the image of the Tyrant as above everyone, a figure whose power was incontestable.

Left to his own devices, the Tyrant would have run a much sparser regime. While he enjoyed a moderate amount of personal luxury and comfort, in truth, his tastes weren't all that extravagant. A few well-appointed rooms and a small cluster of servants would have satisfied his needs. It was power he craved, not gold plated bath fixtures and hectares of marble walls and floors. But the Triumvirate had assisted his rise to power, and they had advised—commanded?—on everything he'd done since. And they'd been quite insistent he live the part, portray an image of spectacle and pageantry to the masses. He didn't know if he agreed completely, but his own masters—and that is what they were, he hadn't lost enough perspective to forget that—wielded vastly more power then he, and though they hadn't compelled him on such matters, it seemed prudent to take their advice. Besides, sustaining his rule meant managing a corps of nobles and powerful ministers serving under him… and most of them lusted after just the kind of ostentatious frill that he himself only tolerated.

His mind was fixed on the battle to come. Eldaron was a strong world, one that had grown enormously in the years of his rule. That had come more from financial support and imports subsidized by the Triumvirate than any of his own personal magic, but it was extremely useful nevertheless. His regime was one of the most oppressive of any on the thousand worlds inhabited by humanity, and fear followed his citizens on a daily basis. But they were also relatively prosperous, the benefit of twenty years of rapid economic growth. That was an aberration, and had he been on his own, he suspected he would have bled the people dry as most other totalitarian regimes did. But the Tyrant, rapacious as any dictator, was no fool, and he knew allowing some of the prosperity to flow to the people was an insurance policy against rebellion, a good bargain in the end.

Eldaron's capital had been unremarkably named Eldaron City, though that particular lack of imagination had happened decades before he had seized power. He could have changed the name with a single command, but he was far too practical to waste funds on such nonsense. He didn't care what the city was called, as long as he controlled it with an iron fist.

He waved his hands. "Out! All of you. I want to be alone!"

The room was usually full of courtiers, business leaders and others in positions of wealth and influence jockeying for position and showing their loyalty with their attendance. The Tyrant could grant wealth and power with a wave of his hand...or take it away just as easily. But today the usual pack of groveling supplicants had been sent away, replaced by army officers and the ministers who ran his military. War was coming, war with an extremely competent enemy, and the Tyrant had no time for routine business.

He considered the status, as the startled soldiers and bureaucrats scrambled toward the large room's exits, tried to reason out when the attack would come. He knew the package had been delivered to Armstrong, and that Sarah Cain had departed that world. He assumed she had gone to the Nest, but he couldn't be sure. And one thing was certain...Darius Cain wasn't going to announce his intentions. He would come fast and hard...without warning. One day the skies over Eldaron would be filled with his assault ships. The Tyrant knew he had the strength to destroy the Black Eagles, but he was still afraid. Any man who was about to face Darius Cain and his pack of killers in a fight to the death was scared...or insane. Or both.

*   *   *   *   *

The prisoner heard the familiar clang as the locking bolt on his prison's door disengaged. It was a familiar sound, one that had signified many things over the years. Food, interrogations, beatings...all began with that same noise.

This time would be different, though. He would allow his visitor to come in, to get close. He wouldn't move. He would sit against the wall, head down, shoulders hunched forward in the same pose. He would communicate the message his captors had longed to see...that of a broken man whose sanity was finally gone. He would look passive, weak. But in his mind, something stirred, a fire almost forgotten, but not quite. The prisoner would fight one last battle. Here, now.

He heard the footsteps come closer. He had more than one

visitor. That's okay, he thought. Even better maybe. He only needed to attack one, quickly enough—hard enough—to make the others take him out. Perhaps he had just enough strength remaining to kill his victim. One last taste of vengeance before the peace of death…

"How are you today, my old friend?" The voice was familiar. The Tyrant. The prisoner had almost forgotten what a smile was, but now he had to struggle to hold one back. Fate had given him a gift, and now he knew it was time for his plan. The Tyrant always had guards when he visited, and they would almost certainly gun him down if he attacked their ruler.

I must be quick. I will only have an instant to kill him. Then it will be over.

The prisoner knew many ways to kill a man, with everything from a nuclear weapon to bare hands. But he could feel the weakness in his body. The fighting styles he'd learned long ago were mostly beyond his physical ability now. He would focus, put every scrap of strength remaining to him into one final attack. He'd initially been concerned mostly with provoking his captors to kill him, but now the Tyrant had come, and he could feel the ache, the unstoppable urge to kill the man who had ruled so long over his torment.

"No answer?" The Tyrant's voice was closer, but the prisoner still looked down, unmoving. He would not give his target the slightest warning. He was stay as he was, the battered, destroyed hulk of a man…until it was time.

"I know you have grown weak. But perhaps you have a bit of energy left for me, no? We have known each other for a long time now…who if not I can you call your closest companion?" The Tyrant's voice was loud, yet almost friendly, just a twinge of mockery slipping through.

Stay. Don't move, don't look up. No matter what he says. Make him come closer…

"Still no response? Come now, are you truly so broken? So weak you sit there, incapable of even looking at me?"

The prisoner could feel his tormentor approaching. Closer… but not close enough. Not yet.

"So, after so long, we have finally broken your will. Now you sit there, like a worm, your mind gone, the defiance you so proudly displayed blown away on the wind." His voice was becoming more taunting as he continued.

Not yet…

"I had even come to find some meager respect for you, my old friend…so much so it pains me to see you like this, crushed, defeated."

The prisoner could feel the Tyrant, hear he was close. But not close enough.

"But in the end, you are just like the others. Your strength was a lie, that indomitable will a pathetic façade."

Footsteps again…coming closer…

"I am disappointed. I thought you were a man, but now I see you are merely a worm, just like all the others."

Take a deep breath…then focus. You'll only get one chance, a second or two perhaps, maybe less…

"I would punish you for your failure, for your pointless attempts to pretend you had a spine. I despise weakness, but a fraud is even worse. I would have you fed to the fangworms right now…but despite your failing, you are still useful. For a short while. And then, I myself will cast you into the…"

The prisoner lunged, his mind focused on his moves, his will, not broken as the Tyrant believed but channeling for an instant the warrior he had been, forcing his atrophied muscles to exert the last bit of force that remained to them, to launch his withered body at his target.

His head snapped up, and his eyes focused on the Tyrant's. In an instant, he saw the gloating, mocking expression vanish, replaced by a look of fear, of outright terror. He savored the image, and his hands pushed out in front of him, reaching for the Tyrant's neck. One thought dominated his consciousness. This is your last battle…do not fail.

The Tyrant reacted, too late to avoid the blow. The prisoner was on him, striking hard, his hand slamming into the Tyrant's face. It was a killing blow, one of many the prisoner had learned in his years of combat, and he executed it perfectly. But his strength failed him, his rapid strike a bit too slow. The Tyrant dodged to the side, changing the impact point of the blow... just enough.

The Tyrant fell to the side, screaming in pain as the prisoner's hand moved past his stricken head. Blood poured from his mouth, and he dropped...first to his knees and then to the ground.

The prisoner knew he had failed, that his strike had not been a lethal one. He tried to swing his body around, to move in for another attempt, but then he heard the sounds, distant, muffled. He felt the impacts, slamming into him. His arm, his chest. But there was no pain, just a vague awareness. His attack had used the last of his strength, and now he felt himself falling, the impact on the ground, hard, but also without pain.

He had failed...fate had denied him his vengeance. But his ordeal was over, and he could feel himself slipping away, the blackness taking him. He heard a voice, pained, forced. "No... we still need him alive..." Then even that was gone, and he heard nothing but the sounds of waves crashing against the rocky coast.

Chapter 14

APS Zephyr
Zed-4 System
1,200,000 Meters from Gamma-Hydra Warp Gate
Earthdate: 2319 AD (34 Years After the Fall)

"Battlestations!" Jamie Wheaton's voice was calm, but that didn't lessen its imperious nature one bit. She was *Zephyr's* commander, and her ship was facing an oncoming enemy. Battle was almost upon her, but she was cool and focused. She had seen combat before, against an enemy more fearsome that a group of pirates, and she knew what to do.

Her mostly-rookie crew was another matter, and all the more reason for her to stay cool and under control. One hint of fear in her tone would undermine the morale of the entire crew. No, they had to see their captain completely unconcerned about the vessel now accelerating toward them at 3g. She was the source of the strength they would need to get through what would be, for most of them, their first battle.

Zephyr had come through the warp gate as planned, and Wheaton had done her best to try and hide her ship. But there were no asteroids nearby, and no particulate clouds heavy enough to provide cover…at least none close enough to the gate. So she maneuvered to the best spot she could find and powered down, with only scanners and basic life support operating.

Then nothing happened. Hours went by…then a day. She'd been almost ready to give up, to suggest to Elias that they had made an error, that Gamma-Hydra III had been the pirate's true course. But then, finally, *Zephyr* picked up the unique energy readings caused by a warp gate transit.

The pirate vessel slipped slowly and cautiously into the system, crawling out from the warp gate, clearly searching for *Zephyr*. Wheaton felt a wave of disappointment. This pirate captain knew what he was doing. He was cautious, and he wouldn't be easily fooled. Still, she kept *Zephyr* on minimal power, hoping to get lucky, waiting to see what happened. If the pirate was going to find her ship, he would have to do it on his own. She wasn't about to help him.

The pirate accelerated slowly into the system, its thrust barely 1g. Then suddenly it fired its engines hard, blasting at 3g. Wheaton knew immediately, and a few seconds later she got her confirmation. The AI announced that the pirate's thrust vector was consistent with a course directly toward *Zephyr*.

She was surprised, not so much that the pirate located her ship but that he was closing for a fight. *Zephyr* wasn't a battleship by any measure, but Wheaton was sure her vessel was more than a match for any pirate ship.

Maybe he figures we're all rookies here. Close, but not close enough...

Zephyr's crew might not be battletested, but her captain was... and Wheaton was determined to bring her people through their first fight, whatever it took.

"So, no dice, eh?" Elias bolted through the hatch onto *Zephyr's* small bridge. "I figured they'd find us. There really wasn't much to work with as far as hiding places.

"Yeah," Wheaton replied. "Still we had to try." She sighed. "Now we're back at a dead end...and we've got to explain this when we get home."

"Dead end?" Elias shook his head. "No, we can't lose this trail. Not now."

"What can we do? They're coming at us hard. We're going to have to destroy them"

"No."

"What are you talking about, Elias? What do you suggest we

do? Run? Let them attack us and don't fight back?" There was confusion in her voice, and a little resentment. She was fond of Elias Cain, too fond perhaps. But *Zephyr* was her ship, and she didn't react well to anyone stepping onto her turf.

"We disable her. We fight like pirates ourselves…and then my people board her."

Wheaton stared back, a look of shock in her eyes. "That's insane, Elias. We don't fight like pirates. They have needlers for that…we don't. Our laser cannons aren't precision weapons for targeting specific systems." She started shaking her head. "No, it's not possible. And how would your people even get there? We don't have assault craft. You'd have to go in the regular shuttle, no armor, no breaching gear. You'd have to find an access port…and hope like hell you can dock with it. Or jury-rig something to breach the hull."

"It's all doable," he said simply, calmly.

"Since when are you the expert in naval tactics?" she snapped back. "And even if we could manage it, you've only got twenty agents. We have no idea how many pirates are on that vessel… and they're experienced at fighting aboard ships. Your people aren't."

"We know they took heavy losses in the fight on *Carlyle*. There can't be too many of them left, especially in fighting condition."

"According to Captain Marne," she answered sharply. "Who was half crazed out of his wits when we picked him up…and who's been in sickbay ever since, unconscious most of the time."

"That doesn't mean what he told us wasn't true. If the ship's captain ended up in the cargo hold with time to blow the doors, you can bet there was one hell of a fight on that ship. I'm willing to bet on what Marne told us."

"But you want *me* to bet my ship to give you that chance."

"We started this to find out what happened, Jamie. If we don't at least get some prisoners…" He stared at her, and she saw something in his eyes. Pleading? Desperation?

Why is this so important to him? It can't just be the attack on Carlyle, as costly as that was. Is he really in that much trouble back home? Does

he see this as a way to put himself back in the good graces of his superiors?
"Why?"

He stared back at her, a confused look on his face. "Why what? Why do I want to catch this pirate?"

"No. What are you really after?" Her voice was serious. "I know it's more than capturing a pirate."

Elias paused, his eyes flashing toward Megan Berry and the other two officers on *Zephyr's* bridge. Then he leaned in close and whispered, "I believe there is a major crime ring, one spanning a vast area, perhaps even all of Occupied Space." He paused, looking at the others again before continuing, his voice even softer. "And I believe it extends into the Atlantian government in some way. Corruption...more than any of us have imagined. And possibly worse. And this pirate ship is my only lead to learn more about what is truly going on."

She listened to his words, felt his breath on her ear. What he was telling her was extraordinary...and dangerous. But she realized at once she believed him. Whether that was rational judgment or something else was a question she couldn't answer. Still, if she was going to act on Elias' suspicions, she wanted to know more. She *needed* to know more.

"Ensign Berry...time to engagement range?"

"Twenty-one minutes, Captain. Based on target's current velocity and acceleration." Berry sound nervous, her voice a little shaky.

Wheaton had done everything she could to bolster the morale of her crew, but they were about to go into battle. It was natural for her people to be on edge.

And watching me whisper up here with Elias isn't helping. I've got to take this off the bridge.

She leaned even closer. "Let's go into my office. If you want me to risk my ship to try to take prisoners, I need to know what you know. Everything you know."

Elias looked like he might argue, but he kept silent and just nodded his head. Then he followed her through the hatch into the small compartment she used as an office.

"Captain, we've got full scanner data in. That's an Atlantian Patrol ship. She's got ten thousand tons displacement on us... and she outguns us too. We've got to reverse course and make a run for it." Treven was edgy, and Yulich could hear the fear in his first mate's voice.

Black Viper's captain sighed. Running from a Patrol ship was a dicey proposition. The Atlantian vessel not only outgunned his vessel, she probably had more thrust as well. But that wasn't what was truly troubling him. He'd have put his navigational skills up against some random Atlantian Patrol commander's. But even if he could outrun this enemy ship and stay out of weapons range, he knew he had no chance of evading it entirely. If he made a run for it, the Atlantian ship would follow. And with its damaged engines firing at full power, *Black Viper* would leave a trail leading right back to base. That was not an option, at least not one Yulich was likely to survive.

He was already in trouble, he knew that much. If he knowingly led an enemy ship back to base, he'd lose whatever chance he had of keeping his head. The Black Flag was not a forgiving organization, and maintaining the secrecy of its pirate bases was sacrosanct. So that left only one option. Fight it out.

"Run where?" he finally said. "She's as fast as us, Lars, or damned close. We might outmaneuver her for a while, but we can't outrun her, not in the long run. And if we can't shake that vessel, we can't go back to base."

Yulich stared at the plot. *Black Viper* would be in weapons range soon. He figured the Patrol ship had the same sized laser cannons as his vessel, though he knew the enemy had more of them. But if he was right, at least the Atlantian didn't outrange him. His guns might even be a surprise to them. Few pirates bothered with the expense of such heavy weapons. If his people could shoot well enough, maybe they could make up the difference in turrets. It was a chance, at least.

"You think we can take her? But we're outgunned and we've got damage." Treven was trying to hide the fear in his voice, with only marginal success.

"You know the rules as well as I do. What do you think will happen if we run to base with a bogey on our tail?"

Treven's face twisted into a frown, and he stared back at Yulich. Finally, he just nodded his understanding.

"At least this way, we've got some chance to win the laser duel. If we can damage her engines we can slip back out of range and really outrun her. Then we can get through one of the other warp gates and work our way back to base by some roundabout route."

Treven didn't look convinced, but he didn't offer an alternative.

"Very well," Yulich said, taking his first mate's silence as acceptance. "Then let's give ourselves every chance we can. I want the laser cannons as strong as we can make them. Get a team down there to run a bypass from the reactor around the regulator circuits. Let's see if we can pump a few extra gigawatts through those turrets, bump our range a few thousands kilometers. We'll give these Atlantians a little surprise."

"But the guns will blow out, Captain. I don't even know if they'll handle one shot at that throughput, but even if they do, they won't last long."

"What options do we have? We can't win a conventional fight. But if we can score a critical hit or two, we've got a real chance to disable her and get away...or even destroy her..."

I wonder if blasting an Atlantian Patrol ship will enough to pull my ass out of the fire...

"I guess it's our best chance." Treven still didn't sound too confident, but he was trying to make the best of it.

"It's our only chance." Yulich's eyes panned to the display showing the relative ship positions. "Now, let's get it done. We'll be in range in a few minutes...and I damned sure want us to be firing first..."

*   *   *   *   *

"Firing range in three minutes, Commander." Berry's voice was cool, calm. Wheaton was impressed with her young officer.

"Very well, Ensign." She paused for a second then added, "Confirm gunnery status." She'd given the order twice already, and gotten confirmation both times. But she figured a third time wasn't going to hurt anything. The AI had crunched the firing plots, and it was updating them in real time. At just over 60,000 klicks, her two gunners would confirm the AI's data, possibly adjusting it slightly, the 'spin' a good gunner could put on a shot. In theory, the computer's targeting solution was perfect...save for one thing. There was a crew on the other end, and they were trying like hell to fool their enemies with evasive maneuvers, last minute acceleration or deceleration. It didn't take much to miss a target two hundred meters long from sixty thousand klicks away.

"Gunnery reports ready to fire, Commander."

Wheaton just nodded, and she looked down at the chronometer. Two minutes.

She wished for a moment that Elias was on the bridge. She didn't need any support. Wheaton was a combat veteran and she was perfectly capable of commanding her ship against a pirate. But she didn't like thinking about him down in the bay, crammed aboard *Zephyr's* only shuttle, ready to lead his agents into battle. His people were armored, at least partially, but Hyperkev breastplates and fragile survival suits below weren't heavy protection against firearms. She found herself wishing Elias and his people wore powered armor, like the Marines had during the Second Incursion. At least then it would take more than one lucky shot to take him down...

Zephyr shook hard, and she felt the heavy fabric of her harness dig into her chest and abdomen. She knew immediately what had happened, and the alarms that sounded a second later only confirmed her analysis.

"Damage report," she snapped at Berry, as her eyes dropped to the countdown clock. *Forty-five seconds to go. How? Their guns aren't any heavier than ours. I'd swear to it.*

"Hit amidships, Commander." Berry paused, partly buckling a bit under the stress of battle, but mostly because she was waiting for data to come in. "Primary port power coupling severed...backups engaged and functioning. Two compartments have lost containment. Structural integrity compromised in several locations. Minor fires in data center one and cargo hold two."

Not critical...but damned close. We dodged a bullet on that...

Her eyes flashed back to the chronometer. Thirty seconds. Then, again: *How?*

They must have overloaded their guns...probably a direct bypass to the reactor.

It was a risky strategy, one that could cause a massive blowout at any time. But it was a damned good idea too...especially for a damaged pirate engaged and outgunned. She thought for an instant about doing the same thing, but she killed the idea almost instantly. First, it was downright reckless. And second, she didn't have time. It would take a lot more than the...twenty seconds...left on the counter.

No, just hope their guns take long enough to charge that we get our first shot off before they hit us again. If that backup power line fails, we're as good as dead.

"Ten seconds." Berry's voice was distant, slipping through her own thoughts.

She leaned back in her chair, absent-mindedly checking her harness. She could almost feel the ship shaking, imagine the impact of the enemy's next shot. *Almost...*

"Five seconds." Berry's voice had lost its earlier tension. Whether that meant her tactical officer had conquered her fears, or just that she was numb, Wheaton didn't know.

She could hear the seconds counting down, though no one was reading them off.

Three.

She tightened her hands on the armrests of her chair.

Two.

She sucked in a deep breath. Her gunners were good, but

they were inexperienced in actual combat. Would they hold it together, score a hit when they had to?

One.

She closed her eyes, feeling the vibrations as her ship's reactor poured energy into the laser turrets. She felt a rush of relief. They'd gotten the shot off.

She'd just turned toward her screen to check the scanning reports, but before she could focus, *Zephyr* shook hard and went into a wild spin, her harness slamming hard into her body as it held her in her chair. An instant later, the power went out on the bridge, plunging her into total darkness...

Chapter 15

"The Nest" – Black Eagles Base
Second Moon of Eos, Eta Cassiopeiae VII
Earthdate: 2318 AD (34 Years After the Fall)

"You are going to tell me everything you know…that is not up for debate. The only question is how much of you will be left when you do." Darius Cain stared at the cowering figure in front of him. His mother had brought the messenger with her. He'd told her the ring had come from Eldaron, but not much beyond that. And that wasn't enough for Darius. Not even close.

"You know who I am, don't you?" His tone was pure malevolence. Normally, he wasn't above a bit of acting, playing the role of the monster people thought he was to achieve an end. But the darkness in his voice this time was one hundred percent genuine. If there was a chance—any chance—his father had not been killed on that ship seventeen years before, he was going to find out. And he didn't give a damn what he had to do to make it happen.

The prisoner was cowering, hunched over on the floor in front of Darius. He was naked, his cell empty, devoid of any furniture at all. He'd been stripped and fed nothing but water and nutrition pills for three days and forced to sleep on the floor. His surroundings were all white, the walls, the floor, the ceiling. Even the door virtually disappeared into the endless white expanse when it was closed. But the man hadn't been otherwise physically harmed. Yet.

"Now, I am going to give you one last chance to tell me everything. And I do mean everything. Who you spoke to, what they told you word for word, your surroundings on Eldaron... everything. And remember, whatever fear you have of your Eldari contacts, they are lightyears away. You are my prisoner now, and you are in the stronghold of the Black Eagles. There is no escape from here, no hope for you at all...save my clemency. You will die if I order it. You will be tortured in ways your mind cannot even imagine—all it would take is a word from my mouth. So remember all you have heard about me—the legends, the rumors—and multiply it by ten. You are at the very gates of hell, my friend, hanging by a thread. And if you do not tell me everything I want to know, I will cut that thread and cast you into a horror you cannot imagine."

Darius wasn't the sadist his many detractors made him out to be. He was normally unemotional, a consummate professional who conducted his operations as cleanly as possible. But this wasn't business...it was personal.

"Please, General Cain..." The prisoner's voice was shaky, choked with tears.

"You have very little time," Darius said coldly. "And you are wasting it..."

"I...I was hired to...to bring the package to Armstrong and deliver it to Sar...to your mother..." His voice trailed off.

"Continue," Darius said, standing over the messenger's pathetic form like a statue, hard, unmoving.

"I...I didn't know what was in the box...and they told me not to look. It was still sealed when your mother opened it. Ask her! It was!"

"Someone gave you this box then. Who?"

"He didn't give me his name...he wore a uniform...it was white with gold trim all over it."

"You'll have to do better than that," Darius said. "And look up at me when you speak. You are a man, aren't you, and not a worm?"

The miserable creature straightened a bit, twisting his head to look up at Darius. His face was wet with tears. "The whole thing was white, with gold trim down the pants, and all over the jacket." He paused, sucking in a deep breath as he did. "And the hat," he added, as if he'd just remembered another detail that might help satisfy his tormentor. "It was black, with more gold on it...some insignia on the front..."

Darius nodded. He'd studied the library computer's information on Eldaron, and the description was ringing true.

Eldari High Guard, the Tyrant's personal regiment. Most of his senior officers hold commissions in the unit in addition to their command postings. So, it is Eldaron, almost certainly.

Unless someone was seriously trying to trick him...which was always possible.

But not likely here. Too much else fits.

"Tell me about how you were recruited...about the people you saw, the places."

The prisoner looked down again, the stress of maintaining Darius' terrible gaze clearly too much for him. "I was on Eldaron. I had delivered a priority package there from Novastar Shipping. I am a native of Tarsus, a bonded courier. I've worked for most of the transport concerns there..."

Darius stared down for a moment without saying a word. The prisoner's story lined up. If the Eldari were behind this, it wouldn't make sense to use one of their own people...too much risk he'd talk. Darius didn't enjoy inflicting pain on people, but he had no doubt he could get whatever information he needed out of a captive...and the Eldari command would know that too.

Better to send someone who knows nothing but what you want your enemy to discover...

"You know I will check on that, don't you?" His tone became even more frigid than before, like the sound of death itself. "And if I find out you are lying to me...you will beg for death every second, but it will be slow indeed in coming..." He let the threat hang in the air. His reputation had done half the work for him, but a little reminder never hurt.

"It's true...I swear."

"I believe you...but I need more. Who approached you? How did you meet them? Did you go to them or did they come to you? Describe everything you saw...and I mean right down to the pile of dogshit in the street you stepped in." Darius' voice was firm, but he pulled back just a little on the ominous tone. The prisoner was cooperating. "Tell me...tell me everything," he said, leaning down until his eyes glared right at the captive's. "Tell me all I want to know...and you may make a live prisoner yet."

*   *   *   *   *

"He told me everything he knows. He shit himself half a dozen times, but he finally opened up." Darius was looking across the table at his mother and Erik Teller. His old friend and second in command was used to the way he did things, but Sarah was having trouble hiding her discomfort.

"That's...good, Darius," she replied, trying to hide her concerns.

Darius held back a sigh. It was the same as always, the rush to judgment. He hadn't hurt the prisoner. There had been no branding irons, no pliers pulling out fingernails, no drugs that would turn him into a vegetable. He'd have gotten worse on half the worlds of Occupied Space for a lot of infractions. Sure, Darius had threatened the prisoner, and allowed the man's own fears to run away with him. But he hadn't so much as slapped the bastard across the face. Yet here it was again, the discomfort, the silent condemnation. What was he supposed to do? Let his father rot in a cell somewhere...or, if he was dead, allow his murderers to go unpunished? To spare one man the scare of his life?

"He is unharmed, mother," he finally said, his tone betraying his impatience. "He could use a solid meal, but other than that he's perfectly fine. A little shaken up perhaps, but no real damage."

She just nodded. He felt a rush of anger. He hated the illogic, the inconsistency people applied to their moral judgments. He knew his mother would do anything to save his father. But even as intelligent a woman as Sarah Cain was tentative, hesitant to accept what had to be done. If Darius had not existed, if his mother had been compelled to act alone, he didn't have the slightest doubt she would have done whatever had to be done to try and save his father. But his existence freed her of that necessity, made him once again the ally everyone craved... but the one all treated with a certain discomfort.

"I am going to launch the expedition, mother. As soon as I can organize everything. And I am going to do whatever it takes to find out about father...and get him out of there if he is still alive." His tone was cool, professional, though inside his emotions were running wild. The thought of seeing his father again was overwhelming, but the pragmatist at his core realized the chances of finding Erik Cain alive were slim. But that had no place in his decision. He'd go to Eldaron even if he knew his father was dead. He would go for vengeance. He almost scared himself thinking of the horrors he would unleash on the Eldari if they had killed his father.

"I knew you would," Sarah replied. "That's why I am here." She paused, sounding troubled. "And that's why someone sent me the ring, because they want you to attack. And that makes me unsure I should have come. I couldn't bear the thought of your father being held prisoner, thinking himself lost and forgotten...but he wouldn't want you to march into a trap for a small chance of saving him."

"It's not his decision, mother. Nor yours. I am going." His voice was like iron, and it was clear to anyone listening that nothing would change his mind...not any argument, not danger, not even the virtual certainty he'd be walking into a trap. "You may stay here, or you may come along. But if you decide to accompany the expedition, understand now, I will do what I have to do to ensure victory. *Whatever* that is. You and I judge things differently sometimes, but this is my operation, and I will run it as I see fit." He paused, staring into her eyes intensely.

"Understand what I am saying. If I have to crucify half the Eldari government to find out what happened to father, that is exactly what I will do." He paused. "If I have to crucify *all* of them...then that is what I will do." If you don't want to be part of that, stay here." A short pause. "Please."

She looked at him for a few seconds, and he could see from her face she was confused by her own inconsistent thoughts. Finally, she just nodded. "I will go."

*   *   *   *   *

"Black Eagles, I am speaking to all of you, as a group, and also as the thousands of individuals you are, for this is something each of you must decide for yourselves. We have come together, outcasts mostly, refugees, political fugitives, the cast-offs of a hundred worlds...and together we have become the most formidable fighting force mankind has ever known." Darius stood at a small podium in one of the landing bays. The soldiers of the Teams were deployed before him, and the rest of his veteran warriors were watching on their screens, from the wardrooms, duty posts, even their quarters. Every Black Eagle was listening with rapt attention to what their leader had to say.

"I will be leaving the Nest shortly, to lead another mission, a planetary invasion that, to me, is the most important we have ever undertaken. But it is not like the others, for we have not been hired by a combatant government, nor will this fight be the culmination of an existing political conflict. My reasons for this assault are personal, and its purpose is to free a prisoner... or extract vengeance for that captive's death if I should find he had been slain." His voice was cold, as frigid as that army of grizzled veterans had ever heard from their commander.

"I will not order any Black Eagle to join me in this mission. You did not become part of this organization to serve the needs of one man, even your commanding general. The Eagles are a brotherhood, and we fight for each other, not the needs of any one man. So you must each decide, will you come with me or will you stay behind? There is no paymaster on this mission, no great riches to be won, but I will cover the costs and wages of all those who join me from my own resources."

He paused again, and when he continued, his voice was somber, his words slower. "Before you decide, know this. The information that has led me to launch this invasion was deliberately sent, presumably to provoke exactly this action on my part. Again, I say, listen to me, and take this to heart when you decide what course of action to take. The attack force will almost certainly move right into a trap, one no doubt devised by the mysterious enemy we faced on Lysandria...and again on Eris. We have almost no solid data about them, but we know they are out there...and with this most recent series of events, I have come to believe they have targeted the Black Eagles, and that this is all part of their effort to destroy us. But, I say loudly, for all to hear, others have tried to defeat the Eagles, and none have succeeded. And all who have tried now lay buried under the ruins and dust of their worlds. The Eagles are not so easily vanquished, and I will go to the planet Eldaron, with any of you who will come with me, and together we will prove this. Whatever trap has been set, we shall turn on our enemy. We will show them the true strength and power of the Black Eagles."

He hesitated again, taking a deep breath before continuing. "This is a sacred quest for me, for I believe the prisoner of Eldaron is none other than General Erik Cain...my father. He has been thought dead for many years, but I have reason to believe he survived the destruction of his ship so long ago..." His voice hardened, a barely-contained rage energizing every word he spoke. "...that he was held prisoner, indeed that he may still be alive, a captive in some Eldari cell."

Thoughts of his father held prisoner, tortured, alone for so many years drifted through his mind...images of the wreck of Erik Cain, imaginings of what years of helplessness would have done to so independent and defiant a man. And with each mental picture his anger grew, a swirling cloud, like the birth of a star, an elemental fury almost unimaginable.

"I will go to Eldaron, alone if I must. And all who join me will have my undying gratitude. But those who feel this is not their fight, who do not wish to walk wide-eyed into a trap... there is no shame in this, nor will I hold it against anyone. We are brothers and sisters now, and so we shall remain if I return. And if I do not come back, if this mission claims me, then the Eagles will continue, for we are far greater than any one man, than any thousand. No matter what losses we suffer, what tragedies we endure."

He took a deep breath. "So think, my comrades. Hear what I have said, and consider deeply the deadly dangers of this mission. Then make your choice. Log into your accounts on the network, and enter your decision." A pause. "Today. For this operation must be dispatched as quickly as possible, and preparations begin tomorrow."

He stared down at the podium for a few seconds, and then he looked back up and added a last comment. "Before I sign off from this address, I would like to add one last thought. Twelve years ago, when we fielded the first ragged company of Black Eagles, I could hardly have imagined where we would end up. There are fourteen left from that first group, men and women who have shared every moment of this wild ride. But an Eagle is an Eagle, and each of you are part of that tradition. You were with us in spirit on that first mission, when we landed one hundred ten bodies on Ventara...and when seventy-nine of us came back. And we are still one...our oldest veterans and our newest additions...and all those lost on our battlefields over the years."

Another pause. "And we shall always be one...each of us, whether he or she goes to Eldaron with me or not. No matter who or how many return from that world. As long as one of us endures, the Eagles will never truly die. You have all been my life, my comrades. I say to all of you now, fare thee well, whatever comes next. And never forget...never forget...that you are a Black Eagle."

*   *   *   *   *

"Have you tallied the results yet?" Darius Cain walked into the large but Spartan office of his second-in-command.

"Yes," Erik Teller replied. "And you're not going to believe it."

Cain stopped and turned toward his friend. "Bad? I was hoping at least half would come with me...but I guess asking people to walk into a trap with you is a heavy lift..."

"It's almost unanimous, Darius. More than ninety-nine percent."

Cain sighed softly and looked down at the floor. "I thought at least some of them would come with me..."

Teller smiled. "Darius, they all want to go with you. Almost to a man."

"It was ninety-nine percent to go?" Darius was genuinely surprised, and it cut through his normal discipline. "I never imagined..."

"They would follow you into hell, my friend...and so would I."

"No," Cain said flatly. "You have to stay here and command the Nest."

"That's not true, and you know it. The two of us have gone on every major mission. The Nest is perfectly fine with its permanent staff."

"I need you to stay behind, Erik. This mission is different..."

"No...it's not different. It's exactly the same." Teller paused, staring at his friend for a few seconds before he continued. "And you are more to me than even a brother. I've known your father as long as I have conscious memories, Darius. He was like another parent to me. I was named after him." Another pause, as he fought to keep the emotion from his voice. "And my father fought in the Second Incursion too...and he didn't come back either. But I know he is dead. They brought back a body...I saw it. But if there is a chance your father is alive..."

"What about the Eagles, Erik? What if I am leading them to their destruction? This enemy is powerful...you know that. And we know nothing about them. I never imagined the entire corps would volunteer to come. Maybe I should only take half."

"I understand your concern, Darius, but you are wrong. You can't save the Eagles by making them something they are not. The men and women know that...that's why they all voted to go with you. If you make half of them stay behind, order them to sit idly by while their comrades, the brothers and sisters who have fought at their sides in a dozen battles, leave to face the greatest struggle of their lives, you will destroy them...in a way far more complete than honest death in battle. Would you leave them knowing they let half our number go off to fight, weaker for their absence? To wonder for the rest of their lives if their friends and comrades would have survived had they been at their sides? Is that what you think you have instilled in them after so many years?"

"But what if I lead them all to destruction?" Darius' voice was nervous, uncertain, emotions he rarely displayed.

"Then we will fight our last battle...together, like the brothers in arms we are. Though I do not believe there is anything on Eldaron that can destroy us, whatever the Tyrant may have convinced himself." Teller stood up and walked toward Cain, putting his hand on his friend's shoulder. "We are with you, Darius. All of us. And together we will go to Eldaron, and find out what happened to your father...and God help anyone there planning to trap us. We will show them what the Black Eagles can do."

Chapter 16

Confederation HQ
Beneath the Ruins of the Ares Metroplex
Planet Mars, Sol IV
Earthdate: 2319 AD (34 Years After the Fall)

"Roderick, I understand your hesitancy. I know you are uncomfortable with what you had to do...if you weren't that sort of man, you'd have found me on the other side of your coup. But we all did what we agreed was necessary, and you cannot afford to be indecisive now. You did what you did to save Mars...and you will fail in that effort if you do not command forcefully. All of this will be for nothing."

Vance leaned back in his chair, silent, hearing Astor's words but not quite processing them fully. He'd tread as softly as he could since the coup, imprisoning only those he had to, and most of them under house arrest or in commandeered hotel rooms. Only a few, like Boris Vallen, languished in true prison cells.

But the thirty-two men and four women his people now held in custody now were different. They had attempted their own counter-revolt, one that was quickly defeated, but not before almost three-hundred civilians had been killed or wounded in the fighting.

"Thirty-six executions? Is that what you think we need?" Vance looked up at his senior general.

"Yes, Roderick. That's exactly what we need. And you know

it." Astor paused. "You're letting your guilt at seizing power interfere with your judgment. Innocent people are dead because of this failed revolt. Almost two hundred are in the hospital. This isn't about going after political rivals. It's about punishing a group of murderers."

"Who did the same thing I did…just less successfully."

"That's horsecrap, Roderick, and you know it. If these were purists, democratic zealots trying to overturn your regime and restore the council…that would be bad too, but it would be different. And perhaps there would be cause for clemency. But that's not what happened here. This was an attempt to seize power…by a small group of mostly wealthy individual for their own personal gain. There is no ideology here, no cause of freedom. Just a group of criminals and traitors…who need to mount the scaffold."

"Perhaps…"

"There is no perhaps, Roderick. You planned your takeover because you knew it was necessary…and we all backed you. Now, you must follow through. You must *lead*. You owe it to those of us who risked all to aid you. You owe it to Mars." Astor glared at Vance, his frown expressing both frustration and understanding.

"I know you're right, Arch. I lived through the Shadow War and both struggles with the First Imperium. And my gut tells me this new enemy is going to be at least as bad. Unless I am very wrong, thousands will die—millions—and I will send our soldiers and naval crews to their deaths in battle. I won't like it, and I will live with the memories for the rest of my life." He paused briefly. Still, unilaterally pronouncing death sentences on thirty-six Martian civilians…" His voice trailed off.

"It is your responsibility now, Roderick. I don't question the pressure of your position, the guilt and doubt and worry it must carry with it. But you took it, and now you are the sole authority in the Martian Confederation." Astor paused, staring at Vance while he took a deep breath. "You must use that authority, and you must not allow doubt to deter you from what you know is necessary."

Vance sat still for a moment, and then he just nodded.

I know you're right, Arch. I just don't know if I can do it...

* * * * *

"Where is he?" Xavier Melander sat on one end of the long sofa, his head turned, looking down at his companions.

"He's in his office, Xavier." Archibald Astor's voice was soft, subdued. He'd gotten through to Vance, convinced him he had no choice. And in five minutes, thirty-six men and women would die...they would die because Roderick Vance had ordered it. Astor knew he had convinced Mars' dictator, but in the end, the responsibility for the act would always lay with the man who had the power. And that man had made it quite clear he wanted to be alone.

"I've known him for a long time, longer even than most of you. He was colder when he was young, quicker to do whatever was necessary. I daresay, the thirty-five year old Roderick Vance would have ordered these executions without hesitation." "But he has seen too many things, borne the guilt for too many dead. He is a different man now...probably a better one, yet I fear it will make what he must do more difficult for him to accept." Andre Girard was old. He looked to be in his mid-seventies, but that was illusion, the result of an active life and fortunate genes—as well as the rejuv treatments he'd received his entire adult life. He was actually one hundred eight years of age, and he'd been one of Vance's top agents during the First Imperium and Shadow wars. He'd been retired shortly after the Fall, but he'd gone to Earth the year before at Vance's request, to check out the status of the Jericho settlement without the knowledge of the council. What Girard had found, and the survivors he'd brought back with him, had been the beginning of the sequence of events that culminated with Vance's coup.

"I'm afraid you are right, Mr. Girard." Duncan Campbell was sitting off to the side, in a large chair. His eyes had been on

the large screen, watching the coverage of the imminent executions, but now he turned toward the others. "We must look to
support him…and guide him. Roderick Vance is a good man,
and that is a rare thing. But though he must lead through this
crisis and command all authority himself, I believe we also have
an obligation in this. We must support him, and as General
Astor did in this circumstance, guide and advise him. We must
not allow him to carry the load by himself. I fear it is more than
any man can bear."

"Agreed," Melander said, nodding his head as he did. "The
four of us will work together. We are promised to Roderick's
service already, but we will go beyond normal duty. We will add
our strength to his, do whatever is necessary to ensure that the
Confederation survives this crisis. Because I believe with all my
heart that when Mars is again safe, Roderick Vance will lay down
his power as promised and reconstitute the ruling council." He
paused, and then he extended a hand. "Are we agreed?"

Girard was the first to respond. The old spy leapt from his
seat and leaned forward, placing his hand on top of Melander's.
Duncan Campbell followed suit, placing his own palm atop
Girard's.

Archibald Astor watched with a smile for a few seconds.
Then he stood up and walked over. "I am proud of you all…
and I am with you. Whatever it takes. Whatever we must do to
prevail in this."

On the screen behind them, a man stood before a firing
squad, his hands shackled to the wall above his head. The sound
on the display was muted, but it was obvious he was shouting,
begging for clemency. He stood there for a few seconds, no
more than ten, struggling with his shackles, his face covered
with tears. Then his body tensed and slumped forward, held up
only by the chains bolted to the wall.

The four men turned and their eyes were fixed on the flickering screen as two soldiers unlocked the shackles and carried the
body away. They all stood silently and watched, unmoving as
the scene was replayed over and over…thirty-five more times.

Vance looked down the length of the table. "Good morning, gentlemen. We have much to plan, and little time. Let us begin, shall we?"

Vance's voice was coolly professional, with no hint of emotion or guilt. Everyone present knew that didn't mean Mars' dictator didn't feel those emotions, but it was clear he had put them in their place. Vance had spent the previous night alone in his residence, and he'd given himself few hours to work out the self-pity and remorse. He had never been much of a drinker, aside from his well-known weakness for fine wines, but he'd gone well beyond a bottle of pre-Blight Bordeaux or an Arcadian Pinot Noir, engaging in what was commonly called, an all-out drunk. But one night was all the time he had to numb the pain, and he'd greeted the morning with a frigid shower and a renewed determination to do what had to be done.

The four men at the table nodded their assent. They had a variety of expressions on their faces, with varying degrees of surprise at Vance's demeanor. Girard was the only one with a deadpan expression, as if he was seeing in Vance exactly what he had expected, the resolution and strength he had come to expect from his friend.

"Very well…first, let us look to military readiness. We do not know what we face, but the base on Eris was strong and well-defended. The Black Eagles were able to take it, but they had a considerable fight on their hands, and that tells me we'd best be prepared for war. As prepared as we can possibly make ourselves." He looked over at Astor. "Arch, I want you to call up all the reserves, anyone who has had any service with the army or Marines."

Astor nodded. "Yes, sir." There was something in his voice, a thread of concern.

"What is it, Arch?"

"It's the arsenals, sir. The post-Fall budgets have been tight, and worse since the Second Incursion. We can supply the standing forces well enough, but if we have to arm all the reserves, we're going to be on thin ice as far as logistics goes. If we get to the point of launching any off-word expeditions, we're going to have supply problems almost from day one."

"I understand. And I expect the naval situation is no better." He glanced down the table to see both Melander and Campbell shaking their heads, acknowledging the truth of his statement.

"That's not a surprise," Vance said softly. The destruction of the surface cities had dealt a harsh blow to Martian economic prosperity, and the need to relocate to the old underground metropolises—and expand them considerably—had prevented production from recovering to old levels. More than thirty years later, Martian GNP was still twenty-five percent below pre-Fall levels, and the decision to keep the terraforming reactors operating at full power caused a massive drain on the Confederation's reduced resources.

"Nevertheless, as a first priority, we must call up the reserves and bring all inactive naval vessels to full readiness." Vance knew both forces were pale shadows of what they had been thirty years before, even with every second line unit recalled to the colors. But he had what he had, and wishing otherwise wouldn't change that. "I will authorize whatever diversions of available supplies or funds you require."

"For starters, we'll need every millimeter of docking space… not just in the naval shipyards, but anywhere we can get a maintenance staff. Some of these old ships have been in mothballs since the Second Incursion." Melander looked over at Campbell, who nodded his agreement.

"We're going to have to stretch the crews pretty thin too," Campbell added. "We just don't have enough trained reservists."

"Do what you have to do, Xavier. Just let me know what you need from me." Vance turned toward Astor. "That goes for you too, Arch. Whatever you need to get your reserves combat ready…just come right to me. If it's anywhere on this planet, you'll have it."

Astor nodded. "Thank you, sir. I'll see it done."

Vance turned slowly, looking at each of them in turn. "And for the love of God, can we stop with the 'sir' stuff?"

"You are the supreme commander…sir. It is important that everyone address you as such. Informality can spread like a virus, and it could begin to undermine your authority. There hasn't been a peep since…" Campbell's voice tapered off.

"Since the executions?" Vance finished the statement without wavering in the slightest.

"Yes," Campbell said softly. "Since the executions."

"Well that is why we did it, isn't it?" Vance said. "At least we're getting what we paid for." He paused, but he didn't show any signs of his emotionality from the previous day. "And I understand the need for certain conduct for public consumption…but when the five of us are alone, call me Roderick. And if this makes it easier for you all, that's an order."

"Yes, s…Roderick." Astor turned each way, looking for a second at each of his cohorts. "I would say the next most important thing is to address our logistical problems. You're going to need to nationalize the factories, at least for the duration of the crisis. We need every industrial facility that can be converted to producing ammunition and military supplies switched over at once. We'll need enforced overtime schedules for trained workers so the plants can run around the clock."

Vance sighed. He'd known that was coming…and he realized he didn't have a choice. But it wasn't going to be well-received. The Confederation had a profoundly capitalistic system…indeed, most of the incredible development of the first century of colonization had been the result of the great founding families, who'd considered reinvesting their profits to be a civic duty. That system had created a massive amount of wealth for those elite clans, not least among them, the Vances. But it had also produced a century-long economic boom, and turned a few scattered colonial settlements into a Superpower that had rivaled those on Earth in economic activity if not in population.

"There's going to be trouble over that…and you all know it."

Though perhaps less than there might be. The heads of the biggest concerns are prisoners right now, unlikely to complain too loudly about anything…

"Call it temporary," Astor said, "and give them government

bonds in compensation. They're not in a position to say no. They'll take that and be glad to have something in return."

"What about the polar reactors?" None of them had wanted to address that, but Melander had finally done it.

Vance sighed. The reactors had been running for a century without more than a few brief pauses for maintenance and refueling. The very spirit of every Martian was bound up in the notion that one day, their children or grandchildren would be able to step out onto the surface, with no breathers or pressure suits, no cold weather gear. The reactors consumed over twenty percent of Martian output, a constant, crippling drain. But shutting them down would have a disastrous effect on morale.

"We'll keep them running for now. If we take away the people's hope for the future as well as their current freedom, we're going to have a hell of a morale problem." He turned toward Girard. "But Andre, I'd like you to get me an idea of just what is involved in shutting those units down...and restarting them again. Quietly, of course. We don't need rumors flying around. Just a contingency plan if we end up needing it."

"Consider it done, Roderick."

"So that brings us to one last item for now. Allies."

"Allies?" Melander sounded confused. "We've been isolationist for three decades, Roderick. We don't have any allies."

"You're right, Xavier. And it's time we did something about that. Can you handle the fleet mobilization yourself?"

Melander looked back confused. "Ah...yes, I'm sure I can. But Admiral Campbell..."

"If you can take care of the fleet, I was planning on asking Admiral Campbell to take a bit of a trip for me." He turned toward the retired naval commander. "I'd like you to go to Armstrong, Duncan. You did that once before for me...do you remember?"

"It would be hard to forget. Forty-five gees all the way? And a crash landing at the end. If Sarah Lin...Cain hadn't been the surgeon she is, I doubt I'd have made it back."

"Well, we're in a rush, but perhaps not quite the same as last time. I still want you to take one of the Torches, but you don't need to push it so close to the edge this time. But you know Sarah Cain...and she will trust you. The Marines are our natural ally in this. Sarah was at Eris. She knows we're facing something none of us can fight alone."

"The Alliance Marines were an amazing force," Astor said, "but there's very little left of the Corps. Are they the place to start in the hunt for allies?"

"Don't underestimate the Marines, Arch...even in their twilight. Yes, I think they're a good place to start. And don't forget, Sarah is also Darius Cain's mother. And we're going to need the Black Eagles in this."

Vance saw a general round of nods around the table. *They all agree. Or at least they don't disagree enough to argue.*

"Anything else?" Girard asked.

"As you mention it, Andre...yes. There is one more thing, but only if you feel up to it."

Girard glared back, his eyes fiery with defiance. "After all we've been through—and what we just started—don't tell me you're going to start treating me like an old man *now*."

Vance smiled. It was brief, and it gave way quickly to the seriousness of the matters at hand, but it was genuine...and far from the first grin Andre Girard had inspired over the years.

"Well, I had to ask you, *old* friend." He smiled, again for only a few seconds. Then he said, "I'd like you to go to Arcadia and talk to William Sanders and his mother Kara." Arcadia was a republic, one where the citizens were engaged and had a real say in their governance...a relative anomaly in Occupied Space, and one Vance knew existed only due to the continued efforts of Kara and her son.

"William's father was the leader of Arcadia's rebellion after the Third Frontier War, and the Sanders are the oldest and richest family on that prosperous world. If you can convince the two of them that we face something that will endanger all of human space, you might bring them over. And Arcadia is one of the strongest of the former colonies. They will be a crucial ally in any war that may come."

Girard nodded. "Of course, Roderick. Eighty years as a spy

crawling around in the shadows alone, trying to remain unseen, to avoid making an impression. So why not make me a diplomat now?"

Chapter 17

APS Zephyr
Zed-4 System
1,200,000 Meters from Gamma-Hydra Warp Gate
Earthdate: 2319 AD (34 Years After the Fall)

Spinning…out of control. Blackness. Jamie Wheaton's hands had slipped off her chair, but the heavy restraints held her in place…painfully. She could feel her shoulder jerk hard, the wave of agony that followed. It was dislocated at least, and maybe worse. But it was the darkness that seized her attention. The lights were out, the screens, everything. It went on for what seemed like an eternity, but which some part of her realized was only a second or two. Then the emergency lights came on.

"Damage to main power couplings, Commander. The reactor deactivated at once to prevent containment loss." The voice was odd, almost serene. The ship's AI.

She heard the words, and they slammed into her like a sledgehammer. The reactor was down. That meant *Zephyr* was dead.

Wheaton's head snapped around. Megan Berry was still at her station, pounding away at the keys, trying to generate some kind of response. And an instant later she got it. The main workstations came back on, the light of their displays dimmer than usual.

Battery power, Wheaton thought grimly. Enough for some lights, some computers…but nothing close to enough to fire the lasers.

And that means we're finished…

She sucked in a deep breath and exhaled hard. After fifteen years of service, and half a dozen battles against the First Imperium, this was not how Jamie Wheaton had imagined she would die.

Wait…

She felt a flush of energy…not hope perhaps, but not despair either.

"What is the status of the reactor?" she snapped back to the AI. Then she looked around the bridge, her mind deep in thought, estimating the elapsed time since the last enemy shot. *Forty-five seconds to recharge…and another fifteen to reconfigure for our attitude change, maybe thirty. The force from the blown compartments had sent* Zephyr *into its nasty roll, and that had been enough to trash the enemy's firing solution. At least without a hurried update.*

"Reactor appears to be undamaged, however, a full diagnostic will require thirty-seven point five minutes to complete."

"That's thirty-seven minutes longer than we've got," she snapped back. "Flash start the reactor. Now."

"Commander, a flash start under current conditions is ill-advised. I estimate a twenty-two percent chance of critical failure if…"

"Just do it," she barked. "That's an order." She gripped her armrests again, more of an instinctive action that one that served any purpose. She tried to ignore the wild gyrations of her ship, and her years of experience as a spacer came through for her. She couldn't say the same thing for the other two officers on the bridge. There were chunks of vomit floating around and plastered to the walls. Her eyes darted over to her tactical officer's station. She'd never seen a human being's skin as sickly white as Megan Berry's.

A few seconds later she heard a strange sound, one that went through her like a banshee's howl. Her mind raced, wondering what chilling death cry her vessel was making, but another few seconds later it stopped. An instant after, the lights went on, and the nonessential displays came back to life.

"Emergency restart completed, Commander. The reactor appears to be functioning within acceptable parameters."

"We didn't blow up," she said softly to herself. "I'll take that."

She glanced down at the screen on her workstation. "I want 2g thrust along current facing." She had no idea what vector changes would result. *Zephyr* was spinning out of control, which meant her engine facing was constantly changing. She didn't know where her ship would go, but she didn't care. She just knew she didn't want to be where the pirate had aimed his lasers at what he'd thought was a helpless target.

"Enemy vessel has fired, Commander. The laser blasts were approximately 800 meters from our port hull."

She let out a long breath. *That was too close. But now we've got another minute.*

"Charge the lasers. And stabilize the ship. Maximum efficiency without regard to crew comfort."

"Yes, Commander," the AI replied smoothly.

A second later the ship pitched hard...and again as the thrust vector moved. Then there was a series of smaller nudges, the compressed gas positioning jets, methodically canceling out the momentum causing *Zephyr's* spin.

Wheaton sighed softly as the wild roll slowed, and her ship returned to its normal bearing. "One gee forward thrust," she snapped. The forward movement might throw a curve to the enemy's targeting, but mostly, she just knew some Earth normal gravity would help her people maintain whatever efficiency they had left to offer.

Her eyes dropped down to the status bar. *A little over half charged*, she thought. *Sixty-one percent.* She was squinting to see the small number next to the illuminated bar. *Not enough...*

"Hold thrust now," she yelled suddenly. "Bypass safety regulator...open the conduits to the laser turrets to one hundred percent."

Two can play this game...

And two can blow their ships to bits trying it...

"Commander, I advise stron..."

"Do it!" she roared. "Now!"

We have to fire first. Or blow ourselves to bits trying...

*   *   *   *   *

"I need you to pay fucking attention!" Yulich was in a rage, and it was clear to everyone else aboard *Black Viper*. "You can't miss in this kind of battle, you imbeciles. Every shot we take at this power level could be our last. And that ship is perfectly capable of blowing us into dust." He paused, staring down at the com unit, fists clenched in frustration. "You miss again, we die. You understand me?"

He knew he was being unfair. The sudden evasive maneuvers by the target—just when he'd thought they were helpless and without power—had taken him by surprise as well as his gunners. And the targeting AI too. But there was no room for reason or understanding. This was a fight to the death...and it wasn't going to last much longer, whoever won.

"Understood, sir." The voice on the other end of the com failed to inspire Yulich. He knew his people were near the end of their ropes. Pirates attacked freighters...and they didn't take the kind of losses his people had boarding one. They certainly didn't take on Patrol ships. They ran when confronted by the authorities...lived to fight another day.

Only it was looking very much like his people wouldn't have another day. There was nowhere to run. He'd made a gamble transiting through the warp gate, a bet that the mysterious contact had not been pursuing *Black Viper*...and he'd lost. The Atlantian had been waiting just inside the system, too close for him to make a run for it.

His only hope now was to disable that damned Patrol vessel. And for a brief moment, he'd thought his people had done it. He'd have bet his five biggest hauls that last shot had scragged her reactor. But less than a minute later, she had power again... and his gunners' shots missed by almost a kilometer when she unexpectedly fired up her engines.

He looked down at the display. *Ten seconds until full power... until another shot. Probably our last*, he thought grimly, *so make it count, you guys...*

Five seconds.

His mind was focused on the Patrol ship, as if he could will his laser bursts to hit. He felt the knot in his stomach, the unmatched tension of a deadly battle, a fight to the death.

But whose death?

He focused on the countdown. Three...two...

Black Viper shook hard, and a second later he could hear a series of muffled sounds.

Secondary explosions.

His eyes dropped to the display. The power was out, the screen dark. But he knew it was past time for his guns to have fired. "Shoot," he yelled, grabbing hold of the com unit. "For shit's sake, fire the damned lasers!" But he knew...he knew even before he got the response from the gunners. The lasers were out.

Black Viper was doomed. He and his people were as good as dead.

*　　*　　*　　*　　*

"I repeat, you are ordered to surrender immediately." Wheaton's voice was firm, thick with anger.

She knew she'd come within a hair of losing her ship and that only a desperate gamble—and enough good luck to win that wager—had saved them all. She'd been careless with this pirate, failed to anticipate what moves his own desperation might induce. Her skill hadn't brought her people through the fight. Luck had.

Her body was still tense, but she could feel the fatigue pressing in, the utter exhaustion that followed a close escape from death. The adrenalin rush was fading away, but the tightness remained in her gut. The worst of the crisis had passed, at least for *Zephyr* and her crew, but those feelings subsided slowly. There was a familiarity to it all, one that flashed her thoughts into the past. It had been almost fifteen years since she'd been in combat this intense, but now the recollections began to flood back into her mind.

It's like nothing else, that feeling. Terrifying, horrible, unimaginably awful…and yet there is something else there too. An exhilaration? No, not exactly…

She hated battle, despised the danger and the death that accompanied it. But she'd never felt quite so awake, so alive, as she did during a desperate struggle. It was almost as if…as if she knew that those instants were her at her best, her mind clear and capable, her focus almost total.

Is that it? Do I really believe my best moments are those when I stare back into death's cold eyes?

She was disturbed by the thought, but she refused to indulge an argument with herself, at least not now. She still had work to do. If she could get the pirates to surrender, Elias and his people wouldn't have to forcibly board.

And risk getting killed…

"Still no response, Commander." Berry's voice was hoarse. The young officer was trying—and failing—to hide her exhaustion.

Wheaton held back a sigh. She couldn't say she was surprised. Pirates didn't tend to surrender. They knew what awaited them, and most of them thought dying in battle was preferable to humiliation and public execution. Normally, Wheaton wouldn't care. She'd be just as happy blowing away another pack of cutthroats and murderers. But this time was different. They needed a prisoner.

She shook her head and leaned down toward the com unit. "Captain Cain," she said, pushing every bit of formality she could muster into her weary voice, "there is still no response." She'd become quite informal with her passenger and ally, but now she felt she should put all that aside. Cain was going into danger, and the more he thought like a soldier, the better chance he had of coming back. The thought of distracting him in any way, of being even tangentially responsible for his death or injury, was extremely upsetting to her.

"Very well," came the sharp reply. There wasn't a trace of hesitation in Cain's voice. "We're going in, Commander."

"Understood, Captain," she replied, trying hard to match the crispness of his tone. "Good luck."

Be careful…and come back in one piece.

*   *   *   *   *

Elias Cain stood next to the bulkhead, right at the front of his small team of agents…waiting. He was clad in black, a heavy suit of body armor over his survival suit. There was a carbine in his hands, and a belt slung over his shoulder with extra clips. But he was most conscious of the heavy pistol hanging from his side. The stun gun didn't have a lot of range, but it was the most important piece of ordnance his boarding party possessed. If he'd wanted the pirates dead, he could have sat back in *Zephyr's* wardroom and watched as Jamie Wheaton blasted the helpless vessel to atoms. But he didn't want them dead, not all of them at least. He needed information. And that meant he needed a prisoner.

He tried to keep his mind focused as he waited for the shuttle to dock with the enemy ship, but he was distracted by something inside, a feeling in his stomach. Fear, tension. He'd been in combat before, when his team had raided various criminal enterprises, but he'd never seen anything like the action his father and brother—and even his mother—had. This would be a real battle, a fight to the death against an enemy that had nothing to lose. A situation far more like war than the police actions he'd experienced before.

"Ribis, as soon as we get in, I want you to take Tiergen, Jalte, and Zimmer. You've got one job. Find the reactor and secure the containment equipment. As quickly as you can. The last thing we need is some desperate pirate blowing the magnetic bottle just to take us with him."

"Yes, sir," the agent snapped back. He turned and moved back toward the others to relay the command.

Cain knew the enemy reactor was damaged, but his gut was telling him it wasn't completely scragged…and that meant a loss of containment would be disastrous. He had no idea where the reactor was on the pirate ship, but he knew his people would have to find it or they would all risk destruction. Portable radiation detectors would point his people in the right direction, but without any idea of the ship's layout, there was no way to be sure how long it would take them to get to the control area. They would just have to do their best. And if they failed, win or lose the battle, it was as likely Elias Cain was leading his men into a nuclear holocaust as anything else. He suspected the pirate captain would destroy his ship as a last act of spite against a force that had defeated him. He wanted to be repelled by such a senseless act of destruction, but he suspected he might take the same action in the pirate's position. And he *knew* what Darius would do…

"Everybody else, we have to win this fight, first and foremost, but we also need at least one prisoner. So blast away, but when the enemy fire dies down, hold back until I can assess the situation. If we scrag them all, we will have wasted the entire boarding effort…and any of our comrades who fall will have died for nothing."

He looked back over the twenty agents of his team, wondering for a moment how many they would face on the pirate ship. By all accounts, the enemy had suffered heavily when they boarded *Carlyle*…and it was likely they had suffered additional casualties to Wheaton's laser cannons. *There could be just a few survivors…or we could be outnumbered and outgunned.* He just didn't know.

There was a loud noise, the clang of metal on metal. A few seconds later, the com line crackled to life and the voice of the shuttle's pilot blared from Cain's headset. "We're docked, Captain. Just give the word when you're ready, and we'll blow the enemy's outer hull."

And then we'll be in combat…

"Alright," he said onto the main com line, "it's time. We're here to get information on a potential plot that affects not only Atlantia, but possibly all Occupied Space. I want every one of you at your absolute best, and I know that's what I will get." A short pause. "Lieutenant…you may proceed. Blow the hull."

He stepped back a meter and waited for the charges to blow…and an instant later the bay shook hard as the carefully-positioned explosives detonated. Then he could hear the mechanism in the shuttle activate, extending the umbilical through the hole in the enemy's hull and sealing it off from space.

About twenty seconds later, the lieutenant's voice was back on the com. "You're good to go, Captain Cain. You should have life support in the enemy ship, but I'd suggest survival gear anyway."

"Acknowledged." He flipped the com to the unitwide frequency. "It's time," he said, as he pulled the clear hood up and over his face, attaching it to the connectors along the neck of the survival suit. "Full life support gear, everyone." He could almost feel the collective groan. The survival suits were incredibly uncomfortable, especially with the hoods drawn. But he didn't care. Uncomfortable was better than dead. A lot better.

"Okay, let's go…" He took one last look to confirm everyone had their gear in place. Then he put his hand just over the switch to open the hatch. He paused for an instant and turned back toward his people.

"And remember, get me a prisoner!"

*   *   *   *   *

Yulich stared down at the weapon in his hand, a small sub-machinegun. There were guns in the locker with greater hitting power, but *Black Viper's* captain was after mobility. The corridors and passageways snaking their way through his ship's lower levels were narrow and crisscrossed with conduits and structural elements. Better to carry something small than to try and navigate down there with a heavy assault rifle.

He stood around the corner from the spot where the enemy's shuttle had attached itself to *Black Viper*. He knew every centimeter of his ship, and he figured his people would have a good vantage point here.

He could hear the creaking sounds as the enemy shuttle attached to his ship's hull. It didn't sound like a normal breaching tube, which made sense, because he hadn't expected an Atlantian Patrol ship to carry any assault shuttles. He hadn't been able to confirm what exactly was out there. The shot that had taken his lasers offline had blown his whole scanner suite to charred rubble as well. The reactor was still running, at about thirty percent output at least, but otherwise, *Black Viper* was a wreck. She'd served him for ten years, through more raids than he could easily recount, but that was all over now. His ship was doomed.

And us with her…

There was nothing left to do but make the invaders pay for every centimeter of her broken hull. And he intended to do just that…at least as much as he and ten survivors could do before they were wiped out. He guessed a few more of his people were still alive, trapped behind jammed bulkheads or too badly wounded to move. Lars Treven was among those Yulich knew was dead. He'd seen his first mate cut in two by a collapsing girder while they were still on *Black Viper's* stricken bridge. The two had served together for a long time, and Treven was one of the few men Yulich had called friend. He hadn't dealt with the grief yet. He'd pushed it back, refused to let it work its way into the forefront of his mind. And the way things looked, he'd never have to face it. He was likely to join his friend, and very soon.

"Alright, you men, listen and listen good. These bastards could have blown us out of space if they wanted to, but they're boarding instead. We've got something they need, and that means this isn't over yet." That was all for show, to work his few remaining fighters into a frenzy. If Ivan Yulich knew one thing for certain it was that this battle was all but over. There was nothing left but to go down fighting…and deny his ship to the enemy.

"We hit them hard as they're coming out, but then we fall back down the main corridor toward engineering, fighting all the way."

And then, when it's really over, I'll end it. Black Viper is mine and nobody else's, and I'll be damned if I'll let them have her.

He heard a loud clang, and an instant later a door blew out into the corridor…and armed men poured out. They paused for an instant, getting their bearings and locating the defenders before shooting. But by then Yulich's crew had opened up, raking the corridor with deadly fire.

He saw one of the invaders drop…then another. One of the stricken men lay in the middle of the corridor unmoving. The other was pulled back into the compartment by his retreating comrades.

A loud cheer rose from Yulich's crew, and he could see out of the corners of his eyes as they pumped their arms into the arm.

Let them go, he thought. *Anything to keep their morale up a little longer…*

But he knew things would get tougher. He was still thinking that when half a dozen small spheres came bouncing down the corridor.

"Grenades!" one of his men shouted, and then the hallway erupted in blast of smoke and flame.

Chapter 18

Marine Headquarters
Planet Armstrong, Gamma Pavonis III
Earthdate: 2319 AD (34 Years After the Fall)

Catherine Gilson stood next to her office's outside wall, a single stretch of floor-to-ceiling hyper polycarbonate, offer a sweeping view of the parade grounds twenty meters below. She was watching the recruits run by, organized by platoon, each with its drill sergeant close behind, driving the exhausted trainees forward. They looked a little ragged, but that was to be expected. The new class was only a week into their two-year basic training regimen, a staggeringly difficult program that saw fewer than thirty percent of participants graduate. Most of the rest dropped out, taking the option for a free return trip back to whatever world they had come from. But not all the attrition would come from the quitters. A fair number would die trying to get through the program, she knew. Marine training was designed to produce the best possible fighters, whatever that took…and that sometimes meant putting men and women in dangerous situations. The armor instruction on Armstrong's moon was particularly dangerous, and there were always fatalities among the second year men and women when they arrived at Jax Base to learn how to move around a frigid near-vacuum in a twenty ton suit of nuclear-powered armor.

Gilson's mind flashed back, years before…to Camp Puller on Earth, where she had endured the torments of the Marine training program. Back then it had been six years, something she couldn't imagine now, and it had been heavy in remedial education, with dozens of classes designed to bring its often illiterate trainees up to high standards of educational achievement. The Corps had recruited mostly from Earth's horrific slums back then, offering a way out of the misery for those who had what it took to become Marines.

Gilson's strategies had been somewhat similar, opening the door to a Marine career to all citizens of former Alliance worlds, many of which had fallen on hard times after the Fall...and had suffered again during the Second Incursion. They weren't the hellholes Earth's Cog-peasants had endured, but a few of them were close. A career in the Marines meant a chance at an education, and to be part of an organization with a storied history and high standards of excellence. But the Corps demanded much in return, far more than most could give.

That pitch had lost some of its appeal with the growth of the mercenary companies. They too offered an escape from poor worlds and dismal lives. And they held out the promise of riches, the profits of a life spent at war for gain. Gilson liked to imagine the allure of the Marines would appeal more to those she really wanted to recruit...but then she remembered herself the day she'd gotten off the train at Camp Puller, young, angry, there only because the alternative was so much worse.

How would I have responded to a recruiter for the Wildcats or the Lightnings? Not to mention the famous Black Eagles? Am I just lying to myself if I say I would have walked through the gates of Puller? Turned down enlistment bonuses and promises of riches to be won?

She put the thought out of her mind, mostly because she suspected she wouldn't like the answer. Besides, despite the competition, the Marines hadn't had too much trouble filling their meager quotas. The Corps she led was the slimmest shadow of what it had been at its peak, and it had survived only because she, and a band of old officers like her, had refused to let it die. And service with the Corps carried one benefit the mercenary companies couldn't match—Armstrong citizenship upon retirement, a chance to live on a prosperous world that enjoyed a wide array of constitutionally-protected freedoms. And, however much the Corps had shrunk, it still held much of its reputation…and Armstrong was a peaceful world as a result, a place few would even contemplate attacking.

She turned and walked back toward her desk. The Corps was indeed smaller than it had been, but its Commandant's workload seemed as deep as ever. She had pages of reports to go through, as many of them dealing with Armstrong's civil government as with the Corps itself. The planet had been a small, unimportant colony when the Marines moved their operations there after the colonial rebellions. The Corps had been vastly larger then, and it had virtually taken over the entire planet. Later, it fought one of the great battles in its history there, when thousands of Marines struggled under Erik Cain defending it from the Shadow Legions. From that moment on, Armstrong belonged to the Corps, in every way that mattered.

Gilson was effectively Armstrong's head of state as well as the Corps' senior officer, though it was a bit more complicated than that. There was a civilian Assembly as well, and a Speaker who presided over that body. In theory, the two branches shared equal power, and they had to agree on all major decisions. In practice, the Assembly, half of its members Marine and naval veterans, did whatever Gilson wanted, rubberstamping anything she sent their way. Armstrong was the Marines' planet, through and through, most of its industry dependent on the Corps' technology, which Gilson had freely licensed to promote economic growth. Armstrong's industrial output was exported to a hundred other worlds, and even the purest civilians couldn't argue with the way the planet had been governed.

Gilson sat down at her desk, making another effort to focus on her work. But she still couldn't concentrate. She read a sentence, maybe two…and then her mind wandered back to the same subject. Finally, she slapped her hand down on the desk in frustration.

Why would she leave without speaking to me? It's not like her. What could have made her behave so impulsively?

Sarah Cain was one of Gilson's few true friends, a veteran with a service record almost as long as the Commandant's. They saw each other frequently, had a regular weekly lunch together. Sarah was the Corps' unofficial second-in-command, one of the very few remaining veterans who had seen service in all four of mankind's wars of the last sixty years. The two had known each other for all that time, and they had served together on many campaigns.

But something was wrong now. Gilson knew Sarah had gotten a mysterious visitor...and that she had disappeared immediately after. But that was all she knew. And that had her very worried.

Gilson's first reaction had been to fear some sort of abduction...but then she realized that simply wasn't possible. No one could have gotten into the Marine hospital with enough force to subdue her and all those around her. Sarah was a surgeon, but she was also a Marine, and that meant she would never yield without one hell of a fight. Even if someone had managed to subdue her without raising a general alarm, they could never have escaped unnoticed. Or gotten offworld. Any unauthorized vessel lifting off would have been detected and intercepted. Armstrong space was well-defended. The small remnant of the fleet had come under the Corps' control when Augustus Garret had finally retired and gone back to his family's home on Terra Nova. It was a small armada, but one perfectly capable of observing every ship leaving or approaching Armstrong orbit.

Some private vessels had left over the past few days, but nothing out of the ordinary. Unless Sarah had commandeered one of them. But why would she want to slip away? What could have come up that would cause her to leave, keeping her reason a secret? It didn't make any sense. But Gilson couldn't stop herself from trying to figure it out.

Where did you go, old friend? And why?

*   *   *   *   *

"Thank you for seeing me without an appointment, General."

"It is my pleasure, Admiral Campbell. It has been a long time…since just after the Second Incursion if I remember correctly." Gilson gestured toward two small chairs sitting in front of the window wall.

Campbell nodded, waiting for Gilson to sit before he did. "Yes, your memory is impeccable." His voice became somber. "I believe it was at Erik Cain's memorial service."

"Yes…could that have really been more than fifteen years ago?" She shook her head slowly. In some ways it seemed so distant…yet in others like yesterday.

"I'm afraid so, General. I must say, I am gratified to see the Corps still intact. I shudder to think of where mankind would be if your people hadn't been there during the Shadow War… and again when the Second Incursion struck."

"Yes, we've managed to survive, though it was very tentative for a while. But things are better now, quite a bit better. Our technology has fueled a bit of an economic revolution on Armstrong, and our finances are actually quite stable. Indeed, I have been considering activating a third regiment if things continue to go so well." She paused. "Though that's not for public consumption yet."

"That is of course good news, General," Campbell replied with a smile. "Which I will certainly treat with the utmost discretion. And from what I hear, your use of the Corps' military technology to spur civilian industry has been extraordinarily successful. I'm told the standard of living on Armstrong is the envy of Occupied Space."

Gilson returned Campbell's smile. "Well, considering how many trillions of credits the Alliance spent developing that tech…not to mention what we retrieved from damaged First Imperium gear, it's no wonder we've seen a decent return. At least some of it can be used for productive purposes as well as destruction."

The two sat quietly for a few seconds before Gilson spoke again. "So, not that I'm not happy to see you, but I imagine you came for a reason beyond reminiscing about old battles?"

Campbell nodded. "Yes, I'm afraid I did." He paused, looking uncomfortable for a few seconds. "Before I begin, may I ask where General Cain is? I have come to speak with her as well as you, but I was unable to contact her at the hospital."

Gilson looked down at the floor for a few seconds. "I'm afraid I don't know, Admiral. She has disappeared. We don't suspect any coercion or foul play, but I am frankly at a loss to understand what would have made her sneak away. I cannot think of any circumstance that would cause her to leave without informing me."

Campbell frowned. "Yes, that does sound very unlike her." He paused, a concerned look on his face. Finally, he sighed and said, "Well, I will brief you, General, and you can pass the information on when you see her." He didn't sound at all satisfied, and it was clear he was worried.

Gilson nodded. "So what have you come to discuss?"

He paused and took another deep breath. "First, you need to know that Roderick Vance has assumed control of the Confederation."

"Control?"

"To be specific, he has launched a coup—with the support of the commanders of both the army and navy."

Gilson stared back at Campbell, her decades of Marine discipline keeping any reaction from her face. "And with your support as well, I assume?"

"Yes," Campbell said, a little defensively. "I supported his action. I still do. That is why I agreed to come see you."

"I know Roderick Vance well enough to assume that this was not a traditional power grab. He is not that kind of man." There was no surprise in Gilson's voice, at least none Campbell could detect.

"No, General, he is not. He reluctantly decided to move forward after the council repeatedly refused to take any action about what he sees as grave threats to the Confederation...and all human space. You are familiar with the recent events on Earth and Eris?"

Gilson nodded.

"Mr. Vance believes there is a much greater danger than a single slaving ring, and after his discussions with Darius Cain, he became even more convinced there is some kind of enemy gathering in the shadows, one that could be as dangerous as Gavin Stark...and the Shadow Legions."

"That is quite a leap, Admiral," Gilson said, though her tone suggested no real doubt. "I would discount it out of hand if it had come from almost anyone else. But I learned long ago to trust Mr. Vance's instincts."

"That is why I am here, General. Mr. Vance controls the Confederation absolutely...all its military and espionage assets. He has taken steps to prepare, though we do not know what we will face. He sent me to inform you...and to ask for your aid, to request that the Marines once more ally with us to face whatever is coming."

Gilson took a deep breath. "Mr. Vance knows we will support him." There was something in her voice, a hesitancy. "But the Corps is not what it was, even during the Second Incursion. With our obligation to defend Armstrong, I doubt we could field an expeditionary force larger than two thousand strong. And that would require calling in our primary reserves."

"Mr. Vance was hoping you would issue an all-out call for your veterans to return to the colors." His tone suggested he knew the gravity of what he was asking.

"Admiral..." Gilson started to answer, but she paused uncomfortably.

"General Gilson, Mr. Vance understands what he is asking... but you better than anyone knows the terrible cost we have paid in the past for waiting too long, for ignoring warning signs until open war was upon us."

"But most of those veterans now have lives elsewhere... careers, families. They have served, done their share. They are Marines, of course, as they will be all their lives. I believe they would return to the colors in a true emergency. But I couldn't ask that of them unless I was sure...and I would have to tell them what enemy they face. How could I uproot them, drag them halfway across occupied space, when I can't even tell them who they will be fighting? Would they even respond to such a vague call?"

"There is only one way to find out, General."

Gilson was shaking her head. "How could I? And if we were to go that way, to mobilize for war, we would need armor, weapons, supplies. The cost would be staggering." She paused. "The Corps barely survived the cutbacks following the Second Incursion. Can I risk its current stability, put all we have worked to achieve at risk...on a hunch?"

Campbell nodded slowly. "I understand, General. But I could ask you similar questions. Can you risk not preparing now, take the chance that your people are unprepared when the enemy reveals himself? Do you not put the lives of your existing Marines in danger by not readying the Corps for what may be coming? Even your veterans...if you wait too long, will they return to the ranks too late to make a difference? To go down in a lost cause? Or do they stay where they are, and die in the ashes of their adopted homeworlds, because we did not take the steps necessary to defend against the coming onslaught?"

Gilson sat quietly looking across the desk at her guest. Finally, she leaned back in the chair and said, "You don't pull any punches, do you?"

"Not with something this important. If Roderick Vance didn't believe we faced a coming storm, he would not have sent me here. If I didn't believe it, I wouldn't have come...nor would I have supported his coup." He paused, maintaining eye contact. "The question is what do you believe, General? You cannot take such a step because I ask it, or even because Roderick Vance asks it. You can only consider what I tell you, look at the evidence yourself...and make a decision."

Campbell hesitated again, the room completely silent. Finally, he said, "So, General Gilson...will the Corps join us?"

Chapter 19

Black Viper
Zed-4 System
1,200,000 Meters from Gamma-Hydra Warp Gate
Earthdate: 2319 AD (34 Years After the Fall)

Elias whipped around the corner, firing on full auto. The assault rifle was a basic model, at least by the standards of the hyper-velocity guns leading edge military forces like the Black Eagles used. But those weapons fired iridium or depleted uranium slugs, and the high-powered coilguns propelled them with enough force to blast right through the hull of a ship like the corsair. And if he'd wanted to crack open the pirate vessel like an egg, he could have sat back and watched while *Zephyr* blasted away at long range.

He ran down the short corridor, spraying his fire in front of him as he did. It was as much to keep the pirates under cover around the corner as to actually hit anyone. He had half a dozen of his people right behind him. They'd been pinned down too long, the two sides tucked in around the corners, exchanging ineffective potshots. But Elias knew time wasn't on his side.

Ribis and his people were somewhere in the ship, trying to find the reactor so they could set up a defensive perimeter and prevent the surviving pirates from cutting off the containment field. But there were only four of them. Even if they did find their way to engineering and take control, the pirates could always assault and recapture the place. And they would only need a few minutes to shut down the magnetic bottle and obliterate the ship—and everyone on it. He didn't know if the pirates would choose such a desperate course of action, but he was certain they knew what to expect if they fell into the Patrol's hands...at least under normal circumstances. Summary execution was the standard penalty for piracy, and this group of buccaneers had no reason to expect anything different.

Elias and his people had forced their way onboard covered by a cluster of grenades—half the total they possessed. But that had only worked because it was a surprise...and the enemy had been distracted long enough to allow his people to advance and seize the first intersection of hallways. The pirates had fallen back, and Elias' people had taken down three of them as they ran. But he doubted it would work again. His agents didn't have any smart weapons, sophisticated drones that would navigate around corners and the like. If he'd ordered his people to throw the rest of their grenades, more than likely, the enemy would have just dropped back from the corner far enough to dodge the blast.

"Ooooph..." Elias heard the sound, and its meaning was clear enough. One of his people had been hit.

That's four, he thought, glumly reviewing the casualty list in his head.

Elias gasped hard, struggling to suck in a lungful of air. He could feel his heart beating, like a bass drum in his chest, and he felt dizzy, lightheaded. Elias Cain was no coward...not even his rivals would call him that. But he wasn't a soldier either, or at least he hadn't been. He'd raided a few criminal enterprises, but those were typical law enforcement actions, where his people had huge numerical and equipment advantages. That didn't mean he couldn't have been killed hitting some smuggler's holdout—he'd seen agents go down more than once—but this was different, a more even struggle. He was on unfamiliar ground, without a significant numerical superiority. He had been an agent for years, but this was his true baptism of war.

He felt something in his stomach, a rolling, uncomfortable sensation. He realized it was fear. He'd been afraid before, certainly, in operations...and in that brief second on Mars when he'd realized he was in an assassin's crosshairs. But this was like nothing he'd felt before. He was in the open, relying on his suppressing fire to save him, to prevent one of his enemies from leaning around the corner and putting a bullet in him. Any instant could be his last...he could almost feel the phantom bullets, ripping into his chest, putting him down. It was an odd feeling, terrifying, but also invigorating in a strange way. His body flooded with adrenalin, and his mind crackled with alertness. He'd never felt more awake, more aware. His eyes locked coldly on the corner with focused intensity, staring for the slightest shadow that might warn him of an enemy's movement.

Okay, he thought, trying to stay focused. *Almost there...*

He lunged forward, twisting to the left as he pushed off into the intersection. He whipped his rifle around to the side, spraying the perpendicular corridor with fire. The move was bold, reckless...but this time it was also effective. There were three pirates crouched down in the hallway. His fire hit two, at least. One fell back as multiple rounds took him in the chest, and the second stood transfixed, his hands clutching at his neck, where a growing flow of scarlet blood marked his mortal wound.

The third pirate reacted, bringing his rifle around to fire back, but Elias' momentum took his past the intersecting corridor before his opponent's fire blasted through. Elias landed hard, his knees slamming painfully into the cold deck. He loosened his legs and went into a makeshift combat roll, using the last of his inertia to hop back to his feet. He spun around, popping his spent cartridge as he did and reaching around for a fresh one.

Four of his people had followed his lead, leaping across the open gap and shooting down the hallway as they did. The return fire had stopped...his people had taken out the last pirate. But it hadn't come without cost. One of his agents was face down in the intersection, and he could see from the massive pool of blood expanding out from under her that she was dead. The others were still on the far side, and he motioned for them to stay. He crept up and looked cautiously around the corner, confirming the last enemy was down. The pirate was a gruesome sight, riddled with bullets, his blood splattered all over the walls.

"Alright, let's go," he snapped, turning his head, looking at the groups of agents on either side of the intersection. "Follow me." Elias knew there had been more than three pirates facing his people...and that could only mean one thing. The three dead men lying in the hall were a rearguard, left behind to hold off his people while their comrades fell back.

Back to engineering. The perfect place for a last stand...and a final way to strike back if they lost the fight.

"Move it...we've got to get to find the engineering section. Now!"

Before Ribis and his people get overrun...and some desperate pirate blows us all into plasma...

*   *   *   *   *

"I'm alright," Ribis growled as he pulled the end of the makeshift tourniquet tight around his left arm. "You just keep your eyes open. We don't know this ship, and they could come from any direction." He groaned as he tugged harder. The ammunition strap was thick canvas, and he had trouble holding one end tight with his teeth as he pulled hard, trying to secure it enough to stop the bleeding. They had found the engineering section almost immediately, but no more than five minutes after they got there, at least ten pirates showed up. The Atlantians had managed to push the enemy assault back, but not before Ribis took a close range blast in the arm.

Pam Jalte hesitated, a concerned look on her face as her eyes dropped to Ribis' bloodsoaked arm. But after a few seconds, she just nodded her acknowledgement and turned to face the main access corridor. She was pretty sure they'd hit at least two of the attackers...but that meant a minimum of eight were still in action. And though she hoped Ribis would survive his wound, there was no way he was picking up a gun and firing any time soon. So that left three of them.

Shitty odds.

She might have suggested they fall back, but she knew why they were there. The pirate ship was doomed, even if its crew managed to kill every one of the boarders. Commander Wheaton wasn't about to let a helpless pirate go, even less so if twenty Patrol agents had been killed in a failed boarding op.

No, these guys are running on pure desperation...and that means we stay here and defend this reactor.

There weren't many things on a spaceship the captain couldn't do remotely, but shutting down the fusion reactor's containment field was one of them. Even a microsecond's interruption was enough to vaporize any vessel...and allowing a remote override of such a vital system invited an enemy or saboteur to try and send a counterfeit command, and destroy a ship without a shot fired. It was core to spaceship design and operation to keep the field up and running at all times...and to scrag the reactor instantly at the slightest sign of trouble.

Jalte turned her head as she heard rattling sounds over her head. *They're crawling through the ducts, trying to get around and hit us from behind. Or both sides at once.*

She looked back at Ribis. His eyes were closed, his breathing shallow. It looked like the tourniquet was working fairly well, but he'd already lost a lot of blood.

He might survive, but he's out of this fight. And in no shape to run the show now...

"Ed," she snapped at Zimmer, "try and follow the sounds overhead...figure out where they're heading and cover that approach." She didn't like the idea of their flank being protected by a single man, but there were only three of them. And she was betting that most of the pirates would still come at them from the front.

She was still wondering if she was right...or if she should have sent Tiergen with Zimmer, when the enemy opened up again, and she dove behind the console she was using as cover. She hit the ground harder than she'd intended, knocking the wind out of herself, but she shook her head and struggled hard to focus. She crawled to the end of the workstation and peered around the edge…just as four of the pirates came running around the corner, charging right at her position.

She tried to pull her rifle around, but it was long and wedged behind the console, and she lost a second, perhaps two…precious time she didn't have to spare. Then one of the pirates fell. There was a spray of blood, and she could see that the right side of his face was gone as he fell forward.

One down…at least Tiergen is on the ball…

One of the pirates was almost upon her. She struggled to bring the rifle around, and she pulled the trigger. She hadn't had time to aim, but she managed to get off a round before he got to her. The pirate fell hard as his stricken leg gave out. The wound wasn't critical, but she could tell it was painful.

No time…

She rolled over and tried to bring the rifle up, to target the next pirate, but she was too late. He was standing over her, his own weapon already extended. She tried to lunge out of the way, but she knew it was too late.

The shot took her in the shoulder, and she could feel it shattering bone and tearing muscle. For an instant, it was almost clinical, an awareness of the damage but not real pain. Then it hit her, a wave of agony like nothing she'd ever experienced. She felt the howl escape her lips, an involuntary response, and she lay back, helpless, unable to even make herself move. The side of her face was splattered with her blood, and through the pain she could feel the wetness all over her neck and her arm.

The wound was bad, but survivable if she got help. But she knew there was no hope, and she could see her enemy through teary eyes, leveling his weapon for another shot. The killing shot.

She was dead…she knew it. Just an instant, and it would be over. She would never see home again…her family.

There was a sound, a gunshot that somehow registered in her failing ears louder than the others in the melee swirling all around her. *That was it*, she thought. *Am I dead?* But then she saw her enemy falling backwards, a bullet hole right between his eyes.

"Jalte?" she heard. The voice was familiar, and through the pain she found it somehow comforting. "Pam," it said again. "Can you hear me?"

She tried to move her head, but the pain was unbearable, and she let it drop again. She realized the firing had stopped. Then she felt motion, someone moving around, stopping, looking down at her.

"Just stay still, Pam. It's over…we took the ship. Try to rest. We've got a medteam on the way."

Her vision was blurry, fading, and she knew she was slipping into unconsciousness. Her throat was dry, and she couldn't force out any words. But she recognized Elias Cain standing above her…and she had a single thought before she slipped into the darkness.

We won.

*   *   *   *   *

"Okay, *Captain* Yulich, it is time we had a serious talk." Elias pronounced the pirate's rank as if it was a curse. "Apart from your attack on the *Carlyle*, and the murder of its entire crew save one…you have to answer to me for the losses among my own agents. I had six dead and six wounded taking your vessel, *Captain*. That's sixty percent casualties seizing the ship that you refused to surrender. The ship you used to attack *Zephyr*, and the one you tried to destroy with my people on it. So, let's just say that you are going to tell me everything—absolutely everything—I want to know. Starting now."

Yulich sat in the chair, silent, unresponsive, his arms and legs shackled. He'd taken a few flesh wounds in the fighting, and while none of them were serious, Elias figured they hurt like hell. *Good*, he thought, staring into the prisoner's eyes, somewhat surprised to see there was still defiance there. Elias fought back the urge to beat the resistance out of the son of a bitch.

He had a passing thought, wondering what kind of unspeakable dungeon Darius had built into his Nest, what kind of hell awaited captives who had killed Black Eagles, as this pirate and his crew had killed Elias' agents. Elias had long told himself he was above such behavior, and he'd condemned his brother as a traitor and a barbarian. Now, staring down at the man responsible for the deaths of Captain Marne's crew as well as six of his own men and women, he felt different thoughts. Images passed before his eyes, the faces of the dead, the image of Pam Jalte in sickbay, her wrecked shoulder so bad, the medic had been forced to amputate her arm. The anger was pulsating within, threatening to overrule his self-control.

He would try to reason with this man, to obtain his cooperation without resorting to means he had always despised. But if that didn't work, he knew he would no longer allow his actions to be constrained by within his former limits. There was something going in Occupied Space far more dangerous than the destruction of one valuable cargo. And this pirate, and the other two still-living members of his crew, were the only leads Elias had.

He suddenly realized he was subconsciously beginning to justify actions he didn't even know he would have to take. He was going to learn what he needed to know. And the words that came to his mind made him think of his brother's was of doing things...*whatever it takes.*

"You and your men face a death sentence on Atlantia...and on any other civilized world whose spacers you have victimized. It is a fate you richly deserve, but if you cooperate fully, I am prepared to intervene on your behalf for commutation and a reduction of your sentence."

Yulich remained silent, no reaction at all.

"I see you are a tough one. Certain death awaits you, and you spurn your only chance at salvation? The deal I offer you is the best you will get, I can promise that. Is saving your miserable hide really so unimportant to you?"

Yulich managed a mocking smile. "And what is your promise worth? Do you think I would believe anything you say? I tried to die with my ship...and take you and your pack of dogs with me, but I failed. So, why don't you just go ahead and kill me?"

"I have no intention of killing you." Elias remained calm, not letting the pirate's taunting words anger him. "And fortunately, your ship, while damaged, has been secured. I can promise you, we will take it apart, bolt by bolt to uncover all its secrets. Com records, nav data, even particulate residue. You'd be surprised what a Patrol forensic team can accomplish."

Yulich glared back, silently. It looked for a moment like he was going to say something, but finally he just looked away.

"I know you are not some lone wolf pirate, Captain Yulich. The cargo shipment you intercepted was highly classified, yet you were able to intercept it. That means you had a source of information inside the Atlantian government." Elias slid to the side, angling so he was again looking right into the pirate's eyes. "So either you had a personal contact…or you are part of some larger organization. I am inclined to think it is the latter, and I believe you can provide me useful information on such a cartel…size, scope, base locations."

"You are insane," Yulich growled. "Do you know what they would do to me?" The pirate's face twisted into a frustrated knot, as if he was angry with himself for saying anything.

"I can promise you protection," Elias countered.

"Ha!" Yulich spat. "Protection? From them? You don't know what you're talking about. You are nothing to them. You don't even know what operatives they have in your government." A jagged smile slipped onto his face. "Yes, of course they have people there, that is how they operate. You have no idea what you are dealing with. You think you offer me my life? It is not yours to give. If the Atlantian authorities don't kill me, they will. And there is no way you will be able to stop them. So spare me your empty promises. Shoot me if you will, but stop boring me to death with your pointless questions."

Elias stood for a moment, silent, thinking. He felt a cold feeling, a sudden realization that whatever he had expected to find, the truth was even darker, more ominous.

He's resigned to death, completely sure they will find him

and kill him. What could cause such fear that a man would seek death over offers of salvation? What am I chasing?

He didn't know what to say, what to do. Amnesty and protection were all he had to offer. If Yulich didn't believe either was possible, there was no way Elias was going to get him to cooperate.

How can I convince him I can keep him safe? Or scare him as badly as his former employers? Of course...

Suddenly, he turned back toward the prisoner. "Do you know my name, Captain Yulich?"

"What?" the pirate captain asked, a scowl on his face. "Yeah, you told me. Elias. Elias Cain."

"Is any part of that familiar to you?"

"No, I've never heard of you. Does that make you feel less important?" The mocking tone was back.

"No, not at all," Elias said, his voice firm and even. "But I thought you might recognize my last name. My father was Erik Cain, General Erik Cain."

"Yeah...I know who he was. So your father was a big hero. What do I care?"

"Well, it's not my father I thought you might know about. I'm going to take you to see my brother, Captain. He can protect you if he wants...even against whatever pack of bottom-feeding criminals you worked for. And he can get information from you too, I'd wager. I seriously doubt he would be as restricted by...shall we say ethical constraints?...as I am."

Yulich stared back, a confused look on his face. Then the expression vanished, and he went white as a sheet.

"Yes, Captain, I think you finally understand. I suggest you think about just how abrasive and defiant you want to be with my brother. He's far more likely than me to get...rough."

"Your brother is Darius Cain?" The fear was thick in Yulich's voice.

"Yes, Captain. He is. And I have it on good authority the Black Eagles are quite gifted at...extracting information."

Yulich's eyes were wide, his skin pasty white. He looked at Elias as if he was staring into the yawning pit of hell.

"I think I will wait until we get there to dig deeper into all of this. Darius and his people will have a much easier time of it than me." He turned and walked away, forcing himself not to turn back. He didn't need his eyes to hear Yulich's heavy breathing…and something that sounded a bit like whimpering.

He wondered if it was the right move to bring Darius into this. He'd made an uneasy peace of sorts with his estranged brother after the whole Mars-Eris episode, but there was still a lot of bad blood between them. He still disapproved of Darius' way of doing things, and he wondered what it meant that his mind had gone right to threatening Yulich with the same methods. He was worried about what was happening…on Atlantia, along the interplanetary trade routes, in all of Occupied Space. But did that justify what he had for so long condemned? Was he losing his principles? Becoming more and more like his brother?

He didn't know, but he would think on it all, he was sure. But first he had a more difficult task.

How the hell am I going to convince Jamie to take Zephyr all the way to the Nest?

Chapter 20

Planet Terra Nova
Alpha Centauri A III
Earthdate: 2319 AD (34 Years After the Fall)

Augustus Garret stared down at the small headstone. He was kneeling, his knees damp from the morning dew on the soft grass, more brown now than green with the approach of winter. There was stiffness in his legs, an ache in his cold knees. Rejuv treatments or no, Garret felt every bit his age, especially in his mind. He was old, and he thought mostly now of days passed, companions gone. He went through his daily routine with the discipline born of a military life, but there was always a shadow of sadness upon him, an exhaustion that made every action an effort. He felt like he was done, as if his life had been stretched too far. Perhaps he should have died in one of his battles, he often thought, cut down at the climactic moment...a hero's death. A fitting end for the great admiral, one for the history texts. But that hadn't been his fate, and he simply went on, marking time as the increasingly empty months and years passed by.

Cemeteries were relatively rare on the worlds of Occupied Space, cremation generally serving as the standard disposition for the deceased. But Terra Nova had retained the custom, at least in the old Alliance sector, and the families who called that area of the declining world home continued to bury their dead.

The stones marking the graves in the century and a half old

Garret family cemetery were mostly native granite, gray and featureless, like most things on Terra Nova. But not this one. It was Columbian marble, an extremely rare strain in a striking midnight blue. Blue had been Charlotte's favorite color.

Charlotte...

Charlotte Evers had been dead for many years. So many, Garret surprised himself every time he did the calculation. She had been young when she died...far too young. And Garret knew she had died because of his actions. He had lived an entire life since that day, fought a series of cataclysmic battles and, in the process, he'd become perhaps the greatest hero known to mankind. But he still remembered that one day as if it had just happened. And the pain was fresh, as biting as it had been then, so long ago.

He had failed to save her, driven by his youthful arrogance to attempt too many things at one time. He had destroyed an enemy battleship, turned the tide of a crucial battle, but he'd been too late to get back to her dying ship. He'd been sure he could do both, or at least he'd convinced himself, so he could justify going after the damaged enemy first. But rescuing Charlotte, and the others on her crippled vessel, had been a step too far. By the time he'd gotten there she was dead, frozen in her quarters. They were all dead.

It wasn't the first time he'd failed her. He had abandoned her years before that fateful day, to go off to the naval academy and begin a military career, one that would take him further than he could have imagined. He hadn't admitted it to himself for many years, at least not in direct terms, but now he realized the harsh truth...that day he'd chosen glory over love. There wasn't a doubt in his mind he'd loved Charlotte. He loved her still. But he'd told himself he would come back to her, that he would request a post on Terra Nova after graduation. He'd believed it when he said it, with all the foolishness an ambitious young man in love could conjure. But it was never reality, and years later he'd come to realize that she had known it all along, even that rainy day at the spaceport, when he'd held her one last time before boarding his shuttle...when they'd sworn they would be together after he finished at the Academy. Now when he remembered he understood, the way she'd held on to him, the desperation in her grip. He had masked his pain with false promises, but Charlotte hadn't. She had known he was leaving her forever. He was sure of that now. He'd broken her heart that day. He had been the most important thing in her life, but she hadn't been for him. There was one mistress that had come before her, that took him away. The call to battle...to glory.

It almost seemed absurd to him now that he would have returned to a posting on Terra Nova after graduation. The young Augustus Garret had been almost comically ill-suited to a desk job on a backwater world, and whatever lingering chance there had been that he would have chosen to that path was shattered when the Second Frontier War began. He graduated at the head of his class, bound for service with the frontline fleets...and he jumped into his career with both feet, distinguishing himself in a series of junior officer postings before he at last got what he'd longed for his entire life, a ship of his own to command.

Wasp had been a fast attack ship, just the kind of posting suited to an arrogant young officer new to command. The 'suicide boats,' as the fast but lightly-armored vessels were informally called, employed extremely aggressive tactics, taking great risks to attack heavier enemy vessels. It was on *Wasp's* bridge that the young Garret issued the commands that destroyed an enemy battleship...and lost the love of his life.

It was a choice...your choice. You chose glory, and that devil's bargain certainly paid off. You got your glory, more of it than any man could withstand. But that is all you got. All you have. The cost of such renown is steep, all consuming. And you paid its price.

His life would have been vastly different if he hadn't boarded that shuttle, so much so he could hardly imagine it. Would he live in Bluestone Manor with Charlotte, his life's love still alive and at his side? Would they be surrounded now by children and grandchildren, living a quiet life, one of relative obscurity, without the fame and glory that followed the great Augustus Garret wherever he went?

Would we have been happy? Or would I have just resented my choice, mourned for the life of glory I had imagined but that had never been?

He sighed softly. He knew some questions didn't have answers, at least not meaningful ones. He had done what he had done, and there was little to be gained by rethinking what was long past.

"I love you, Charlotte," he said, softly, almost inaudibly. He kissed his fingers, as he always did, and pressed his hand against the headstone, holding it there for a few seconds before he slowly rose to his feet. He stood still, staring for perhaps half a minute before he turned and walked down the path leading to the cemetery's main gate.

Garret had failed Charlotte in life...but he had been doting in death, an obligation he felt to show his devotion in whatever pathetic ways he could now that it was far too late to do anything meaningful. The charade only mocked him with its pointlessness, but he was resolute nevertheless. He had brought her home after she died, and he had the magnificent blue marble imported for her headstone. Was it for her? Or to claw at him every time he came, a form of self-flagellation, as if by his own pain he could reach her, make her know how sorry he was. Her grave had been covered in flowers for seventy years, something he'd arranged throughout his long and storied naval career, though he had gone decades without ever returning to Terra Nova himself. But when his last war was done, the great admiral had come back...to a home that no longer felt like home and a family he hardly knew.

He walked through the cemetery's main entrance, a large masonry arch with a heavy iron gate. It was shabby, like most constructions on Terra Nova, and one side of the gate hung at an angle, as if it would fall from its mounting at any moment.

He turned onto the main path, a gravel road leading up a small hill, toward the rambling manor house the Garret family had called home for 180 years. The Garrets had always been moderately prosperous, but when Augustus finally returned home fifteen years before, he'd come to realize his fame had lifted the family's fortunes. He was happy that his various nieces, nephews and cousins faced a less tenuous existence, but he also felt it was somehow wrong, as if his family's fortune had been paid for with the blood of thousands of spacers and Marines.

"Admiral Garret?"

Garret looked up, the voice shaking him from his thoughts. There was a man approaching. He looked to be about seventy years of age, but Garret had learned to notice the telltale signs of rejuv treatments, and he suspected the visitor was well over one hundred years old. Maybe even a match for his own 108 years.

"Yes," Garret replied. His voice was somber, still somewhat distracted. Visiting Charlotte's grave always put him in a pensive state of mind. "I am Augustus Garret. What can I do for you?" Garret kept walking slowly down the path, waving for his visitor to come along.

"My name is Andre Girard, Admiral. Roderick Vance sent me to speak with you."

Garret's eyes brightened at the mention of Vance, and turned to face the visitor. "And how is old Roderick?" He remembered his first impression of Vance. He'd thought the Martian was a bit of a cold fish, not very likable. Garret generally trusted his initial evaluations of people, but he'd had to admit he had been wide of the mark on Vance. The Martian spy had proven to be a reliable ally through the horrendous series of wars mankind had endured... and a good friend too.

"He is well, Admiral." A short pause. "There is no way to say this except to just blurt it out. Mr. Vance led a coup that seized total control of the Martian Confederation. He now rules as absolute dictator. He was quite insistent that I tell you this bluntly, with no parsed language."

Garret stopped in his tracks and turned toward Girard. "Roderick Vance?" He'd known Vance as a perfectionist, a hard-driving taskmaster...but he'd never seen the slightest sign the man had craved power, certainly not enough to take such a radical and risky action.

"Yes, Admiral. I understand the news may be surprising, at

least without context. But I am here to bring you up to date on events that caused Mr. Vance to act as he did. I believe when you know everything, you will understand."

Garret felt a familiar feeling, one that had become less frequent in recent years consumed by boredom and routine. But he hadn't forgotten what that tight feeling in his gut usually tried to tell him. Something was wrong, that much was clear. But he pushed back against the adrenalin burst, the impulse to ask a hundred questions, to dive into whatever was happening. His days of being on the front lines of each new disaster were over.

"Go on, Mr. Girard." Garret was old, far older than he looked. And while the rejuv treatments had kept him alive and biologically younger, inside he felt ever one of his 108 years. War, death, pain of loss…he'd experienced it all, enough for ten men. He was done. But he was still curious, and it drove his need to know more. Anything that prompted Roderick Vance to mount a coup had to be damned serious.

"Well, Admiral. It started on Earth. Mr. Vance had instituted a program to provide aid to a group of promising villages there, tracking their growth and progress. He hoped to turn them into nodes around which a second phase of assistance could begin to expand the recovery…" Girard told Garret about the slaving ring, the destruction of the base on Eris, Vance's suspicions, everything.

"That is intriguing to say the least, Mr. Girard, but I think Mr. Vance is jumping to some hasty conclusions. Perhaps the pirate ring was simply a large criminal organization, with no political or military ambitions and no other…tentacles."

The two had been walking toward a large, rambling house, built mostly from the local granite, and now they stood outside the front door. "Let's go inside, Mr. Girard. You have come a very long way. At least I can offer you some refreshment."

Girard nodded. "That would be most appreciated, Admiral."

Garret put his hand on a small scanner plate and the door unlatched with a loud click. He pushed it open and gestured for his guest to step inside.

"Welcome to Bluestone Manor, Mr. Girard. The home of

the Garrets for almost two centuries." There was an odd tone to Garret's voice, something mildly derisive.

They walked into the main entry. It was large, clearly intended to be the foyer for a grand and important house. But there was a shabbiness to it too, as if it had never quite lived up to what it should have been and now had begun to succumb to time's relentless passage.

Indeed, all of Terra Nova seemed less than it should have been. Earth's first interstellar colony predated the Superpowers...and all the wars men had waged in space. It had been founded by waves of optimistic settlers, courageous men and women who had left Earth behind to travel through the first warp gate ever discovered and build a new life. And among those on that first colony ship there had been several Garrets, who quickly took their place among the new world's leaders.

But, as with many things, early promise withered, and the future failed to live up to the past's dreams. Terra Nova lacked significant metal deposits and other resources a world needed to develop and expand a modern economy. Its early history was marred by repeated plagues, as the local pathogens outwitted medical science for half a century. And perhaps, most damaging of all, the discovery of hundreds of warpgates had opened a universe of new and more promising worlds to colonization...a number that steadily increased until nearly a thousand planets had human beings living on them.

"Welcome back, Admiral. I trust your walk was satisfactory." A gray-haired man stepped into the hall and nodded to Garret. "May I get anything for you and your guest?" he asked, walking across the room and taking Garret's jacket.

"Yes, Carson. Mr. Girard and I will sit on the terrace." Garret turned toward the Martian. "Iced tea? It's homemade...I have the leaves shipped in from Zambara."

"That would be very nice, Admiral. Thank you."

Garret turned and nodded toward his attendant.

"Right away, sir." The man walked slowly through the door from which he'd entered.

Garret angled his head toward his guest. "This way, Mr.

Girard." He gestured toward a different doorway, one in the center of the rear wall."

Girard nodded and followed Garret through the door. It led to another room, a large sitting area of some kind, with a series of glass French doors along the back.

"Straight through those doors, Mr. Girard. Bluestone Manor is a bit of an old wreck, I'm afraid, but I think you will find the terrace a most pleasant space. It is my favorite spot."

Girard gently pushed open one of the doors, and he stepped out onto a large outdoor space. The floor was covered with the same blue stone as the rest of the house, and the rails were cream-colored balustrades. The Martian stared out over the landscape, rolling hills surrounding a rich valley. There were neat rows of small trees, orchards of some kind, and a small river meandering through the property in the distance.

"This is quite lovely, Admiral." Girard paused for a moment, taking a few steps and putting his hands on the cool stone of the balustrade.

Garret knew his guest was thinking of his own home, the tunnels of the Martian cities, the recycled air and water, the artificial light. Even before the domes had been cracked, the environment had been artificial. Garret had spent his life in space, aboard one ship or another, and he thought he understood. It was so easy to forget how pleasant natural air felt, the sensation of a cool breeze...

"Thank you. I do like it out here. Terra Nova is a dying world, at least economically...but it has its appealing features as well." Garret turned and gestured toward a table, just as Carson emerged from one of the doors carrying a tray. "But please, let us sit and continue our discussion. And enough of the 'admiral' formality. I know Augustus doesn't exactly roll off the tongue, but..." He let his voice trail off.

"Very well, Augustus...and I am Andre." Girard sat in one of the chairs, watching as Garret gestured for the servant to leave and reached out to grab the pitcher on the table.

"So, back to where we were, Andre..." Garret poured a glass and set it down in front of his guest. "...as I was saying,

I have the utmost respect for Mr. Vance, but the existence of a slaving ring, however repugnant an enterprise, is hardly conclusive evidence of a larger organization...certainly of one powerful enough to threaten Mars, or Occupied Space itself."

"There is more, Augustus. Darius Cain has spoken of a mysterious force his soldiers encountered during one of their operations...apparently a large body of very well-trained troops he was unable to explain or identify."

"What do the Black Eagles have to do with this?"

Girard looked right back at Garret. "It was the Black Eagles who destroyed the base on Eris. Mr. Vance was unable to convince the Confederation council to take definitive action on its own."

Garret leaned back, a surprised look on his face. "And Darius Cain thinks there is something going on? Something beyond just the slavers?"

"That is correct." Girard picked up his glass and took a drink. He smiled and looked at the glass for an instant. "This is very good, Augustus. Thank you."

Garret nodded. He was silent for a moment, his mind jumping onto the problem, as it always had years before. Finally, he asked, "The council's intransigence...was that why Roderick launched the coup?"

"Yes, essentially. The Black Eagles destroyed the base, and Mr. Vance urged the council to take the matter seriously...but they would not be swayed from their policy of isolationism. In the end, Mr. Vance felt he had no choice. He is convinced there is a major danger out there, an enemy we know little about...but one he considers a threat to all Occupied Space."

"I still fear Roderick may be overestimating the danger here, but I have learned to take his judgment seriously. Very seriously indeed. But even if he is correct, what does he want me to do?"

Girard looked back with a surprised expression. "He wants you to join him in facing whatever is coming, of course. As you have in the past."

Garret stared back at his visitor, a non-committal look on his face. Slowly, almost imperceptibly, his head began to move back and forth. "I'm sorry, Andre...Roderick has my respect and my best wishes, but I have nothing else left to offer."

"Adm...Augustus, how can you say that? You are the greatest living naval tactician. *No one* would argue otherwise. You have been at the forefront in every desperate battle."

"Yes," Garret said, his voice wistful. "But I have nothing left to give. My fleets are gone, nothing remains of them save a few old ships in Cate Gilson's care. My crews are dispersed... and many are dead, lost in those battles you speak of." He took a deep breath, and stared at Girard with glassy eyes. "I am old, my usefulness is behind me. Mankind will always face crises... it is in his nature that he can never long enjoy peace. But it is time for a new generation of warriors to lead the fight, men and women with the energy and capability to stand in the breach, as I...and many others once did."

Girard sat silently, watching Garret as if he was waiting for the old admiral to change his mind. Finally, he said, "Admiral Garret, Mr. Vance was confident that you would join him...and give all you have to this new fight." His voice was tentative.

"That is precisely my point, Andre." Garret's voice was firm but soft, touched with sadness. "I have nothing to give. I am an old man, alone...no longer the admiral commanding a great fleet. I am a memory, a reputation too heavy to sustain itself. If I could help I would, but my time is past."

Garret turned and locked eyes with Girard. He felt the crushing weight of all the years, all those who had once been at his side but who were now gone. Charlotte, of course, but also Terrance Compton, Elias Holm, Erik Cain...

He had outlived his peers, at least most of them, and his strength was gone. "Tell Roderick I am sorry," he said sadly.

Chapter 21

"The Nest" – Black Eagles Base
Second Moon of Eos, Eta Cassiopeiae VII
Earthdate: 2318 AD (34 Years After the Fall)

"Nest Control, this is the Atlantian vessel *Zephyr*. I am Captain Elias Cain, and I wish to speak to my brother immediately." Elias stood in front of the main display with video communications activated. He expected tight security at the Nest, and he figured it could only help him cut through it if the officers in the Eagles' command center could see he was the image of his brother.

Being a twin should have some use...

"Atlantian ship *Zephyr*, this is Captain Rolf Anders, the current duty officer. I am sorry, but General Cain is indisposed for the immediate future. We are currently on high security protocols, which disallows the approach of any non-Eagle vessels. As such, we cannot authorize your approach. If you wish to leave a message for your brother before departing, I will be sure it is delivered to him."

"To hell with that, I need to speak with my brother now!" Elias' voice was a primal roar. He hadn't come all this way to see Darius only to be sent away by one of his guard dogs.

"Again, Captain Cain, I'm afraid there is nothing I can do for you at present. Our alert status precludes allowing your vessel to approach."

"Then bring my brother to the com unit. I need to speak

with him." Elias tried to keep his expression neutral, but inside he was vacillating between anger and concern.

"I am sorry, Captain…General Cain is not available at this time. If you do not wish to leave a message, I must insist that you depart." Anders' voice was businesslike, but Elias thought he detected a hint of uncertainty.

What the hell is going on? Why won't Darius come to the com?

He stood silently for a few seconds, focusing intently at the face on the screen.

Damn Darius and his people. It's almost impossible to read them…

"Captain Anders, with all due respect, I have come a very long way to see my brother, and I am not about to turn back now."

Anders' expression was unwavering…almost. Again, Elias had a vague feeling something was wrong. "Captain Cain, I am very sorry, but I cannot allow your vessel to proceed."

"Then shoot us down, Captain. Kill your general's brother. Because we are not leaving until I see Darius." He turned toward Wheaton. He'd just laid down a heavy challenge for her vessel. It wasn't his decision for *Zephyr* to proceed…and risk the wrath of the Black Eagles.

She paused for a second, and then she simply nodded. Elias felt a surge of strength, and he stared back at the display, waiting for Anders' reaction.

"Captain Cain, I reiterate…you are not to approach the Nest. If you do so, your vessel will be engaged and disabled. I cannot account for your safety in such a circumstance, nor that of anyone else on board. I urge you to turn around now while you still can."

"Well that's not going to happen, Captain," Elias said, his voice like solid steel despite the churning in his stomach. "My brother and I have not always gotten along, but I do not believe he would fire on me. And I don't think he would look kindly on one of his minions killing me…and the sixty other people on this ship."

"Captain Cain...please understand. I do not wish to attack your vessel..."

"Then don't," Elias snapped back, running his hand under his neck to signal the com officer to cut the line. He turned toward Wheaton, letting his poker face slip a bit.

"He's your brother, Elias," Wheaton said softly. "He won't let his people fire on us."

Elias managed a weak smile and a quick nod, but he didn't answer.

I wish I was as sure of that as you...

*   *   *   *   *

"I am sorry, Captain Cain, but this was the only way I could allow your people to approach the Nest." The officer stood outside the hatch of the shuttle, clad in a perfectly-pressed dress uniform. "Allow me to introduce myself. I am Major John Cranston." He paused. "The acting commander of the Nest at the present time."

Elias stepped slowly through the narrow opening. The landing bay was massive, like nothing he had ever seen. He knew all about the success and power of Darius and the Eagles, but it was still something that was hard to appreciate until you actually saw it. There were at least a dozen shuttles lined up, most of them copies of the one that had just fetched him, but a few of them larger, clearly designed to haul significant cargoes. *Or for some military purpose...*

His eyes fixed on the officer waiting for him, but he caught a glimpse of the squad of troops standing behind, fully armed. He suspected there were others too, ones he couldn't see. *Probably a sniper or two. Am I in someone's sights now? Almost certainly. The Eagles don't fool around with their security. But then they can't, can they?*

"I understand, Major." Elias wasn't sure what to do...salute? Bow? Finally, he just extended a hand. "It's a pleasure to be here."

Cranston took his hand firmly. "I'm afraid I must insist on some business before me move on to any further niceties…or the reason for your visit." He turned and gestured to a woman standing behind him. "This is Doctor Hind. I'm afraid I must insist on a positive ID before I can allow you outside of this landing bay." A short pause. "Fortunately, in your case that will be a simple process. A small DNA sample is all we need to instantly match against General Cain's. If you are indeed his twin brother, we will have a result almost at once."

Elias nodded. "Certainly, Major."

"If you will just open your mouth, Doctor Hind can collect a saliva sample."

Elias nodded again, this time toward Hind. "Whenever you are ready, Doctor."

Hind stepped forward, swiping a small swab just inside Elias' mouth. She took a few steps back and inserted the sample into a small reader. The bay was virtually silent for five or ten seconds until Hind looked up and said, "It checks. He is an identical genetic match to General Cain."

Cranston nodded. "Thank you, Doctor. Dismissed." His expression was slightly more relaxed, though Elias noted he did not dismiss the armed detachment. "Shall we go to a conference room and discuss whatever matter brought you to the Nest unannounced?" His tone was congenial, though there was a small hitch when he noted that Elias' arrival had been unexpected. "Where are my manners?" Cranston added a second later, still struggling to hide the uneasiness in his voice. "Are you hungry or thirsty? Can I offer you anything before we begin?"

I can see the Eagles don't like surprises. Of course not. Darius always liked to know exactly what was going on. And Elias knew how little his brother truly believed in. It was just like Darius to assume any surprise was a bad one.

"No thank you, Major. To be honest, I'd very much like to see my brother as soon as possible." He paused, wondering why Darius hadn't come to the bay to meet him, why Cranston had introduced himself as acting commander of the Nest. The Cain twins didn't get along very well, but Elias had never known his twin to avoid a conflict, to be hesitant to go toe to toe with him. And whatever else Darius Cain was, he certainly wasn't the officious type, prone to ceremony and layers of aides between him and a guest.

"Captain Cain...I'm afraid your brother is not available at this time."

Elias stared back at the Eagle officer. "They told me that already, Major Cranston. What exactly does that mean? Because though we have fought tooth and nail on many occasions, I know damned well my brother would have come to this bay to meet me...if only to pick a fight with me. So, please tell me what is going on if you..." Elias paused. "Is he injured? Is he..."

"General Cain is not hurt, Captain. Nor is he ill."

Elias felt a wave of relief. He'd begun to seriously worry something had happened to Darius. "Then why can't I see him?"

Cranston made a face, as if he had finally decided to divulge something he'd have preferred to keep secret. "Because your brother is not here, Captain Cain." A pause. "He is not on the Nest."

*   *   *   *   *

Elias sat at the conference table, a stunned look on his face. Major Cranston had tried to make him comfortable. There was a glass of water in front of him, almost full, with barely a centimeter missing. The plate of food to his side was completely untouched.

"My father?" he said simply. "Alive?"

"Perhaps, Captain Cain." The hard edge was gone from Cranston's voice. Whatever lingering doubts he'd had about Elias Cain had been dispelled. "But I must caution you that there are many possibilities. Even if the ring is genuine, your father may still be..."

"Dead." Elias' voice was soft, distracted. "Yes, of course he may be dead. Indeed, he has been dead for seventeen years as far as I am concerned. The change is that he may be alive."

He tried to imagine Darius' reaction when he got the news. He could almost see his brother ordering his soldiers to prepare to invade Eldaron. Nothing could have stopped him, not the danger, not even the likelihood that it was a trick, that their father was indeed dead as they had believed for so long. Darius would rescue Erik Cain...or he would avenge him. Elias shuddered to think of what his brother would do if the Eldari had killed their father. He felt a kneejerk urge to condemn that kind of bloodshed, but there was no emotion behind it. If the Eldari had truly held their father prisoner for so long, if they had killed him...Elias found himself wishing his brother's worst upon them.

"When did Darius leave?" Elias' thoughts were wandering, disorganized. His mother had been here...indeed, she had been the one who discovered the ring. *She went right to Darius*, he thought, feeling a momentary resentment that his mother had chosen his brother first.

No, that's not fair. Darius has the power to do something...I don't. He understood that...he even agreed with the logic. But it still stung.

Cranston hesitated. "Not long ago..."

"I'm not trying to pump you for classified details, Major. I just want to know where things stand."

"The expeditionary force left four days ago, Captain Cain. Your mother went with them." Cranston sounded tense, even giving such general information.

Whatever else, Darius has his people disciplined. And they're all as suspicious as he is.

A cold feeling ran through him. "Wait...that ring couldn't have just found its way to my mother after so long. This *has* to be a trap."

"Yes," Cranston said. "I am inclined to agree with you, Captain."

"If Darius and the Eagles attack...that is just what whoever sent the ring wants. They could be walking into an ambush."

"Yes, Captain. Indeed, that is almost certainly the case. But General Cain is not so easy to defeat, nor are the Black Eagles." Cranston was trying to sound confident, and some if it seemed genuine. But Elias could hear worry there too.

Elias' mind went to Eris, to the mysterious organization behind that base, and the slaving ring it supported on Earth. Then he thought about *Black Viper* and the attack on *Carlyle*, the level of intelligence gathering it took to learn the schedule and course of the secret shipment of STUs. It couldn't all be a coincidence. The slavers, the pirates…and now Eldaron.

It can't be chance. It all has to be related.

"I know my brother is very skilled, Major…and the Eagles' reputation precedes them wherever they go. But to walk straight into a trap…"

"There was no choice, Captain. If there is any chance your father is still alive, the general had to go. And the men and women had to go with him. He did not order anyone to undertake this mission. He asked for volunteers."

"How many volunteered?" Elias asked, wondering how large a force his brother had with him.

"They all volunteered, Captain. The entire mobile force is en route to Eldaron. And whatever is waiting there, whoever thinks they are clever enough to trap the Black Eagles, they will have a rude awakening." Cranston's tone broadcast confidence, but Elias could still hear the slight doubt still lingering behind his words. And something else? Disappointment perhaps…at being left behind?

"You wanted to go too." Elias hadn't intended to verbalize the thought, but it just popped out.

"Of course, Captain. This will be the Eagles' greatest test." Cranston's guard dropped a bit, and the level of his concern became clearer. "Our thoughts are with those who travel now to the great battle, yet we all must fight our own demons. We have our duty, for the Nest must be manned and defended, but we long in times like these to seal our armor and march into the landers alongside our comrades…to hit the dirt of the target

world. Every Eagle longs to follow General Cain, to save his…
your…great father. Or to avenge him."

There was dreamy a quality to Cranston's voice, one of
remembrance. Elias was sure in that moment that John Cranston had been one of Darius' field officers, probably a highly
valued one. He understood. Darius had assigned this man to
protect his stronghold when the field army was deployed. It was
an honor, a sign of trust…yet it carried with it a cost, at least for
a veteran like Cranston.

Elias saw much of his father in the Eagle major, and he
knew, for all Erik Cain's longing to live in peace, he had never
been able to stay back from the front lines when war called.

"You are here because my brother trusted you, Major."

Cranston smiled, and he looked at Elias as if he had just
seen something unexpected in his commander's sibling. "Yes,
Captain. He has good reason to. I saved his life. Twice." He
paused, then he rapped his hand against his thigh. It made an
odd sound, like he was slapping metal. "The second time cost
me this. Turns out I've got a rare genetic disorder. Regeneration won't take." He sighed softly. "Nothing to do with the
half-soldier except put him in command of the base…"

Elias wanted to say something, but he had no idea how to
respond. Finally, he just said, "Major, I know my brother well,
and the one thing I'm sure of is that if he assigned you here
it's because this is where he needs you. Where the Eagles need
you."

Elias was surprised how the veteran officer had opened up
to him. It seemed wildly out of character. *Is it because I look
just like Darius? But he knows who I am…and my brother and
I are nothing alike. Nothing.*

But he began to wonder. He'd always taken the fact that he
and Darius were very different as a given, but now he began
to think about it. He liked Cranston, and he found that he
respected the man. Everyone he'd met in the Nest had made a
good impression on him, and he found himself regretting all the
times he'd declared them criminals and mercenary killers.

He felt unsettled. He'd grown comfortable with his beliefs,

with his baseless prejudices, but the past weeks had shattered his view of things. He'd found the government he'd believed in to be riddled with corruption and dishonesty...and those he'd considered villains to defy that simplistic characterization. He felt a longing to see his brother again, for the two to talk...truly talk.

And my father...is it really possible...

He felt his stomach twist into a knot. But if there truly is one massive enemy behind all of this...they surely know how strong Darius' Eagles are. Any trap they set would be powerful enough to destroy them, almost certainly.

Of course! That's the whole point of this! They want to destroy the Eagles, get them out of the way.

"I have to go, Major. Immediately."

"I'm sorry, Captain, but I've given you highly classified information. I'm afraid I can't allow you or your ship to depart until the general returns from Eldaron."

"*If* he returns, Major! You *must* let me go. I can help him."

"Captain, I understand how difficult it is to wait while..."

"Please, Major...I have to fight this battle with my brother." He hesitated. "It is my struggle too." Another pause. "You have my word, Major. I will do nothing to endanger my brother...or the other Eagles."

Cranston stared back, his hard impassive face slowly softening. "I would be violating the general's orders, Captain."

"Do you really think Darius would want you to keep me here? I understand orders, but my brother could not have anticipated that I would come to the Nest while he was gone." He stared at Cranston, locked eyes with the officer. "Don't be a martinet, Major. Let me go help my brother..."

Cranston sat silently for a moment. Finally, he said softly, "You must promise not to speak of anything you have heard here. Not the slightest detail. To anyone."

Elias nodded. "You have my word, Major." He extended his hand, feeling a deep pang of guilt as the Black Eagle grasped it tightly. Elias Cain considered himself a man of integrity, one whose word meant something. He had never before broken it, at least not about anything as important as this. But he knew even as he shook Cranston's hand, he would not be true to his promise.

He would tell someone what was going on, though he would break his word not for betrayal, but to help Darius and the Eagles the only way he could devise. Because, he had a feeling that even the Black Eagles were in too deep this time.

*   *   *   *   *

"I need your help again, Jamie." Wheaton had been waiting for him when he docked. He caught the smile on her face when she first saw him. She had heard all the legends about the Black Eagles too, and as soon as he saw her face, Elias knew she'd been worried since he'd left *Zephyr*.

"Of course, Elias. We've come this far, haven't we? What do you need?"

His eyes darted toward the crewman standing alongside the docking controls...then back to Wheaton. She understood immediately. He wanted privacy.

"Let's go to my office," she said, keeping her voice as businesslike as possible.

Elias nodded, and he followed her through the hatch and down the corridor. They were both silent until they stepped into the tiny room she used as a workspace, and the hatch closed behind them.

"So," she said, "what do you need me to do?"

"I need to go somewhere. As quickly as possible. And I mean brutal g forces, strain the engines to the breaking point fast."

She stared back, a troubled expression on her face. "We came all this way to have your brother interrogate the prisoner...and now we're not even taking him to the Nest? We're just leaving...and going somewhere else?" She paused. "Elias, you know I support you...but don't you think we are in enough trouble already? We need to go back to Atlantia."

"My brother is en route to Eldaron, Jamie." Elias blurt out the words. "He has his entire attack force with him. That is why we are leaving."

"Eldaron? What is on Eldaron?" She sounded confused. The Tyrant of that world had a fearsome reputation, but for all its ruler's reputed cruelty, Eldaron had never been aggressive with the worlds around it.

"Perhaps nothing," he said softly, a touch of sadness clinging to his voice. "Perhaps my father."

"Your father is dead," she said, her voice tentative, sympathetic.

"Perhaps not. Darius had evidence that he might still be alive. A prisoner on Eldaron."

She stared back with a look of astonishment on her face. "My God..."

Elias just nodded and looked back at her.

"Okay, Elias. We will go to Eldaron."

"No."

"No?" she said, a confused look on her face.

"Not Eldaron, not yet."

"Then where do you want to go?"

"Armstrong." His gaze hardened, his plan taking shape in his head. "I want to go to Armstrong. As quickly as we can get there."

Chapter 22

Central Command
The Citadel
Planet Eldaron, Denebola IV
Earthdate: 2319 AD (34 Years After the Fall)

"What in the nine rings of hell is going on?" The Tyrant's voice echoed across the high-ceilinged room, the caustic edge of it giving no doubt to anyone present he was not in a patient mood. Eldaron's absolute ruler was standing in the lift, looking out over the command center with a crooked scowl on his face.

The officers present had almost agreed not to wake the Tyrant, at least not until they had a good idea what was going on. The failure had begun with a single satellite, and it had at first appeared to be a minor malfunction, nothing important enough to disturb the sovereign...and risk the often unpredictable results of his temper. But then it spread through the system, one unit at a time, until the planetwide com networks were completely down. The ground backup units were still functioning, providing emergency transmissions to the military and other vital services. But the entertainment networks, the news broadcasts, and almost all civilian communications were out... as well as orbital scanning capabilities.

"We don't know, sir." The colonel on duty was trying to keep his voice steady, but a healthy dose of fear was apparent despite his best efforts. "At first we thought it was a mechanical

failure on one satellite, but now it has spread to all the others...
and it is moving to the ground stations as well. It is beginning
to look more like some kind of cyber-attack now. But we can't
trace it at all. The systems appear to be fine, diagnostics check
out 100 percent. But nothing is functioning."

"I would say that means they are not *fine*...wouldn't you,
Colonel?" The Tyrant walked into the center of the control
room, his heavy boots slapping down hard on the polished
stone floor. His rage hung over everyone, and the officers and
other personnel hunched tensely over their workstations, trying
to avoid his attention.

"No, sir." The colonel struggled to keep his voice firm.

The Tyrant turned and looked out past the colonel across the
rest of the room. "Listen to me, all of you...I want answers,
and I want them now! How could our entire communications
system just collapse..."

His voice trailed off, and he snapped his head back to the
colonel. "Were there any scanner contacts before this happened?" The Tyrant felt his stomach clench. *Could it be...?*

"No, sir. None. I checked it twice."

"Then check it again!" The Tyrant shook his head. He wondered if the Eagles could have arrived already. It was far ahead
of even his most aggressive projections. He knew when Sarah
Cain left Armstrong, and he could guess how long it had taken
her to get to the Nest. No matter how he looked at it, that didn't
leave enough time for planning and preparation...not for a full
scale planetary invasion. One Darius Cain almost certainly suspected was a trap.

Or was it enough time? Are they that good...that much better than everyone else?

The thought that Cain might have mounted his invasion
so quickly was terrifying. He didn't believe it, not really. The
Eagles were the best, he knew that much. But still, they couldn't
possibly live up to all the legends about them.

Could they?

"I want functioning orbital scans immediately! I don't care
what you have to do. Launch another satellite if you have to.

But we can't be naked up there, with no idea of what is happening. And I want all military units placed on full alert. Now!" The Tyrant's voice was cracking, shaky. The officers in the control center took it as anger, rage...the unspoken threat of what he would do if they failed to do what he commanded.

But it wasn't rage, at least not entirely. It was fear.

*   *   *   *   *

"The advance team reports mission complete, sir. The virus has been introduced, and it appears to have spread throughout the Eldari communications networks. Preliminary scans suggest all but ground-based backup com is down."

Darius Cain sat at his station on *Eagle One's* bridge. He had a smile of sorts on his face, but it wasn't one that suggested happiness. It was a symbol, rather, of satisfaction at watching a plan begin to unfold, one that would bring unimaginable devastation to his enemy. Darius Cain was already considered a brilliant strategist, but he had resolved the invasion of Eldaron would be his masterpiece...a battle he intended to see executed with a level of precision even his Black Eagles had never imagined possible. He was walking knowingly into a trap. But he planned to turn the tables...and spring his own trap on his enemy.

The ground stations won't do them any good. Tom Sparks created this virus, and it's beyond anything they have. It will compromise all of their communications, not just the satellites. Just a few more minutes...

"Order the team back, Captain. And give Lieutenant Bellows my personal compliments on a job well done." Darius didn't move his eyes from the screen as he belted out the order. He'd been a little nervous. The stealth shuttle was new, the latest thing out of Sparks' laboratory. It hadn't been tried out, not really. Darius didn't like testing out new equipment in an actual combat situation, but needn't have worried. Everything had gone magnificently. From what he could tell, the Eldari hadn't the slightest idea a hostile ship had even moved into orbit, much less docked with one of their satellites and injected a virus into their network.

"Yes, sir," came the reply, as sharp as a razor. The Black Eagle's fleet didn't see as much action as the ground forces, but the ship crews were every bit as elite as the line regiments. Many of the captains and senior officers had even seen service with Augustus Garret, and they had brought with them the skill and excellence they'd acquired fighting under history's most brilliant naval commander.

It had been thirty-five years since Gavin Stark had used his secret stealth ships to devastating effect in the closing stages of the Shadow War. One of the undetectable vessels had managed to sneak into Mars orbit and launch the attack that devastated that world's surface cities—and others had inflicted almost as much damage elsewhere. But the scientific marvels had all been destroyed during the war, and the secrets of their construction lost. For the next three decades, scientists and researchers had struggled to replicate the technical marvels, but all had failed. Until the Eagles' chief engineer, the former Marine research chief who had developed half the technology used to fight the First Imperium, had finally made a breakthrough. Tom Sparks' new technology couldn't hide large ships or vessels operating above a maximum power level. But the Eagles had just proven conclusively that it worked perfectly on a small shuttle.

"Prepare to launch assault squadrons." Darius took a deep breath. The Eldari were now blind, at least in space. The rest of the Eagle fleet could close without detection. And when the fighters went in, they would deal another blow to an enemy that didn't yet know it was under attack.

"All squadrons report ready to launch on your command, General."

Fighters had been a crucial component of the fleets that had fought against the First Imperium and the Shadow Legions. But they had mostly passed out of use by the small navies the former colony worlds had managed to maintain. The small attack ships remained highly effective in combat, but few vessels were large enough to support squadrons…and the immense maintenance contingents it took to keep them flying. Even Cain's Eagle vessels only carried six fighters each, a fraction of the massive attack wings that had gone to battle with Augustus Garret. But the Eagles' craft were highly advanced…and usually the only ones in a fight. And that made them doubly useful.

"*Eagle One* and *Eagle Two*…launch fighters. All other squadrons remain on standby."

"*Eagle One* and *Eagle Two*, launch," the captain repeated. A few seconds later, Cain felt the shaking, as *Eagle One* launched her half dozen birds.

He still stared at his screen, watching as the small symbols representing the fighter squadrons appeared next to the larger icons labelled *Eagle One* and *Eagle Two*. Major Darryk was at the head of the twelve small ships. The Eagle's flight commander was one of the best at what he did. *The* best, Darius Cain believed. And he was leading this small strike.

The Eagles' fighters weren't going after enemy squadrons, nor even warships. Eldaron, by all accounts, had a strong army, but no navy to speak of. The Eagle fleet would establish total local space superiority the instant it reached the planet. No, the fighters were on a very special mission, one that Cain was sure would surprise his enemy…and clear the way for his Black Eagles to fight their way to victory…regardless of whatever trap the Eldari had laid for them.

He stared straight ahead, unmoving. He was here for personal reasons, but he'd pushed that aside now, clamped down on all indiscipline. He was cold, his mind clear, focused. There was no emotion…no fear, no hesitation, no pity for those he was about to attack.

Darius Cain was a man, one like any other in many ways. He wasn't as immune to abuse as he liked to believe, the invective he knew was hurled at his name in the shadows of a hundred worlds. He felt hurt…and love and guilt and regret, the way any man did. His thoughts often wandered during the nights, images of the people of Occupied Space floating in his head, running, trying to flee from him. He wondered how many regarded him only with hatred…and fear. But those thoughts were not in his mind, nor gauzy images of a child and his father, years before on the snow white Atlantian beaches. Not now. He had cast aside his humanity…his iron discipline slamming down over every thought, every impulse. He was a shadowy revenant, a feral beast with one thought in his mind.

The hunt has begun…

*   *   *   *   *

"Eagle strike force, this is Eagle Leader. Approaching final break point. All birds, confirm navcom settings." Kevin Darryk had been a Black Eagle for eight years…and the first one to pilot a fighter. He'd been a rookie Eagle—but a veteran fighter jock—when Darius Cain's mercenary company had launched *Eagle One*. And when that great ship began its first voyage, it carried six fighter-bombers in its assault bay. Darryk had been in the lead bird the first time that squadron launched, and he had remained the Eagles' strike wing commander ever since… even as *Eagle Two* and its brethren expanded the fleet and the fighter group.

He'd struggled at times to attract experienced pilots. Few of the planetary navies maintained fighter corps anymore, and the cadres from his own day had been withered by the losses in the Shadow War and the Second Incursion. Casualties in all services had been bad in those conflicts, but the fighter wings had always taken the heaviest losses. There was no argument…any fleet commander would risk a bunch of four or five man fighters to preserve a battleline of dreadnoughts with a thousand crew on each. He couldn't argue with the math, but he'd had to work his ass off to build up the Eagle's fighter group…especially to the quality demanded of everyone who put on the black uniform.

He listened as each of the eleven other birds in the strike force acknowledged. The Eagles had sixty fighters-bombers in total, but only two squadrons had launched on this mission.

Eldaron was not a naval power, and the few vessels it possessed would be no threat to the Eagle fleet, even if any of them returned from their pickets at the system's warp gates. There had been a patrol at the Eagles' point of entry, two frigates, old rustbuckets that had no place trying to engage anything like the Eagle vessels. Cain's fleet had burst into the system, jamming all communications within 100,000 kilometers. Less than two minutes later, both of the Eldari frigates were balls of glowing plasma...and not a warning message had gotten through.

"Three, two, one...break." Darryk gripped the throttle of his fighter, angling it hard and feeling the pressure of six gees slam into him as his ship's engines fired, changing his vector as he entered orbit. The twelve birds of his command had executed similar maneuvers, and each of them blasted off in a different direction. They had their targets, and they all knew what to do. Darryk felt the tension he always did during an op, but his confidence was stronger. He'd trained these men and women, and he didn't doubt they would complete the mission with the pinpoint precision it required.

"*Eagle One* C, here. Entering upper atmosphere now."

"*Eagle One* D...entering atmosphere."

They all checked in, one at a time, until finally, Darryk tapped the throttle and guided his ship downward. "Eagle Leader... entering atmosphere," he said.

That's all twelve. Time to do this...

His ship shook hard as it skimmed the thickening air. Darryk had piloted plenty of fighters in space, but very few in an atmosphere, where gravity and the thickness of the air presented the pilot with an entirely different set of issues. Few ships designed for use in space were streamlined and structurally-reinforced for deployment in an atmosphere. But Darius Cain had demanded his strike force be capable of both space and planetary operation, and Tom Sparks had made it happen. One of Darryk's first lessons as a Black Eagle had been that Darius Cain gets what he wants...so the grizzled old pilot brushed off his rusty atmospheric doctrines and ran the Black Eagles' crew through a basic training course.

"Eagle strike force…arm your payloads." He turned slightly and looked back toward his gunner. "Arm the bombs, Stef."

"Arming now, sir." Stef Kross was young, much too young to have served during the Second Incursion, the last time large fighter formations had gone into battle. But she'd been so persistent, Darryk had finally given her a chance…and she'd proven to be a natural, a gunner who could beat the AI's targeting nineteen times out of twenty. He'd been so impressed, he'd assigned her to his own fighter. And he had never regretted that decision.

Darryk just nodded, and he looked back to his screen.

Two minutes, twenty seconds, he thought, staring at the plot.

He tapped the throttle, making a minor adjustment. He planned to put the two nuclear warheads exactly on target.

The ship shook again, harder this time. The atmosphere was getting thicker, and Darryk was bringing his bird in on a steep trajectory. He wanted to complete this mission and get the hell out…as quickly as possible. If that meant a rough ride, so be it. He knew the Eldari communications and scanning networks were supposed to be down, but he didn't plan to take any more chances than absolutely necessary. The enemy might not have fighters, but his ships were going to pass barely two klicks from the ground…and the Eldari damned sure had surface to air capability that could blow his squadrons from the sky.

General Cain wouldn't have given the authorization if the enemy networks were still active…

He believed in Darius Cain, and he knew the veteran mercenary cared deeply for his soldiers. But he also knew this mission was different. The normal rules didn't apply. And if those ground batteries still had tracking capability…

One minute…

He looked down at his screen. The course was perfect.

"Alright, Stef…coming up on first target location."

"I've got it, sir." He could see her in his peripheral vision, working the controls, adding her gunner's intuition to the AI's plot.

"Thirty seconds…the ship is yours, Stef."

He leaned back in his chair, looking out the cockpit of the

fighter. It was night over this side of Eldaron, but he could see the twinkling lights of a city below. His eyes panned to the scanning screen. Still nothing. No incoming attacks.

He couldn't help but smile. He didn't know how Darius Cain had managed it, but he knew the Eldari com systems were a mess. If they weren't, he'd have half a dozen rockets on their way up to blast his fighter to atoms.

He felt the ship pitch slightly as Kross applied a tap of thrust to position for the drop. Another few seconds passed, and then he felt it. The sudden lurch as the five megaton warhead blasted out of the fighter's bay and into the Eldari atmosphere.

He leaned forward and hit the throttle, firing the engines again at six gees. That bomb had a twenty second detonation timer...and Darryk wanted to be as far away as possible before it blew.

A blinding flash turned night briefly to day...and a few seconds later, the fighter shook wildly. His hands were on the throttle, correcting the ship's course to account for the shockwave that had just hit it.

"Alright," he said as he brought the gyrating fighter back under control. "Three minutes to second target...and then we can get the hell out of here.

Well, if the Eldari didn't know we were here before...they damned sure do now.

*   *   *   *   *

"It was a nuclear detonation, sir. An airburst. We've got runners coming in, reporting on several similar explosions." The colonel was tapping at the side of his headset. "Still no communications...even the land lines are out now."

The Tyrant's was in his office, just off the main floor. The palatial room had a movable wall that closed it off from the command center, but it was fully retracted now. The Tyrant sat at his desk, watching his officers trying to manage the crisis...

without scanners or communications. It was the Eagles, it had to be. His trap was ready...his well-laid trap. But now it was *his* people panicking, running around like ants after somebody kicked the anthill.

"Are they missing their targets?" The Tyrant stared at the colonel, his eyes burning into his subordinate like two lasers. "They seem to be random airbursts...mostly over rural areas."

"No," came a voice from outside the office. "They are not missing. They are hitting exactly where they intended." The Tyrant heard footsteps, heavy combat boots rapping on the polished floors of the command center, and then General Omar Calman walked into the room. Calman was the Tyrant's senior general, and the overall commander of his forces. He was also one of the few Eldari who could stand up to the planet's ruler and not languish in fear at the Tyrant's fluttering eyelash.

"General, it is about time. I called for you when this all began." There was an edge to the Tyrant's voice, but it wasn't as hard as usual. Eldaron's dictator had been nervous about facing the Black Eagles, even with a ten to one advantage in numbers...but now he was downright terrified. He knew Calman was a skilled general, and he needed his commander in place now, directing the defense of the planet, not worrying about covering his ass.

"I never got any message. The com lines are down everywhere. I can't even get a report from units in the field."

The Tyrant turned and looked around the command center with a disgusted look on his face. "I want communications restored, and I mean fucking now!" His voice was coarse, his fists clenched at his side. The men and woman all around him stared back in abject terror. But not one of them offered a suggestion on how to proceed.

It was the inevitable byproduct of totalitarian rule. The room was filled with friends and relatives of highly-placed officials who had lobbied for prestigious posts for their sons and daughters and other dependents. Skill had been far from the first prerequisite for an appointment to the Citadel's command staff, and now it was showing. These people had prospered by exercising caution, and by pandering to the egos of their superiors and their ruler...not by making any daring suggestions.

"We're not likely to get any com back in the near future... even if by some miracle we figure out how the networks were corrupted." Calman's voice was cold, hard. He was as much a participant as any in Eldaron's corrupt hierarchy, with two sons and a daughter comfortably placed in upwardly mobile positions. But the old general himself was raw and gritty...and far from devoid of military skill. It was clear he knew what was going on, even if no one else in the command center did. "Those airbursts aren't intended to destroy cities...or even military bases. They're laying down EMP...and a lot of the supposedly hardened equipment we've got is turning out not to be. My information is spotty, but we've got whole units with nothing more than rifles still functioning. In some cases, not even those."

"How is that possible?" The Tyrant's anger momentarily overcame his fear, and he glared at the general.

"Don't ask me, Excellency. I didn't handle requisitions. Perhaps you should start by asking why your minister of production has a residence that rivals your palace." It was a bold thing to say to the Tyrant, especially when he was already angry and scared. But it was clear Omar Calman didn't give a shit.

The Tyrant felt a flush of fresh anger, but he held it in check. Not many people spoke to him the way Calman had just done, but there wasn't time for that now. The Black Eagles were coming...he knew it now, almost certainly. And that meant he needed his general. And Calman was right. He realized suddenly how much he'd allowed himself to be manipulated by those who used flattery to gain his favor.

It's the power...it's like a drug. And these parasites exploit that. But now I need to be strong. I need to focus on the real fighters. It is time to destroy the Black Eagles. Stay focused. Win this battle. And then you will rule over a hundred worlds...

"Very well, General," he said, gaining control over his emotions. "What do you propose we do?"

"First we need to get some runners in here. We need to communicate with the capital area forces at least. The other cities are as good as lost."

"I will not give up on..."

"Your Excellency," Calman said, making sure his voice was at least moderately polite as he interrupted his sovereign, "If there's an attack coming..." – and his tone left no doubt he expected an attack – "...it will be decided here. They've got to take the capital to control the planet, and they know it. The main fight will be within twenty kilometers of the Citadel. And we can't communicate with the other cities anyway. All our focus must be here."

The Tyrant was silent for a moment, staring back at his general. People did not speak to him the way Calman had. And they certainly didn't interrupt him. But fear was firmly in control. He turned toward the colonel. "You heard the general. Go and get him fifty runners. No, a hundred. Anybody young and in good shape."

The colonel snapped off a nervous salute. "Yes, sir." He turned. "Captain, go and..."

"I said *you*, Colonel. Now go before I get truly angry." He could tell the colonel thought the task was beneath him, but he realized the sooner they all understood there was no time for that nonsense the better. He'd pampered his senior officers, allowed them to become pompous, ruling over those they commanded with the same prerogatives he invoked in dealing with them. But *they* were not the Tyrant...only he was. Now they had to be soldiers. They had to defend their world against the most terrifying enemy any of them had ever faced.

He turned back around as the colonel raced toward the hatch. "What else, General?"

"We need to contact the Omega units." The secret regiments the Triumvirate had dispatched to Eldaron were hidden in underground bunkers, ready to move out and surprise any Eagle invasion force as soon as it landed. But the com lines were down, just like all the communications on Eldaron.

"Yes," the Tyrant said, struggling to hide his fear. "We must activate the Omega units. Do it at once."

The general nodded. Then he turned back toward one of

his aides. "Go, Captain. I want you to make your way to the main Omega HQ immediately...then come back here and confirm their alert status."

The captain snapped off a salute—and a second one to the Tyrant standing next to the general—and he raced off to carry out the order.

"We must not panic," Calman said quietly. "We must keep the Omega forces hidden until the enemy has landed and engaged."

"Perhaps we should release them immediately." The Tyrant was being driven almost entirely by fear, and it was obvious in his voice.

"No...I mean, I recommend against that, sir. Tactical surprise was always a key part of the plan. We should not deviate from that now. We must lure the Eagles down."

"Very well, General," the Tyrant said, his voice soft, weak. "We will wait."

"And then when the enemy has landed, we will release the Omega units from the bunkers...and we will surround and destroy the invaders." Calman's tone was powerful, confident... mostly, at least. But there was something else there too, well-hidden but still detectable. Fear.

Any man would have felt fear. The Black Eagles were coming.

Chapter 23

Atlantian Capitol
Planet Atlantia, Epsilon Indi II
Earthdate: 2319 AD (34 Years After the Fall)

"The funds have arrived, Mr. President...and they have been distributed as you instructed." Asha Mazeri sat across the desk from Armando DeSilva. Her tone was pleasant, respectful, but DeSilva could see there was tension beneath her demeanor.

Well, it's not every day you launch a coup...

Still, he'd never seen her so edgy before. She'd always been remarkably calm, whatever the situation.

She must be under pressure to get this done. Who does she really work for? What have I gotten myself into?

"Very well, Asha. We shall proceed as scheduled." DeSilva felt acid in his stomach. He was attempting to remain calm, at least outwardly, but in truth he was scared to death. The people of Atlantia were disinterested politically, and he had used that to great effect over the years to maintain his power. His propaganda ministry had worked tirelessly to portray his administration in the most appealing terms...and it had put just as much effort into discrediting potential adversaries.

But that success had begun to wane. The people ignored the imposition of new laws when they were first enacted, accepting at face value the claims they were necessary and beneficial. More recently, though, signs of discontent had become widespread...and DeSilva feared his next election would be his most difficult. And if he lost, everything he built would fall apart. He controlled the law enforcement agencies and the entire justice system, and he'd used it to terrorize his enemies and enhance his own power. But if he lost his grip on the instruments of government power...

No, it was unthinkable. DeSilva lived for power, for control. And if he lost, there would be no holding back the investigations. A new Atlantian administration would almost certainly uncover all his misdeeds...and he would find himself in prison instead of sitting at the president's desk in the Capitol.

"The operation will begin just before dawn." The plan was a brilliant one, and DeSilva had to admit that Asha had been mostly responsible for its development. He'd initially planned a straight out coup, but Mazeri had urged him to consider something more elegant. The Atlantians were a crusty lot, by and large, and while they often ignored politics to their detriment, they were likely to react violently to any attempt to seize absolute power. The operation needed cover, she had argued, something that would deflect the peoples' attention...and stall opposition to his power grab. If it was done right, she had said, the people will embrace it. DeSilva had been shocked when she'd first suggested the idea, but the more he considered it, the better it sounded. There would be more casualties of course, but that was of little account.

"Very well, Mr. President. I shall see to everything on my end. And this time tomorrow, you will be the absolute and unchallenged ruler of Atlantia."

DeSilva smiled. He liked how that sounded.

*   *   *   *   *

Buck Tomlinson walked slowly down the street, enjoying the cool morning. Tomlinson was an early riser...he always had been. He loved this time of day, the quiet, the chill in the air streaming in from the sea. In another hour the streets would begin to fill, the people of Eastport moving to jobs and heading toward the markets.

The town was the planet's third largest, but that meant little on a world as rural as Atlantia. There were perhaps 10,000 residents, including a fairly large community of retired Marines, attracted by the beauty of Atlantia's rocky coastline—and the fact that Erik and Sarah Cain had chosen the ocean world as their home after retirement.

Tomlinson was a veteran himself. He'd been one of Erik Cain's Marines in the Shadow Wars, though as a private he'd never met the legendary general in person, not until he'd followed him to retirement on Atlantia. In the small town culture of ocean world, Tomlinson encountered Cain many times, and the two had even played cards on several occasions. Tomlinson had gone back to war with the general during the Second Incursion—and he bitterly mourned Cain's death in that conflict.

He walked toward the small square that overlooked the harbor, taking his usual seat at the café just a few steps from the water's edge. He took a deep breath. He'd lived on Atlantia for more than thirty years now, and he still hadn't gotten over the freshness of the sea breeze. He smiled as the café's proprietor walked over.

"Buck…nice morning, isn't it? You want your usual?"

"Magnificent, my friend. A great day to be alive." He paused, looking out over the calm waters of the harbor. "Yes, Bill, the usual." He'd ordered the same breakfast every day for at least ten years…and every day, Bill Wentz still asked him if that's what he wanted.

Wentz nodded and turned to walk back inside.

"Bill, what is that?"

Wentz turned abruptly. "What is what?"

"That transport parked next to the dock. Have you ever seen it before?"

Tomlinson knew it was the kind of thing people made fun of in small towns, but the truth was he knew almost everyone in Eastport, and there was something out of place about the large black truck.

"Can't say that I have, Buck. But what's of it? Just a truck someone left there."

"At this hour?" Tomlinson stood up. "I'm just gonna have a quick look."

Wentz made a face. "Whatever you feel like, Buck. I'll get your breakfast."

Tomlinson turned and walked toward the truck. It was black, with no windows. He tested the doors, and they were locked. He knew it was probably nothing, but he had a strange feeling…a kind of foreboding. The type of thing he'd experienced on the battlefield, when a bombardment or attack was about to commence.

He had an odd thought, wondering what Erik Cain would have said. The image of his old general was still in his head when it happened. There was a flash, so quick he had no time to even acknowledge it. Then he was consumed instantly, vaporized in the nuclear fire.

*   *   *   *   *

Armed men filled the streets in front of the Capitol, just as they were doing in every other city across Atlantia. Everything seemed like a normal response to a terrorist attack, and few noticed that many of the detachments were moving into residential neighborhoods, breaking into houses and taking away their occupants.

In each place, where screaming families were shoved roughly into unmarked black transports, neighbors looked on, wondering with a chill if they'd had terrorists and radical supporters living so near. They applauded the raids, shouted their support to the law enforcement authorities they were sure were reacting to the horrifying events of that morning. Images from Eastport had dominated the news coverage. There were thousands dead in the nuclear blast, and the town itself had been wiped away. It was a horror the quiet people of Atlantia could hardly comprehend. And they cried out to find and punish those responsible.

But those arrested had nothing to do with terrorism. They were, rather, the citizens deemed most likely to resist increased government control, to question too pointedly the reaction to the Eastport attack. They protested their innocence, even as they were dragged away, but no one listened. Atlantia was in a frenzy, and accusation equaled guilt in the minds of most.

Hundreds were arrested, all across Atlantia. Some were taken to special prisons, the ones suspected of having information on other potential resistance. They were destined for very aggressive—and unpleasant—questioning. But most of those arrested were driven directly to government facilities in remote areas. They were unloaded and herded into dark basements and concrete warehouses. One by one, they were pushed down to their knees…and an officer moved behind them, firing a single shot into each of their heads. There were no trials, no formalities, no appeals. DeSilva had decided to move quickly, to sweep away all potential resistance while Atlantians were focused on the attack.

Whole families had been arrested, and they went together into those terrible execution chambers, even the children. Pleas for mercy were ignored, even for the youngest present, who swiftly followed their parents into death.

The executioners were clad in Atlantian police uniforms, but many of them spoke with strange accents…and none of the unfortunates executed that day ever knew the men who murdered them were not Atlantians at all, but operatives of Asha Mazeri's organization…and the allies of Atlantia's president.

*   *   *   *   *

"My fellow Atlantians, it is with a heavy heart that I now address you all." DeSilva wore a black suit, perfectly-pressed, and he spoke with a strong and clear voice, edged quite deliberately with a touch of both sadness and anger.

"Our world has just experienced the greatest tragedy in its

history, an atrocity of immense proportions. Over ten thousand of our neighbors and friends are dead, killed by cowards and murderers…villains who have lived among us, nurturing their hatred and their radical agendas. I can say nothing that will help the thousands of our friends and neighbors who were killed, nor can I ease the pain we all feel. Nothing can do that, and I fear we will long grieve for those lost." His voice deepened, took on an ominous tone.

"But I can assure all of you that those who have committed this terrible act will pay for it. Already, arrests have been made…and it has become clear that a terrible cancer has grown in our great society. It is difficult to imagine such evil, and worse to think of it existing all around us, but such is the case. And as your president, I swear now that I will see that everyone involved in this horror is held accountable."

DeSilva gripped the edges of the podium and sucked in a deep breath, pausing as if he was fighting back a wave of sorrow.

"Our arrests have already begun to provide us information, and I regret to tell you all that we have found evidence of other plots planned or underway. I promise you now, each and every law-abiding citizen of Atlantia, that I will not rest until we have uncovered every root and branch of this evil, and I can step up to this podium and assure you all that there is no more to fear.

"But that day is not today, and now I must take the necessary steps to ensure the safety of Atlantia and its citizens. Effective immediately, martial law is declared. All assemblies of more than three people are prohibited. Enhanced surveillance protocols will be in effect. All elections, both local and national are hereby postponed indefinitely…

*   *   *   *   *

"It is done." Asha Mazeri was alone, her room dark save for the small light on the com unit's display. "Everything has gone according to plan."

"That is good, Agent Mazeri. I am most pleased to hear this. Your involvement in the debacle with the *Carlyle* was of great concern to us. However, the successful delivery of Atlantia to our control is likely to pardon your earlier failure and restore your fortune."

"Thank you, sir. I can assure you that Atlantia is ours."

"Contact us again in three days with an update." As usual, the com went dead immediately.

Asha breathed hard. She felt a cold feeling in her stomach. She'd been terrified every moment since the botched operation involving the STUs, and every sound had filled her with the terror that her assassins had arrived. There wasn't a doubt in her mind that any failure on Atlantia would be her last. The Black Flag did not easily forgive. Its demands were great, as were its rewards. Asha felt relief, but she also worried about her control over DeSilva. She had influence, certainly, but he was a loose cannon. She had handed him enormous power, and she was concerned how he would handle it. Would he be as pliable to her suggestions now as he had been? Or would he feel he didn't need her as before?

That, she knew, would be a fatal mistake for DeSilva. The Black Flag could easily kill the president and replace him with a more pliable figure. But that would be her end as well. Indeed, DeSilva's unpredictability wasn't a real danger to Black Flag control of Atlantia. She had placed agents throughout the new government, even in the president's security detail. The Black Flag could kill DeSilva with a single command. But another failure—and the need to bring in outside assistance—would be her end. She was sure of that.

She sighed and stood up, turning to look at herself in the mirror. She hadn't seduced DeSilva yet. She'd planned to, but something had told her to keep some powder dry.

Perhaps now is the time. I must do everything I can to maintain my control.

She reached up and undid two buttons on her shirt, wiggling around a bit until she thought she looked her best. *Time to congratulate the president...*

Chapter 24

Main Assault Bay
Eagle One
Orbiting Planet Eldaron, Denebola IV
Earthdate: 2319 AD (34 Years After the Fall)

"Darius, you can't do this." Erik Teller stood amid the controlled chaos of *Eagle One's* assault bay. Around him, hundreds of Black Eagles—combat units mostly, but also technicians, launch coordinators, and a dozen other types of support personnel—bustled around, performing their duties with a level of efficiency no other combat unit could hope to match. The noise was almost deafening, but a close inspection revealed that the entire swirling mass was a perfect image of organization.

"I have to, Erik." Darius Cain stared back at his oldest friend and second-in-command. "And you know it." Cain's voice was calm, measured. But anyone who knew him understood just how stubborn he truly was. There was probably something in the galaxy more difficult than getting Darius Cain to back down once he'd made a decision, but it wasn't anything that came to mind easily.

"But once we secure the planet…"

"Erik, stop. Don't play dumb with me even if it is the only way you can make your argument. Nobody knows how smart you really are like I do. If my father is still alive—and yes, I realize that's a huge 'if'—I have to go after him immediately.

Taking the planet, defeating whatever they have waiting to trap and destroy us, will require time. And it only takes a second to put a bullet in a prisoner's head." He turned toward his armor hanging on the rack against the wall, but then he paused and looked back. "You know I have to take them by surprise, do anything I can…"

Teller's face was twisted into an uncomfortable frown. Darius was aware of his friend's concern, both on a personal level and as the Eagle's executive officer. But he also knew Teller truly understood, in a deeply personal way. Both men had lost their fathers in the war history had come to call the Second Incursion. But James Teller had been gunned down leading a desperate assault…and he'd died in front of three hundred of his own troops. There was no mystery, no nagging doubt about what had happened to him. But Erik Cain had been presumed dead in the destruction of the ship carrying him home. And now it looked like he might have survived, at least for some time after his reported death.

Finally, Teller just nodded. "I understand. But what about the Eagles? The assault? We need you."

"The assault is planned out to the last decimal…and you can lead the main effort as well as I can." He hesitated, then before Teller could object he added, "And don't give me any nonsense that isn't the case. Because we both know it is."

Teller didn't answer for a few seconds. Finally, he said, "I'm just nervous, Darius. We both know this is a trap. And there has to be some relationship with what happened on Lysandria and Eris. Even the disappearance of the lost platoon on Karelia." He paused. "We shouldn't underestimate whoever this is we're facing."

Darius stared hard into his friend's eyes. "I don't underestimate them, Erik. This will probably be the hardest battle we have fought…which is why I have obsessed over every detail. There is nothing I wouldn't do to make us as strong as possible. But you in HQ is the same thing as me in HQ. We built the Eagles together, old friend, and there is no one in the galaxy I trust as much as I do you. I've had a million doubts about this operation, but your role in it has never been one of them."

Teller stood still for a moment, and he even managed to force a brief grin of sorts in response to Darius' praise. But his expression darkened again, and he said, "Still, you know what a crazy risk you are taking. You'll be in the middle of the enemy's stronghold while a war rages all around you."

"I won't be alone. I'll have the Teams with me."

Teller frowned. "Two hundred of you...against a planet's armies? Deep in their largest stronghold?"

"Our two hundred best, Erik. And every one of them a volunteer." Darius had asked his troops from the Special Action Teams to join him in a raid intended to find and extract his father from captivity. It was a breathtakingly dangerous plan, made worse by the almost total lack of intel on Erik Cain's location...or even any idea if he was truly still alive. Darius had felt guilty asking any of his people to join him, and he'd been stunned when every single member of the teams had not only volunteered, but had outright demanded to go...with such intensity he suspected he'd have faced the first mutiny in Eagles' history if he'd refused to take them all. Darius had been almost speechless, touched deeply by the devotion of his soldiers.

"We're not two hundred taking on all their armies...the entire Black Eagles corps is fighting here, not just a force of special operators. And when we're through, whoever is behind this *trap* won't know what hit them." Darius realized he had slipped into his rally mode, the persona he adopted in battle to inspire his troops. He was surprised, as he often was, at just how effective his words often were...even with a grizzled veteran like his second-in-command.

Teller just nodded, but Darius could see the jolt he'd given to his friend, the blast of confidence. Erik Teller was a brilliant tactician, and not a single fact about the operation had changed. But Darius could see Teller was more energized. Ready to do what had to be done.

"Darius..." The voice came from behind him, and he recognized it immediately.

"Yes, mother," he said, turning to face her. "What can I do

for you?" He figured she was there to follow up on Teller's argument, to urge him to stay in headquarters rather than drop right on top of the enemy's main fortress. But she surprised him.

"I need you to tell your chief surgeon that I'm landing with the medical services."

He paused for a moment, just staring back at her. "No," he finally said. "Absolutely not."

"Darius," she said, her voice as firm and cold as his own, "I've been patching Marines and other soldiers together for more than fifty years. I'd wager I've made more combat drops than you or any other veteran you've got, so don't tell me I can't do my job." She paused and glared at him with an intensity that revealed he hadn't gotten all of his stubbornness and will from his father. "Because going down with the med teams is my second choice, and it's taking all I have to stand back and let you go after your father without me."

Her voice cracked slightly, but she maintained her gaze. "I haven't been a combat Marine for a long time...and I know I'll just distract you. And that will only get you killed...or your father, if he is really down there. But if you think I'm going to wait up here while thousands of soldiers are fighting to free Erik, you're crazy."

He opened his mouth to argue, but he closed it again. He realized she was right. She was his mother, and beyond that he carried a lot of guilt about how things had gone after his father's disappearance. But she was a Marine, and by all accounts, the best trauma surgeon in Occupied Space. And she was a Cain.

"Very well, mother," he said. "I will advise Dr. Lagrange at once." His voice was odd, a touch of defeat in it perhaps, but also pride. Sarah Cain was ninety years old, but she was still every bit the Marine...and as much the source of his own inner strength as his father.

And he was damned glad she hadn't insisted on going in with the strike team. He had an idea what an epic argument *that* would have been.

"They knew exactly where to hit us. Our anti-missile defenses are strong, but they are clustered around the cities and military installations. With the scanning net and coms down, we had no warning at all. Not until the detonations." Colonel Matias Davidoff spoke firmly, confidently, though he still stood rigidly at attention. General Omar Calman was the supreme military commander on Eldaron, and he had a way of making everyone around him nervous. But it wasn't Calman who threatened to shake Davidoff's confidence. The veteran colonel was accustomed to reporting to the general. However the man standing behind was one he'd rarely seen in person—and had always feared.

"Our military equipment, at least, should have been shielded against EMP, Colonel, should it not?" The Tyrant spoke softly, with no hint of the rage everyone present knew he had to be feeling. "Can you explain why almost everything is dead—communications, scanners, transports, armored vehicles? Why is my army a disordered mess, crippled and panicked in the wake of a pending invasion?"

The Tyrant had managed to get control of himself since he'd left headquarters with Calman. He knew he was at least partially to blame for the blithering throng of sycophants that infested HQ, but now he found himself craving the company of capable subordinates, brave men and women ready to face whatever was coming…and he found them to be far too rare in his service.

But Davidoff was no coward, nor a brown-nosing yes man. He was nervous, that much was obvious, but the Tyrant suspected he would hear the truth from this man. And right now, the truth was what he needed.

"Excellency, our specifications for military equipment are quite clear with regard to shielding requirements…" The colonel's voice trailed off.

"Yes, Colonel, I am aware of that. So, would you please enlighten me as to why, in spite of the specifications, nearly all of my military hardware has been turned into useless junk before a single enemy soldier has set foot on Eldaron?" His voice was hardening, rising in volume. He wasn't yelling, not yet, but he was losing control over his frustration.

"Excellency, every order we have placed has corresponded with the specifications, but…"

"But?"

"That is not always what we receive." Davidoff paused, and he swallowed hard. "Indeed, it is almost never what we receive." Another nervous hesitation. "Excellency, you must be aware of the level of…corruption in some of the ministries. Procurement is perhaps the worst of all."

The Tyrant could see Davidoff struggling to stand firm, to maintain his composure as he answered directly and firmly. Eldaron's ruler did not like complaints or accusations against his cronies. Men had been killed for less, but now things had changed. The Tyrant felt an icy chill in his bones. *Darius Cain* was coming for him. The *Black Eagles* were coming. Indeed, they were already here. He had no time for profiteers and corrupt lords who worked him over with flattery while they were feathering their own nests. Not any longer. Now he needed hard men, fighters. He needed soldiers who could stand up and face an enemy like the Black Eagles.

The Tyrant stared back at Davidoff. *This is a brave man. I don't know how many there are like him in my service, but I need every one of them now.* "You will take over the field command of the forces deployed around the citadel," he said, noting the surprise in the officer's expression. "And I am giving you your star, General Davidoff, to match the level of your new responsibilities." The Tyrant turned toward Calman. "See that the newest member of our general staff gets everything he needs, General Calman."

Calman nodded, a small crack of a smile on his lips. He'd been trying to get officers like Davidoff promoted over well-connected sycophants for years. "Yes, Excellency."

"Thank you, Excellency." Davidoff managed to keep his tone calm and even, but it was clear he was almost in a state of shock. He'd half expected a firing squad when the Tyrant had approached with Calman. The debacle now unfolding around the capital wasn't his fault, but the last twenty years of Eldari history was strewn with the bodies of innocent scapegoats who had gone to the scaffold.

"I expect much from you, General," the Tyrant said coldly. "Starting now. I don't care how you do it, but I want these defenses ready when the Black Eagles land. That means scanning, communications…and certainly it means functioning weapon systems." He paused, staring at his new general with a withering gaze. "Do you understand me, General Davidoff?"

"Yes, Excellency."

The Tyrant nodded and turned around on his heels. Calman glanced over at Davidoff, and his expression virtually shouted out at his subordinate, a single desperate plea.

Find a way…

*   *   *   *   *

The landing craft bucked hard as it tore through Eldaron's thick atmosphere. Darius Cain stood in his armor, motionless, bolted to the heavy racks along the ship's interior hull. There were thirty-nine other Eagles in the assault lander…and four identical vessels coming down alongside. Two hundred men and women, the elite of the Black Eagles, were approaching the very center of the Eldari defenses.

The Eagle fleet had entered orbit and destroyed every Eldari satellite. Even if the enemy managed to get the viruses purged from their systems, their orbital capability was gone, replaced by the Eagle's own com stations. The battle was yet to truly begin, but Cain's warriors had undisputed control over planetary surveillance and communications. It was a huge advantage, and one he was sure they would need. He had force assessments for the Eldari military, but he suspected the enemy had more hidden somewhere…or they'd never have picked a fight with the Eagles. Whatever happened, his people were going to be outnumbered. Heavily.

Darius had fought many battles, and his armor felt like a second skin. He felt fear in battle, of course, and the pressure of being responsible for so many lives, though he'd learned how to manage it all, to put it aside and concentrate on the job at hand. But he was distracted this time, uncertain. He'd struggled to stay focused on the mission, to treat the operation like any other, but he'd found it to be far more difficult than he'd imagined. His father...was it really possible? Could he be alive after all these years? And if Erik Cain *was* alive, could Darius rescue him? Somehow find where he was being held and get there before the enemy killed him? Or would he arrive too late, only to find his father dead after fifteen years of captivity?

He felt something else too...a rage deep inside, an almost elemental need to seek out and destroy everyone responsible for his father's abduction. Despite the fear and the dark reputation the Black Eagles endured, Darius had always conducted his affairs with a high level of calmness and rationality. He and his soldiers had designed their campaigns to minimize destruction and collateral damage. But he couldn't feel that urge in him anymore, the impulse to control suffering. All that remained was a fiery anger, a hatred so deep he had no idea how to control it. When he'd seen the virus take effect and cripple the Eldari ground defenses, he'd felt a powerful urge, a desire to launch a massive nuclear assault, to bomb the defenseless planet into radioactive dust. The thought that his father might still be down there had stayed his hand, but he wondered now what he would have done if that had not been the case, if for example, he knew his father was already dead. Would he have destroyed a world for vengeance, unleashed death on 25 million people because of his own rage? He didn't know...and he wasn't sure he wanted to.

The lander shook again, pulling Darius from his daydream. He rolled his eyes upward, toward the combat display inside his visor. Five kilometers to landing. His AI was displaying the incoming scanner feed from the dish under the lander. His small strike force was approaching a city. It was large, with a cluster of skyscrapers in its central area. But it was dark now, and silent. The viruses and EMP had done their jobs, and not a single blast of defensive fire lit the inky night sky.

By all accounts, the Eldari capital was one of the largest metropolises in Occupied Space, the pride of the planet's Tyrant and the result of two decades of almost inexplicable economic expansion. And he was about to invade it with two hundred troops.

He looked to the side of the shimmering image projected in front of him. The longer-ranged display was bright with blue icons. Landers, over a hundred of them, Black Eagle forces coming down all around the perimeter of the still dark and silent city. Those forces would land outside the city's defensive perimeter, but Darius' small force was coming down right on top of the Citadel, the Tyrant's main fortress and command center.

It's just as likely they've got him stashed in some mountaintop retreat or a prison in the middle of nowhere.

He shook his head, at least as much as he could bolted into the lander.

No...he's no place else. If they have him, he's here. You've faced men like the Tyrant before. The paranoia that goes hand in hand with totalitarian power. If he has a prisoner like father, he'd keep him close. In the most protected area of his domain.

I hope.

"Landing in one minute." The AI's voice reverberated in his helmet.

He glanced at his indicators. Everything was green, just as it had before launch...and the two other times he'd rechecked on the way down.

"Unitwide com," he said quietly to the AI.

"Unitwide com activated," came the immediate response.

"Okay, Eagles." Darius said, struggling to put thoughts of his father out of his mind and focus on this operation as coolly as he had all his others. "We're coming down right into the middle of the shit this time, so I want you all running out of these landers, ready to fight. Stay focused, every one of you... and remember, collateral damage protocols are suspended on this op. If you think there's the slightest chance a contact is hostile…scrag it. We're outnumbered everywhere on the planet, but the 200 of us are landing in the middle of an enemy army. We've got three considerations…finding the prisoner, striking as hard as we can at the enemy's command and control capability, and staying alive. Anything else pops into your mind, slap it away and stay on focus. Now, let's get this done!"

"Landing in fifteen seconds," the AI announced just after Darius had finished.

He took a deep breath. The ships were coming in fast and steep, and that meant the landing would be a rough one. He remembered his father's descriptions of the old Gordons and Liggetts the Marines had used years ago. They weren't even ships, not really, just open frameworks with five or ten Marines bolted in. *Talk about a rough ride…*

The Eagles' landing craft were fully enclosed and solidly built, not comfortable in any sense of the word, but not quite the trip down the Gordons were either.

Darius felt his body pressed hard against the front of his armor as the lander's braking jets fired. A few seconds later the craft shook again as it touched down. The Black Eagles were on Eldaron.

"Alright, let's move," he shouted into the com as the locked bolts retracted and he hopped down from the rack. The other Eagles in the bay were doing the same thing, and a few seconds later, the ship's AI dropped the back hatch, and armored soldiers began pouring out.

Darius looked around as he stepped out onto the Eldari street. The landers had come down at the edge of a small park. Three of them had landed on a wide grassy area, now blackened from the braking jets. The other two were partially in the street. It looked like a main thoroughfare, but it was deserted now, save for a few parked vehicles. Half a dozen Eagles were already running toward them, making sure no enemy was using them for cover.

Darius glanced up at his display then back to the street around him, getting his bearings. They were in an area of the city about three klicks north of the main business district. *Right where we're supposed to be*, he thought as he turned around and looked up.

There it was...the huge chunk of stone the Eldari called the Spur. At least in the days before the Tyrant had built his fortress atop the four hundred meter high rock. Now it was known as the Citadel.

"Let's go. Get organized by team and spread out. We move forward on a five hundred meter frontage." Darius looked back toward the city center. Normally, five ships coming down in the middle of an enemy defense perimeter would have triggered every alarm imaginable, sending waves of troops down on the invaders. But the Eldari capital was dark, its scanners and communications networks dead. No doubt people had seen the glow of the landers' engines as they swooped down, but even that information would be hard to communicate. Still, Darius Cain wasn't one to take chances.

"Captain Kring, is your satellite uplink functioning?"

"Yes, General. I have full two-way communication with the battle computer on *Eagle One*."

"Very good," Cain said. "Any contacts?"

"Looks like nothing within two klicks, sir. At least nothing that looks like an organized response." Kring paused. "It looks like chaos down here, General. I doubt they're going to be able to organize anything to hit us before we get to the Citadel. And the main attack force is less than five minutes out."

Just as planned...hopefully two regiments of Eagles coming down just outside the city will give them enough to think about while we find our way inside...

"Alright, Eagles...let's get going. Our best bet is to find some drainage outlet or utility conduit and come up from the bottom." Darius looked up at the hulking monstrosity of the Citadel itself, a massive, shadowy fortress protruding a hundred meters above the rocky peak. It was dark, but he knew that was deliberate, that the heavy guns ringing its circumference were silent for lack of targeting data and not because they'd been knocked out by the EMP. The Eldari had been stunningly unprepared for the EMP attack, but Darius knew better than to suspect the substandard equipment extended to their nerve center. No, the Tyrant's inner sanctum would be fully shielded, he was sure of that. His two hundred elite commandos had no chance mounting a frontal assault...at least not until the main force pushed through and linked up with them.

So he had to find another way in...and he had to do it quickly.

"Captain Horssen, position a team a klick off of each flank and assign two to cover the rear." Darius' order was crisp and clear. His battlefield persona was taking over, pushing back the scared, angry son, at least for a moment.

"Yes, sir," came the reply, every bit as sharp and confident as the original order. The Black Eagles' Special Action Teams were as professional as soldiers got...and every one of them loved Darius Cain and knew exactly what was at stake.

Okay, father....if you're there. I'm coming.

"Let's move out!"

Chapter 25

Martian Council Chamber
Beneath the Ruins of the Ares Metroplex
Planet Mars, Sol IV
Earthdate: 2319 AD (34 Years After the Fall)

"Roderick, I'm sorry to disturb you, but we just got some intelligence I thought you needed to see right away." Andre Girard stepped into the non-descript room that was serving as the office of the absolute ruler of the Martian Confederation. Vance had selected it almost immediately after securing his hold on power, deliberately rejected the ones his staff had suggested in favor of his own rather drab choice. Most of his underlings were confused by the selection, but Vance's closest cohorts understood. Mars' dictator had enough guilt for seizing control the way he had, and the last thing he wanted was to bury himself in palatial surroundings and the trappings of power.

"What is it, Andre?" Vance had a surprised look on his face, but he quickly pushed it aside.

He'd been the head of Martian Intelligence for a long time, and it was still a little uncomfortable having another layer between him and the incoming reports from the Confederation's spy network. Vance had long maintained operatives throughout Occupied Space, combatting the isolationist directives of the council by ensuring that he had a constant flow of fresh intelligence at all times.

But now, Andre Girard occupied Vance's old post, and the

aged eyes of that experienced operative had the first look at reports coming in. Vance hated the added distance between him and his agents, but he'd decided he couldn't adequately do his old job and rule Mars as well. He'd offered the position to Girard the instant the old spy had returned from his unsuccessful attempt to recruit Augustus Garret, and the two old friends had played their respective roles ever since. Vance didn't want to give up the job he'd held for nearly half a century, but he knew what had to be done. And Girard didn't want it at all, but he too realized he had no choice, and he graciously accepted.

Girard walked across the room and looked at his old friend. *My God, he looks tired*, he thought, realizing he couldn't fully understand the pressure Vance had taken on himself.

"It's Atlantia, Roderick. Somethings going on there. Something big."

"An attack?" Vance looked up, his concern obvious in his expression.

"No, not exactly. A media blackout. Riots. Some fighting in the streets." Girard noted Vance's gesture for him to sit, and he plopped down hard into one of the guest chairs. "If I had to guess, I'd say a revolution of some kind...a coup." He hesitated on the last two words...they hit too close to home.

"Any details? Any idea who? Or how it went?" Vance felt a cold feeling in his gut. He'd had no warning about Atlantia, no sign any kind of trouble was imminent. But somehow, he was sure it was related to the other incidents. It was intuition, perhaps, nothing based on real data. But he was sure about it nevertheless.

"The reports are sketchy so far. We've only got two operatives on the whole planet, as you know. Atlantia isn't a place we expected trouble."

"And that's where the trouble usually comes from..."

"True enough, Roderick, but let's not jump to any wild conclusions. All we really know is there is some kind of unrest going on. And there has been some fighting."

"What about Elias Cain? Any word on him?" Vance felt a wave of concern.

"Nothing. There are no reports of his whereabouts, none at all. As we were aware, he was in some level of disfavor, largely as a result of his trip to Mars." Girard paused. "But if he has been arrested—or worse—we haven't heard of it."

"We wouldn't have, would we? Not if they handled it right." Vance was worried about Elias...and he felt responsible for his troubles at home. Elias had only come to Mars at his request. Vance knew the Atlantian government had become increasingly statist and paranoid, but he'd been surprised by the level of fall-out Elias had experienced. He'd almost sent an official communique to try to clarify the matter, but he decided it was as likely to make things worse as help.

Vance stared at his desk for a few seconds, thinking. Finally, he looked back at Girard. "I need to know what happened to Elias Cain."

"Roderick, I understand your concern, but the situation on Atlantia is very fluid. We have extremely limited intel, and if we push too hard we could lose what few assets we have there."

"I understand, Andre...and you are right. By every measure of risk/reward, by every aspect of tradecraft, your logic is unassailable. Save for one thing. If Elias Cain is rotting in some prison cell, he is there because of me."

And if he's dead, shot in the back of the head and thrown in a ditch somewhere, that's my fault too.

"I want to know what happened to him, whatever it takes." There wasn't a hint of doubt in Vance's tone.

"Very well, Roderick, I will try.

*   *   *   *   *

"I'm sorry I am late." Andre Girard came jogging into the conference room, the quickness of his pace presenting an image out of sync with his advanced age.

"You are a walking advertisement for rejuv therapies, Andre." It was Archibald Astor's voice, though there was little question they were all thinking the same thing. Girard had been the old-est agent in the Martian service when he'd retired some years before. But he'd come back to embrace his new duties with a level of energy and aggressiveness few could have predicted.

"I don't want to interrupt the schedule, but I have new information from Atlantia." His eyes fixed on Vance's. "I don't know if you want to see this privately first."

"No, Andre. I have no secrets from anyone in this room." He looked up at the new arrival. "Sit. And tell us what you have."

Girard hesitated, his eyes briefly pausing over the single new presence in the room. He didn't have anything against Katarina Berchtold, but he didn't trust her either. But Roderick Vance apparently had decided she was reliable, and that was enough for him. At least for now. "First, Elias Cain is alive." He paused. "Or, at least he was not killed during the coup on Atlantia."

Vance's eyes widened. "That *is* good news. But how can we be sure?"

"Because he is not on Atlantia. Indeed, he left some time ago on the patrol ship *Zephyr*. Apparently there was some pirate activity, and he was sent to investigate."

"Elias holds a fairly high rank in their organization. Why would they send him to investigate a routine pirate raid? It doesn't make any sense, even if he is…"

No…not an ordinary pirate raid. Atlantia was on the verge of shipping out their first batch of stable trans-uranics. Could that shipment have been captured…?

"STUs," Vance said firmly. "It must have been their first shipment of STUs from Glaciem. The freighter must have been taken by a pirate, and they sent Elias to investigate. It makes sense. If, through some miracle, he succeeds in catching the pirate and recovering the cargo, he is rewarded with a pardon for whatever crimes they feel he committed by coming here. If he fails, it is the last straw…and they can use it to discredit him, overcome public resistance to cashiering a Cain. We all know his name is the only thing that kept him from being arrested the moment he returned to Atlantia."

"But the *Zephyr* has disappeared, Roderick."

"Destroyed?" Vance felt his stomach tighten.

"No. Not according to our sources at least. The word is the Atlantians don't know where the ship is. They've sent out investigatory missions, and they haven't found any indications that she was destroyed. All Atlantian Patrol ships carry special black boxes that are ejected in the event of an emergency. So if *Zephyr* had been attacked, she would have left the box behind."

"Unless she was destroyed instantly, with no warning. But what could have done that? No, Elias must have found something...some clue he decided to urgently follow."

"Perhaps it was a fortuitous development." Girard looked around the table as he spoke. "By all accounts, the coup was a power grab by the existing government. Our sources suggest there were massive payoffs of military officers, local politicians, business leaders...and a huge series of arrests as well. It appears the government jailed anyone they couldn't buy."

"Atlantia doesn't have those kinds of resources, especially not if they lost their first STU shipment." Vance spoke grimly, as if he had already come to an unpleasant conclusion. "We planned the coup on Mars, and the five of us controlled the army, navy, and intelligence services...and we have been in our positions for decades. We are well-known throughout the Confederation. The Atlantian government, on the other hand, consists mostly of relatively new arrivals from Earth. They attained and kept their positions largely through the Atlantians' disdain for politics. The situations are as different as any two such could ever be. And yet we all know what the Martian coup cost. Can you imagine the expenses involved on Atlantia...where the prime movers had to buy or undermine the equivalent of each of us? Where they had to secure control of the military and the media? The cost must have been enormous, many times Atlantia's GDP."

"You think they had support? Off-world support?" Admiral Melander was nodding as he spoke. "It's starting to make a disturbing kind of sense, isn't it? Criminal activity like slaving to produce revenue...to fund efforts to seize power on various worlds."

Girard nodded. "My thinking exactly. And it leads to an inevitable question. Who is next, after Atlantia? What other worlds are in the crosshairs? And when will the next one fall? Tomorrow? A month from now? A year?"

"Or what worlds have already been suborned more quietly? Are there government officials on other worlds, men and women who have already been bought and paid for by this organization? How many spies and operatives do they have, even now working to expand their influence on a hundred planets...a thousand?" Duncan Campbell sat back in the plush conference chair looking out at his comrades. "Occupied space has been far from calm these last few years. Yet we have speculated that this enemy that seems so new to us has been in existence for some time, have we not? Perhaps before we think the future, we should look back, try to identify worlds where totalitarian or other suspect governments have seized control...or simply where elected officials have behaved suspiciously. We might more effectively find a trail to our adversary in the past rather than the present."

Vance looked over at Campbell. "You know, Duncan, I am inclined to agree with you. The base on Eris was a massive construction. I can't even imagine the resources it took to build it in secrecy...or how long it was under construction." He sighed and panned his gaze across the table. "Indeed, though I know this is a truly disturbing thought, I think we must begin to acknowledge that this enemy we face, the one about which we know almost nothing, has been in operation for far longer than we had imagined. Years, almost certainly. Perhaps even decades."

The others stared back, their faces showing varying degrees of discomfort at Vance's words. But no one offered any argument, nor even a hint of disagreement. Vance saw the grudging agreement in their faces, and he realized his speculation was most likely correct.

He felt a numbness, a withering cold that passed through his body. He'd thought things were bad. He'd believed that with enough certainty to launch his coup. But the thought that the unseen enemy had been lurking in the shadows, plotting for years, threading its tentacles throughout Occupied Space, was profoundly disturbing. Had they been there even during the Second Incursion? Had they lurked in the shadows, maneuvering to take advantage even as the military forces of mankind fought another desperate war against the First Imperium?

"What about Mars?"

Every eye in the room turned to focus on Katarina Berchtold. She had been silent until then.

"Mars?" Melander asked. "What do you mean?"

"I mean, might this enemy have agents on Mars? Might they not have personnel in key positions? Or even sleeper agents in place, waiting for the orders to make a move, to assassinate Roderick, for example…or any of us?" Berchtold paused then added, "Even if we assume the six of us are beyond suspicion, how many people are in key positions in the government and the armed forces? How much trouble could they cause? The chief engineers on the fusion plants, a high-placed army or naval officer, someone in a position to poison the food supply or sabotage vital industry…"

She paused and looked around the table. "We sit back and feel confident because the most powerful people in the old regime are imprisoned, disconnected from their networks. What about senior officers, the heads of the government ministries… even men and women who have joined our cause, seemingly sincerely? Or perhaps a prison guard, willing to look the other way as Boris Vallen passes communications back and forth with his people?"

Vance felt an urge to argue, but he realized she was right. He and his cohorts carried so much guilt about their actions, they had failed to look clearly within their own house, to suspect everyone and to take whatever steps were necessary to ensure no enemy exerted influence within the Confederation.

Berchtold had not been part of the coup. Indeed, she had been a victim of sorts, arrested and taken from her home that fateful morning. Ironically, the one person present Vance had not initially trusted had opened his eyes.

"Andre, Katarina is correct. I'm going to need you to take a close look at all key personnel outside this room. We need to know for sure that they are reliable...and if we have enemy agents among our senior personnel, we must eliminate them. Now."

"Yes, Roderick," Girard said softly. He glanced briefly toward Katarina. "Are we certain everyone in this room is reliable?"

Vance frowned. He knew Girard was only being cautious. His compatriots had taken a terrible risk supporting him, and he knew asking them to trust Berchtold required another leap of faith, especially since everyone knew the two of them had a long history of squabbling over various issues.

But I do trust her. I can't explain it, but I just know. And I have to believe in my own judgment.

"Yes, Andre. I trust everyone in this room with my life."

Girard just nodded, but Vance caught the unspoken message: 'You are doing just that.'

Chapter 26

Madarasa Plateau
Outside Eldaron City
Planet Eldaron, Denebola IV
Earthdate: 2319 AD (34 Years After the Fall)

Explosions ripped through the night sky as the guns of the Citadel opened up on the clouds of landing craft dropping swiftly toward the ground. The weapons were modern…heavy railguns and hypersonic rockets, but they were firing blind. The Eldari Citadel itself was fully-operative, its weapons and computer systems shielded against the Eagles' EMP attack. But the sensory inputs were gone, the satellites and ground stations that fed into its targeting systems. And the Black Eagles had the most sophisticated countermeasures in Occupied Space.

"We've got two landers hit, Colonel. Moderate damage to one, but they were able to engage reserve systems and land without casualties. The other is worse…they tried to make an emergency landing, but they were too badly hit. They came down hard…four dead, ten wounded."

Erik Teller stood in his armor, immobile, bolted into the lander as he listened to the incoming report. His ships were almost on the ground, and he'd only had two hit. He hurt for every Eagle who was killed or wounded in combat, but two hits was nothing for an opposed landing, especially against a world as strong and technologically advanced as Eldaron. He'd known the virus and the EMT blasts had been effective, but he was only just realizing *how* effective.

"Colonel Teller, Cornin reporting. My lead elements are deployed...moving out to secure the beachhead. Resistance is moderately heavy but disordered and scattered. Initial losses are light. I'm still bringing my tail elements down, but eighty percent of the regiment is on the ground."

"Very well, Colonel. See to your regiment. The Blues are right behind you, estimate nine minutes out." Teller nodded to himself, at least as far as he could in the confines of his immobile armor.

So far so good. Another few minutes and we'll know just how badly the EMP hit them.

He felt the pressure slam into him as the ship banked hard, positioning itself for landing. Teller knew he should have stayed back on *Eagle One*, come down with the later waves. At least according to any reasonable command doctrine. But neither he nor Darius were wired that way, and it had taken considerable effort to resist the urge to land with the lead elements instead of at the tail end of Cornin's Red Regiment.

Most of the Reds were already down, and from the reports he'd been monitoring, things were going better than he'd dared to hope. The Eldari were virtually paralyzed, their communications net a shambles, and their heavy equipment had largely been neutralized by the EMP. On a normal op, Teller would have had a broad smile on his face as he waited to land and congratulate the Eagles on yet another quick victory. But he knew *this* was anything but a normal mission. The complete disruption of the Eldari defense grid was good, but he doubted it would be decisive. Whatever mysterious force had baited the Eagles to attack here—and he didn't think for an instant it was the Eldari Tyrant acting on his own—they had something up their sleeve. And Teller knew it would be trouble when they unleashed it.

Still, despite his concern for the trap he knew was waiting for them, that wasn't what was truly troubling him. He had faith in the Black Eagles, and he knew they could face any fight that came their way. But Darius was out there somewhere, deep behind enemy lines with only 200 men and women. The cream of the Eagles were cut off and driving their way deeper into the heart of the enemy's stronghold.

I hope. For all I know they could have been wiped out already.

He was struck by the oddness of his thought, that his oldest friend could already be dead, lying in some ditch outside the Eldari Citadel, and he wouldn't know. *No*, he thought angrily, pushing back the doubts. *Darius is the best warrior I've ever seen. He's a survivor.*

He believed it, mostly at least. But the hint of doubt hung over him, like a shadowy darkness. He struggled to put it out of his mind...he had duty now. He had to take care of the Eagles until Darius returned. But he couldn't quite banish the concerns, the guilt he felt at not having gone with his friend... even though he knew that hadn't been an option. Somebody had to lead the Eagles...and make damned sure whatever trap was waiting out there didn't get the better of them.

That's all you can do for Darius now, you damned fool. So get your head out of your ass and do it!

He glanced at his display. Thirty seconds to landing.

Back in the shit again...as deep as we've ever been...

*   *   *   *   *

"Let's go...get that gear up to the front." Matias Davidoff was clad in full powered armor, a luxury few of his soldiers enjoyed. Even a planet as wealthy as Eldaron was limited in the number of powered infantry units it could support...and half of those had been caught out in the EMT blasts, where their shielding proved inadequate to prevent their circuitry from being fried. So, instead of having over a thousand armored infantry in the line, he had less than 200...and 800 elite soldiers, trained in powered operations were now wearing fatigues and whatever scraps of hyperkev or other partial armor they'd managed to scrounge up and sharing a few boxes of assault rifles that had been stored in a secure location.

Even rifles and other equipment had been devastated by the Eagle's surprise attack, the processors and circuitry that made the sophisticated guns work burnt out and useless. Davidoff didn't care for the idea of sending his men to the front in pairs, with instructions for the second to grab the rifle after the first had been killed, but he hadn't had any choice, not at first at least. But now he was finally getting a few weapons deliveries from the Citadel. He knew there were thousands of guns stored in the great fortress, along with grenades and ammunition. Most of it was old, ordnance that had been replaced with newer equipment but never discarded, but none of that mattered now. A ten year old gun was a hell of a lot better than no gun at all.

He looked over and saw that the soldiers delivering the weapons were hesitating. They were Citadel guards, not his own troops, and his authority over them was questionable. Most of the men assigned to the Citadel got there through some sort of patronage or connections, and it was clear the soldiers on the trucks had no desire to see the front lines up close. And Davidoff was far from sure they'd follow his orders to do so.

"Sergeant Patrillo," he roared. His helmet was fully retracted, and he shouted across the blasted field.

"Sir!" Patrillo was a grizzled non-com, a career Eldari soldier whose service dated back further than the Tyrant's rule. He ran over and snapped to attention in front of Davidoff.

"Sergeant, assemble a platoon and *escort* these gentlemen to the front line units. I want you to see to the distribution of these weapons personally."

"Yes, General."

"You have authorization to take any actions you deem necessary to ensure that these trucks get to the front. Do you understand me?" He spoke loudly enough for the cluster of men standing around the trucks to hear him.

"Yes, General. I understand." Patrillo's voice left no doubt in anyone's mind he fully understood what Davidoff meant by *any actions*. He turned and raced over to the trucks, shouting out commands to the stunned drivers.

Davidoff stood and watched the non-com for a minute, turning away once he assured himself the Citadel guards were obeying. He turned toward a crew working off to his left, setting up a medium-sized dish. The equipment was from the Citadel, just like the assault rifles, more outdated stuff that had been stored instead of trashed. But once it was set up—and the hundred portable units he had were distributed to key units—the dish would give him at least some limited communications. It would be far from perfect, but enormously better than nothing, which was what he had now.

The battle wasn't going well. Indeed, it had been a debacle. Facing troops like the Black Eagles required organized and well-equipped veterans, but his men were in total disarray, most of them without communications, many even without functioning weapons. He had hoped to hit the LZs quickly and hard, to try to keep the Eagles off balance. But those legendary warriors poured out of their craft and snapped almost immediately into formation. Then they turned toward the masses of Eldari soldiers circling their landing craft and fell on them with an almost unimaginable ferocity. There were wounded streaming back all across the front, and without effective com, Davidoff could only imagine how many more of his men were dead or dying along the battlelines.

He was pouring reserves forward as quickly as he got them, but so far nothing had even slowed the momentum of the Black Eagles. The new arrivals were generally better-armed, many units having re-equipped from the supplies trickling out of the Citadel. Still, the Eagles were sweeping them aside as quickly as he sent them forward. He figured he had numerical superiority of at least five to one, but it wasn't going to matter, not unless he could get his troops rallied and reordered.

He looked over the convoy, his eyes catching the nervous look in the drivers' eyes. He knew they were trying to figure a way to just drop their deliveries here and dash back to the Citadel. No doubt they would have already, but Davidoff was radiating an aura of barely controlled fury...and Patrillo had managed to communicate without a spoken word that he was perfectly willing to put a bullet in each of their heads.

Davidoff shook his head.

This is why we have such trouble facing an enemy like the Eagles. They have discipline, certainly, but they fight because they are fighters, because they have pride and dedication. They will stay in the battle if their officers are killed, continue the struggle even as their ammunition dwindles to nothing. How do we fight that? With conscripted soldiers and corrupt officers? What do my men fight for? Eldaron? Or the Tyrant? Are they one and the same, as we all must believe? Is this war truly for our planet, our families? Or do we merely served some scheme of the Tyrant, some play he is making for even greater power?

The Eagles have no such questions. They fight for themselves, and for their comrades. And they have Darius Cain at their head, not a man who seized power over the bodies of his betrayed allies. How can we hope to beat them?

Davidoff shook his head, as if the motion would banish his dangerous thoughts. It was not his place to question such things, only to do what he could with the resources at his disposal. He had numbers...and that was all he had. He had to find a way to use that advantage, or the Eagles would run right over his army. Then he would die, either on the field...or at the hands of an enraged Tyrant.

*   *   *   *   *

The Eagles were professionals who had fought most of their wars as dispassionately as men and women can endure battle. But this one was different. The steely nerves and cool execution were still there, but the Eagles carried something else with them on this campaign, something fiery and uncontrollable. It was anger, pure rage. Erik Cain was a legend, not only to the Marine Corps, but to honorable fighters everywhere. And he was the father of the Eagles' beloved leader. The very thought that the Eldari had kept Cain a prisoner for so many years filled the Eagles with indignant rage. Their battles had always been business, professional endeavors treated as such. But this one was personal.

Jordyn Calfort was along the front line of the Eagles' rapid advance. Her platoon had been one of the first to hit ground, and now they were with the forward line, heading toward the enemy Citadel. The fortress was still almost forty klicks away, nothing more than a shadowy mass off in the distance. Its weapons were engaged, but without its satellite tracking systems it was firing randomly. She'd had one casualty, a KIA, from the bombardment, but mostly the enemy's long range fire was a nuisance and not a real danger.

"Lieutenant Calfort, the enemy are trying to form a defensive line two klicks ahead. We're attacking in three minutes." Captain Tonn's voice was high-pitched, very feminine-sounding. But that fooled no one who knew the veteran officer. Priya Tonn had made nine combat drops as a Black Eagle, and the diminutive company commander had racked up an astonishing number of kills, while also distinguishing herself, first leading a platoon, and now a company.

"Understood, Captain. My people are ready to go." *They've been ready since we hit ground...*

No one seemed to know for certain, but it was the army's worst kept secret that General Cain had led the Teams to infiltrate the enemy Citadel. Every Black Eagle knew the only way to help the General was to take that massive fortress and hook up with his trapped force...whatever it took.

The Eldari had fallen back all morning, but now they were finally making a stand. They'd picked a good position, a high ridge slicing across the open plain, offering sweeping coverage of every potential approach. It was a first-class killing ground, just the kind of spot Calfort would have chosen to mount a strong defense if her people had been under attack. In most situations, it would be a difficult place to assault, one that offered few alternatives to a brutal frontal approach...exactly the type of situation that significantly negated the Eagles' operational advantages and compelled them to accept heavy losses. But the

Eldari forces were still severely disordered, their weapons and communications systems not yet recovered from the effects of the Eagles' disruptive attacks earlier in the campaign.

Normally, Calfort would have hoped for orders to go around, to put up a skirmish line facing the enemy and execute a flanking maneuver. But the enemy's numerical superiority made an outflanking move almost impossible. Besides, there were advantages to keeping up the continuous pressure, squeezing every drop of benefit from the enemy's disorder. She knew the Eldari were shaken, that a hard attack now was the right move. But there wasn't so much as a tree on that open plain...

"Lieutenant Calfort..." It was Tonn again. "Commence your attack!"

"Yes, Captain," she said. Then she toggled the platoon-wide com. "Alright...let's move. I want everybody across that plain as quickly as possible. Keep firing all the way...I want their heads down. And we get across as fast as we can. No stopping for anything."

She took a deep breath and hopped up over the small hillside in front of her. "Attack!"

*   *   *   *   *

The trio of fighters streaked through the dawn sky, leaving long white trails as they ripped over the city at almost four times the speed of sound. The birds had already fired their missiles, and now they were flying low, blasting what looked like a freight monorail line with their autocannons. They'd left a long line of blasted concrete pylons behind them, along with the smoking wreckage of one train unfortunate enough to have been traversing the line at the wrong moment.

Kevin Darryk banked his craft to the right, angling for the meandering river that snaked past Eldaron's second-largest city. Nordberg was a manufacturing center, the place the Tyrant had centered his heavy industry and basic materials production—all the dirty and polluting factories he hadn't wanted marring his magnificent capital.

"That's enough on the rail line. It'll take them long enough to replace a kilometer of tracks. I want to take out those bridges before we head back to rearm."

One glance at the display told him his wingmen were following him, their formation tight, as close to perfect as he'd ever seen. There had been no fighting in space to speak of on this campaign, but he was glad his fighter wing was earning its pay. Everyone knew the Eagles had been baited to attack Eldaron, and while just what was waiting for them was still a mystery, Darius Cain's warriors believed they could handle anything that came at them. Still, confidence wasn't the same thing as arrogance, and the Eagles' battle plan had left no contingency unaddressed.

It was clear the war on Eldaron would be won or lost around the capital, so that is where the Eagles landed. The invasion was a surgical strike, with everything landing right around Eldaron City…where Cain had expected the bulk of the defenders to be deployed. The plan mostly ignored the planet's other cities, but not entirely. Darryk and his squadrons of fighter-bombers had been charged with attacking airports, rail lines, roadways…any transport assets that could be used to rush reserves and supplies to the capital. Normally, a campaign like that would be costly, forcing the fighters to fly close to the ground-based defenses. But most of those were still down, and the few that were operational lacked effective targeting data. The Eagles' squadrons had been running constant sorties all night, and they'd only lost one bird—and that had been a lucky shot.

Darryk angled his fighter down, diving at the first of a series of bridges spanning the two-kilometer wide river. There were four of them in total, connecting Nordberg with the rail lines and highways that led toward the capital, just over a thousand klicks to the west. Cutting them all would cripple the flow of troops and materials to the front lines.

His eyes glanced at the ammunition readouts. *Hmmm, lower*

than I'd like.

"Okay, we're running low on ammo, so let's split up, each take out one of these things. Then we can hit the last with whatever we've got left." Splitting up a three-ship formation was against almost every operating principal of fighter-bomber tactics...but it was the only way to completely cut the westward flow of armaments and reserve troops. Darryk was a fighter jock all the way, but he never forgot the thousands of Eagle troops around the capital...waiting to see what the enemy managed to throw at them. And taking out those bridges was the way he could help the ground pounders.

"Strike Two, take the second target, Strike Three the third. Then we'll reform and come back and hit the fourth before we head back to base."

"Acknowledged."

"Understood, Strike One."

Darryk smiled. He could hear the confidence in his pilots' responses. "Break," he said, pushing his throttle forward and accelerating toward the first bridge. His fighter ripped through the atmosphere, bouncing around hard in Eldaron's thick air. But Darryk was focused, his mind on one thing...his target.

The bridge was coming up in front of him, growing larger with each passing second. He'd been approaching at an angle, but now he tapped the throttle to the side, bringing his bird around until it was coming straight over the road that led to the crossing. His hand tightened around the firing controls as he angled lower, bring his guns to bear.

The massive plasti-crete and hypersteel structure loomed ahead, an astonishing structure by the standards of man's colony worlds, and a product of Eldaron's massive and growing economy.

Millions of megacredits, Darryk thought, *more than most planets could imagine spending on a single project. But that's not going to stop me from turning it into a pile of debris...*

He squeezed the trigger, and the dual autocannons of his fighter opened up, their hypervelocity projectiles leaving a glowing trail as they ionized the air around them. A single missile could have destroyed the bridge, but Darryk had fired them already, so he had to tear this new target apart bit by bit. He watched as the depleted uranium rounds tore into the surface of the bridge, chunks of shattered plasti-crete flying around, exposing the steel structure below. He angled the throttle after he zipped past the bridge to come around for a second pass. He could see the target was pockmarked with giant holes, but he hadn't severed it...not yet.

He looked down at the ammo readout. He had barely enough left for one more run...but he had to save something for the fourth bridge. If he left any connection from Nordberg to Eldaron City, there would be a steady flow of arms and men heading toward the front lines. And he knew his people were working on borrowed time. It would take at least an hour and a half to rearm and get back...and sooner or later, the Eldari would get at least part of their air defense network back online. His people had taken out a number of defensive installations, but he knew there were more, underground and in armored strongpoints. If they came back online, his next bombing run would come at a much higher cost.

He stared straight ahead, his eyes focusing on the worst-hit section of the bridge. One of the structural supports was severed, and there was only one remaining. He angled the fighter, heading straight for that point. The targeting display was projected in front of him, and he nudged the throttle until the lines matched up. Then he pulled the trigger, spraying the exposed girder with fire, tearing the tortured metal to shreds. The middle section of the bridge seemed to hover in space for a few seconds. Then it collapsed, twisted girders and huge chunks of 'crete falling into the murky brown water below.

Yes! Darryk's eyes moved to the ammo display. *About 600 rounds left. Not much...but maybe enough...*

He brought his ship up, moving toward the rally point. He could see the distant white trail of one of his birds, heading toward the same position. A quick glance at the widescreen display showed him his other wingman, coming up on his six.

"Report," he snapped into the com. He could see that they'd

both taken down their targets. What he really wanted to know was if they had any ammunition left to attack the fourth.

"Strike Two, here. Target destroyed. I've got one short burst left in my guns then I'm out."

"Strike Three. Target destroyed. My guns are dry, Major."

He nodded. About what he'd expected. He figured they could still take out the fourth bridge, but there was no room for error. "Three, return to base. Two, on me. We're going in." There was no point in Strike Two staying around. With its guns dry, it couldn't do anything even if the Eldari unleashed some previously unknown air force. Better they get back and get rearmed and refit…and clear the way so his bird and Two could get in and out that much faster.

"Two, do you see those center supports on bridge four?"

"Yes, Major. Got 'em."

"It'll take some serious accuracy, but I think that's the easiest way to take the sucker down with what we've got left." A short pause. "Follow me in, and finish off anything I leave standing."

"Got it, Major. On your six."

Darryk nudged the throttle forward, diving toward the last bridge. He came in lower, far lower than he had on the first attack. His bird was streaking across the river, barely a thousand meters over the rippling water. But he was going lower still, and as the target grew larger ahead of him, he pushed the throttle hard, dropping to five hundred meters…three hundred…one hundred…

He could almost feel the river below, the torrent his fighter created as it zipped along barely thirty meters over the river. The bridge was just ahead, but now he dropped again, to twenty meters. The main support pylons were coming up, right in front of him as he came in ten meters below the bridge's road surface. His hand tightened, and he stared intently at his targeting screen. He took a deep breath and held it.

No room for any mistakes…

The AI was aiding his targeting, but the final shot would be his. It was 99% math and 1% gut feel, and the intuition was his part, the last touch that made a good shot a great one. *Now*, he thought, as he pressed the trigger.

The first pylon blew apart as the stream of hypervelocity particles took it dead on. Darryk's finger loosened, saving the last of what he had for the second support. He pressed again, the rest of his rounds blasting out in less than a tenth of a second, ripping into the massive column of reinforced plasti-steel. His shot carved out a huge chunk, but about a third of its circumference remained. He didn't know how, but the bridge was still standing. And his guns were bone dry.

He felt his stomach lurch, the feeling of coming so close but not getting the job done. He'd have to come back...and if the Eldari got some of their defenses working, he was going to lose people on that attack. All because he hadn't hit that pylon hard enough...

"Yeeeeeahhh!" he heard on the com, and his eyes darted back to the display. His finger hit the rear camera controls, bringing up an image of the collapsing bridge...and Strike Two zipping up right after his bird.

Strike Two had done it, placed his last few rounds perfectly, and finished the job Eagle Leader had begun. Darryk pumped his fist hard and screamed, "Yes. That's fine shooting, Strike Two! Damned fine shooting!" He paused, taking one last look as the bridge tumbled into the water below. "Now let's get back to base!"

* * * * *

Darius couldn't feel the knee deep water as he moved forward, but he could hear it splashing around his armored legs. Cain had been grateful for his armor many times, though usually it had been the combat effectiveness of the fighting suit he appreciated. There was likely fighting ahead, and he suspected those offensive and defensive capabilities would once again be welcome. But right now he was just happy to have a couple centimeters of airtight osmium-iridium alloy between him and the sewer he was walking through.

Not to mention the cool, fresh recycled air. I can't even imagine the stench out there...

It wasn't easy to move quietly in powered armor, but he slowed down a bit and tried to walk more carefully. The deeper they got into the complex without being discovered, the better. Not just tactically, but because the news that an infiltration force was loose in the Citadel might cause the Tyrant to take decisive action against the prisoner.

Assuming there is a prisoner.

Darius Cain found himself flip-flopping back and forth about whether he truly believed his father was on Eldaron, or if it was all just an elaborate hoax. It didn't really matter...if there was any real chance Erik Cain was alive, Darius knew he had to investigate. But even his legendary discipline was failing him, the anticipation of seeing his father again after so many years playing havoc with his focus.

And if he's not here? If it was a hoax...or worse, if he is here, but you get there too late? What then? The truth is, you let yourself buy into this, to hope to see him again. You allowed emotion to rule your judgment. What will it do to you if it was all for nothing? Or if he dies because you came here and forced the enemy's hand?

Darius didn't have any answers, but he could feel the darkness in his mind, and it gave him a pretty good idea how Eldaron would suffer if they killed his father. Despite his reputation, he'd generally been just and rational during his campaigns, reluctant to shed any more blood than was absolutely necessary. But if he found his father murdered by the Tyrant's soldiers, he knew his heart would cry out for vengeance, that it would rule his mind. Then they would see the monster the legends made of him. If Erik Cain died at the hands of his captors, Darius knew he would leave the planet a lifeless graveyard. He might live to regret such savagery, to mourn the innocents who died alongside the guilty. Indeed, he knew he almost certainly would. But he was just as sure that wouldn't stop him.

"General Cain, the forward scouts have found an ingress

point. It appears to lead up into a maintenance area below the Citadel." Captain Alcabedo's voice was crisp, focused.

"Any sign of the enemy?" Darius knew they were lucky to get so far without running into a guard or a patrol.

No, more than luck. It's Tom Sparks and his tech, Kevin Darryk and his pilots…all my people. We kicked the anthill, and the Eldari are up there in a panic trying to get their shit together…instead of guarding access points in the bowels of their fortress…

"No, sir. The forward pickets request permission to move up into the corridor and scout it more thoroughly."

Darius heard his officer's voice from the speakers inside his sealed helmet, but he knew the captain was close by. Ernesto Alcabedo was one of the longest-serving veterans in the Black Eagles, a man who had joined the colors when Darius and Erik Teller commanded three hundred troops and a single spaceship. He'd served for years now in the Special Action Teams…and more recently as Darius Cain's babysitter.

That role, informal but nevertheless one he took very seriously, had come about when Darius had gone to Mars to meet with Roderick Vance. Erik Teller had eventually given up trying to convince his friend the trip was too dangerous, but he'd resolutely demanded Darius take a detachment of guards with him everywhere he went…and the Eagles' number two had filled that roster with the hardest core warriors to ever wear the black uniform. And he'd put Ernesto Alcabedo in charge of the detail.

The guard detail had been disbanded when Darius returned to the Nest from Mars, but Alcabedo seemed to regard his own assignment as a permanent one, and he'd been hanging as close to the general as he could without outright disobeying orders. Darius had found it amusing at first, then annoying. But he'd stayed silent and allowed the officer to continue in the role. Of all the things in the vast galaxy, Darius Cain knew that true loyalty was one of the rarest, to be valued and appreciated when found…even when it annoyed the hell out of you. He didn't think he needed a bodyguard…but he did need men and women like Ernesto Alcabedo. And he knew he wouldn't keep them if he didn't respect and value them. And since Alcabedo was going to follow him around like a puppy anyway, he figured he might as well make the veteran captain his aide.

"Yes, Captain. I want a full team to move up and scout the area. Push another team deeper down this sewer line...see if there are any other exit points nearby."

"Yes, General."

I just wish I knew where anything was in here...

The Eldari data networks had proven to be carelessly safe-guarded, and the Eagles had been able to secure strong intel before launching their attack. About everything but the Cita-del. There was no information about the Tyrant's great fortress, none at all. Darius understood the paranoia of Eldaron's leader. Indeed, he knew it was a necessary survival trait for a dictator. But it also meant he was completely blind in these tunnels, with no idea where the detention cells were.

"Captain, remember, we need information. Advise the for-ward teams to deploy their stun guns. I want a prisoner."

*   *   *   *   *

"The Eldari forces are being slaughtered, General. We must engage soon, or they will be destroyed. Shall I order the lead formations to assemble?"

"No." The reply was cold, final. There wasn't a shred of doubt in Albrecht Trax's voice.

"But sir..." the aide said tentatively, hesitant to argue too strongly in the face of the general's steadfastness.

"Major Diomeni, I needn't remind you that the Eldari are expendable in this operation. Indeed, all of Eldaron is. We have only one purpose, one overriding mission to accomplish. Destroy the Black Eagles. It is of little consequence if the Eldari forces, the Tyrant...or indeed this entire planet, survive."

Trax stared back at the display. The screen was divided into eight rectangles, each feeding in a report of a different section of the battlefield. The areas being reported on covered a range of several hundred kilometers, but the data on each was similar. Eldari forces fighting well initially, despite their lack of communications and equipment, but falling back in disarray as each formation was assaulted by the Eagle forces.

"Indeed, I have yet to find an instance of the Eldari standing before a concentrated Eagle offensive, regardless of numerical superiority. We can only ascertain that they are incapable of doing so."

"That is true, General, but the Eldari are without communications, and much of their ordnance was rendered inoperative by the EMT strikes."

"Which were effective largely because of the inferiority of the Eldari equipment." Trax's voice was heavy with disgust. "No, we cannot consider the native forces to be of any use save baiting the trap...and that is why we must wait before we strike, why we must remain in our shielded bunkers without giving the enemy any opportunity to detect our presence."

The major cleared his throat, likely as much to gain a few seconds to work up his courage than because he really needed to. "May I remind you, sir," he said tentatively, "that we have suffered some equipment failures as well, despite our superior ordnance and our position in shielded bunkers?"

"That is true, Major. Clearly, the Eagles' weapons were enhanced somehow to produce an EMP spike far above norms for nuclear detonations. But the attack was a minor inconvenience to us...yet it virtually obliterated the Eldari forces' capacity to resist. They are getting what they deserve."

The general paused for a few seconds, his mind deep in thought, face twisted into a frown. "Still, the Eldari must pose enough of a threat to compel the Eagles to bring down all their forces. Our best reports suggest that only two of four operational regiments have landed as of yet. If the Eldari fall too rapidly, the Black Eagles will keep their reserves on their fleet... and they will have maximum mobility to counter our strike. Or, perhaps more unfortunately, half of the company will be able to escape once they become aware of the size of our forces...and the lethality of the trap we have set for them. Trax's confident voice faltered a bit when he mentioned Eagle forces escaping. His orders had been made perfectly clear to him—destroy the Black Eagles, all of them. And he had seen how the Triumvirate handled failure.

"Perhaps we should provide at least some limited support, sir. At least enough to stabilize their forces. We must coax the Eagles to land the remainder of their combat units, after all." Diomeni's voice was halting, tentative. It was clear he didn't like watching allies hung out to dry...but even more apparent that he was hesitant to challenge General Trax too strongly.

Trax looked up from the display and stared at Diomeni.

"We cannot release *any* of our primary combat units, Major. Not yet. The Eagles have faced Omega forces before, and the chance that they will recognize the true threat we pose is too great. But we will dispatch what we can to stiffen the Eldari lines...weapons, communications equipment, ordnance that will not seem out of place in their hands." He paused. "And armored vehicles. There were no tanks deployed when the Omega forces engaged the Eagles on Lysandria, and therefore no reason they would connect such forces to us. It is likely they will attribute them to some Eldari secret corps, an armored reserve the Tyrant had kept hidden. Perhaps they will even determine that such a force is the trap they are no doubt expecting. Indeed, if that is the case then we shall gain doubly from their early deployment."

Trax stood silently for a moment, considering his own words. Then he said, "Yes, release the armored force. They are to launch an attack against the Eagles' flank. Then the enemy will be compelled to bring down reserves to face the new threat."

Tanks had virtually disappeared from ground warfare since the Fall. Few of the worlds of Occupied Space had the industry to build large numbers of the heavy combat vehicles...and transporting them across space was incalculably expensive. Even the Triumvirate was severely limited in what it could produce and move. But destroying the Black Eagles was the highest priority operation currently underway, and no expense had been spared setting a trap that would destroy Darius Cain and his elite warriors.

"General, the operational directives for the armored vehicles stipulate that they are to be deployed with infantry support."

"Yes, Major, but if we send out any of our infantry, the Eagles will know who we are. They may even abort the invasion and escape." He left unspoken the fact that every officer in the force ranked colonel or higher—and possibly major too—would likely lose their heads if that happened. "No, the armor will attack alone."

Trax paused, slipping deep into his thoughts for a moment. "And activate full Endgame protocols for the armored units, Major." His voice was deep, almost grim. "We can't risk having the Eagles take any Omega soldiers prisoner…"

Chapter 27

"The Nest" – Black Eagles Base
Second Moon of Eos, Eta Cassiopeiae VII
Earthdate: 2318 AD (34 Years After the Fall)

"What the hell is going on, Rolf?" John Cranston burst into the control room like a force of nature. He was dressed in his duty uniform, but the state of his hair—and the fact that the buttons of his jacket were out of order—told Rolf Anders he had awakened the Nest's provisional commander when he'd sounded the alarm.

"I'm sorry to disturb you, sir. It's probably some kind of misunderstanding. But we've got ships coming through the Gravis warp gate."

Cranston moved up behind Anders, staring down at the captain's display. "Any contact?"

"Negative, sir. We have issued the standard challenges." The Eagles were extremely defensive of their base, and there was a series of communications issued to unauthorized vessels approaching the Nest. The first was polite, a businesslike announcement that the ship was encroaching on secured space and instructing it to change course. By the third broadcast, very specific threats were being made, strong enough to chill the blood of most unwelcome interlopers. But the approaching ships had ignored the warnings and continued toward the Nest.

Cranston stared down at the screen, and he felt a knot in his stomach. One lost ship he could buy...maybe. But icons were still coming onto the display as the scanners around the warp gate picked up new vessels emerging. They were all lost? None of them had active com systems? Not likely.

"Bring the Nest to red alert, Captain." Anders had already initiated condition yellow, one that had heightened the readiness posture of the Nest's defensive personnel. But red alert was a full war footing, an order to prepare to repel an imminent attack.

"Yes, sir." The control center was bathed in the red glow of the battle lamps. The alarm sounded throughout the massive complex. On every level, in dormitories and quarters, in workshops and rec areas, the Black Eagles were being called to arms. The frontline regiments were gone, off fighting on Eldaron. But the Nest was far from defenseless. Cranston commanded an impressive force, and the Black Eagles base was well-armed and able to defend itself. But ships kept pouring out of the warp gate, more than twenty already, and the provisional commander began to worry.

Who is launching an attack this size? Who would dare? Who even could?

He leaned over Anders, reaching out and opening a com line. "This is Major John Cranston of the Black Eagles." He'd almost added, 'commander on site,' but he'd stopped himself. There was no reason to broadcast that the Eagle's feared field army was gone, off on a mission and unavailable to bolster the defenses of the Nest. Though he was fairly certain that whoever had launched this attack was well-aware of that fact.

"You are hereby directed to decelerate at once and reverse course, returning to your warp gate of origin. If you fail to obey this command within thirty seconds, we will consider you intent hostile and respond accordingly." He flipped a switch, cutting off the line. He didn't have any interest in a reply, not a verbal one at least. If those bastards didn't want to feel everything he had to throw at them, they could show it by turning around and leaving. Now.

"All primary posts report combat readiness, Major." Anders had been monitoring the status display, watching the updates while Cranston was sending his communique.

"All missile stations, prepare to launch as soon as the enemy enters range." Cranston's eyes were on the chronometer, watching the last of the thirty seconds slip away. His choice of the term 'enemy' was clearly deliberate. The fleet, wherever it had come from, had gotten its last chance. Now the Eagles would treat it as an attacking force…and a deadly threat.

Cranston watched as still more ships came through the warp gate, and any doubt he had drained away. This was an attack, one carefully planned to hit the Nest while the strike force was away. He could feel his stomach tighten, as he thought about it. Nobody had hired the Eagles for this mission. No one outside the organization had any idea that Darius and the strike force had left for Eldaron.

Elias Cain. The thought popped into his mind, but he quickly discounted it. Elias knew his brother had gone to Eldaron, that the main Eagle forces were away from the Nest. Cranston had liked Elias Cain; he'd convinced himself to trust him. Now he felt a wave of doubt, a sick feeling that perhaps he should not have allowed Elias to leave.

No, he thought almost immediately, *it can't be him. This is a serious operation. These ships left their bases long before Elias Cain got here. But then who…?*

He stared back down at the display. The lead elements of the enemy fleet were almost in range. "Missile status, Captain?"

"All launchers report armed and ready, sir."

Cranston stared at the screen for a few seconds, watching as the first line of enemy ships entered range.

"All missiles launch."

*   *   *   *   *

"Strike force Alpha, form up on me. Force Beta, position for missile interception." Christos Caravalla stared at the display, watching the waves of missiles moving toward the enemy fleet. His fighters had launched just after the fifth volley, staying close behind the cluster of missiles. With any luck, the enemy ships' point defense arrays would be overwhelmed intercepting the incoming warheads, allowing his fighter-bombers to approach without heavy resistance.

He'd intended to take the entire fighter corps in against the enemy fleet, but there were just too many warheads heading toward the Nest. Force Beta consisted of half of his forty fighters, and detaching them would seriously deplete the power of his attack. But if too many enemy missiles got through, the Nest's surface installations would be wiped clean. Most of the vital areas were far below ground—living quarters, the AI processing center, the reactors. But if the surface was hit hard enough, they'd lose the missile launchers, laser turrets, docking facilities, scanning arrays. The Nest would be besieged, its ability to strike back against its attackers obliterated.

If the fleet had been in port, the ten Eagle warships would have moved up behind the massive missile attack to meet the invaders. But the ships were all gone, dispatched to Eldaron with the strike forces…and the Nest had only its core defensive resources.

Including my forty fighters…

Caravalla was one of the oldest Eagles, an ex-Europan pilot who'd seen combat as far back as the Third Frontier War. He'd worked alongside Kevin Darryk to build up the Eagles' fighter corps, but he had stepped aside and allowed his younger comrade to take command of the offensive element, the sixty fighter-bombers carried aboard the Eagle warships, while he led the forty craft permanently stationed to defend the Nest. The fighters were all the same design, though the older and more battered craft tended to rotate toward the defensive command. And there was no question, the best pilots were assigned the Darryk's strike force, while those with less experience—or old vets like himself, past their primes—were assigned to the Nest-based forces.

Nevertheless, any Black Eagle was a highly skilled fighter, and Caravalla was confident his people would fight with distinction. But looking at the large enemy fleet, he had a feeling that wasn't going to be enough. There were already thirty ships aligned in battle array, and vessels were still coming through the warp gate.

He had no idea who was attacking the Nest, but he couldn't think of a world in Occupied Space that could field a fleet so large. Was it some kind of alliance? A pact of the other mercenary companies making a move on the Eagles? That didn't make sense to him, but he couldn't think of anything else. Getting the Eagles out of the way would open up some lucrative contracts to the others, but it couldn't possibly make up for the losses they were sure to suffer in a protracted battle against the Nest's defenses...not to mention the fact that Darius Cain was still out there, with the Eagle fleet and four crack regiments of troops. Caravalla was tense, focused on the battle at hand. But he shuddered to think of the revenge Cain would take against anyone who attacked and destroyed the Nest.

He watched the display as the first wave of missiles closed on the enemy ships. The attacking fleet's point defense had blunted the volley, destroying two-thirds of the incoming warheads. Now, Caravalla focused as the final dance began...the surviving missiles seeking to get close enough to cause damage to the enemy ships, and the vessels themselves firing their magnetic catapults, throwing out huge clouds of metallic projectiles, seeking to destroy as many more of the incoming weapons as possible before they detonated.

He saw one of the tiny dots on the display expand into a larger circle...one of the warheads detonating. Then another... and another. He watched as the dozen or so missiles that had survived exploded all around the enemy formation. Most of them were too far out to cause significant damage, and they exploded without effect or inflicted minor exterior damage to a nearby ship. But four of them got close. Three detonated within two kilometers of enemy ships, bathing their targets with massive amounts of radiation, causing system failures, melting sections of the exterior hulls, and inflicting heavy casualties on the crews. The last missile got to within 400 meters of an enemy ship, and when the energy of the explosion began to clear there was simply nothing left. Missile and ship were both gone.

The 500-megaton warheads on the Eagle's missiles were throwbacks to the wars of the Superpowers, weapons of a power and production cost that was out of reach to most of the colony worlds since the Fall. But Darius Cain had spared no expense in equipping his Black Eagles…and now this enemy would feel the effects of his wealth and foresight.

Caravalla watched as the second and third waves moved in against the enemy line. Again, the defenders' point defense arrays thinned each volley, but despite all their efforts, missiles were getting through…and as they did, more ships were damaged and destroyed.

"All right, Alphas, prepare to begin attack run. We're going in right on the tail of the fifth wave. We don't give those bastards any time to adjust their point defense arrays." He'd seen the thickness of the anti-missile fire from the enemy ships, and he realized immediately his strike force was going to suffer badly. If they'd been going in alone, without the missiles as cover, he doubted any of his twenty birds would have made it through. But the missiles gave them a chance, and the heavy plasma torpedoes they carried could gut one of the enemy ships with a single hit.

He glanced down at the secondary display. The scanner satellites around the Nest were sending him a live feed as the first of the enemy missiles approached the base. The Eagles' defensive fire had torn into the clusters of enemy weapons…and Strike Force Beta had plunged in as well, chasing down and destroying any warhead that evaded the Nest's fire. In the end, only two missiles from the first wave got through…but the instant Caravalla saw the explosion on his display he felt his throat tighten.

That was a big detonation. Like one of ours.

His eyes stayed locked on the display, watching as the report filtered in. Estimated yield: 511mt.

Fuck, he thought, quickly realizing that the one advantage he'd thought the Eagles enjoyed had just vanished. It wouldn't take too many 500 megaton missiles to scrape the surface installations away. Including the landing bay for his fighters…

He looked back toward the primary display. The fourth wave of missiles had just gone in. The front line of enemy ships had been hit hard, four of them destroyed outright, and another dozen damaged to various degrees. But the second echelon was accelerating, moving forward to support the vanguard.

He tapped the throttle, and he felt his body pushed back into his chair. "Alphas, accelerate at five gees…begin attack run."

He angled his thrust, altering his vector slightly as he followed right behind the fifth wave of missiles. He stayed close… ten klicks behind, as close as he dared. If he moved up any faster he risked getting caught in the damage radius of a detonation. But if he drifted back, he'd give the enemy more time to target his ship.

The rest of the strike force was all around him in a tight formation. But now it was time…

"Strike Force Alpha, break. All ships target and pursue individual targets."

He angled his own throttle to the right. He'd spied an enemy ship on the display. It had taken a significant hit from a missile detonation, but it wasn't a wreck either. Caravalla wasn't going to waste his single plasma torpedo on an almost-dead ship…he had laser cannons for carrion work after his first run. But now he wanted to take on an enemy vessel that had combat power remaining, one that was still a threat.

He leaned back in his chair, forcing breath into his lungs as five gees of pressure bore down on him. He did a quick calculation. The 5g thrust would put him on a vector directly toward his target in three minutes, twenty seconds. And he would reach the vessel in just under four minutes. That was cutting it close. But Caravalla had been in a fighter cockpit the better part of the past fifty years, and he wasn't afraid of a pinpoint maneuver.

He focused mostly on his own target…the strike force had its orders, and there was little he could do now to help them. But he glanced over at the wide area display anyway, taking a quick note of where his pilots were heading. The screen showed all of the fighter-bombers, with two lines extending forward from each. The first showed the current vectors and the second the courses to their projected targets. He allowed himself a brief smile. If all his birds got through and scored hits, they would obliterate the second line of enemy ships.

Whether or not we'll have any place to refuel and rearm—or even land—is another matter.

He watched as a pair of warheads detonated around his target. One was almost ten klicks out, too far to have any real effect. The second was just inside five, too far to cause major damage, but enough to blast the vessel with a heavy dose of radiation...one strong enough to interfere with its scanner array, and it's ability to target his fighter.

Perfect, he thought, feeling the excitement he usually did as he approached a target. There was a touch of the predator in every good fighter pilot, and he was no exception.

He pushed on the throttle, bumping the acceleration to 7g. It was damned uncomfortable, but the sooner he could reach his target, the more cover he'd have from the radiation...and the less chance the enemy vessel would manage to target his fighter before he fired.

The enemy ship was growing, almost filling the screen. The range was displayed just below, the numbers moving quickly as his fighter raced toward its target.

Fifty-thousand kilometers. Well within range...but not close enough to ensure a hit.

The scanners were feeding him stats on the enemy's activities. Their point defense had been completely offline right after the nuclear blast, but now it was coming back. He could pick up defensive missiles firing. Some were clearly targeted at the warheads of the sixth wave, but at least two were clearly aimed at him. His ship was moving at over two thousand kilometers per second, and at that speed even maximum thrust would take a long time to appreciably alter his vector. It was one of the realities of space combat that seemed illogical to those who spent their lives in the atmosphere and gravity of a habitable planet. In space, slower-moving vessels were harder to target, because their thrust could more quickly alter the vector of their movement. A ship moving at high speed was predictable, because its thrust could only slowly alter its trajectory.

He put the missiles out of his mind. They would either detonate close enough to destroy his fighter or they wouldn't. There was nothing he could do, certainly not without giving up on the target. And that wasn't going to happen...

Twenty thousand meters.

His eyes dropped to the status screens on the panel in front of him. The torpedo was armed and ready, the bay doors open. One small tap on the firing stud, and it would be on its way.

Ten thousand meters. Close range by any measure.

But not close enough...

Eight thousand. The enemy ship filled his display. He could see darker areas on the image, locations were the hull was breached, where atmosphere and fluids were escaping.

Hold on...wait...

Six thousand.

Now!

His finger squeezed hard, and he felt the fighter shake as the torpedo launched.

He fought the urge to watch the weapon go in, to confirm that he had scored a hit...he was three seconds out, on a direct collision course for the enemy ship, and he didn't have time. His hands moved rapidly, moving the throttle as if by instinct alone. He pushed forward, increasing the thrust to 9g. He felt the pain, the pressure of nine times his normal weight slamming into him. He held his breath, knowing if he exhaled he'd never manage to force another gulpful of air into his lungs.

He knew only seconds were passing, but each one drew out like an eternity. A few seconds of thrust wouldn't change his vector much, barely a few thousandths of a degree. But he didn't need much of a heading change...just enough to clear the eight hundred meters of the enemy ship.

He could see the icon of the vessel moving across the display, slipping off to the side as his fighter's trajectory was altered slowly...and an instant later the image disappeared from his forward view as his craft whipped by barely a thousand meters away.

He cut the thrust at once, feeling the relief of free fall, sucking air greedily into his lungs. He'd found the effects of high gee
forces harder to endure as he had aged, but that wasn't a consid-
eration, not in the heat of battle. But now, his attack run complete, he felt the effects, and he fought off a wave of dizziness.

It took him a few seconds to regain his focus, but when he
did, he could see the effects of his attack on the scanning display. There was no enemy ship at all, just the residual fury of a
massive fusion blast, mostly likely the result of lost containment
in the vessel's reactor.

Scratch one bogie, he thought, a wave of exhilaration sweeping
over him. Fifty years of warfare, and he had never tired of the
feeling of the kill. That vessel could have bombarded the Nest,
killed his comrades. But he had destroyed it, and it would do
no more harm.

He gave himself a few seconds of private celebration, then
he grasped the throttle again. He hated the idea of more high
thrust maneuvering, but he had to bring his ship around...his
laser cannons were fully charged, and there were enemy ships
remaining to be destroyed...

*   *   *   *   *

Cranston watched on the display as the surface above the
Nest was blasted by one massive explosion after another. The
five hundred megaton warheads were ravaging the frigid surface,
vaporizing the nitrogen snow covering the ground and gouging
huge craters that filled instantly with molten stone. The heat
didn't last long, the lack of an atmosphere hastening its dissipa-
tion. But wherever the deadly weapons impacted, anything built
by man was swept away. Silos, laser turrets, scanning arrays...all
were destroyed as missile after missile slammed into the moon
the Eagles called home.

He had ordered all installations to maintain fire. The remaining missile silos continued to launch, and the functioning laser

arrays kept up their defensive fire. But with each hit, the Nest's firepower declined. Every laser turret obliterated by the fury of a thermonuclear blast, every missile silo buried under tons of caved in rock, reduced the Eagles' firepower. Cranston knew his people were the best...but he also knew war was ultimately about mathematics. You could be ten times better than your enemy, but if they outnumbered you twenty to one, you were fucked.

The enemy fleet had been ravaged, not a ship remaining from those in its first line. But the second line had moved up into position. More than half of those vessels were gone too, mostly at the hands of Caravalla and his pilots, but now a third line had formed up and was advancing. And ships were still coming through the warp gate. Cranston was too old a veteran to try and fool himself. The Eagles weren't going to win this fight.

This isn't a normal enemy. Any of the colonial forces—and even the other merc companies—would have broken off after suffering losses like this. But they are still coming.

His people were outnumbered, and if they couldn't break the enemy's morale, they'd eventually be overwhelmed. He stared at the damage reports scrolling down his display. Two of the landing bays had been destroyed, along with half the surface docks for the big ships. When Darius Cain returned, much of the Eagle fleet would be unable to land. But Caravalla's fighters were a worse problem. There was only one bay still functional, and if that one went, the strike forces would have no place to land. They'd be trapped in space, unarmed and low on fuel. And that meant they would die. All of them.

Cranston felt a wave of frustration move through him. He was a man of action, accustomed to meeting an enemy head on, not sitting five klicks below ground waiting helplessly. But there was nothing for him to do. He couldn't move his garrison forces to the surface, not in the middle of a nuclear bombardment. So all he could do was sit and watch...and wait until his remaining weapons were picked off one by one.

He turned and looked over at Anders. "Captain, I think it's

time to dispatch the Flare."

Anders nodded. "Yes, sir. I agree." Anders turned toward his workstation, turning a lever and opening a small cover over a large red button. He glanced back to Cranston, and at his superior's nod, he pressed it.

The Flare was a small ship located a million kilometers from the Nest, a two person vehicle that was constantly manned and positioned when the Eagle fleet was out on an operation. Duty on the Flare was commonly dreaded, for its boredom rather than its danger. Its crew generally did a 72 hour shift before being relieved by shuttle. While aboard, they endured the dim lighting and minimal life support of a vessel operating on low power. It had two purposes: to remain as undetectable as possible and to make a run for one of the warp gates if the Nest was threatened…and to find its way to the main force, to alert Darius Cain and the rest of the Eagles that their home was under attack.

"Flare alerted, sir. She is activating thrusters, and heading for the Omicron-5 warp gate."

Cranston nodded and sighed. The Flare was the fastest thing in the Eagles had, and she was heading almost directly away from the enemy fleet. And that meant she would easily get away. How long it would take to reach Darius Cain, and what the general would be able to do, remained to be seen. But Cranston realized, as he watched another half-dozen warheads slam into the surface, that he had only one purpose…to dig in underground, to hold onto the Nest at all costs.

"Evacuate all surface personnel," he said grimly. "We're closing the vault in five minutes." The most recent wave of warheads had obliterated the last of the landing bays. He felt a pain in his gut, a wave of guilt at abandoning Caravalla's fighters. But he knew those crews were as good as dead without a place to land. And if he didn't close the vault he risked radiation penetrating to the main facility. Once the last of his surface weapons were destroyed, nothing would stop the enemy from carpet bombing the surface. The Nest's underground facilities were deep, located there for the express purpose of resisting such an attack. But if he intended to hold out, he knew he had to go by the book, whatever the consequences. And that meant closing off all access to the surface...and giving up on Caravalla and his squadrons.

Chapter 28

Below the Citadel
Eldaron City
Planet Eldaron, Denebola IV
Earthdate: 2319 AD (34 Years After the Fall)

"Team Three, bogies coming down the left corridor toward your flank."

"Roger that, Team Five. We've got the approach covered."

"Team Five, we've got your left flank. Four bogies here, all down."

"Team Four, Captain Alcabedo here. We want prisoners, don't forget that."

"Yes sir, Captain. This group put up a fight. We had to take 'em down. But Hemmes and Ferrus are checking for survivors."

"Check, Team Four. Carry on."

Darius Cain stood in the dimly lit corridor, listening to the chatter of his forward teams. He couldn't help but smile at the way they worked together so coolly under fire, snapping warnings and status reports back and forth. That was years of training and experience at work, and he felt a flush of pride at how well his finely tuned machine functioned in action.

His troops had found three more access points from the sewer, but they all seemed to lead to the same main corridor. From the looks of things, this section of the Citadel was more or less abandoned. They'd found a few storerooms full of weapons and other supplies, but the crates were old, covered with years of dust.

Finally, his people ran into an enemy patrol. At first he feared the incursion had been detected, and that a defensive force had been sent to engage his people. But there weren't enough of the enemy for that, and he decided the Eldari were actually searching these old warehouses for weapons that had survived the EMP blasts.

That strike succeeded on a level I couldn't have imagined. How can a planet's whole army be so utterly unprepared for the threats they might face?

He knew the answer to his own question. He'd seen it again and again, even among the forces of the governments who'd hired his Eagles…and the less fortunate ones who'd faced them on the field. Their armies were continually plagued by problems with materiel—shortages and quality issues that resulted not from a lack of funding or technology, but from pure graft. Behind each substandard batch of supplies, he suspected, stood a well-connected magnate, and a pack of corrupt politicians, profiting immensely by supplying inferior goods and pocketing the difference.

That was something that simply couldn't happen with the Eagles. It was anathema to their culture…and there could be little doubt about the punishment Darius Cain would have pronounced on a supply officer who put his comrades at risk through his corruption.

He could hear the distant shots as his forward pickets took out the outmatched and outnumbered Eldari. The Eagles were quick and efficient, and the fight lasted perhaps half a minute. Still, Darius realized, that was plenty of time for the enemy to get a warning out. And even if they'd failed to do so, the disappearance of the patrol would be noticed. His people had gotten as far as they were going to get undetected, and that meant they could expect to fight their way forward the rest of the way.

"Any prisoners?" Darius spoke calmly, professionally. He understood the difficultly of taking captives during a fight like this. Accepting surrenders was one thing, but holding back from killing an enemy who was still fighting was dangerous...and Darius had taught his Eagles to survive their battles, mostly by avoiding foolish chances.

"Looks like two, General." Alcabedo snapped back an answer almost immediately. Darius knew the veteran was mostly concerned with his role as bodyguard, but he had to admit, Alcabedo made a first class aide as well. "One's pretty bad... they're questioning him now, but I don't know if he's going to last long. The other's on the way back now."

Darius hadn't even responded yet when he saw the small cluster of armored figures ahead of him move aside. Two Eagles were walking down the corridor, pushing a dazed, but only lightly wounded, man ahead of them.

"A prisoner, General. One of the Eldari soldiers."

The Eagle had his name stenciled on the outside of his armor, but Darius knew his people well, and he recognized the voice before he even looked. "Thank you, Sergeant Darrow," he said. "This place reminds me of the underground city on Baragon II," he added, instinctively dropping the type of morale-building comment that showed he remembered that Darrow had gotten a medal, and his sergeant's stripes, on that campaign.

Darius had to admit to himself that his legendary familiarity with his men, the almost eidetic ability he had to recall the names and deeds of the soldiers under his command, had failed to keep up with the growth of the Eagles' organization, and he'd come to rely on clandestine reminders from his AI at times. Including the fleet personnel, logistical corps, and Nest staff and garrison, the 6,500 strong ground force the Eagles deployed was part of an overall organization of nearly 18,000 men and women, including some of the most highly-trained specialists in Occupied Space...more than even than his legendary father could have kept track of individually.

"Yes, sir," the veteran non-com replied. "It's a lot like those tunnels. Though the Baragonese put up more of a fight than these Eldari."

"We're just getting started here, Sergeant. I want you to stay sharp. I think we're going to see some of the worst fighting of our careers before we leave…and the only way we're going to get through it is if I can count on the absolute best from my old veterans. Eagles like you, Greg." He'd remembered Darrow's first name, but he wasn't above a secret assist from his AI when he couldn't recall a similar bit of info.

He turned and looked toward the prisoner. The man was bleeding from a wound on his arm, but otherwise he seemed fine. He was scared to death—that was no surprise—but otherwise in pretty good shape.

"I am General Darius Cain." He towered over the unarmored captive, well over two meters tall in his fighting suit. "What is your name?"

The prisoner shied away. He was breathing heavily, but otherwise silent.

Darius popped his helmet, and it retracted behind his head. It was a breach of normal procedure, of course. He'd designed the Eagle protocols to protect his soldiers, and casually opening a helmet could expose an Eagle to gas, radiation…an almost endless lists of hazards on the modern battlefield. But Darius figured the situation was low risk—though the instant the helmet came down he could smell the residue from the sewers that was caked all over the legs. Not deadly, but not pleasant either.

But he wanted to look the prisoner in the eyes, to try to get to him with a combination of intimidation and empathy. He knew he could get information out of any captive, with enough time and lack of moral restraint on his methods. But the quicker he managed to scrape up some decent intel, the better chance he had of getting to his father—if he was even on Eldaron at all—before the Tyrant felt threatened enough to order the prisoner killed. And Darius knew making himself seem more human—and less like a terrifying armored killing machine—could only help him reach this soldier.

"C'mon boy, just tell me your name. I don't want to hurt you." *I don't want to, but I will if you make me…*

As he took a closer look, he could see the Eldari soldier was young…very young. He had to be at least somewhat connected to get himself assigned to duty in the Citadel…but Darius knew anyone with real contacts would be an officer, not a private sent down to fetch old weapons.

Probably the son of a long-service non-com or something like that. No real power, but enough to get him a cushy position in the fortress garrison. Just the kind of person who probably knows his way around in here...

"My name is Camus. Henri Camus." The voice was pinched, shaky. Darius didn't hold that against the kid...there were few people in Occupied Space who could stare up at a force of armored Black Eagles and maintain their calm.

"Okay, Henri...listen to me. You know who we are, right?"

The Eldari soldier nodded gently, as he struggled to maintain Darius' gaze.

"No doubt you have heard many things about me...about all of my people. Some are true, many false...others perhaps exaggerated. The truth is actually quite simple. We are here for a reason, and we complete our missions, whatever it takes. We need your cooperation. You can give it willingly or you can resist, delay us. But that will not stop us...and it will only make this entire affair vastly more unpleasant for you than it needs to be." He paused, allowing the ominous nature of his last sentence to hang in the air.

The Eldari private was losing the battle to retain his composure. His eyes slipped from Darius', dropping to the floor, and his body began to shake.

"There is no need for fear, Henri...not if you cooperate with us. I do not require much of you, only that you lead us to the detention area of the Citadel. There is a prisoner, one who has been captive here for a long time. I am here for him...and when I find him, we will release you, allow you to return to your compatriots."

Camus looked up, forced himself to meet Darius' stare again. He was shaking a bit, but he managed to maintain his gaze. "You will release me?" he said, his voice weak, his tone skeptical.

"Henri," Darius said, his voice as gentle as he could manage, "there is one thing I suspect you haven't heard about me, though it is something that is absolutely true. I have never gone back on a promise; the Eagles have never reneged on a contract. I do not give my word often, but when I do, I keep it." He stared at the captive with a withering intensity. "And you have my word, Henri Camus, if you lead us to the detention area, help us find the prisoner we seek, and do this without treachery, without betraying us to the guards and security forces…then you will be released unharmed."

Darius paused, maintaining the hard stare. Then he added, softly, almost incidentally, "And if you do not…" He let his voice trail off to nothing. Some things were better left to the imagination.

The prisoner stared back for a few seconds, his eyes wide with terror. Darius knew that the Tyrant's servants lived in constant fear of their brutal master. On some level, perhaps, he even sympathized with the poor devil. But that wasn't going to interfere with what he did. He was here to see if his father was the Tyrant's prisoner, and nothing—not enemy soldiers, not devious traps…not even pity for a pathetic common soldier caught in the middle—was going to interfere.

He glared at the Eldari, wordlessly communicating his impatience. A few seconds later, he snapped his wrist, extending the dreaded blade from his armor. "Do you know what a molecular blade is?" he said, his voice becoming darker, more sinister. "It is a knife honed to the width of a few molecules, almost unimaginably sharp. With the strength amplification of powered armor, a blade can slice through a steel girder. For a soft target, human flesh say, the strength of a fighting suit is hardly needed. The weight of the blade itself is more than sufficient to slice a man in half." A pause. "Shall I prove it?"

"No!" the whimpering Eldari screamed, dropping to the floor, unable to make himself look at Darius. "Please…no…"

"Then show us to the detention area!" Darius' voice was frigid, commanding. His words echoed off the walls and ceiling of the tunnel with a force that took even his veteran soldiers by surprise. "You are out of time," he continued, his tone moderating slightly. "It is time to make your choice…"

Jordyn Calfort stared at the display projected inside her visor, sighing softly as she read the casualty figures scrolling by. The battle had been a cakewalk for the first half-day, nothing but advancing after a retreating enemy, one that had been inferior to begin with and had been crippled by the Eagles' stunningly successful cyber and EMT attacks. But eventually the enemy mounted a significant defensive effort. The Eagles had landed close to the Eldari capital, and they'd immediately began driving toward the planet's largest city…and the Citadel that rose above it all like a physical representation of the Tyrant's power. And that compelled the Eldari to choose a place, and try to stand their ground.

The enemy had occupied a long ridge, not enormously high, but enough of a defensive feature to offer them cover…and a perfect field of fire over the two klicks of open ground lying before it. Normally, the Eagles would have put a screening force opposite the ridge and probed around the enemy's flanks, looking for a weak spot to assault. But there hadn't been time. The enemy was still suffering from degraded combat effectiveness, and every hour the Eagles let up, their enemies would have more time to reorganize and to replace fried equipment with new gear. But that wasn't their only reason to attack immediately. General Cain was behind enemy lines, most likely in the bowels of that massive fortress. And the longer it took the main army to break through, the longer he'd be stuck there, surrounded by enemies with only a small force. And there was no way Calfort—or Captain Tonn or Colonel Teller or any other Black Eagle—was going to waste time on wide flanking maneuvers. Not when the boss was in danger.

Her platoon had been part of the attack across the open plain. Two full companies had jumped off, racing across the blackened grasslands as quickly as the powered servos of their armor could carry them. It was difficult to run in powered armor without bounding high into the air—and making yourself a juicy target—but the Eagles were the best-trained force in Occupied Space. Calfort had waddled across the field, just as she'd been taught, sliding her body from side to side to keep herself low, maintaining fire the entire time to keep the enemy suppressed while her people raced toward the defensive line.

Casualties had been light, at least by the standards of the situation. An enemy attacking the Eagles across that ground would lose at least half their number...and they might be wiped out entirely. But Calfort's platoon had only four down, and only one of those was KIA. It was as good a result as she could have hoped for, but it still hurt to lose any of her people.

The enemy had looked like they might put up a serious fight, but the reputation of the Eagles had been too much for them in the end. They broke and ran before her people reached the crest, and they'd suffered terribly as the attackers took position along the ridge and gunned them down as they fled.

Her people had stopped to reorder along the top of the ridge, but she expected the order to pursue any moment, and her platoon was ready. When the orders came, however, they weren't what she expected.

"Lieutenant Calfort, prepare to return to your original position." It was Captain Tonn, and the instant Calfort heard he voice she knew something was wrong.

"But sir, we just took this..."

"Follow my orders, Lieutenant." A brief pause. "There's trouble along the flank of the army...some kind of armored vehicles attacking. The whole regiment is falling back."

"Yes, Captain. Acknowledged." Calfort felt a strange feeling in her stomach. They all knew there was some kind of trap waiting for them on Eldaron...but tanks? Armored units had fought in the Superpowers' last war on Earth, just before the Fall, but no colony world had ever fielded them in significant numbers. They were simply too costly, and the logistical problems and expense of transporting them through space were enormous.

What the hell is coming at us?

*   *   *   *   *

"We can't contact the general, Colonel. It's your call, sir." Antonia Camerici was one of Darius Cain's closest aides. She'd practically begged to accompany him on his mission into the enemy fortress, but he'd ordered her to stay with Colonel Teller. She'd been upset at first, afraid Darius had been concerned she couldn't keep up with the Special Action Teams, that her diminutive stature relegated her to staff work.

But Darius had just looked at her calmly and told her flat out he needed her at headquarters…that he had hundreds, no thousands of great warriors, but no one who could replace her organizational wizardry in the chain of command. Then he told her Teller needed her even more than he did, and he asked her to do everything she could to help him run the Eagles until he got back.

She still smiled recalling the encounter. She knew she was being worked…there were few people who knew how to handle soldiers as well as Darius Cain. But she realized there was truth to what he had said. This was likely to be a very difficult and dangerous campaign…and everything had to run as smoothly as possible. And she knew damned well it was nothing but the truth when he spoke of her administrative skills.

"Bring down the Blacks," Teller said, the disgust in his voice making it clear he wasn't happy with the decision.

"Yes, sir. Sending order now. Colonel Falstaff's people are preparing to launch. Here is the preliminary landing pattern, sir." Camerici had already organized the deployment orders, and now she handed her 'pad to Teller so he could approve or change them. She'd cut it close, bringing the Black Regiment down just behind the current lines. That meant the troopers facing the armored attack would have to hold…or they would lose the LZs. It was a risk, a big one, but then they both knew those were Black Eagles in the lines.

"Cutting it a little close, aren't we, Captain?" Camerici had an odd look on her face. She still hadn't gotten used to hearing her new rank in use. She'd been a lieutenant the last time the

Eagles suited up, and it was her performance on that op as much as anything that had gotten her the promotion. "The Blues are getting slammed pretty hard over there, and it will be…what, an hour?…before Colonel Falstaff's lead elements are down?" Evander Falstaff commanded the Eagles' senior regiment, 1800 of the most grizzled veteran on the Eagles' roster.

"Forty-nine minutes, sir." A pause. "From the moment you give the order."

Teller forced a brief smile. "Very well, Captain. I am giving the order."

Camerici was cool under pressure, and she calmly relayed the command to *Eagle One*. In less than an hour, fresh troops would be landing right behind the existing lines…as long as those lines held. She knew they were gambling…if the Black Regiment came down on enemy-occupied ground it would be a disaster, but she didn't allow her doubts to interfere with her judgment.

Camerici was young to be an Eagles captain, and fairly inexperienced, at least by the standards of Darius Cain's famous mercenary company. Most of the Eagles' officers were veterans of other military services, but she had been a civilian the day she had walked into the recruiting station, to the snickers of several of her larger, stronger classmates. By the time the notoriously brutal Eagles training program was over, however, Camerici was graduating with honors…and her detractors had long since washed out. She was still the only one from her class to be commissioned an officer.

She set down her 'pad and looked at the large display unit set up at one end of the makeshift headquarters. The long lines representing troop positions were moving…mostly back as the Eagles shifted to deal with the new threat. Her eyes focused on the flank section, to the two lines that marked the position of the battalion facing off against the tanks.

"Hang on you guys…hang on. Help is on the way."

And if you don't hold on, the Black Regiment is going to come down into a world of hurt.

"Let's go! The Blues are catching hell up there, so move your asses. First battalion, we're going straight in. Second battalion around the right flank." Evander Falstaff stood just outside the hatch of the lander shouting into his com. His external speakers relayed the chaos outside his armor, the heavy blasts of the enemy tanks and the higher-pitched sound of the Eagles' assault rifles. He could tell immediately the fighting was intense.

Only half his people were out of their ships yet, but there was no time to lose. Ian Vandeveer's Blue Regiment had hung on, stopping the onslaught of the enemy tanks and grimly holding the LZ, but they had paid for it in blood. Now it was the Black Regiment's turn, and Falstaff would be damned if he was going to give his people time to hang around and scratch their asses while their comrades were fighting and dying on the line. Ideally, he'd have all his people formed up before he engaged...

But then when did 'ideally' ever fit into war?

"All platoons move forward as soon as you're formed up. We'll get the larger units organized later."

It wasn't optimal to send his people in piecemeal, but right now time was more crucial than perfect order. His people had to take the pressure off the Blues...and break up the enemy attack before it sliced through into the rear of the Eagles' position.

Tanks...Falstaff had never faced off against a large force of them, but he had some idea of the doctrine involved. These were monsters by all accounts, behemoths on the scale of the old MBTs the Superpowers had fielded on Earth. They were bristling with weapons and heavily-armored, difficult to damage...even for the Eagles in their cutting edge fighting suits. But Darius Cain's legendary paranoia had come through once again, and the arsenal the fleet carried included a wide array of supplemental weapons, ordnance designed for a variety of eventualities that might occur on the battlefield. Including hypervelocity rockets capable of destroying even the heaviest main battle tanks.

Falstaff's first thought was to concentrate the weapons, create several powerful spearheads to attack through the enemy formation. But he didn't have enough ordnance for that, so he handed them out two to a platoon...and he sent those platoons forward as soon as they were ready. The fight would be slower, dirtier—and bloodier—but there was no choice. Those tanks had to go...whatever it took.

*   *   *   *   *

"Fucking hell, look at that monster." Jan Kelly peered out from the hastily-dug trench, watching the tank approach. It was more than six meters long and its armored hull was covered with weapons. She had her whole platoon dug in, and she'd ordered them all to stay down. She had seen just what the autocannons on the massive vehicles could do even to fully-armored troops. Calvett's platoon had been caught in the open and shot to pieces, barely one in three surviving to get back to cover. She didn't intend to let the same thing happen to her unit.

"Alright Sergeant...let's get that thing deployed." Emilio Versagio was her platoon sergeant and one of the best in the regiment. Versagio had been an Eagle even longer than she had, but he was happy with his stripes and his position closer to the fighting men and women and content to leave officer training to more ambitious types. Like Jan Kelly.

"Setting up now, Lieutenant." Versagio's voice was gritty, determined. But he was frustrated too. The HVRs were tricky weapons to deploy, and few of the Eagles had more than basic training with them. Even an elite fighting corps couldn't prepare equally for all eventualities...and tanks had not seemed a likely problem in the Eagles' battles against a bunch of fledgling colonies that had been cast onto their own resources since the Fall.

Kelly looked back out at the tank. It was heading straight at the trench...and it was getting closer. "Hurry it up, Sarge... and move to the right. See if you can get a shot at that thing's flank as it closes in." The HVRs were enormously powerful weapons, with their own nuclear power supplies and a heavy frame designed to absorb the enormous kick of launching a heavy rocket at over four thousand meters per second. Even a fully-armored Eagle would find himself slammed back hard by the kick from an unbraced HVR. Still, even for all the weapon's hitting power, the chances of scoring an outright kill tripled if the shot was aimed at the flank of the vehicle instead of the more heavily armored front.

"Yes, Lieutenant," Versagio snapped back. Then: "Quince, Barnes...get your asses over here and help me move this thing."

Kelly dove down below the berm as the tank opened up, the heavy autocannon rounds tearing into the dirt and rocks along the lip of the trench. Her eyes darted up instinctively toward her display, checking the casualty reports. She felt a rush of relief. No casualties. *That won't last...*

She shuffled down the makeshift trench, reaching out to stabilize herself as she stepped over the broken, flooded ground. She could see Versagio about twenty meters ahead of her, struggling to balance the heavy weapon on his shoulder. It was at least a two-man weapon by any reasonable standard—and three by the book—but the platoon sergeant was managing fairly well by himself, at least until the two troopers he called staggered up through the muck and grabbed onto the launcher's front and back.

Kelly stopped for a few seconds and glanced again at her display. Her second team was already in place about sixty meters behind. Sergeant Mimms had set up on the other side of a small rise. His people had the launcher in place, but their section of line was quiet, and Kelly wondered if she should redeploy them. *No,* she thought...*it won't stay quiet. The enemy wants to get all they can from the surprise of these tanks, and that means we're going to get hit all along the line...*

She moved forward again, crouching down below the lip of the trench, the nuclear-powered servos of her armor pushing through the knee-deep mud. It was an uncomfortable way to move, but she had to stay in cover. Even the osmium-iridium alloy of her powered armor was too weak to stop the heavy autocannon rounds slamming into the piled up dirt and rocks in front of the trench.

She looked ahead, tapping the button near her left index finger to bump up the magnification of her visor. The image tightened on Versagio and his two troopers, blurring a little at first then sharpening again as her AI compensated. The launcher was almost ready.

She pushed forward another few meters then stopped to check her recon. She didn't dare lift her head and take a look, but the company had four drones in the air, circling the battlefield. She tapped into the closest one, getting a look at the tank approaching her platoon from a different angle, almost directly on the opposite side. There were more vehicles moving forward too. Three were heading toward Mimms' position, verifying her gut feel that her people would face attack all along the line. Another three were rumbling forward about a thousand meters behind the lead tank, now less than a klick from her trench line.

She shuffled the rest of the way toward Versagio's position, stopping a few meters from the platoon sergeant. She was silent for a few seconds, letting her number two finish prepping the weapon. Then she said, "Better make this shot good, Emilio. We've got three more of these monsters coming up behind. And another three approaching Mimms' position on the other side of the hill."

"That doesn't give us much room for error," the grizzled sergeant replied. There was no panic in his voice, nothing but the grim tone of a veteran who knew what the battlefield demanded of him.

"No, not much." *None*, she thought to herself. *Less than none. There's no way we can take out seven of these things…not before they run over us…*

Versagio didn't answer. He was hunched over the targeting mechanism. The tank was heading toward the launcher's previous position, hosing down that section of trench with fire. But the weapon wasn't there anymore…and in another hundred meters it would give the waiting sergeant a clean shot at its flank.

Kelly watched silently, understanding exactly what was happening. She knew they'd have to move again after this shot... the enemy would know there was a HVR here as soon as they fired. And if three or four MBTs opened up with such pin-point targeting, not even the trench would be enough to save her people.

C'mon, Emilio...c'mon...

She knew her sergeant was one of the best. But even he had only used the HVRs in training, and not much even then. But there was no one else she'd have rather had at that targeting scope, herself included.

Versagio stood still, crouched below the edge of the trench, his helmet close to the targeting screen. He waited...waited...

Shooooom...

Kelly could hear the missile firing, the strange sound the electronic catapult made as it accelerated the projectile almost immediately to eight times the speed of sound. There had been no way to adequately secure the launcher itself along the edge of the trench, and it was pushed back hard, twisting a few degrees and slamming into the back wall as its bracing failed. Versagio had positioned it as well as he could, but the slick mud just didn't provide the kind of support needed to handle the recoil of such a powerful weapon.

She jumped back instinctively, moving away from the launcher. She snapped her head back, checked to make sure none of her people had been injured. Again, they had been lucky. The heavy rocket launcher could have killed even an armored trooper if it had hit him directly enough. But it had missed them all, and it was buried halfway into the back of the trench.

Kelly heard the explosion as she was staring at the launcher, and her eyes were still moving to the display to assess the shot when Versagio's voice echoed in her helmet. "Yes!" the non-com shouted, momentarily losing his discipline and celebrating.

Her eyes finally fixed on the display, focusing on the footage from the closest drone. She saw the smoke first, a thick black column, rising slowly above the battlefield. And below it was an inferno, flames licking ten meters into the sky above the skeletal wreckage of the massive tank.

Yes, she thought, repeating Versagio's sentiment. But the excitement was short-lived. One dead tank was a good thing... but there were six more heading their way.

"Nice shooting, Emilio. But time's not our ally. Let's see if we can get that thing dug out and move our asses...before the others open up on us.

$$*\qquad*\qquad*\qquad*\qquad*$$

"Alright Eagles, let's do this. These tanks are chewing up our people on the ground, and it's time we do something about it."

Darryk nudged his throttle forward, bringing his bird down at a sharp angle. The drones were feeding him a constant stream of intel, and he could see the tanks spread all across the field, three large lines of them moving toward the Eagles' hastily-dug trenches. The first echelon of tanks had been pretty badly chewed up...Falstaff's Black Regiment was the Eagles' elite, and they were acquitting themselves with their usual distinction. But there were a lot of tanks, and it was going to be a near run thing by the time it was done...and a bloodbath no matter who won.

That's without airpower, he thought grimly. *We might have a few things to say about that...*

"Strike teams...begin final attack run. First pass, HVRs... then we come around again with autocannons." The fighter-mounted HVRs were bigger versions of the semi-portable weapons the Black Regiment was currently employing in its desperate attempt to defeat the enemy tank force, and a solid hit would obliterate even one of the giant vehicles. Autocannons presented a different equation. Enough hits with the smaller projectiles could destroy a tank, but Darryk knew his fighters would have fly much lower...and within range of the vehicles' AA arrays. His fighters had enjoyed the luxury of virtual impunity to enemy fire, but he knew he'd take losses doing close in strafing runs on the tanks. But the fighter wings were Eagles too, and he had no intention of watching the troops on the ground slaughtered so he could keep his own people safe.

He brought his fighter in straight at one of the enemy behemoths. His AI did the preliminary calculations, displaying the targeting scope on his main display. Against another aircraft, he'd have adjusted the computer's calculations, inserted the instinct a good pilot had for offsetting his opponent's evasive maneuvers. But the tanks were big lumbering vehicles, crawling across the broken plain at fifty kilometers per hour. He didn't change the plot at all...he just pressed the button to fire.

The fighter kicked hard as it loosed one of its two missiles, and Darryk looked down at the scope, watching the tiny yellow icon move closer to the tank. Suddenly, there was a small flash on the screen...and the tank was gone. Direct hit!

He moved the stick to the right, bringing himself around to target another vehicle with his second missile. He spotted a group of six moving forward. They were all identical, but there was something about the way one of them was moving, where it was positioned. It was some kind of command vehicle...he was sure of it.

He banked down and drove right toward the cluster of tanks, locking his targeting systems on the one that had caught his eye. The AI crunched its numbers and almost immediately displayed the firing solution. He tapped the throttle, slowing slightly and moving to the right to match the AI's plot. His fingers tightened over the firing stud, and with a feral grin on his face he loosed his second missile.

Another hit! Two for two!

He felt the wave of satisfaction, the feeling of a job well done. He knew on one level he'd killed other human beings, that they had probably died horribly in the twisted, burning wreckage of their tank. But those people had been trying to kill his comrades, his friends. And he knew he had probably saved the lives of some Eagles...the ones who would have died fighting those two tanks.

He glanced at the strike force display. All his people had launched their missiles. *Sixty shots at a seventy percent hit rate,* he thought to himself. *Over forty of those Godforsaken tanks gone.*

"Nice shooting...all of you," he yelled into the com. "Now let's see what we can do with our autocannons. Darryk angled his ship, bringing it into a steep dive toward the surviving tanks. He'd already spotted his first target, and he was going to go right down its throat...

His eyes snapped around to the strike display. One of his birds was gone. He was still trying to figure out what had happened when the com went crazy.

"I've got SAMs locked onto me, Major."

"Me too...I'm picking up multiple launch sites. Looks like something mobile."

"Yeah, they're on the move. They're blanketing the sky with targeting beams."

Another icon disappeared from his screen...another of his fighters gone.

He felt a wave of frustration, anguish for the crews he'd just lost.

You knew it couldn't last...sooner or later, they had to get their defense grid back online.

No...that can't be it. We blasted their anti-air emplacements to scrap...I'd bet my life on it. So what the hell is this?

He stared down at the enemy tank, feeling an almost irresistible urge to follow through, to rake it with his autocannons. But then he heard the high-pitched whine of a target lock. One of the enemy ground installations had him. If he broke off now, he had a chance...a good one. If he stayed on target, he'd have a cluster of missiles on his ass within half a minute. And he'd never shake them all.

He still hesitated, thinking about taking the risk. But then his training kicked in. Black Eagles were professionals, and they didn't throw away their lives in pointless displays. Besides, he wouldn't be making the choice just for him. He had twenty-seven other fighters with him, and they would do whatever he did.

"Break off," he said, spitting the words out like they tasted bad. "Full evasive maneuvers. Return to base."

His eyes dropped to the display, to the wave of missiles now rising from the battlefield…and he realized not all of his people were going to make it…

Chapter 29

"The Nest" – Black Eagles Base
Second Moon of Eos, Eta Cassiopeiae VII
Earthdate: 2318 AD (34 Years After the Fall)

John Cranston stared at the display. The Nest's surface scanners had been swept away by the enemy bombardment, and the control center screens were almost blank. But the seismic detectors were still feeding in data, and the AI had estimated that fifty gigatons of warheads had detonated on the surface.

That means the bays are completely gone, and all the docks too. Caravalla's people are lost...and our weapons are destroyed. At best, we stand a siege...we hold on down here, resist any enemy attempts to penetrate to the main areas. And then we wait, hoping against hope the general and the strike forces can get back in time.

"Captain, I want the garrison battalion deployed half on duty, at all times. All potential areas of forced ingress are to be fortified and defended at all times. I want regular sweeping patrols covering the entire Nest." He paused for a few seconds then added, "We've got one job now...keeping these bastards out of here."

"Yes, sir." Anders stared down at his workstation, punching at the keys to execute Cranston's orders.

"Vault door status?"

Anders glanced over at the display. "Holding, sir. Exterior temperature is rising, but still within acceptable parameters."

Cranston grunted. The vault door was a fifty meter thick fortified barrier that closed off the main access tube from the surface. It was about as strong as a door could be, but it was still a physical construction…and that meant the enemy could get through it if they tried hard enough. Even the hyper-steel of the door would vaporize if they dropped a nuke directly on top of it. And then they'd have access to the Nest.

And that will be the end of it all…

Cranston was a Black Eagle, and he had the same confidence the others had, an almost cocksure attitude about what his people could achieve. But he was a realist too. He didn't doubt his people were vastly superior to the attackers, but he also realized they were trapped, that the enemy had numbers and initiative.

Hell, they don't even have to come down and fight us…all they need to do it get through the vault door and start dropping nukes down here…

There might not even be a fight in the halls of the Nest… just an extermination. But he couldn't do anything about that. All he could do was ready his people for a fight.

"All support personnel are to arm themselves at once. Engineers, stewards, trainees…everybody. I want backup teams assigned the garrison squads immediately."

There *was* one thing he was sure of. If the enemy came down to the Nest, *every* Eagle would fight. Every damned one. But he didn't really expect the enemy to send soldiers into the teeth of desperate resistance. They had other ways to strike at the Nest.

*   *   *   *   *

Christos Caravalla stared out of the cockpit at the rich blackness of space surrounding his tiny craft. He'd been in the control seat of a fighter of one kind or another for half a century, and he understood enough to realize he had reached the end of the road. All his people had.

He could see on his display the pounding the surface of the Nest had taken. The docking stations and landing bays were gone, obliterated in a nuclear holocaust. With the ships of the Eagle fleet away at Eldaron, that meant his people had no place to land. No place to refit or rearm.

He'd ordered his squadrons to regroup on the far side of the moon, away from the enemy fleet. It was a temporary respite, but at least it gave him time to think. He didn't fool himself that he'd devise some plan that offered his people a chance at survival...but if they were going to die, he was determined they should die well, striking at the enemy any way they could. The fighters had fired all their torpedoes, but they still had some power left for their laser cannons. And enough fuel for one more good attack run. Caravalla had twenty-four fighters left, sixty percent of what he started with...and far too few to take on the enemy fleet alone with any hope of victory. But they might take out a few ships, and since the alternative was waiting to be hunted down and destroyed, any price they could extract was better than none.

"All ships, arm laser cannons. Prepare for attack run." He stared down at the schematic displayed on his screen. "We're going to swing around in a tight orbit. The tracking satellites are all down, so we don't have data on the enemy deployments, but my gut tells me we can come in on the flank of the vessels bombarding the Nest. That'll give us a chance to do some real damage be..." He cut himself off. Adding, "before we're destroyed" to his speech wasn't going to do anything to rally his battered force. They all knew they were on a suicide mission—there was no reason to dwell on it.

"Alright, Eagles...follow on my lead." He nudged the throttle, working the thrust up to 2g, and he saw that the rest of the fighters fell in behind him. He smiled as he watched, proud of the precision his battered squadrons managed to maintain.

If we're going to die, let it be with some dignity...and dishing out some hell to our enemies.

He increased the thrust gradually. Three gees. Four. He eased back slightly. He wanted to build as much velocity as he could without breaking orbit. The moon's gravity would help his fighters whip around, changing their vector as they progressed.

He knew they wouldn't have much time. The enemy ships would react immediately...especially after the price his people had extracted in the earlier fighting. So his fighters had to be coming in hard when they swung around into detection range.

He glanced down at his nav controls. Four gees was the maximum acceleration...anything higher would push his ship out of orbit. He knew it would only be another minute before his force would come around, and their last battle would begin. He'd been so focused on the specifics of the attack, he had barely considered the full implications. But now he realized in clear terms...he was leading his people to their deaths. They might take down some of the enemy's vessels, but now it came to him coldly, harshly. In a matter of minutes, perhaps half an hour, he and his people would all be dead.

Better to die in battle than wait to run out of power and life support...

But the thought was still a stark one, and he had to make an effort to get it out of his mind. It wasn't so much his own life... he'd been at war for half a century, and he'd known that any one of the hundreds of missions he'd flown could have been his last. But he mourned for his pilots and crews, the men and women he was leading to their deaths.

There's nothing you can do. They are dead already. This is about how they die...

He took a deep breath, eyes fixed on the scanner.

Almost there...

Suddenly, his screen lit up with icons, ships coming into scanning range. The AI displayed the enemy vessels with small red triangles.

"Okay, Eagles...here we go..."

His eyes dropped to the display again. More red triangles had moved into view. He was about to look away, but then he froze. There was something else, on the very edge of the screen. A row of icons, small yellow circles. He squinted, reading the designation listed next to each of them.

Unidentified vessel.

*   *   *   *   *

"I think those are burrowers, Major. I read a dozen or more, positioned all across the surface." Anders was flipping switches on his workstation, reviewing the data coming in from the few remaining scanners buried beneath the surface. "Yes," he said, "I'm sure of it. There's nothing else that could create that kind of vibration in the rock."

Cranston sat quietly in his chair, staring out over the Eagles' compact command center. He sighed softly, trying to keep the sound to himself. He couldn't understand why the enemy didn't just blast the vault door. Perhaps they lacked decent intel on the Nest, didn't know where it was. Considerable effort had been made to hide the main entrance to the Black Eagles' base.

The burrowers were a more indiscriminant weapon system, the kind of thing an enemy would deploy if they didn't understand the layout of the target. The high-yield warheads would dig into the rock of the moon's surface before detonating, gouging out great craters with each detonation. The Nest was buried deep, but the burrowers would work their way down eventually...and when they did, the Eagles base, and all the personnel in it, would be obliterated in the fury of a final thermonuclear blast.

This enemy knew what they would need to destroy us...and they knew the fleet would be away...when to strike. Who is this?

Cranston realized it didn't matter. He suspected that whatever mysterious enemy the Eagles had encountered on Lysandria and Eris was behind the attack. But he still knew almost nothing about them, other than this demonstration of just how much power they could deploy. Even if he could figure it out, he couldn't get the information out. He and his people would be dead soon.

Cranston felt the anger building inside him, the frustration. The Black Eagles were many things, but even those who hated and despised them acknowledged they were an elite corps, the best at what they did.

And now we're going to die like rats caught in a trap.

He stared at the display, trying to think of a way to strike back, to take the fight to the enemy. But there was nothing. Only the bitter taste of defeat.

*   *   *   *   *

"Who are they?" Caravalla's com had exploded. It seemed like every one of his ships had sent out a message, reporting the mysterious vessels on the scanner, or asking who they were.

I have no idea who they are. More enemies? Friends?

He stared at the display, but the AI had not updated the labels. That meant there was still no positive ID. But that changed almost immediately.

"Attention Black Eagles." The deep voice blasted from his com. "Attention Black Eagles, this is Jarrod Tyler in command of the Columbian fleet. We are here to assist you in your struggle against these invaders."

Jarrod Tyler? Caravalla knew Columbia's dictator and General Cain had a relationship of sorts, but he was surprised Tyler would come so quickly and forcefully to the Eagles' aid. Still, now that he thought about it, the intervention made sense. Tyler was a highly suspicious man, far more apt to see threats where none existed than to ignore ones that were real. And Columbia and the Eagles did share the Eta Cassiopeiae system. A huge fleet of warships coming through one of the warp gates was sure to arouse Tyler's concern.

He felt a wave of excitement as the realization set in. The battle wasn't over yet. Far from it. Indeed, Tyler's forces were about to move into combat range...and the enemy vessels were spread out, deployed to bombard the Nest, not face an attacking fleet.

He hit the button to activate his com. "General Tyler, this is Captain Caravalla, strike force commander for the Nest. My fighter squadrons are deployed, but the rest of the Nest's surface weapons have been knocked out. The enemy is bombarding the surface, attempting to reach and destroy the main facility."

"Very well, Captain. We'll put a stop to that soon enough. My forces will be engaged in less than a minute. Then we'll show whoever this is what happens when outsiders invade Eta Cassiopeiae." Tyler's voice was firm, grim. There was a coldness there, one almost devoid of emotion. Tyler had no bloodlust, not even any evident anger against the invaders. But Caravalla knew without a doubt that wouldn't stop him from exterminating every one of them if he could.

"Your aid is most welcome, Mr. President. On behalf of the Black Eagles, please allow me to thank you...and to wish your forces good fortune in battle."

Caravalla switched his com back to the strike force's frequency. "Alright, things have changed just a bit. Now, we're supporting the Columbians, so break formation and go pick your targets. It's time to send these bastards to hell."

Chapter 30

Below the Citadel
Eldaron City
Planet Eldaron, Denebola IV
Earthdate: 2319 AD (34 Years After the Fall)

"There's an entrance to the detention area just ahead." The Eldari captive's voice was weak, his fear coming through with every word. But he seemed to have accepted that his best chance of survival was to cooperate with the Black Eagles. He was scared of the Tyrant, certainly, but he was no less afraid of Darius Cain. And Cain and his people were a lot closer.

Darius stared at the prisoner, his gaze alone reducing the Eldari to a near state of panic. "Where is the cell, Henri?" Darius' voice was cold, ominous. "He has been here a very long time. I know you know who I am speaking of, and if you don't tell me what I want to know…" He let his voice trail off. Nothing he could have said would match the horrors he suspected his captive's mind would produce.

"It is a special cell, at the very end of the main hall."

Darius nodded. Then he toggled the unitwide com. "Alright, Eagles. We're going in…and we can damned sure expect some serious trouble. We know this is a trap, that we were lured here. Whether or not Erik Cain is in the detention area, the enemy knows that is where we are going. We have been fortunate not to have run into more resistance so far, but we can be sure that respite is at an end."

Darius could feel his heart pounding. He was consumed by emotions...the tension before battle, and anticipation of seeing his father after so many years. His prisoner's confirmation that there was indeed a special prisoner who had been held for many years beneath the Citadel was a cause for encouragement. Perhaps Erik Cain *was* alive. It was hard to imagine in any terms that felt real. Darius had lost his father when he was seventeen...before he'd left Atlantia, before he'd become a mercenary, before the Eagles. Everything that had happened since, the years that seemed now like most of his life...it had all existed in a reality where Erik Cain was dead.

Despite the captive's words though, Darius knew the mission could still end in disappointment, in finding it was all a hoax, that Erik Cain was indeed dead. And he already felt the guilt for leading his people into an ambush, into a fight he almost certainly knew would be a bloodbath. If it proved to have been for nothing...he couldn't imagine the pain of so many of his loyal soldiers killed for no purpose.

There were positive feelings too, though, beyond just hopes that his father was alive. Satisfaction that he had come this far, certainly. And pride in his warriors, and in the loyalty they had shown him. The Black Eagles were mercenaries, they fought for pay. But to a man they rallied to their leader, agreeing—no, demanding—to follow him to Eldaron, whatever the danger. He'd always been dedicated to his Eagles, but now he truly realized how special a group of misfits he had assembled.

Darius stepped forward, moving toward the front of the two hundred armored men and women crowding the passageway. He was pushing the prisoner before him, and Alcabedo was close on his heels.

"General...I think you should stay in the center of the formation." There was obvious concern in his voice.

"Yes, Ernesto, I know you do. And I want you to know I appreciate your efforts." He paused. "But there are some things a man must do, some times he must lead."

"Yes, General, but..." Alcabedo's voice trailed off.

"Don't worry, Ernesto. I've been in battle before." Darius took a deep breath. "Alright, Eagles, the enemy has to know we're here, and the fact that we've seen so little resistance suggests they're waiting for us somewhere...probably behind this door. So I want everybody ready for a fight."

He motioned toward the two men standing by the hatch holding an explosive charge. "As soon as the door blows, we go in...and we take the entire detention area. And remember, you are all Black Eagles...so whatever is waiting in there, you will know what to do. And God help whoever stands in our way."

He stepped back and nodded. The two men at the door affixed the charge and walked back. They crouched down and one of them looked toward Darius.

Here we come, father.

He turned toward the soldier and nodded again. An instant later, the door was blown apart...and the Black Eagles surged forward with a terrifying fury.

*   *   *   *   *

"Fuck." Jan Kelly looked out over the field. There were burning tanks everywhere, the thick black smoke rising in a hundred columns above the broken ground. The fighter strike had been devastating, and the enemy armored vehicles had been stopped in their tracks, ravaged by the constant attack runs. But the fighters were gone now, the ones that escaped at least, and it was up to her people to finish off the surviving tanks. Major Darryk's fighter-bombers had broken the back of the enemy force, but Kelly knew her people would have to hunt down the survivors and destroy them one by one. She didn't doubt they could do it, but she knew it would cost.

She was still looking up at the darkening sky, the heavy clouds of black smoke obscuring the otherwise bright sunshine of midday. Darryk's people were out of sight already. Indeed, they were off her scanner. She still looked up after them, grateful for the intervention that had restored her line, but sorry for the unexpected blast of AA fire that had taken down a number of them before Darryk managed to pull them out. Kelly had no idea where all that AA had come from so suddenly, but she had no doubt what it meant. The Eagles had lost their air support. No group of fighters, not even the state of the art machines the talented Eagle pilots flew, could go up against heavy ground-based AA. At least not for close support. And that's what her people needed.

"Alright platoon, listen up." *She finally forced herself to look down from the sky. The fighters are gone, and they're not coming back. Not unless you take out all that AA.* "Those hotshot pilots took out a ton of tanks, but now it's our turn. We're moving out in three minutes...search and destroy all across the field. The job's simple. Find tanks...and blow them to hell."

She'd gotten the orders a few minutes earlier. The entire battalion was moving forward to hit the rear echelon of the enemy tank force...before it could pull back and redeploy. Taking it out was going to cost, probably heavily. But she knew it was better than letting them reorganize and pick another point of attack. As long as they were out there somewhere, they were a threat. Better to destroy them now. Eagle officers didn't like to see their people killed and wounded, but the job came first. And the Black Eagles did what had to be done. Always.

"We're not picking up any enemy infantry, but we're going to have a section protecting each HVR team...just in case." That was one thing Kelly couldn't figure out. The Eldari had somehow managed to acquire a large force of main battle tanks...but they didn't support them with infantry when they deployed. It didn't make sense. Tanks were rare in post-Fall warfare, but the doctrines on their use were well-known.

Whatever. Don't question it when the enemy makes a gift to you of their mistake.

But it still nagged at her. She didn't have a lot of respect for the Eldari or their military, but she knew they weren't stupid. So why such a foolish error?

She glanced up at her chronometer. One minute.

"Everybody ready…we go over the top in one minute. I want those tanks dead, but that doesn't mean I expect to see any stupid shit going on out there. Stay low, zigzag across the field. The strafing runs tore the ground to shreds. You've got lots of craters and blast holes out there. *Use them.*"

It was basic infantry tactics, and she realized her people had been trained again and again in all of it. But she also knew that it always helped to review before a fight, to remind her people of everything they already knew. Even Eagles were scared in battle, and fear had a way of overriding judgment. Even veterans could make stupid mistakes, screw-ups that got them killed.

She took a deep breath, twisting her foot around, looking for a hard bit of ground in the muddy trench, a good jumping off point. Then she pushed off, propelling herself up and over the lip. "Let's go," she shouted into the com, and she crouched low and moved out over the blasted, smoky plain.

*   *   *   *   *

"Yes, Lieutenant. Understood." Jordyn Calfort's voice was crisp, more a result of her skill at hiding fatigue than anything else.

"And good luck, Lieutenant." Antonia Camerici sounded tired as well. Calfort knew Darius Cain's communication officer well. Calfort had been a last year trainee when Camerici had arrived at the Nest, and the two had become friends. Camerici didn't look the part of an Eagle, slim and no more than a meter and a half tall, but Calfort knew better. Antonia Camerici had her headquarters position because of her extraordinary organizational skills, not because she couldn't fight. Calfort had seen her friend remind more than one hulking doubter, as often as not with a trip to the infirmary.

"Thank you, Lieutenant." Calfort was a believer in formality on the battlefield, even though Camerici was 'Antonia' to her in all other circumstances.

Calfort was sitting in the foxhole she had dug herself a few hours before. The orders had been to stop and hold, but when the Black Eagles paused on the battlefield, they put that time to good use. Calfort's people weren't engaged at the moment—the enemy forces they had been pursuing had pulled back out of immediate combat range. But that didn't matter…this was still a battle, and Eagles were trained never to be careless. So the first thing her people did was to dig some hasty works, a series of foxholes and small trenches that would give them some cover if the enemy reorganized and launched a counterattack.

Her people had been advancing toward the enemy capital… and the Citadel that rose ominously above it. Fortresses, especially above-ground ones, were a bit of an anomaly in modern war. In a battle of rockets and lasers and hyper-velocity railguns, no physical construction could stand up to a focused bombardment. But this battle was different. The Eagles were on Eldaron because there was a possibility that Erik Cain was being held prisoner inside those massive stone ramparts. And now Darius Cain was in there too, along with the Teams, the 200 best of the Eagles. Blasting the Citadel to rubble would kill them all. So the Eagles would have to take that fortress the old-fashioned way. But first, they had to get there.

She flipped to her unit's frequency. "Prepare to move out. The entire line is advancing in five minutes."

She muted the com and sighed softly. The flank attack had stalled the advance toward Eldaron City, and the fact that the enemy had possessed a large force of tanks had been a surprise. But the Black Regiment had landed, and the fighter wings had strafed the armored column mercilessly. The last report suggested the lead elements of the Black Regiment were chasing down the last dozen surviving tanks.

Now it was time to resume the advance. Calfort's mind was in the same place every Eagle's was. With the general. Darius Cain had landed before the main force, he and his 200 picked troops infiltrating the Citadel, searching for Erik Cain. It had sounded daring in the briefing, an adventure worthy of the Black Eagles. But now, in the mud and grit and blood of the battlefield, her viewpoint was changing. Cain's plan looked risky, downright reckless. She saw the desperation in it now, the reality that the Eagles' leader was walking directly—and deliberately—into a trap. She felt the tightness in her gut, the fear. For herself, of course, but also for Cain. Like virtually every other Eagle, she practically worshipped the man. Darius Cain was a warrior who could lead thousands of troops in battle but take the time to ask a soldier about some vague personal fact the two had discussed for a few seconds a year before. He was a true leader, and she felt lucky to follow him.

If he's even still alive.

The Citadel was jamming all communications in its immediate area. That wasn't a surprise, but now she felt the true anxiety of not knowing anything about what was going on in there. And she knew Camerici—and even Erik Teller—were just as in the dark. They all had to trust in Darius Cain's abilities, force themselves to believe that somehow, he and his two hundred warriors would manage to survive against all the forces of the enemy in their stronghold.

She glanced down at her rifle, checking it thoroughly. "Run a quick diagnostic," she snapped to her AI. She knew her armor was fine, but it didn't hurt to check again. Once they resume their advance, there wouldn't be much time to spare. *Hopefully.* The first delay had cost them hours…time they could have used to move to General Cain's relief. Whatever brilliant tactics Cain might employ, however fiercely the Teams fought, no one believed they could take the entire Citadel alone. The main forces in the field had to do it…and then link up with Cain and the Teams inside. And her platoon was dead in the center of the line moving on the enemy capital. Any more delays would only reduce the chance of reaching the objective while General Cain was still alive.

"Let's move out," she snapped into the com. "Fouks, Lewiston…I want you out five hundred meters. We should have some clear ground, but I don't want either of you getting careless." The two scouts tended to be aggressive to the point of craziness. It was typical, a personality trait common among those volunteering for recon training. But she didn't care. They worked for her now, and she damned sure wasn't going to let them get themselves killed for nothing.

She climbed up out of the foxhole and started forward. Her drones had kept tabs on the enemy. They had pulled back five klicks, to their prepared lines at the outskirts of the city.

That will be a bloody assault, she thought grimly. *But then we're in. And the Citadel will be next.*

*   *   *   *   *

"I want those emplacements ready in twenty minutes. No excuses."

The lieutenant snapped to attention. Davidoff had walked up behind and taken him by surprise. "Yes, sir." The voice was squeaky, cracking. It didn't fill Davidoff with confidence. But he'd have to wait until they actually failed before he could tear them down.

General Matias Davidoff was walking along the defensive works his people were manning—and hastily repairing—his eyes darting from one strongpoint to the next. The position had been prepared in advance, built to be as strong as field fortifications could be. But Davidoff had been angry to find much of it half-completed or poorly designed. The Tyrant had long planned his great trap, but he hadn't watched those around him carefully enough, the courtiers and sycophants who bowed and scraped in his presence then stole like bandits behind his back.

Davidoff wasn't one of them. In fact, people like that sickened him, and he had long suffered, his career slowed by less capable officers who were more adept at playing political games. But while they had practiced how to work the system and schemed to gain advances and the largesse of the Tyrant, Davidoff had learned how to lead soldiers in battle. And now he had the Tyrant calling him every thirty minutes, asking what he needed and promising him whatever support he requested.

Davidoff suspected the Tyrant would order the deaths of the very officers who had so insinuated themselves into his court if he but asked for it. But he had greater concerns now, first and foremost among them, keeping his army in the field.

Davidoff found himself disgusted with the Tyrant. Eldaron's dictator had picked a fight with the Black Eagles of all people, but he hadn't even paid personal attention to his own preparations, nor listened to reliable officers who gave him unpleasant reports about real problems. Davidoff knew that General Calman had tried ceaselessly to convince Eldaron's dictator that his ministers were weakening the military with their graft. But the Tyrant had only seen growing numbers of troops, and half-finished works looked strong enough to his untrained eye.

Indeed, though General Calman was a bit more of a manipulator than Davidoff himself, the senior Eldari military commander was also a highly skilled officer. He and Davidoff had often discussed the problems...and the implications they held if a real war ever came. But both of their warnings fell on deaf ears.

Until now...when we're supposed to fix twenty years of neglect immediately. And under fire. Fire from the Black fucking Eagles!

The Eagles had been lured to Eldaron, and their invasion of the planet was no surprise. Or at least it wasn't supposed to be. The Tyrant had shared his plans with his most senior generals...and he spoke cheerfully of the rewards that would accompany victory. But the Eagles' cyber-attack on the planet's com lines and the perfectly-placed EMP bursts had thrown the defensive plans into turmoil, one grossly exaggerated by substandard equipment and poorly constructed works. Davidoff had been consigned to routine duties, far from the primary chain of command, when Calman had finally convinced the Tyrant to name the general field commander of the Citadel-area forces. Davidoff appreciated Calman's confidence and support, but he also knew it was a booby prize of sorts—to face off against the most dreaded military force in Occupied Space, without even enough functioning rifles for his soldiers.

If Calman thought our forces had any chance, he'd have taken the command himself. Fuck.

Davidoff realized most of the soldiers in the lines—and even the senior officers—didn't know this fight had been provoked. They believed the Eagles had been hired by some other planet, brutal mercenaries sent to conquer their homeworld. They felt a wave of patriotism, an urge to defend friends and family. Davidoff knew it was all nonsense, but he had used it nevertheless. He whipped his men into a patriotic frenzy before sending them to battle, two men sharing a rifle.

Before you sent them to their deaths...

He had only one other advantage over the Eagles. Numbers. And he used them as well as he could, sacrificing thousands of soldiers in repeated attempts to slow the enemy advance. But his efforts had been in vain...until the mysterious armored force had emerged from its bunkers and hit the Eagles' flank. Davidoff knew the Tyrant had off-world forces waiting in reserve, but their size and composition were mysteries to him. He'd asked half a dozen times for them to be committed, but each time he'd gotten a vague refusal. Then he'd finally realized. The Tyrant didn't control them.

Who are they? And when the hell are they going to commit the rest of their strength?

Davidoff had lost almost ten thousand troops already, a third of his total strength. The tank attack had been a welcomed diversion, but it had been launched unsupported by infantry, and the Eagles had committed reserves and beaten it back. He'd gotten twelve hours' respite out of the whole affair, but nothing more. Now the Eagle forces facing his line were advancing. The final struggle for Eldaron City would begin soon, perhaps in less than a day. And he had no doubt how that battle would end.

Unless those mysterious troops intervene. Soon.

*   *   *   *   *

"Admiral, we've got something on the scanners. Looks like a ship coming through the Betalax-4 warp gate." The tactical officer's voice was firm, but it was clear there was urgency to his report.

Gaston Allegre's head snapped around. The commander of the Eagles' fleet was an old navy veteran, who had fought alongside Augustus Garret against the First Imperium and the Shadow Legions, and he relied as much on experience-driven intuition as he did on meticulous analysis. And he didn't like the feel of this. Not one bit.

"Send out an advisory, Lieutenant. This system is declared off-limits to all traffic. Any vessels transiting in are advised to immediately decelerate and return to their origin point. Violators are subject to seizure or destruction." The Black Eagles weren't nearly as bloodthirsty as their reputation suggested, but Eldaron was a war zone, and Allegre planned to treat it as such.

"Yes, Admiral." The communications officer forwarded the command. "All vessels and scanner buoys are broadcasting your warning, sir." A pause…then: "More activity, Admiral. It looks like multiple ships coming through now." Another pause. "And no response to our warning, sir. All contacts appear to be establishing a thrust vector toward Eldaron."

Allegre frowned. His gut feeling had been right. This was trouble. "I want the scanner buoy data immediately, Lieutenant. On my screen." He paused, taking an impatient breath and staring down at his display. "And feed it through the AI. I want a full analysis."

"Yes, Admiral." The tactical officer hunched over his workstation, his fingers moving across the controls, carrying out Allegre's orders.

The Eagles' naval commander was staring at his own screen, experienced eyes focusing on the raw data coming in. Numbers of ships, tonnages…energy outputs. It all painted an increasingly grim picture. He knew it before the AI confirmed his analysis. It was a battle fleet coming through, almost certainly.

And a big one, he thought, watching as ships continued to

transit. *And they can only be here for one reason.* His ships were already outnumbered, but enemy forces continued to pour into Eldaron's system.

He leaned back in his chair and sighed. *We worried about a trap, but only on the ground. Whoever our enemy is, they thought bigger than we did. If the fleet is destroyed, the ground forces will be trapped... and they'll run out of supplies before long.*

In that moment, Allegre had no doubt the ground forces would encounter more unpleasant surprises. An enemy who could deploy a fleet like the one now assembling around the warp gate would have more waiting than a force of tanks. But that wasn't his problem. Colonel Teller would handle whatever happened on the planet. Allegre's duty was clear. The fleet was his responsibility...and it looked like he was facing one hell of a fight. Perhaps a hopeless one. But even so, he felt his combat reflexes come to life, and he stared ahead with the cold expression of the focused warrior.

Eagles die when the need arises, but they never go down without a fight.

He turned toward the tactical officer. "Get me Colonel Teller. Now!"

*   *   *   *   *

Erik Teller stood still, staring out at the formation maneuvering in front of him but seeing nothing...nothing but his imagination's depiction of an enemy warfleet advancing across the blackness of space. He'd known all along the Eagles had walked into a trap on Eldaron, but he hadn't imagined it would come in the form of a spacefleet. Most colonies struggled to keep a few old rustbuckets in service...and he was unaware of any power that possessed a force strong enough to overwhelm the Eagles' fleet.

Yet there it is.

His eyes fixed on the display projected inside his helmet, the scanner readings Allegre had forwarded to him. There was no question...the Eagle fleet was already outgunned, and more ships were coming through the warp gate. Whatever chance Allegre's people had, it depended on them adopting a strong battle formation. And they couldn't do that in Eldaron orbit.

"Work out your battle plan, Gaston," Teller said, his voice firm, decisive. "And get Colonel Kuragina's people on alert. I want them down here before you break orbit."

Teller had kept the last Eagle regiment uncommitted, ready to intervene anywhere there was a threat. But if the fleet was going to break orbit, he wanted those troops on the ground... where they were accessible if he needed them.

Instead of sitting on a bunch of ships about to go into a nearly hopeless battle.

He didn't like thinking of losing the fleet...and he realized that if the enemy destroyed the Eagles' ships, there was little chance the rest of his forces would ever leave Eldaron. But it was pointless to keep the White Regiment onboard, where they could die in defeat but do nothing to aid victory. Better to have them on the ground, deployed and ready to fight. He was sure he would need them before long. He'd been confident his people could handle whatever trap the enemy sprung...until now. The emergence of the enemy battle fleet had made him rethink what they were up against, and he began to wonder if the Eagles had finally met their match.

"Yes, sir," Allegre replied. "We'll have Kuragina's people ready to launch in thirty minutes. With your permission, I will expedite the landing operation. I'd like to ensure we have enough time to build some thrust before we engage the enemy fleet."

"Very well, Gaston. Handle the op however you feel is best. Just get Kuragina and some reserve supplies down here before you leave orbit."

"Yes, sir."

"And, Gaston..."

"Yes, Colonel?"

"Fortune go with you and your people. And remember, you are all Black Eagles."

Albrecht Trax sat still for a moment, smiling. He'd finally gotten the message he'd been expecting. He had held back his forces, waiting for the Eldari army to do its job. He hadn't looked to them to defeat the Eagles...or even hurt them very badly. But he had hoped a defending force that outnumbered the attackers six to one could at least compel the commitment of the Eagles' entire strength. But the Eldari were disorganized, and much of their equipment had been destroyed by the preliminary cyber and EMP assaults. In the end, the Eagles had only committed two of their four regiments. And that had tied his own hands.

Trax's deployment of his tanks had forced the Eagles to land a third regiment, but they still had one in reserve aboard their ships...and the Eldari had been pushed back to the outskirts of their capital. Trax wanted to release his warriors, to sweep out from their hidden bunkers and overwhelm the engaged Eagles. But his orders were clear. Not until all four regiments were on the ground. None of the Black Eagles could escape from this trap.

Now that had finally happened. The last of the Eagle ground forces were on the way down. His info was sketchy... the Eldari scanning network was still disabled, its satellites and dishes destroyed. But he had a few hidden scanners of his own, enough at least to tell him the skies were full of Eagle landers.

He knew immediately it was nothing on Eldaron that had provoked the action. His tanks had been destroyed, and the rest of his forces were still in their hidden bases. And the Eldari were in wholesale retreat, fleeing back to their last line of defense outside the capital. That could mean only one thing. The fleet had arrived.

Eldaron was a trap for the Eagles...everyone knew that, even Darius Cain's warriors. They hadn't been fooled, he reminded himself, they had come willingly. Honor had left them no option. Their devotion to their commander had compelled them to brave whatever dangers awaited them. And their confidence fed their belief that, whatever they found on Eldaron, they could defeat it. He suspected they had come expecting a hard and costly fight...but he doubted anyone in the Eagles' ranks had truly feared defeat. They had been so dominant for so long, he suspected the concept of actually losing a fight had been all but lost to them.

But the trap was more complex than anyone on Eldaron knew...even the Tyrant. For when his people sallied forth to the surface, they would outnumber the Eagles six to one. And unlike the pathetic Eldari levies, his troops were all fully-powered infantry, just like the Eagles. Their equipment was a match for that of Cain's soldiers...and they were well-trained. He'd read the reports from Lysandria—the scant intelligence that had made it back from that defeat—and he knew the Eagles outmatched his people man for man. But not one for six.

He smiled as he considered the scope of the plan. His army was only part of the great trap the Triumvirate had laid for Darius Cain and his mercenaries. Indeed, there were forces in motion in multiple locations. While the Eagle powered infantry was wiped out on the ground, their fleet would be destroyed in space. And far away, the fortified moon they called home would also be destroyed, their reserves and support forces wiped away. When the fighting was over, there would be nothing left of Cain's forces. Nothing at all, save legend.

The plan was magnificent, perfect. The final and complete annihilation of the Black Eagles. And the rewards for those who led in this great victory would be enormous. Albrecht Trax would be the man who had directed the destruction of the greatest fighting force in Occupied Space. He would present Darius Cain's broken body to the Triumvirate himself...and when he did, he would be named supreme military commander of the Conquest...and he would lead the massive forces of the Triumvirate forward to conquer all of Occupied Space.

He turned slowly, staring over his communications officer. "All units are ordered to full alert, Captain," he said, his voice charged with excitement. "The attack begins in one hour."

Chapter 31

A battle raged fiercely, vessels thrusting all around the frozen moon the Black Eagles called home. Waves of missiles detonated across the cold, empty battleground, the fury of nuclear fusion creating hundreds of short-lived miniature suns. Most exhausted their energy harmlessly, too far from target vessels to cause serious damage. But a few came close enough, and ships died as their hulls melted, and as radiation fried internal systems and killed crew.

The invading fleet had been a large force, but the Nest's defenses and Christos Caravalla's relentless fighter attacks had worn it down. His fighters sliced between the enemy formations again and again, blasting away with their laser cannons. With their plasma torpedoes expended, the fighters were reduced to carrion work, seeking out and destroying already-damaged ships...and they embraced this role with abandon, swinging around behind incoming missile volleys and completing the jobs begun by the heavy warheads.

Caravalla stared at his display, his eyes fixed on the sixteen icons representing his surviving ships. He had launched with forty, but he pushed that thought aside. It wasn't the moment to mourn those lost. There would be time for that later. Now, there was a battle to fight...and victory still hung in the balance.

When the Columbian fleet entered energy weapons range, the final struggle began in earnest. Jarrod Tyler had long maintained one of the most powerful fleets in Occupied Space, and he had dispatched all of it to the aid of his neighbors. Now his cruisers opened fire with their x-ray laser batteries, the deadly bursts of focused light slicing into their targets, blasting enemy ships into twisted wreckage.

The enemy's fire was no less deadly, and as the battle continued, Columbian ships began to die. It began with a light frigate, a small vessel positioned on the flank of the formation, but soon there were heavy cruisers in the center bleeding atmosphere and shaking with internal explosions, their own fire lessening as their turrets were knocked out one by one.

Caravalla was a veteran who had seen many battles, and he knew this one would be close. The enemy fleet, as it had first arrived, would almost certainly have overwhelmed the Columbians. But the Nest's deadly defenses had claimed their price before they were destroyed, and it was a crippled force that stood against Tyler's navy.

"Okay," Caravalla said into the com, "form up on me for another run." His fighters were worn down. The crews were exhausted, their fuel supplies quickly running out. But before Tyler's people had arrived they'd consigned themselves to death. No matter what losses they suffered now, if even one of them survived, their situation had improved. As long as the battle was won. And to a man, they were determined to do whatever had to be done to make that a reality.

There are thousands of Eagles down there, he thought, *trapped five klicks underground, and their survival depends on this fight...*

Caravalla pushed on the throttle, feeding power to the engine. He felt the pressure building as he increased his acceleration to 3g. He didn't go any farther, though his ship could handle well over 10g and his crew could survive that as well, at least for a brief period. But his fuel supply couldn't. When his reaction mass was gone, his fighter was helpless. His reserve batteries could maintain life support for a while, but the battle would be effectively over. And he was determined to stay in this fight until the bitter end.

"Same as last time…follow me to 50,000 kilometers then break and pick your targets." His eyes focused on the display, on one of the big enemy ships. It was almost dead center in the formation, and that meant he would have to pilot his ship through 100,000 klicks of enemy defensive zone to close. But the target was spewing out air and fluids from a dozen great wounds in its hull…and Caravalla could feel that one good strafing run would finish the giant. He could feel it, the need to kill that ship, the raw energy of a feral predator. These people had attacked his home, killed his fellow Black Eagles. Now it was time to send them to hell.

He stared straight ahead, nudging the throttle to the side, changing his vector to a direct line toward his prey…

*   *   *   *   *

"The enemy fire is weakening, General Tyler."

Jarrod Tyler stood on *Lucia's* flag bridge, gripping the handhold next to his chair and staring at the main display. There wasn't a hint of emotion evident, not elation, not the slightest discomfort for the thousands his people had just killed.

"The center division is to close and maintain full fire. The flanks are to accelerate and move around the enemy formation." His voice was cold. "None of them are to escape. Not one. We must send a message to anyone who would dare send warships to Eta Cassiopeiae."

"Yes, General." The response was crisp, sharp. The men and women who served Jarrod Tyler knew quite well what their leader expected of them, and for all his coldness and the brutal side of his rule, they loved him and gave him their unfaltering loyalty.

Lucia shook hard as an enemy laser blast took her amidships. Tyler's flagship was barely a heavy cruiser by pre-Fall standards, but it was a large and powerful vessel relative to current fleets.

The Columbian navy wasn't the strongest in Occupied Space, but it was in the top tier. Its weapons and equipment were modern, its crews well-trained career military. And it was led by Jarrod Tyler.

Tyler had been the commander of Columbia's military during the Shadow War, when the planet had been invaded and devastated by the Gavin Stark's Shadow Legions. He had assumed dictatorial powers during that emergency, in accordance with Columbia's constitution, and when the crisis had passed, he dutifully surrendered them back to the duly-elected government.

The young Tyler had no interest in governing and no stomach for politics, despite the fact that his wife, Lucia, had been the planet's president for almost fifteen years. But as the years slipped by, he saw the fickleness of the electorate, the way they finally cast Lucia and her compatriots aside for the empty promises of political rivals. The new government dismantled Columbia's strong military, and they channeled the funds that had gone to support it into a series of programs designed to increase their hold on power. They ushered in a period of heavy regulation and corruption the likes of which the politically naïve Columbians had never seen. And then the Second Incursion began… and Columbia was invaded yet again, this time by the robot legions of the First Imperium.

The planet, which had once been almost fanatical in its approach to self-defense, was caught utterly unprepared. Tyler came out of retirement, called his veterans back to the colors, and they held the invaders at bay, at enormous cost, until Erik Cain arrived with the Marines. The fighting was desperate, and thousands were killed…including Lucia Collins. Columbia's castoff president had taken to the battlefields, rifle in hand, and rallied the people everywhere she went. She organized militia battalions, led desperate defenses of towns and cities…and she died in the final battle, holding the line while the Marines landed behind the enemy's flank.

Jarrod Tyler changed at that moment, his soul freezing in an instant like liquid expelled into deep space. He was devastated by the loss of his wife…and he blamed the people of Columbia.

For those they had elected, for their shortsightedness. They were too foolish to make their own decisions, he decided, too unwilling to educate themselves to make wise choices at the polls. They had to be led...controlled. Prevented from allowing their folly to ever again cause such suffering as the planet had endured in the war just concluded.

Tyler was again the hero, the savior of the planet, and the remnants of the army were fanatically loyal to him. Once he'd decided to seize absolute power, the actual coup itself proved almost comically easy. His soldiers were devoted, and after the losses they had suffered, they had their own resentments toward those who had left them so unprepared for the terrible conflict.

The battered population had no will to resist, and Tyler quickly disbanded the entire apparatus of democratic government, installing himself as the absolute and unquestioned ruler, with a small band of military officers as aides. He made no effort to disguise the fact that he was a dictator, established no ineffectual assemblies or congresses, no rigged votes or plebiscites. He ruled with a naked fist, and his justice was swift and merciless.

Yet that justice was, for the most part, just as well. Tyler was an anomaly, a strongman not driven by ego and lust for power. He viewed his position as an obligation, a duty...and while his growing paranoia caused him to look at almost everyone with a certain degree of suspicion, he interfered little in the day to day affairs of his people. The planet quickly recovered its economic prosperity. Corruption, at least in government, virtually ceased to exist. Tyler was a zealot, with no interest in securing personal gain from his position...and those who pursued corrupt paths soon found themselves mounting a scaffold or shot against some dull gray wall in a non-descript cellar.

Columbia's dictator was popular too, and resistance to his rule was almost non-existent. Some said, quietly and in small groups, that even though they were prosperous and well-protected, the loss of freedom was too high a price to pay. But the vast majority of the population looked at the rapid rebuilding since the war, the economic boom that had continued for over a decade, and they barely thought of the liberty they had once possessed.

"Entering short range now, General."

"All units, continue firing at full." Tyler knew the battle had reached its final stage. He had already dispatched his flanking forces, and now there was nothing left for his center except to drive right down the enemy's throat, firing all the way. It was a slugging match, ship against ship, with victory hanging in the balance.

*   *   *   *   *

"General Tyler, I thank you, on behalf of General Cain and the entire Black Eagles company. Your intervention was not only timely, it was downright crucial. Had you not come to our aid when you did, the Nest would surely have been destroyed." Cranston spoke slowly, solemnly. His voice was professional, but there was emotion there too, the true gratitude to an ally who had not only fought alongside the Eagles, but who had also suffered terrible losses in doing so.

"We are allies, Major Cranston, and that is something my people take very seriously. Never has there been a doubt in my mind that the Eagles would have succored us in our time of need, and we too stand by our obligations to a friend."

"Again, General, you have our eternal gratitude. I am certain General Cain will wish to repeat our thanks when he returns, but on my own authority, I request that your people forward us the names of those lost in this battle, so that we may honor them alongside our own dead in our logs and histories."

"We will do so with honor, Major...and respect for a truly worthy ally." Tyler paused. "I just received an update as well. None of our vessels are able to land fighter-bombers, but Captain Caravalla and his surviving crews have been recovered. I'm afraid they had to ditch so that our shuttles could pick them up...but we are taking steps to secure the fighters themselves as well. We will hold them until you are able to restore landing facilities."

"Thank you, General." The relief in Cranston's voice was obvious. He hadn't imagined any of Caravalla's people had survived. "We had almost given up hope. Until we managed to restore this single com line, we were completely cut off from what was happening around us." He tried to ignore the fact that eleven surviving ships meant that almost three-quarters of Caravalla's people had been lost.

"Several of Captain Caravalla's people required medical care, which they are now receiving." Another pause. "I must commend you on the bravery of your fighter crews, Major. I cannot express how crucial their repeated attack runs were to our ultimate victory."

"Captain Caravalla is an old school veteran, General. So he survived?"

"Yes, Major. The Captain was among the wounded, but my medical team assures me he will live."

Cranston nodded. "Again, General, my thanks."

There was a brief silence, and then Tyler said, "I understand that much of this is best discussed later, in person rather than over open com channels, but do you have any idea where that fleet came from?"

Cranston paused. The communication was fully encrypted... and to his knowledge no one had ever breached Eagle protocols. But he knew of Tyler's reputation for paranoia, and he decided to humor it. "Yes, General, I believe we have encountered this enemy before...though I'm afraid we have extremely limited intelligence about them. And we had no idea they were capable of mounting an attack of this size."

Cranston wasn't sure this enemy was the same that the Eagles had faced on Eris and Lysandria, but he wasn't a strong believer in coincidence either, and there seemed to be few alternate theories.

"Perhaps we can have a brief conference...if you can be spared for a short while."

Cranston looked around the control center. His first impulse was to politely decline. It just felt wrong to leave his post after the Nest had suffered such extensive damage. But Tyler was important…and the only reason every Eagle in the Nest wasn't dead now.

Besides, he thought, looking around at the cool competence surrounding him, *they all know what to do. They don't need me hanging over them.*

The Eagles were professionals, and throughout the Nest they had sprung into action, repair crews working through prioritized lists, other personnel dividing into teams to assist the technicians and engineers. The entire base was a beehive of focused activity…and Cranston knew his people could do without him for a few hours. What they couldn't do without was Tyler's protection, at least until General Cain returned with the fleet.

"I'd be happy to join you, General Tyler," he finally said, "but I'm afraid my only egress at present is an emergency tube leading to the surface. And I haven't got a functioning shuttle or a bay to launch one from. I'm afraid you'll have to send someone to get me."

"My pleasure, Major. Send the coordinates when you are ready, and I'll have a shuttle there in thirty minutes."

"Very well, General." He gestured toward Captain Anders. "Send the coordinates," he said, momentarily holding his hand over the com unit.

Anders nodded. "Yes, sir."

"General Tyler, we're sending the data now. I'll go suit up, and I'll be there in forty minutes. I'm looking forward to seeing you."

And he was. The Black Eagles weren't used to needing anyone's help, and the entire organization had become infused with Darius Cain's cynicism. They were as good as they were partially because they didn't *expect* anyone else to come to their aid. So when someone did, they truly appreciated it…as a rare and admirable act.

The Eagles and the Columbians had always had friendly relations, but now Tyler had put his own forces at risk, and Columbians had died in the battle, fighting bravely to save the Nest.

Most people would appreciate such an act, but to the Eagles it went far deeper. It was a debt, a significant one. And the Black Eagles always paid their debts.

Chapter 32

Obelan Foothills
Five Kilometers from Eldaron City
Planet Eldaron, Denebola IV
Earthdate: 2319 AD (34 Years After the Fall)

"Colonel, take your first battalion now and set up a defensive line. "I'll get over there and bring your second battalion right behind." Erik Teller was standing in the middle of his command post snapping out orders. Kuragina's entire regiment was fresh, but only one battalion was ready to move forward immediately. The other half of her unit had been dispersed to assist with the unloading of supplies. It would take twenty minutes to get them formed up for battle...and right now he didn't have that time.

His eyes darted up at the display inside his helmet. There were so many icons on the one side of the projection, it looked like a single pulsating light. His AI had been updating the scanner reports for him, providing strength estimates for the units now moving against his rear. He'd stopped listening when the numbers hit twenty thousand.

"Yes, sir. I'll have my lead companies on the march in three minutes." It was a precise figure, but that was typical for Cyn Kuragina. Her White Regiment had always been one of the three "line" units the Eagles fielded. The Black Regiment was the elite, the senior force right after the Teams. But since the fighting on Lysandria the year before, Teller had realized that Kuragina had forged her battalions into a force every bit as effective as Colonel Falstaff's Blacks. It was as much random chance as anything that the White Regiment was uncommitted, but if he'd had to pick a force for a desperate holding action, it would have been the diminutive but tough as nails Kuragina and her battle-hardened troops.

"Very good, Colonel." He paused. "And, Cyn…you're going to be massively outnumbered. Just try to slow them down, at least until we can get some more troops deployed." His voice was thick with concern. Kuragina would be leading a vanguard of 700 Eagles to somehow hold off thirty times their number… at least until he got the other half of her regiment up there.

"Don't worry, sir. Black Eagles don't worry about enemy numbers." Her voice was remarkably calm, but Teller could hear the concern there too.

"Use anything you can get…cover, terrain, anything. Just hold them off until we can get reorganized."

"Yes, sir. You can count on us."

"I know I can, Colonel."

He cut the line, turning his head and looking out over the small headquarters. The Black Eagles had a lot more tooth and a lot less tail than most modern fighting forces. Darius Cain wasn't just a tactical genius. His administrative and organizational skills—and Teller's as well—had been as crucial to making the Eagles the efficient force they were.

He switched the com frequency. "Captain Camerici, I want the White Regiment's second battalion recalled immediately and formed up for battle. I will be leading them forward myself."

"Yes, sir." There was a hitch in her voice. Teller knew it was concern about him moving up to the front lines. He sighed.

How many times have I given Darius shit about that? But we're in big trouble here…and I've got to stop this new force from breaking through. Somehow. He shook his head. *And if Darius was here, I'd be telling him to send someone else…*

"The forces attacking the main enemy line are to disengage and pull back at once," he said

There was a pause. "But, Colonel…the reports from the front suggest that the enemy is on the verge of breaking…"

"Yes, Captain, but we've got a huge force moving against our flank and rear."

And unless I'm completely wrong, we're going to find these troops are a hell of a lot better than the Eldari levies.

"I want Falstaff's Black Regiment to redeploy immediately. They are to move east to support Camerici's people against the new attack. Cornin is to pull his Reds back three kilometers and dig in facing the Eldari forces. Once his positions are prepared, I want one of his battalions to man the defenses. The other is to withdraw and move to the flank to relieve Vandeveer's people. Once the Reds are in place there, Colonel Vandeveer is to pull the Blue Regiment back to this location to serve as a mobile reserve." He paused. He realized he had hit her with a tidal wave of orders. "Is all that clear, Captain?"

"Yes, sir. Clear." She was already relaying his commands to the various officers involved.

Teller just shook his head. He'd never seen a tactical officer as sharp and fast as Camerici. Even in an organization like the Black Eagles, she stood out.

"I'm heading to Kuragina's position to get her second battalion moving. When Colonel Vandeveer gets here, he is in command of headquarters." He paused. "Until then, you have my proxy, Captain. You're in charge."

"But, Colonel…" Camerici sounded shaken…in a way she hadn't while discovering a huge enemy force moving against the army's rear. Teller had just effectively put her in command of a dozen superior officers."

"You understand the situation better than anyone else here, Antonia."

And I think I trust you more than anybody else here too.

"You can handle it. And Vandeveer will be here soon."

He better be…because I'm going to need those reserves.

Then he turned and jogged over the hill toward Kuragina's command post.

He knew one thing for sure. Everything that had happened

so far had been preliminary. The real test had just begun

*   *   *   *   *

Darius Cain's eyes stared out though his visor, watching the enemy soldiers fall as he fired his assault rifle again and again. He had the weapon set to three-shot bursts, and every time he pulled the trigger, an enemy died. He was a consummate professional at war, an artist with the weapons of death, but there was something different at play here. No matter how much he tried to pretend this was a normal mission, the fact that he might be less than fifty meters from his father, the man he'd thought dead for so long, dominated his thoughts.

Darius had always been cool under fire. He and his soldiers had killed only because their jobs demanded it...and they didn't draw satisfaction from violence. Until now. He relished every kill, every strike against the force that had brought him here, that had perhaps held his father prisoner for years. He knew those he gunned down were common soldiers, not at all responsible for whatever the Eldari Tyrant had done to his father. But the cold fact was, he didn't care. He held all of Eldaron responsible for their leader's actions...and his mind seethed with what he would do to them if they had killed his father.

Ernesto Alcadebo was right next to him, firing with the same gusto, though his urgency was born of different motivations. The Eagle captain considered it his overriding duty to keep Darius Cain safe. And gunning down enemy soldiers before they had a chance to shoot the general was the most straightforward way to accomplish his goal.

There was no doubt in Darius' mind his people were expected. The doorway into the detention area had opened into a large chamber, thirty meters square, and there were at least fifty enemy soldiers waiting. But Darius had brought two hundred Black Eagles with him, and though only a dozen and a half had managed to pour into the room with him, they had cleared it of the enemy in less than half a minute. The Eldari soldiers wore sectional body armor, but it wasn't self-contained and nuclear-powered like the Eagles' fighting suits. The hyper-velocity coil-guns Cain's people used tore through the breastplates of the defenders, ripping their bodies to bloody chunks in an instant.

The first fight was over, but the large anteroom had over a dozen hallways leading off in every direction. *Cells*, Darius thought. It wasn't a surprise that the Citadel had such a large detention area. Governments like the Tyrant's tended to arrest a large number of citizens, a necessary effort for one trying to maintain a brutal dictatorship and crush all opposition. But Darius hadn't come to bring freedom to Eldaron's oppressed political prisoners. He had come for a single captive. And he knew he was running out of time.

"Where?" Cain shouted to his captive. "Which of these corridors?" There was death in Cain's voice, and the prisoner feel to his knees, whimpering and begging for his life. Darius reached down and grabbed the fool by his hair, lifting him up with a single powered arm. He extended his blade on the other side, and held it a few centimeters from the terrified man's face. "This is your last chance, Henri…tell me which corridor or I will cut you into quivering chunks right now."

The miserable Eldari screamed in pain, but he managed to fight through his fear and agony long enough to hold out a shaking arm. "That one," he managed to rasp softly. "Down at the very end."

Darius stared for a few seconds, trying to decide if he believed the man. This would be a moment for treachery too, though he doubted the Eldari had the courage for that…and the prisoner had to know that whatever happened in the next few minutes, Darius would find a way to repay betrayal.

The room was filling with armored figures, more of the Teams pouring in. "I want a single Team down each of these corridors. Conduct a quick recon, but don't get too far from here." He believed his prisoner, but not enough to forego check-ing out the other hallways. "Ernesto, organize three Teams and come with me."

Darius took a couple steps and stopped, turning to stare back at the terrified captive. "And bring him," he said as he moved swiftly toward the designated corridor.

Alcabedo rushed to keep after him, gesturing for the designated Teams to follow him. He grabbed the prisoner himself, dragging the man roughly behind him until he was able to hand him off to one of the troopers.

Cain stopped in front of the closed hatch and paused for an instant. He looked like he might be thinking of how to unlock the door when he whipped up his assault rifle and opened fire on full auto. The tiny shards of hardened iridium left the weapon at almost 5,000 meters per second, and when they struck the metal around the edge of the hatch, both target and projectile vaporized.

It took less than a second for Darius to blow a large hole on the edge of the hatch, and then he leaned forward and shoved it open with all the force his fighting suit's servos could manage. The door let out one loud creak, and then it tore off its track, falling to the ground into the corridor.

Darius' rifle was already down in front of him when the hatch gave way, and he opened up almost immediately, targeting the half dozen Eldari troops standing in the corridor.

The hall was long, two hundred meters or more, and there were small doors on each side. Cell doors, Darius thought, feeling a surge of unfocused anger when he wondered how many of the occupants of this prison had committed no greater crime than speaking freely or seeking to protect their families.

Whatever I find, that kind of thing is over here. When I leave, if Eldaron survives it will no longer bow under the rule of one who calls himself Tyrant.

Darius wondered for an instant if he'd ever heard of a dictator who actually took the title Tyrant. It was supreme arrogance, but he couldn't help but admire the honesty of it…the sheer brazenness. *But that won't stop me from spilling every drop of his blood…*

He ran down the hall, and he could feel his heart pounding in his ears. Sweat poured down his neck, his back, making his armor even more uncomfortable that it usually was. But he ignored it all. "Have a Team cover the rear," he snapped to Alcabedo. He didn't know the layout of the Eldari prison, and he suspected the way they had come was the only entrance…but there was no point taking chances.

"Already done, General."

Darius nodded, a cumbersome gesture in armor. *Of course you did*, he thought, allowing himself a fleeting smile. Ernesto Alcabedo was one of the Eagles' best, and he took his job as bodyguard very seriously. But he hadn't faltered in his regular duties, not an iota.

Darius stopped abruptly. The corridor ended in front of a door, similar to the others, but a bit larger. *This is it*, he thought…and he summoned all his discipline, all the calm he could muster. He took half a step back and aimed his rifle at the locking mechanism. He was more careful this time, concerned about any rounds or debris going through the door…and hitting anyone inside the cell.

I'm have come, father. I have come for you…if you are here.

He took a deep breath and opened fire.

*   *   *   *   *

"Stay down, you fucking assholes. These aren't Eldari toy soldiers firing pop guns. Those are hyper-velocity rounds coming in, and they'll rip your suits open like you'd pop a can of beans." Joseph Trent was crouched low, peering out over the small ridgeline at the enemy position a klick and a half to the east.

Trent was a sergeant, but he didn't hold a sergeant's post. He was Dan Sullivan's backup as company commander, and one of the few non-coms in the whole outfit who had a direct line to Darius Cain. The Eagles were a precision outfit, and in the field they usually stuck pretty close to regs, calling each other by proper ranks and the like. All except Joseph Trent. No one called him by his names, first or last...or even his rank. No, to everyone in the Eagles, from newly recruited private to the regimental commanders and above, Sergeant Joseph Trent was known as Bull.

No one was sure whether the name had attached itself to the veteran non-com because of his size and enormous build... or because he was stubborn enough to pound his way through an obstacle with his head. But however it had come into the Eagles' lexicon, Bull Trent was one of the great heroes of the organization, a man Darius Cain had personally decorated half a dozen times.

Darius had tried to promote Bull as well, but the pigheaded sergeant had refused, insisting he was a non-com at heart, and that's what he would stay. Nevertheless, ability could not be long denied in an outfit like the Eagles, and though his fatigues still bore the three stripes of his official rank, it had been a long time since he'd stepped onto a battlefield to do a sergeant's job.

"Bull, it looks like we've got another attack coming in...I'd guess brigade strength this time." Dan Sullivan's voice blasted into Bull's helmet. Sullivan was another over-achiever, a platoon commander who had taken over company command on Lysandria...and performed brilliantly. Cyn Kuragina's entire White Regiment had been deep in the fiercest fighting on that world, when the Eagles had been surprised by several thousand well-equipped troops emerging from hidden positions. Just like now. Only there were a hell of a lot more this time.

"The boys are ready, Cap. They come out of those trenches and we'll blow 'em to hell." There were both men and women serving with the Eagles, but Bull Trent had his own way of speaking...and nobody tried to change it. Darius had long decided it was a pointless effort, and the last thing he wanted to do was tinker around with a natural fighting machine like Trent. And there weren't more than a handful of others with the guts to try, even in an outfit as known for ferocity and bravery as the Black Eagles.

Sullivan glanced up at his display. He knew Bull was the kind of fighter who never gave up, never even admitted the possibil-

ity of defeat. But he could also read the data in the shimmering projection just in front of him. There were a lot of enemy
troops over there. A *lot*.

The captain took a look down the line his company had
formed. Bull had them just behind the ridgeline…great cover
against an attack from the enemy's position. The ground rose
slowly from their hasty trench line to the high ground his people
occupied. There was very little undulation, and that meant there
wouldn't be much cover for the enemy forces if they attacked.
It was a textbook killing ground, one he knew troops as good
as his would use well. But he still doubted they could beat back
a truly concerted attack. Not unless the enemy broke and ran.

And that won't happen…not with this enemy.

There was something too familiar about these enemy soldiers. He had seen it before…the discipline, the equipment.

"Bull, do these guys remind you of the enemy on Lysandria?"

"Yeah, Cap. I'd bet it's the same crew, whoever the hell they
are."

Sullivan sighed softly. It was the same force…he was ready
to bet his last credit on that. But what did that mean? What did
Lysandria and Eldaron have to do with each other? They were
far apart, almost on opposite sides of Occupied Space. Lysandria was a backwater, a democracy of sorts that had brought
invasion on itself by provoking a stronger neighbor, one that
could afford to hire the Eagles. Eldaron, on the other hand,
however poorly its military forces had acquitted themselves, was
an economic powerhouse, a strong world ruled by an absolute
dictator.

So where are these soldiers from? There must be 25,000 of
them here, at least. Who could field such a force?

"Cap, it looks like we've got some activity over there…"

Sullivan snapped out of his thoughts…just as something
exploded fifty meters behind him. A huge spray of dirt blew up
into the air, landing all around.

"Mortars," he heard Bull shouting in the com. The sergeant
had recognized the activity along the enemy line…and he'd been
the first one to shout out the warning.

Sullivan ducked low, pushing himself forward, into the soft dirt of the hillside, just as shells began landing all along the line. Mortars weren't an enormously dangerous weapon for fully-armored troops. It pretty much took a direct hit to kill or seriously wound a powered infantryman. But enough of them could drive a force to ground, stalling an advance...or suppressing defensive fire.

"Alright boys," Bull said harshly, "these bogies are going to be coming our way soon, so I don't care how many firecrackers they send over here, your fucking eyes better be where they need to be. 'Cause if you don't blow these bastards away when they're out in that nice open ground, you're gonna be fightin 'em right here...ten of them to one of you."

Sullivan nodded to himself. He'd been thinking the same thing, but once again, Bull had beaten him to it. He wondered if he'd ever seen a more natural soldier than the hulking non-com. He was still wondering when his com unit went crazy, and his whole line opened fire.

His eyes snapped to his display. There were waves of enemy soldiers moving forward. They were all powered infantry, as well-equipped as the Eagles themselves, or nearly so. The moved quickly, covering ground like only powered-infantry could. Their form was excellent, and they moved ahead side to side, keeping themselves low and offering as small a target as possible as they advanced.

His soldiers raked the open plain with fire. Enemy troops began to fall, a few dozen at first...then hundreds as they came closer. The dead soon covered the field, the heaviest concentrations in the lines of fire of the big autocannons. The SAWs and SHWs spat death all across the field, but still the enemy came on. And behind the first wave, fresh lines moved up.

Sullivan peered over the ridge. He knew every shot counted, so he added his own rifle to the fire of his company. He was a crack shot, one of the best in the regiment, and every time he squeezed the trigger, an enemy soldier went down.

But the approaching force just kept coming, despite losses that would have sent most armies reeling in retreat...if not an outright panicked rout. Sullivan couldn't help but be impressed by the courage that was on display. This was a dangerous enemy...that much was obvious. But there was something strange about them, or at least a doctrine that was utterly foreign to the Black Eagles. He had to grudgingly admit that their training and drill was as close to that of his own troops as any enemy he had faced. Yet there was a difference, one that was downright chilling. The Eagles were as fierce as any fighting force that had ever existed, but they valued the lives of their soldiers. Every plan was created to minimize losses. The equipment, tactics, support services...they were all designed to keep casualties as low as possible. Darius Cain set the standard, and down the ranks, every officer, every squad leader...they spared no effort to keep their men and women alive.

This enemy—and Sullivan was sure now it was the same force his people had fought on Lysandria—didn't seem to care about losses. They were willing to incur enormous casualties in their operations...and their soldiers seemed immune to fear. They pushed ahead into withering fire, entire lines serving as little but human shields for those who followed. He wondered how such a force could exist, why well-trained soldiers would follow leadership that valued their lives so little.

Sullivan watched, and his confusion grew. The first wave that had crested the enemy trenchline was almost gone. A thousand soldiers, perhaps, had first stepped off into the no man's land between the armies, advancing quickly under the cover of the mortar barrage. They used cover where it was available, crouched low behind undulations in the ground to block the Eagles' fire. But the terrain was wide open most of the way, and Sullivan doubted more than a hundred of the original thousand were still standing. The others were scattered across the field... dead, wounded, suffering from severe armor damage. But more had come up behind them. And yet more behind that second wave. And they all kept coming.

Sullivan knew his people couldn't hold the ridge, not against such fanaticism. The enemy was almost there, and when they reached the defensive line, their numbers would decide the issue.

His company would fight, and he had no doubt they would kill two for one or three for one. But there were just too many of the enemy.

He wanted to pull back, to retreat now to the secondary line a klick behind. But he couldn't take his company back, not while the rest of the battalion remained. He had to wait for Colonel Kuragina's orders. His people would live or die with their comrades.

He kept firing. His desperation pushed him ever harder, and he directed his rifle with even greater speed and accuracy. He was on full auto now, gunning down every enemy he could. But still they came on.

This is it, he thought. This is where we will die…

"First Battalion, this is Colonel Kuragina. You are to withdraw immediately to the secondary battle line." Sullivan could hear the stress in her usually calm voice, and in an instant he knew what was going through her mind. Did I wait too long?

"Alright, let's go," he yelled into his com. "Evens, fall back halfway to the second line. Odds, stand firm and continue to fire." He paused for an instant. Then: "Bull, I want you with the evens…go!"

He turned and brought his rifle to bear. He and the odds had to buy time, to keep the enemy under fire until their comrades were in position to cover their own retreat.

He pulled the trigger, watching as a cluster of three enemy troopers went down under the withering fire. He tried to stay focused, but the same question hung in his mind.

Did she wait too long?

*   *   *   *   *

"All ships, execute nav plan two…now!" Gaston Allegre's voice was hoarse, dry. *Eagle One's* bridge was smoky, the air heavy with the caustic smells of chemicals and burnt machinery. The Eagle fleet had never fought a battle this intense in space…

but Allegre had. The former Europan officer had served under Augustus Garret, against the forces of the First Imperium and the Shadow Legions. He'd been a junior officer during those early battles, and he'd had no real contact with the legendary admiral then. But he'd returned to Garret's service during the Second Incursion, and he'd moved up to command one of the great admiral's task forces before that war was won.

He still remembered the inspiration he had felt, the way the aura of Garret's skill and confidence bolstered the morale of those who served under him, how it pushed the fear back. He tried to live up to that ideal now, to lead his men and women as he thought Garret would have, to keep them confident and unintimidated, manning their stations with total focus. His people were Black Eagles, some of the bravest and best trained spacers anywhere. But they were also outnumbered. Badly. And they were losing.

Allegre leaned back into his command chair as he felt the 4g of thrust slam into him. There was a good chance the maneuver would surprise the enemy and give his people an opportunity to hit the flank of the enemy formation. The invading ships had slowed considerably since their initial attack run, but the Eagle ships were using most of their initial velocity, only altering their trajectories a moderate amount. The enemy would have to decelerate almost to a stop and then start accelerating in the opposite direction. It would give his people an edge. For a few minutes at least…long enough to inflict considerable damage.

He took a deep breath, his lungs struggling against the gee forces pressing down on him. His eye had caught the opportunity, and he knew the maneuver was just the kind of thing Augustus Garret would have done. But he also knew the advantage would only be temporary. The attacking fleet was simply too powerful. Eventually, the mathematics would prevail. His ships would be destroyed, and the planet—and the entire Eagle ground force—would be laid bare.

He knew his brethren on the planet would fight to the end as well, but losing the fleet would hurt them grievously. The enemy ships would destroy the satellite network Allegre's people had deployed, and the soldiers on the ground would lose most of their intel and communications. At the same time, the enemy forces would regain theirs. The Eagles on the ground would be without resupply, without air support. However well they fought, they would eventually run out of ammunition. The field hospitals would fill to overflowing, with no evac possible.

And eventually, they will fall. Or, even if they somehow win, they will be stuck on the ground, blockaded. And with the Eagle fleet destroyed, there will be no rescue. So, in the end, even victory will turn to bitter defeat.

"We're coming into attack position now, Admiral. Twenty seconds to firing range."

The tactical officer's voice pulled him from his introspection.

"Very well, all batteries are to fire as soon as they are within range. And they are to continue firing at maximum output." Allegre stared straight ahead. "We're going right down their throats on this run, and I want those guns firing until they melt."

Chapter 33

CNS Lucia
Eta Cassiopeiae VII Outer System
Near the Second Moon of Eos, "The Nest"
Earthdate: 2318 AD (34 Years After the Fall)

A Columbian officer and two Marines met John Cranston in the landing bay. They all wore dress uniforms, and they greeted him warmly as he wiggled his armored body through the hatch and stepped off the shuttle. After brief introductions, they led him to an area where he was able to take off and store his armor. Pounding through the corridors of the Columbian flagship in a fully-powered combat suit would be cumbersome at best... and impossible at worst, depending on *Lucia's* exact layout. And it would certainly be inappropriate, downright rude even. Certainly not the way to meet an allied head of state who had extended an invitation. Cranston wouldn't normally have been wearing the suit at all, but the Nest's docking facilities had been virtually destroyed in the battle, and the only way he'd been able to link up with the Columbian shuttle was to meet it out on the moon's frigid surface.

Cranston had brought a small bag with a change of clothes, and he slipped quickly into the uniform he'd brought with him. The Eagles' full dress garb was sleek, devoid of much of the pomp and frill that so often adorned similar attire, but it was striking nevertheless, a black jacket over pristine white trousers and knee-high leather boots. The rank insignia and sparse trim that adorned the shoulders and sleeves were platinum. Cranston paused before rejoining his—what were they? Minders? Honor guard? Probably both, he decided as he looked into the mirror, running his hand down the leg of his trousers, trying to straighten them as much as he could. He frowned as a few of the wrinkles resisted his efforts. A head of state like Jarrod Tyler rated a pressed uniform at the very least, but the situation had been far from ideal, and this would have to do.

The shuttle had picked him up spot on time and ferried him to *Lucia's* docking bay, exactly as Tyler had said it would. He'd had a bit of a fight on his hands back at the Nest when he'd declared he was going alone. His officers had argued fiercely for him to at least take an armed escort with him. But Cranston would have none of it. He wasn't about to play a game of 'who's more important' with Jarrod Tyler over nonsense like that. And, if nothing else, going alone would be a show of trust toward the Columbians.

Who, after all, just saved our lives.

Cranston followed the escort through *Lucia's* corridors. The Columbian flagship's interior was drab, even compared to the Spartan standards of the Black Eagles. He and his companions walked a long way through non-descript surroundings, mostly corridors with endless gray metal walls. Warships tended toward the practical...few fighting vessels wasted productive space on nonsense, but Tyler's flagship took it even further. It all fit in with what Cranston knew about Columbia's dictator. Tyler had a reputation as a dour leader, a hard-driving taskmaster, utterly incorruptible, but also capable of enormous brutality to those he considered enemies. Not the kind of man to approve warship designs with wasted tonnage or needless frills.

Cranston didn't know the design of the ship, but he had the feeling he was being led by an indirect route. *Probably avoiding areas with heavy damage.* He suspected *Lucia* had some sections that were still in rough shape. A damaged spaceship could be a hazardous place, with depressurized compartments, degraded structural integrity, and radiation leaks just a few of the potential dangers.

He'd expected to be taken to a large conference room or some other meeting area, but as he looked around, he felt like they were moving into a quieter section of the ship, far from any formal areas. He looked side to side, noting the large number of doors he was passing. He guessed they were walking through an area of crew quarters, probably officer's country.

The Columbian fleet had fought well in the recent battle—very well indeed—and their skill and armament had proven to be too much for an enemy already weakened in its fight with the Nest's defenses. Tyler's fleet had suffered significant damage—and a fair number of casualties too, Cranston imagined—but they had only lost four ships outright. Given time for repairs, the Columbians would be ready to fight again.

And I don't doubt another battle lies ahead.

The Eagles were accustomed to thinking they didn't need anyone else to fight their wars, but Cranston had shed that bit of personal bravura. Darius Cain's warriors knew they were the best, but they were realists too. The Nest's provisional commander was well aware he'd be dead right now, along with all his people, had it not been for Tyler's intervention. Pride was one of his sins perhaps, but not ingratitude.

The commander of his escort stopped in front of a small door. A single guard stood at attention just to the side. The entry was unadorned, save for a small circle of stars just below eye level on the right. His escort nodded to the sentry and punched at the keys on the access panel. The door slid open.

The lieutenant turned and said, "The General is waiting for you inside, Major." He stepped back and stood alongside the guards, and Cranston understood immediately. Jarrod Tyler wanted to see him alone.

He glanced over at the lieutenant, who nodded in confirmation. Then he turned and walked through the open doorway.

"Thank you for coming, Major Cranston. I am aware that free time is not a resource you possess in any quantity right now. I'd have come to you, but I think if I'd said I was going down to the surface, my security team would have had seven different kinds of fits." Jarrod Tyler stood a few meters inside the doorway, and he stepped forward immediately, extending his hand. Tyler was a tall man, trim with neatly cropped brown hair, fringed around the outside with a light frosting of gray. He looked like a healthy and active man of fifty, but Cranston knew Columbia's ruler was a few months shy of his eightieth birthday.

"Of course, General Tyler. It was no trouble at all. I'm quite certain my people can handle the repairs while I am absent for a few hours." Cranston took Tyler's hand and the two shook firmly. "We are greatly in your debt, General. If not for your forces, I fear the Nest would have been completely destroyed."

"Not at all," Tyler said. The dictator wore a plain uniform, dark gray with almost no adornments, save for a small cluster of stars on the collar. "Indeed, we have long been neighbors. And allies too, have we not? We could do nothing less." Tyler turned and gestured toward a small table with two chairs. "Please, Major, have a seat."

"Thank you." Cranston nodded and walked over to the table, pulling back a chair and sitting. "Yes, General," he said, returning his attention to Tyler's statements. "Of course. Columbia is a most valued ally. Still, it is one thing to sign documents and quite another to stand in the fire to back them. Not all friends are as fair in difficult moments as they are during times of peace and plenty. You and your people have the thanks—and the gratitude—of the Black Eagles."

Tyler nodded. "Thank you. That is indeed something of great value." He paused. "I must confess, Major, I asked to meet with you for reasons beyond the mutual assurances of our alliance. I would never pull you from your duties so you could thank me for keeping my word as an ally. I am not the kind of man who wastes time with such nonsense."

"I had no doubt there was business you wished to discuss, General…or else I'd have likely thanked you on the com and allowed General Cain to make more substantive gestures when he returns."

Tyler nodded. "Before we get to business, you might like to know that we recovered Captain Caravalla and forty-two of his fighter crews. Nine of his craft survived the fighting. We recovered them and are currently providing medical services to your personnel. They are welcome to remain with us until we can find a less cumbersome means of transporting them back to the Nest."

"Thank you, General." Cranston managed a brief smile. "I'd given up on the fighter crews." *Though seventy-seven percent losses is nothing to celebrate.*

Tyler nodded solemnly and looked at his guest for a few seconds. Finally, he said, "I have done my part as an ally of the Black Eagles, Major, and I would have required no other reason beyond friendship to do so. Nevertheless, while I did not take the steps I did to earn gratitude, it is always good when an ally acknowledges an act of good will."

"Please, General, tell me what we can do for you. I'm afraid our combat effectiveness is not at its usual level, but if it is possible, you will have whatever assistance we can give you."

"Thank you, Major. But I suggest you reserve your acceptance until you hear what I have to say. You know that Columbia maintains a high degree of security, that we are constantly seeking to uncover and identify threats to our planet?"

Cranston wasn't sure if it was a question or a statement, but he just nodded and said, "Yes, of course." Jarrod Tyler's paranoia was well known, though Cranston's review of the general's history suggested he had good reason to feel the way he did.

"As I said, Major, there is satisfaction in the act of helping a friend, and I would have intervened for that reason alone. Yet I did have other motivations as well. I have done my part to aid the Eagles. Now I must ask that you do yours...and share information with me."

"Information? What information?" Cranston felt his stomach tighten. He had a feeling he knew what Tyler wanted.

"I have had a number of disturbing reports of strange occurrences in Occupied Space. Indeed, General Cain came to Columbia last year and we discussed the matter." He looked right at Cranston. "I believe the Eagles have discovered more about what is happening...and I would ask that you share what you know with us."

Tyler looked expectantly at Cranston for an instant. Then he leaned forward and added, "I assure you, I am interested in this only for the safety of my world. Columbia has fought many battles, Major, and suffered mightily in them. Few worlds in Occupied Space have seen the horrors we have, invasion after invasion. But when I took my office, I swore she would never again face an enemy unprepared." He paused again. "So, please, Major…tell me what you know about whatever enemy sent this fleet to attack the Nest. This force that seemed to know exactly when General Cain and the fleet and ground forces would be away?" He took a breath. "And one more question, Major… where are the rest of the Black Eagles?"

Chapter 34

Obelan Foothills
Five Kilometers from Eldaron City
Planet Eldaron, Denebola IV
Earthdate: 2319 AD (34 Years After the Fall)

"Get this man out of his armor. Now! If we're going to save his life, we have to start immediately."

Sarah Cain stood surrounded by the hulking forms of wounded men and women. Their fighting suits were rent open and covered in blood. The field hospital had been quiet in the early stages of the battle, and she had marveled at the superiority that Darius' fighters had exhibited, how they used it to minimize their losses. Even the fighting against the tank attack had only produced moderate casualties.

But that had all changed. The soldiers who had emerged from their hidden bunkers weren't the Eagles' equals…but they were a hell of a lot closer than any of the other forces Darius' warriors had faced. And they outnumbered the Eagles by at least five to one.

"Faster, man, faster," Sarah yelled. Those who knew her personally had always marveled at the transformation that took her on the battlefield. Her normal pleasant and easy-going personality vanished, replaced by a vicious taskmaster who had no more use for excuses than Erik or Darius Cain had ever had on the front line. But the Eagles' medical personnel had never encountered her before, and as good as they were, she was something entirely different.

"I'm sorry, Ge…Doctor," the man said, uncertain what to call her. She was a Marine general, a trauma surgeon, and the mother of the Black Eagles' commander…none of which led to a clear conclusion as to what she was on this battlefield. "The rips in his armor got driven into his legs. We're trying to get them out…if we use the plasma torch, we'll…"

"Just get him out of there. Take the legs off if that'll speed things. He's going to lose them anyway." She took a step closer and peered over the unconscious Eagle. "His legs are the least of his problems, Lieutenant. If I can save his life, we can regenerate those."

Sarah looked up at the med tech and nodded. Then she watched as he pulled out the plasma torch and used it to slice off one of the soldier's legs. She moved around, leaning over and making sure the heat of the torch had sufficiently cauterized the stump. Then she backed up slightly, while the tech amputated the other leg.

They hadn't even bothered with anesthesia. The stricken soldier was unconscious, and Sarah knew he would stay that way unless she was able to repair enough of the catastrophic damage he had suffered in battle. And medical supplies were starting to run low. The fleet had sent down a last shipment with Kuragina's White Regiment, but she knew that was the last she'd see…at least until the fleet defeated whatever force had come to challenge it.

Sarah stepped back for an instant as the crew working on her patient pulled off a section of his shattered armor. She watched as they dumped the enormously heavy chunk of osmium-iridium alloy off to the side of the table and moved on to cut another section.

She stepped forward, her gloved fingers probing the massive wound on the soldier's shoulder. There were bits and pieces of metal embedded in the stricken flesh, and she picked out a few of the most accessible ones.

"Five units blood substitute," she snapped off to the assistant standing behind her. "And a trauma-3 cocktail." She looked up and down the exposed areas of the wounded man, searching for an intact vein. "Here," she said, pointing to the side of the soldier's neck. Get your IV set up here."

Sarah hated the death, the terrible feeling of knowing some of these brave soldiers would die no matter what she did, how hard she tried to save them. The men and women on her operating tables now weren't Marines...and she was surprised how little that mattered to her.

She realized she had allowed herself to think of the Black Eagles in the same terms everyone else had, but now, surrounded by them, seeing them in battle, how they worked together as brothers and sisters...she had to admit they reminded her of Marines.

Of course. Darius grew up into a different world, a new reality. But he'd emulated his father, at least as well as he could. These people may be mercenaries, but they understand honor and loyalty too. They are here not for pay, but because Darius asked them to come. They are fighting—and hundreds are dying—to help rescue Erik.

She knew she had misjudged Darius and the military force he had created...and she intended to atone for that sin the best way she could. She would stay in this field hospital, day and night until she literally dropped from exhaustion. But she would save as many of these warriors as she possibly could.

She hunched over the patient, her hands moving all over him. Her hair was tied behind her head, but a small tuft had worked its way free of the elastic and was hanging down in her face. Sweat streaked down her cheeks as she worked against the odds, desperately trying to address the most vital wounds. The soldier's medical AI had done what it could...if it hadn't, she knew, the man would have never made it to the hospital. But now, as she worked closely, she found even more damage.

She was grateful for the way her work consumed her, mind and body. She was a surgeon now, and that was all she had time for. The mother, worrying about her son trapped in an enemy fortress, the wife, desperately hoping the husband she'd long thought dead was actually still alive...they were submerged now, held back by the sheer, brutal necessity for her to focus on the tasks at hand.

"We've almost got the last of the armor off, Doctor," the Lieutenant said, wiping the sweat from his face as his two assistants tugged at the patient's other arm.

Sarah stared back, her face blank. "Don't worry about it," she said softly. "He's dead."

*　　　*　　　*　　　*　　　*

"Colonel Kuragina's lead battalion has completed its retirement, sir. Her second battalion has now reinforced them." Camerici's voice betrayed her exhaustion. She'd been at her post for almost three days straight, but Teller had been hesitant to let her stand down. She was enormously capable at what she did—the best in the Black Eagles, and that was saying something indeed. And right now, lives hung in the balance, the survival of friends and comrades. He needed her where she was, and besides, he suspected he'd have one hell of a fight on his hands if he even suggested she take a break.

I just hope she's not shy about taking the stims. Camerici struck him as the stubborn type, one who would decide she could do what had to be done, without any help, chemical or otherwise. He found such thinking to be familiar—and admirable. As long as it didn't go too far. Eventually her body would give out, no matter what her mind insisted. And the stims could push that moment further into the future.

"Very well, Captain. Casualty reports?" He felt his stomach tense.

"Preliminary so far, sir. Looks like seventy-three dead, one hundred forty wounded."

Teller shook his head. *Thirty percent casualties…and we were still forced back.*

"Are the enemy following up?"

"Not yet, Colonel. Kuragina has the air thick with drones,

and we're getting good scouting reports. It looks like they're trying to reform to follow up. They got badly hurt on that attack. Kuragina estimates close to 2,000 enemy down." Camerici's voice became stronger, a wave of satisfaction finding its way into her otherwise grim reports.

"Yes, her people made them pay for the gains." Teller was shaking his armored head. *But that was on a perfect killing ground, and we burned through a mountain of ammo to do it. The approach to the next line is hillier, with a lot more natural cover. And I'm starting to worry about supplies...*

Teller had seen the battle, at least the start of it. He hadn't been in the thick of the fighting, but he'd led Kuragina's second battalion up to a supporting position, a little more than a klick from the heaviest combat. He'd intended to stay and take the battalion into the battle, but then he got word that the Eldari had launched an offensive all along the line in front of the capital. He'd hurried back to HQ only to find that, by the time he arrived, the single Eagle battalion in position had repulsed the attack, inflicting heavy losses on the Eldari.

If only we were facing Eldari regulars everywhere, he thought. But he knew that wasn't the case. Not even close. He recognized these soldiers who had come pouring out of hidden bunkers all across the field. He'd seen them before...fought them before. On Lysandria. And Darius had fought them on Eris. He had suspected it was the same mysterious enemy who had lured them to Eldaron...and Darius had as well. Now he knew. Whoever was interfering in conflicts across Occupied Space, they had targeted his people. This was intended to be the final battle, the complete destruction of Black Eagles.

He hadn't been able to get through the jamming to reach Darius. Truth be told, he didn't even know if his friend was still alive. And he'd had no reports from Admiral Allegre either. Perhaps the fleet was gone as well, blown to plasma by the same enemy his soldiers were facing on the ground.

This was a trap, alright, and even though we knew it going in, they still managed to take us by surprise. But we're not done yet...and anybody who starts a blood feud with the Black Eagles better make sure they kill us all...

*   *   *   *   *

"Where is the prisoner who occupied this cell?" Darius Cain's voice was like an elemental force, echoing off the ceiling eight meters above. He spun around to face the six Eldari soldiers standing against the wall. "You all know who I am. You've all heard stories about me. Now, you are going to answer me, and you are going to tell me the fucking truth...or you will see a side of me you couldn't have imagined in your worst nightmares."

Darius had burst through the door, ready to find out once and for all if his father still lived, if he had been a prisoner of the Eldari all these years. But all he'd found beyond the door was a rickety old stair leading down to the cell itself. An empty cell. No prisoner at all.

His people had searched the room from one end to the other, but they'd only confirmed what he'd seen the instant he'd run inside. There was no one there.

They'd found some scraps of fabric, and what looked like a worn and filthy tunic stained with blood...along with an old plate and a dented metal cup. There was residue on the plate, the remains of some sort of food. Someone had occupied the cell recently...at least the evidence pointed that way.

Darius picked up the plate and held it up in front of him as he turned back toward the prisoners. "There was someone in this cell...recently enough that the crust of whatever foul swill you feed your prisoners is still on his plate." He walked down the line of Eldari captives, pushing the plate forward, holding it a few centimeters from the face of each guard.

"So what will it be?" He deployed the molecular blade from the sleeve of his armor and turned his other hand to throw the plate to the floor. Then he froze. The bottom of the metal circle appeared to be scratched and scuffed. He'd assumed it was from age and use, but now Darius saw it. Letters...clearly letters. Carved all over the bottom of the plate. EC.

He felt a shiver go through him, and he stared at the plate, confirming what he was seeing. It was clear. Someone had craved the letters "EC" in the plate over and over...at least ten times.

Erik Cain...

So where was he? If his father had truly been in this cell, where was he now?

Darius felt the breath ripped from his body. Was he too late? Had his father been taken from his cell and executed? Had the arrival of his forces caused the death of his father?

"Where is he," he yelled, his voice thick with menace and venom. He reached down with an armored hand and grabbed one of the prisoners, hurling him across the room into the far wall. The man fell to the ground with a sickening thud and remained where he lay.

Darius turned toward the second soldier. The man cringed, shaking like a leaf and begging for mercy in almost unintelligible grunts. But there was no mercy in Darius Cain, not now. He was becoming more convinced with each passing second, the thought playing over and over in his head. His father was dead. He had been here, but the Eldari had killed him. There was something else there too, something dark and hideous, a malevolence he hadn't imagined lived inside him. It gave rise to thoughts more terrible than any he'd imagined before. Images of Eldaron, of the Eldari...paying for what they had done. Of cities burning...and thousands dying.

He reached down, grabbing the second soldier and yanking him up, holding the man's frantically struggling body over his head.

"Darius!"

The voice on the com was familiar, and it reached through the haze of vengeance and terrible violence that had seized him. It was a friend, a new one certainly, but a friend nevertheless.

"Darius," the voice repeated. "The prisoner from this cell is alive...or at least he was." An armored figure burst through the door, and stood at the top of the stairs looking down. He held another Eldari in his armored hand. "There was a fight, Darius. The prisoner attacked his guards…and the Tyrant. He was taken to the infirmary…badly hurt but still alive."

The last words echoed in Darius' mind. *Still alive…*

He turned and looked up at the armored man standing just inside the door. "Axe," he called out, "are you sure?"

"Yes, Darius…as sure as I can be. This man is the head jailor. And I didn't survive so long on Earth without knowing how to get the truth out of someone." Axe pulled the hapless Eldari hard, dragging him out in front of him. "And I made it clear to him what will happen if he's lying."

Darius stood still for a moment, his mind catching up with developments. He'd felt the enormous grief, mourned his father all over again, this time with the guilt of believing his own actions had caused his death. Now there was hope again. His cynicism, the defensive mechanisms he'd spent his adult life building around himself…they called to him not to believe, not to allow hope to flourish again, only to be dashed to bits with more pain and remorse. But he couldn't hold it back. Axe was a newcomer to the Eagles, but Darius had trusted him—and valued his judgment—since almost the moment they had met. The Earther had lived through the Fall, and he'd kept his people safe and alive for thirty years. And now, perhaps, he was leading the way to Erik Cain.

"Let's go," Darius shouted to the twenty Eagles scattered around the cell.

"And the prisoners?" The sergeant standing over the captives looked toward Darius.

Cain had been ready to tear the pathetic Eldari soldiers apart one by one, but now his thoughts were already moving forward. "Stun gun," he said as he ran toward the stairway and bounded up in three steps. He could hear the sounds as his troops fired at the guards. The lucky Eldari faced a few hours of unconsciousness, followed by some staggering headaches…not too bad considering how close they had come to horrible deaths at the hands of a distraught Darius Cain.

"We pulled a schematic from their main computer, Darius.

I've got the location of the infirmary.

Darius slapped his hand on Axe's armored shoulder. "Good job, my friend." He flipped a switch and put himself on the unitwide com. "Alright Eagles…follow me."

$*$ $*$ $*$ $*$ $*$

"My God," the Tyrant wailed miserably, "how is anybody supposed to beat troops like that?" He'd been staring out at the display, watching his shattered forces stagger back in disorder. The Eagles had redeployed to face the Omega units, and they'd only left a single battalion to face his concentrated forces. But the thinly-stretched line of mercenaries had blasted his offensives into bloody disasters. His people had suffered another 2,000 casualties in just a few hours…and the damned Black Eagles were right where they had been, staring out across a hellish no man's land, ready to crush any new attack.

"Your Excellency, General Trax is on your com line."

The Tyrant waved his hand at the officer in a gesture of disgust, but he moved to his chair nevertheless and strapped the headphones on. "Yes?"

"I saw the repulse of your attack. You must launch another immediately."

The Tyrant frowned. The Omega general refused to call him 'Your Excellency" or Tyrant. It didn't seem important in one way, at least not considering the crucial status of the operation. But on the other hand, it was pissing him off to no end. Twenty-five million people on Eldaron, and they all bowed down to him, spoke to him in only the most respectful and subservient tones. And then there was this upstart general, who somehow considered himself to be the Triumvirate's senior official on Eldaron. It was intolerable.

"That's out of the question, General." The Tyrant was scared of Trax, but he put all his will power into trying to hide it. "My forces require considerable time to reform and resupply." *And with what we lost to the EMP bursts, I'm damned near out of supplies…*

"The Eagles must be pinned down, at least. You face less than 600 enemy soldiers…and you have what, 10,000 or more along your lines, and in the city and the Citadel? You will attack now…and you will put more strength into it than you did last time."

The Tyrant felt the rage building inside him, and he saw images in his mind, that arrogant Omega general buried up to his neck as wild Eldari field boars stampeded over him. Or transfixed between two metal pillars, screaming as charge after increasing charge of electricity was pumped through his dying body. The Tyrant knew a hundred ways to punish those who failed to show him the loyalty and respect he demanded…and he'd used them all.

"I will see to it, General," he said, disgusted with himself for yielding so meekly. But there was no arguing with the fact that Trax and his soldiers controlled his future. The Tyrant knew his forces could never defeat the Black Eagles, and if Trax's men failed to do so, that would be the end. He shivered as he imagined what would happen to him at Darius Cain's hands.

"Immediately!" The Omega general cut the line.

"Calman!" the Tyrant roared.

"Sir!" the senior general answered. It was obvious that he, too, was nervous…of defeat perhaps, but certainly of the Tyrant, who was clearly becoming less stable with each passing moment.

"You call Davidoff and tell him I want another attack launched within the hour. And if he values his neck, it will be a hell of a lot more aggressive and successful than that last pathetic display."

"Yes, Excellency." Calman's tone was weak, defeated. It was clear he realized Davidoff had done the best job possible. But the Eldari forces were demoralized, and they had suffered enormous losses. There was still a critical shortage of weapons. If Davidoff ordered a larger attack, it was simple math to realize that half his soldiers would be advancing with clubs in their hands.

The Tyrant sat down hard in his chair and stared out over the command center. He'd been planning this operation for years... the great success that would propel him to the rule of a hundred worlds. But in all his imaginings, it had never been like this. He knew Trax's forces were pushing the Eagles hard, using their numbers to keep Cain's people under constant pressure. But seeing how the Eagles fought, he despaired of ever defeating them. He'd heard all the legends, of course, but now he truly understood. His soldiers were like children compared to these warriors...and if the battle was to be won, it would be Trax and his legions who claimed the victory.

And the Triumvirate will know how badly my soldiers performed...how unready we were for the Eagles. His mind was lost in a sea of fear, and he knew the promise of ruling so many worlds had already fizzled into the mist. He'd be lucky to keep Eldaron. He'd be lucky to keep his head.

"Your Excellency, we're receiving reports from the lower levels. Darius Cain and his soldiers are on the move out of the detention area."

"Where are they heading?"

"Toward the infirmary, Excellency."

The Tyrant felt another flush of anger. *If I find out who talked down there...*

"Alert Force Black," he said. They are to engage the Eagles at once." Force Black consisted of the pick of his personal guard, the eight hundred best soldiers on Eldaron. "I want the Eagles stopped before they get to the infirmary." He paused. "At all costs," he said, his every word an implicit threat.

"Yes, Excellency. Colonel Vialle reports Force Black is already deployed and ready to attack."

"Then they are ordered to proceed...and destroy Darius Cain for me."

"Yes, sir."

The Tyrant leaned back in his chair. His guards were in place, and they knew every centimeter of those tunnels. They were positioned at every intersection, every place they could get a field of fire on the approaching invaders. They outnumbered the Eagle force four to one. There was no way Darius Cain would get to the infirmary. No way.

Still, he felt a tension in his stomach, a nagging feeling that poked at him. There was no way the Eagles should be able to get through. But still...

"Captain Mieren?"

"Excellency!" The captain of the Tyrant's guard stepped out from his place along the wall and snapped to attention.

"I don't want to take any chances, Captain. Too much unexpected has happened already." *And the Eagles are here...and fully engaged. No sense being careless.*

"I have a job I want you to handle personally, Captain."

"I am yours to command, your Excellency."

"Go down to the infirmary...and kill the prisoner for me. Immediately."

"Sir!" The Captain clicked his heels and saluted. Then he turned and moved toward the exit.

No, Darius Cain, you will not get the better of me...no matter how fiercely your soldiers for hire fight...

Chapter 35

325 Million Kilometers from Planet Eldaron
Denebola System
Earthdate: 2319 AD (34 Years After the Fall)

"Eagle *Four's* reactor is down again, Admiral. She's bleeding atmosphere, and Captain Lorne reports he's not sure how long he can keep life support and basic backups functioning."

Allegre felt the words, like crushing blows from an enemy pounding into his chest. He'd never even been close to losing a ship in his time with the Eagles, but his thoughts were back farther than that now, to the deadly struggles of his youth. Ships died by the dozens in those terrible struggles...by the hundreds. He could still remember the voices of the com officers making the reports they knew would be their last...

"Advise Captain Lorne he is to take all steps possible to restart the reactor, at least long enough to get *Eagle Four* out of the line."

The line? You don't have a line, just ten ships, and five of those are blasted half to scrap. Not that the others are far behind.

The Eagle fleet had fought magnificently, and nearly two dozen enemy ships had been blasted to plasma. But the attackers were just too strong, and fresh ships had come up as quickly as Allegre's people could destroy those they were facing.

Allegre knew that, man for man, ship for ship, the Eagles were better than their adversaries. But the numbers weren't equal, not even close, and war in space was enormously dependent upon logistics. Fighting against such a large force had quickly depleted the Eagle ships, making their position increasingly precarious.

First, they expended the last of their missiles...and the enemy reserves still pouring into the system had fresh magazines. Allegre had maneuvered his forces aggressively, struggling to stay in close, to eliminate the enemy superiority in long-ranged weapons. Then he'd sought to use his highly-trained crews to win the battle of maneuver, bringing his vessels in on advantageous vectors. It all helped, but none of it was going to be enough.

Allegre realized his people were going to die, but he had resolved that they would at least die well, fighting to the end. He'd thought, for a passing instant, of making a break for it, trying to extricate his fleet from the doom that was befalling it. But he quickly put the thought out of his mind. Eagles didn't run, and especially not when they would be leaving thousands of their brethren behind. And it didn't really matter anymore. His ships were too far from their exit warp gate, too badly battered to make good any escape attempt.

He looked up as *Eagle One's* lights dimmed for an instant as her batteries fired again. Her reactor was down to about seventy percent output, and Allegre had ordered priority to the laser cannons. He let his eyes drop toward his screen, watching to see if his flagship's latest shot had hit.

He felt a wave of excitement, and he looked up to see the bridge crew shaking fists in the air. There was a general shout, a cheer that he didn't allow himself to join, though he felt the same rush they all did. *Eagle One's* laser cannons had torn into one of the largest enemy ships...and a few seconds later the target lost containment and was consumed in the fury of its own fusion reaction.

They may overwhelm us, but they'll not soon forget the day they fought the Black Eagles...

"Admiral!" There was surprise in the tactical officer's voice.

"Yes, Lieutenant? Report."

"Sir, we've got more ships transiting."

Allegre felt the excitement of the last kill drain away. He had been *almost* sure his people were doomed, but now there was *no* chance. None at all.

"Very well, Lieutenant. Prepare a nav plan to pull us away from the Betalax-4 warp gate. Maybe we can finish off this task force before the new one can reach us…"

"But, sir…the new transits are coming through the Upsilon-2 gate, not Betalax-4."

Allegre's head snapped around.

"Upsilon-2?"

"Yes, Admiral."

Allegre sighed. The Upsilon gate was right on his flank, less than a million kilometers away. Any force coming through there would be in range of his ships in a matter of minutes.

It is over. Nothing to do now but fight until we go down.

"All ships are to maintain maximum fire, Lieutenant."

It was all he could think to do.

*   *   *   *   *

"Colonel, we're running low on ammunition down here." Dan Sullivan was crouched down behind a small rock outcropping. He was staring out at the advancing enemy, taking aimed shots…and dropping a target every time he squeezed the trigger. The attack was a big one, and he knew he should be firing on full auto, taking down as many enemies as he could, but he also had an eye on his ammo supply, and he knew he was looking at trouble if he didn't conserve.

"We're running low across the line, Dan." Cyn Kuragina was tough as nails, and she almost never allowed fear or doubt to creep into her voice. But Sullivan could tell immediately she was worried. *That means the situation is worse than I thought. A lot worse.*

"You're just going to have to manage with what you've got, Dan," she said, sounding almost apologetic. "I'll try to get some supplies up there as soon as I can...but when it gets there, you need to know it's the last you'll see. At least until the fleet gets back." There was another hitch in her voice when she mentioned the fleet. Admiral Allegre and his ships had been gone for two days...and there hadn't been so much as a status report. Everybody was fearing the worst, though no one had yet voiced the concerns verbally.

At least no enemy fleet has shown up and wiped our com network from the sky. Sullivan knew that would be the inevitable result of the fleet's destruction...and the fact that it hadn't happened was some cause for hope.

"Understood, Colonel."

"I'm sending you some reinforcements, Dan. Two companies from the second battalion. I wish it was more, but new enemy forces keep emerging from hiding places all around the city. I have to keep something in reserve."

"Thank you, Colonel. Two companies will be a huge help." Sullivan knew both of them understood the numbers at play... and just how bad the situation had become. He had taken over command of the battalion when Major Julich was wounded. That had been six hours before, and his people had repulsed three attacks since then. But the support he had expected hadn't arrived.

Colonel Teller had dispatched the Black Regiment to link up with the White...and launch a counterattack on the enemy's position. It had been a daring plan, one that defied all military norms...but it also offered the chance to disrupt the enemy rear. A breakthrough would allow Sullivan's forces to destroy a large amount of the enemy's supplies, hopefully crippling their offensive capabilities. At least long enough for the Eagles to regain the initiative. But then more enemy troops emerged from hiding, and they launched a flank attack on the Eagles' overall position. Teller hadn't had a choice. He cancelled the scheduled attack and sent Falstaff's Black Regiment to face the new assault. From all Sullivan had heard, the fighting on that front had been even more brutal than on his own.

"Good luck," Kuragina said. "I've got a company and some

walking wounded working on a backup defensive line, but it won't be ready for at least another eight hours, maybe ten." A pause. "You have to hold until then, Dan. No matter what."

"Don't worry, Colonel. We're Black Eagles. We know what to do." He swallowed hard. "Sullivan out."

He ducked and scrambled down the line. Bull Trent had taken over an autocannon after its crew had been killed, and he was manning the weapon alone. Sullivan could see exactly where the veteran was by the swath of dead enemy soldiers lying in the field in front of him. He jogged over behind the non-com.

"Nice shooting, Bull…but I'm gonna have to have you hand that weapon off. I need you for something else."

"Sir!" Trent snapped back, still firing as he acknowledged his commander's orders. "Perretti, Horn, get your asses over here and take over this gun."

Sullivan watched as the two veterans came running over, each of them crouched just enough to stay behind the gentle rise the company was using for cover. They walked up behind Trent, who fired right up until the instant Perretti took the weapon from his armored hands.

"*Sergeant* Perretti," Trent barked, emphasizing the rank as he did, "We are low on ammunition, so I expect you to actually aim with this fucking thing, you hear me?"

"Yes, Sergeant." Tony Perretti was a troublemaker, a man who had served years in Eagles yet managed to give back every promotion he'd ever gotten through one form of indiscipline or another. But he was a born soldier too, and his extreme reliability on the field of battle had saved him from expulsion…or discipline more severe than a demotion.

He was Sergeant Perretti now, and he was likely to stay that way. He'd made the mistake of becoming too much of a hero on Lysandria, and Darius Cain himself had put the stripes on his duty uniform. The promotion had come with congratulations…and a warning to cut the shit and accept the responsibility he had earned. Perretti was as tough as they came, and he wasn't scared of anyone. Except Darius Cain. And Bull Trent. And both of them had spoken.

Trent watched for a few seconds as the two non-coms got the autocannon back in operation. Then he turned and faced Sullivan. "Where do you want me, sir?"

"This is your Tony Perretti moment, Sergeant Trent." Sullivan was grateful for the helmet that hid his shit-faced grin.

"Sir?"

"With the authorization of Colonel Kuragina, I am herby giving you a field promotion to the rank of lieutenant and placing you in command of the company."

"But sir..."

"Silence, Lieutenant Trent. I know you have fought this for a long time, but in case you didn't notice, we're up to our necks in shit right now. Perretti is doing his duty...and you're fuck well going to do the same. Do you follow me?"

"Yes, sir." The voice was sullen, defeated. But there was a spark there too. Sullivan suspected Trent would prove to be as good an officer as he'd always been a non-com. Better, even.

Which was a damned good thing, because it was going to take everything all of them had to survive this fight.

*   *   *   *   *

"Get the wounded back," Darius yelled into the com. "Set up an aid station closer to the detention area. And clear these corridors!"

Cain and his soldiers had been halfway to the infirmary when the attack began. Enemy troops poured down every corridor, and almost immediately, the Eagles were bogged down and fighting off attacks from every direction.

"Yes, General." Captain Clive was the only surgeon he'd brought with him. Along with two medical techs and half a dozen privates hastily designated as orderlies, he was all that was available to deal with the mounting casualties. The Teams were the best of the best, and they fought with enormous skill and distinction...but they were outnumbered and unfamiliar with the layout of their battlefield. And they knew they had to press on, regardless of position or losses. They had to reach the infirmary. If Erik Cain was truly there, every second was the one the enemy could choose to kill him.

Alcabedo was right next to Darius. *As usual...how does he do that?*

The bodyguard was firing like a machine, putting a three shot burst into every enemy soldier within view. He'd apparently decided trying to get Darius to stay back was a futile effort, so he took it upon himself to try to blast every enemy that came close to the general.

And Darius had to admit, he'd come quite close to meeting that impossible goal.

Darius lunged forward, firing his own rifle as he did. The enemy soldiers were good...clearly these weren't standard Eldari levies. But they were no match for the veteran—and fully-powered—Black Eagles. They lost five, six, seven men for every casualty they inflicted, but Darius knew that was a winning trade for them. He had to keep pushing forward, not only to see if his father was there, but to prevent his forces from getting bogged down.

"I want a Team at each intersection or passageway," he snapped. "We've got to keep the line to the detention area open." He hadn't intended to allow his forces to get this stretched out, but he'd had no choice. His troops had suffered more than forty casualties. And the wounded couldn't keep up with the advance.

He moved swiftly down the corridor, and he whipped around the corner, ahead of Alcabedo and the three other Eagles who'd tried to get in front of him. There were three enemy troops there, and they opened fire almost immediately.

Darius dropped low and fire back on full auto. The enemy shots went over his head, the rounds impacting on the rough stone of the walls, sending shards of rock flying in all directions. His own fire was far more accurate, and in an instant the three enemies were down, their bodies torn almost to shreds by his hyper-velocity rounds. There was a brief clicking sound as his autoloader replaced the spent cartridge.

"That should be the infirmary right up ahead," he said, his com set to the unitwide frequency. "Let's go!" He ran down the hallway, his rifle in front of him as he did.

He stopped in front of the closed hatch. "Plasma torches," he yelled.

Two Eagles pushed their way forward, each of them holding a large plasma cutter. They thrust the tools forward, one on each side of the hatch, and they sliced downward, cutting through the hypersteel like a razor slicing a sheet of paper. In a few seconds it was done, and the two of them kicked the door hard, sending it flying into the room beyond.

Darius pushed past the two of them, leaping first into the room. It was reckless, a stunt for which he would have disciplined any of his people. But Darius Cain the military commander had momentarily lost his control over the persona he now shared with Darius Cain, seventeen year old boy, first hearing his father had been killed. His heart pounded in his ears, and he was shaking inside his armor. That had been the worst day of his life, and now he was minutes from finding out if it was true...or if it had been a fraud all along.

In a few seconds, you'll know...

He looked around quickly, his eyes confirming the room was indeed part of an infirmary. There were medical machines of various types and a row of cots along the side wall. He turned and looked at the beds, frantically searching, feeling the hope he'd so firmly kept under control escaping its bonds, driving him forth with unrestrainable excitement.

He retained enough of Darius the soldier to watch for enemies, but that discipline had been off, below its usual standard. Just enough. He didn't even see the man, he just felt the impact, like a sledgehammer in his shoulder. He staggered backward, but he steadied himself and didn't fall. He had a vague sensation of his soldiers firing, a passing image of the man who had shot him blown halfway across the room, his body shredded by at least a hundred rounds.

Darius felt hands on his armor, those of his Eagles, but he swung his arm back, pushing them away. The wound was bad, but his AI had already packed it with sterile foam and pumped him full of painkillers and stims. He'd deal with it later. Now he had something more important to do.

He pushed through the infirmary, shoving stacks of equipment out of his way with the enhanced strength of his armor. He spun around the corner, this time with his rifle drawn, held in front of him with one arm.

He was staring down a long wing of the room, his eyes moving from cot to cot. He felt the chill of the cold sweat on his neck, and he wondered if he'd even recognize his father after so many years. What torment had he lived through, what profound, aching loneliness? Would he be older? Yes, of course. Would he be changed, hurt? Would he even recognize his own son...a thirty-two year old man he'd last seen as a boy of fifteen?

He pushed himself forward, snapping an order to the AI to increase his visor's magnification. *No*, he thought, looking at a man in one of the cots. *No...no....no...,* he thought, quickly discounting each of them in turn.

He froze. There was a cot at the far end of the room. A man was lying on it, covered to his chest with a white sheet. His head was turned, and a mass of stringy, gray hair hung over the edge of the bed. Then he saw it...the man's arm was along the edge of the bed...bound in a restraint of some kind.

A prisoner...

Darius pushed forward...just as he saw a man coming from the other side of the room. He was tall, wearing the uniform of an Eldari guardsman. He was walking right toward the man in the cot.

Darius' eyes snapped into laser focus. There was a pistol in the man's hand...

*   *   *   *   *

Eagle One shook hard, and a spray of sparks exploded across the bridge. One of the big power conduits had broken loose, and it fell in the middle of the bridge. The two security guards rushed over to secure the flopping cable, but one of them slipped and touched the live end. He thudded to the deck immediately, dead, his body stinking of burnt flesh.

"Get a damage control team up here now, Lieutenant." Allegre sat in his chair, trying to remain as calm as he could. He knew his people would look to him in this desperate hour, and he intended to give them all he had left to offer. He couldn't save them, he knew that. He had no tricks, no tactical wizardry to extricate them from this hopeless battle. But he could show them how to face death…and how to lash out in defiance with the very last of their strength.

"Sir, more ships coming through the Upsilon-2 gate. At least ten so far."

"Very well Lieutenant." He sighed. The enemy already had enough to finish off his fleet. They didn't really need any reinforce…"

"Admiral!" The tactical officer spun around, staring over toward Allegre's command chair. "We've got incoming communications from the arriving vessels."

Allegre felt an odd feeling…he wouldn't have called it hope, exactly, but it was something similar.

"Put it on the main speaker, Lieutenant." He wouldn't normally broadcast something unknown to the entire crew, but he figured they deserved to know what was happening. Whatever that was…

"Attention Black Eagles. Attention Black Eagles. This is Admiral Augustus Garret commanding the Marine Corps fleet. We have come to aid you in your struggle."

Allegre sat still, utterly stunned by what he had just heard. *Is this a trick? Are they trying to fool me, gain an advantage? But why? They know they have us.*

"I want scanning data on those incoming ships, Lieutenant. Now!"

He glanced around the bridge. Even his disciplined crew was distracted, looking around with confused expressions on their faces.

"Seventeen ships have transited, sir. They match the basic size distributions the database has for the Marine fleet from Armstrong, sir."

"It's not possible," Allegre snapped back. "How could the Marine fleet be here? How would they even know we were here?"

"They're requesting visual communication, sir."

Allegre shook his head. *It just can't be.* But he simply said, "Activate visual com."

He stood up, and he found he was subconsciously brushing himself off, straightening his uniform. He didn't really believe Augustus Garret was on the other end of the com line, but just in case…

The main screen lit up…and there was Augustus Garret. He was older than the last time Allegre had seen him—*which one of us isn't*—but he knew without the slightest doubt. It was humanity's great admiral, the man who had, more than anyone, saved mankind from the First Imperium…and from the orgy of self-destruction it tried to inflict on itself in the Shadow Wars.

"Hello, Gaston," Garret said simply. "It is good to see you. It has been, what? Seventeen years?"

Garret stood still, staring into the screen. He wasn't wearing a naval uniform, just a simple set of fatigues over a survival suit. He looked the same as always. His still-thick hair was completely gray now, and his face showed a bit more age, but the stare was the same…warm and cold at the same time. Reassuring…and deadly.

"Admiral Garret," Allegre said, his throat suddenly so dry he could barely force out the words. "How?"

Garret managed a thin smile. "Well, I tried to stay on the sidelines for this one…but what can I say? It's just not in my blood."

Garret turned to the side, gesturing to someone off-camera. "Or, if you mean how did I know *you* would need my help here…"

Garret stepped aside and another man walked into view. Allegre was confused for an instant, but then he saw the face, and he gasped. "I don't under…"

"Hello, Admiral Allegre. I am Elias Cain. I'm sorry if I gave you a bit of a start. I know my brother and I have quite a resemblance." Elias grinned. He and Darius were identical, and beyond hairstyles and clothing, it was almost impossible to tell them apart. At least physically.

Allegre shook his head, trying to clear away the shock he felt. "Mr…" *No, it's captain…* "Captain Cain, I still don't understand."

"Gaston," Garret interjected. "I realize this is quite a surprise for you, and you no doubt have many questions. But I suggest we deal with this enemy fleet before the Q&A session. What do you think?"

Allegre felt strength flowing into his arms and legs, a hot fury driving away the cold numbness of defeat. The enemy fleet was still strong, and the fight would be a hard one. But now he had reinforcements. And he had Augustus Garret.

"I agree completely," Allegre answered, the determination thick in his tone.

Oh no, the battle wasn't over yet. Not by a long shot.

Chapter 36

The Citadel
Planet Eldaron
Denebola System
Earthdate: 2319 AD (34 Years After the Fall)

Darius felt as if time had slowed. His eyes were locked on the soldier with the pistol. Was he just another enemy soldier, responding to his attack? For an instant he thought so. But then he felt a coldness, a realization. The man was here to kill the gray-haired patient. He had no evidence, no reason for certainty, but he knew...somehow he just knew, and he'd never been surer of anything in his life.

Every muscle in his body tensed, an almost electric feeling energizing him, driving his reactions. He had no time for thought, for considering facts, but he didn't have to. He realized instantly...if the Eldari had sent someone to kill that patient, now, in the middle of all that was happening it could mean only one thing...

Father.

His mind wanted to explode, wild thoughts streaming in every direction. But, somehow, the discipline that had always guided him held on, maintained his focus. He had to act, now. Or he would watch his father die ten meters in front of him.

He saw the man moving toward the bed, his arm rising as he did, bringing the pistol to bear. Darius was still moving forward.

It wasn't the best situation for an aimed shot, but he didn't have time to stop. "Single shot," he snapped to the AI as he raised his rifle.

He took a breath and held it as his targeting sight moved over the enemy soldier.

He felt a rush move through him. He was going to make it…he was going to get his shot off first…

Then he heard the sound, an explosion, and even as his finger began to press down on the trigger, it hit him. A small shard of metal, slamming into his ankle. It was a minor wound, indeed, it had barely pierced his armor. But it pushed him forward, and his shot went wide. He was stumbling, and his visor shifted. He saw the floor coming up at him, and instincts kicked in, his body rolling to the side to cushion the impact.

He felt a coldness inside him, and he retched, tasting acidy bile in his mouth. *No,* he thought, a wave of despair coming over him from deep in his mind. He had missed. And that meant…

He whipped around, pushing himself up to his feet. There were waves of pain from the wounded ankle, but he ignored them, indeed, he was hardly aware of them. He was determined to get up, to kill the soldier with the gun. He knew he was too late, but he had to try. Still, he heard the same thing in his mind. *I'm sorry, father…I'm so sorry…*

Then his eyes focused on the cot, the man still lying there. The wall behind was covered in blood, fresh streams of droplets working their way down from a large circular stain. The soldier was gone…no, not gone. Darius saw his feet on the ground, visible behind the cot.

But I missed, I know I missed. And then he snapped his head around and saw the armored figure standing right behind him. Ernesto Alcabedo, his rifle still aiming where he had fired the deadly shot.

The shock hit Darius like a thunderbolt. Alcabedo had killed the enemy soldier…and saved the man in the cot. He stood there stunned for what could only have been an instant, though it stretched out for him, time almost at a standstill while he realized what had just happened. He was finally pulled from his thoughts by the sound on the com, the same words again and again. "General, are you okay?"

"I'm fine, Ernesto," he replied, shaking off the surprise. "Nice shot!"

He moved forward. He knew it was careless, and he could see Alcabedo coming up on his side, rifle out, looking for enemies. Discipline, even the experienced of a dozen battlefields, had its limits. And Darius Cain couldn't wait. He *had* to know. Now.

He pushed forward toward the cot, throwing a stack of equipment out of his way as he did. He stopped at the edge of the bed, and he looked down at the man lying there. His face was drawn, thin from malnutrition. There were scars, the marks of what must have been hundreds of beatings.

He lay under a thin white sheet, and Darius could see the wretched form below. There were bandages in half a dozen places, crusty with dried blood. The captive soldier had said the prisoner been shot...and the man lying in the bed had indeed been shot.

Darius had come lightyears, attacked an entire world to determine if his father was still alive. And now as he stared down at the broken man on the cot, he wasn't sure. Of all the things he'd expected, the traps and the resistance of his enemies, the brutal struggle to break into the heart of the Citadel, he'd been sure he would recognize his father. But the man lying before him was so changed, so withered by ill treatment...

Darius felt a wave of rage, at the way the man had obviously been abused...and at himself. *How could you not know your own father...*

Then the prisoner opened his eyes. They were cloudy, filmy, caked with a dried crust...but even through all of that, Darius could see the piercing blue. Eyes like his, like Elias'. Eyes like a Cain.

He felt his legs go weak, and he struggled to control himself, to hold back the tears, the avalanche of emotions that struggled to come forth.

"Father," he said softly, looking down at the man. "Father it is me. Darius. I've come to get you out of here. To take you home."

The man in the cot turned his head slowly, looking up at the armored figure staring over him. There was disorientation in his glance, and fear. But Darius could see recognition too. It was faint, confused…but it was there. "Marines?" he rasped, his tortured voice barely audible.

Darius was confused for an instant, but then he realized. He was fully armored…and his father would equate that with Marines.

"Open helmet," he said to the AI. An instant later it retracted, and he felt the outside air. It was cooler than the perfectly climate controlled environment of his fighting suit, and the scent of alcohol was heavy. As was the smell of decay, of death.

"Father, it is Darius, your son." He looked down into the blue eyes, saw the uncertainty, the fear. He knew this was his father, that it was Erik Cain lying there. But he also understood the torment, the unimaginable hell he had been through…a prisoner for seventeen years, tortured, isolated. *Of course he doesn't recognize you…you were fifteen when he left.* But he still felt a pang of hurt. He was a feared soldier, a warrior prince, but now all he wanted was for the broken man in the cot to know who he was.

"Erik…Cain…" The man was forcing out the words, and it was clear each syllable was an effort, a painful one. "I…am… Erik…Cain…"

Darius wanted to reach out, to touch his father's face, but his hands were armored…his whole body was wrapped in ten tons of osmium-iridium alloy. He felt confusion, almost panic. He didn't know what to do. He could hear the sounds of battle around him, but he had ignored it all. He was vaguely aware of Alcabedo next to him.

Standing guard.

But he was lost…

"Dar…i…us…"

He stared at the man, at his father, and a single tear overcame his efforts to restrain it, rolling slowly down his cheek. "Yes," he said, his voice choked with emotion. "Yes, father…it is Darius." He gasped for a breath, still fighting to retain his composure. "I'm here to take you home."

"Home…" the man rasped. "Yes…home…" Then he turned his head and looked right up at Darius. "Sar…ah?"

"Yes, father…mother is fine. I am going to take you home… to mother."

"Home," Erik said. His thin lips morphed into a weak, quivering smile. "Sarah."

"Yes, father. Home. Mother."

Darius looked around the room. His people had secured the area, but there was fighting at every approach to the infirmary.

"General…" It was Alcabedo. "We have to get out of here. It's too open, too many approaches."

Darius felt himself return to reality. The joy at finding his father alive was tempered by the danger. They weren't out of trouble yet, not by a long shot. He knew Erik Cain could still die on Eldaron…along with all the Black Eagles.

"Back to the prison, Ernesto. We can set up a stronger position there."

He leaned down and slipped his arm under his father's frail form. Erik shied away from the touch and cried out softly, but Darius scooped him up anyway. He tried to be gentle…as gentle as two large metallic arms could be, but he held his father firmly. They had to get out of here. Immediately.

*   *   *   *   *

Erik Teller stared at the data on the portable display. It was the third time he'd gone over it, and it was telling him the same thing. "Fuck," he muttered softly.

His people had been fighting the new enemy for three days, facing assault after assault. He'd been to every spot on the battlefield, helped pick each position and design each section of fieldworks. He'd been awake for over a week without a break, and he'd overridden his AI's warnings and pumped three times the safe dosage of stims into his bloodstream.

He had shifted reserves back and forth, meeting each attack with enough strength to beat it back. But now the enemy had all their forces in place. And unless he was reading the map wrong—and he sincerely doubted that—his people were about to be attacked on every front, fresh assaults coming in all along his surrounded position.

Erik knew his people had taken out close to ten thousand of the new enemy…and nearly twice that many Eldari levies. But they had lost heavily as well, and most of his units were down to half strength or less. He'd burned the last of his drones on the most recent scanning sweep, and the data was sobering.

Twenty-thousand, he thought grimly. *They've got twenty-thousand in the line, even after all we killed…all powered infantry like us. And another seven thousand Eldari troops in the trenches in front of the city.*

He was proud of the Eagles. They had fought as well as they ever had, as well as *any* soldiers ever had. But there was a limit, and Teller feared he was looking at it now.

I'm sorry, Darius. Are you even still alive in there somehow? Have you been able to hold out in some remote corner, you and the survivors of the Teams? Or have they run you all down, wiped you out? Did you die wondering where we were? Why we didn't take the Citadel, why we didn't come to your aid?

Teller just shook his head. He'd imagined what defeat would feel like, wondered how he would face death when it came for him.

And now you will see, you will understand what all those who have fallen to your arms felt, feel the coldness of failure and destruction.

"But if we must die," he said to himself, "we will die well." He felt his mind clear, the uncertainty fading away. The Eagles' last battle would not be marred by doubts and fears. He owed that much to Darius. And the Eagles. And himself.

"Activate corps-wide com," he snapped at his AI.

"Activated," came the response.

"Attention all Black Eagles. The enemy is about to attack us all across the line. I don't need to tell any of you how outnumbered we are. How low on supplies and ordnance. I don't need to tell you we face many thousands of enemies, fully-armored and powered like us. No. None of this matters. None of it will affect our actions in the coming battles." He paused, pushing back an errant thought about what Darius would have said in this situation.

"No, I need only say one thing to you, and I know with certainty that each of you will truly, deeply understand the meaning. You are Black Eagles, every one of you. And that is all you need to know, all you must think about as we enter this fight." Another pause. "Stand with me, my brothers and sisters, fight by my side as you have so many times before. And remember... Black Eagles never yield."

He cut the com line, and his eyes dropped to the display. There were great thick lines on it, masses of enemy troops so dense the individual icons were not recognizable.

"Colonel!" Camerici's voice...excited, almost hysterical. He'd never heard her like that.

"Yes, Captain?"

"We have incoming communications, sir. It's Admiral Allegre, Colonel."

"Admiral," Teller said, finding it difficult to keep a flash of excitement out of his voice. "It is good to hear from you. We'd almost given up hope."

"It was a tough fight, Colonel." A short pause. "I'm afraid *Eagle Four* and *Eagle Six* were destroyed..."

"We feared you were all lost, Admiral. Considering what we've encountered down here, I imagined the enemy fleet was overwhelming in strength."

"It was, Colonel. We were on the brink of destruction."

"So what happened, Admiral? How did you turn the battle around?"

"We had a little help."

Teller shook his head. "I don't understand, Admiral. Help?"

"Yes, sir. We got reinforcements at the last moment."

Teller still didn't understand. "Reinforcements? Who reinforced you?"

"I did, Colonel Teller." The voice was low-pitched, serious but pleasant in tone as well. "I knew your father, Colonel. Quite well. An extraordinary man, and a good friend too. And I know you as well, though I'm afraid you were a young boy the last time I saw you."

Teller listened, focusing on the voice, the familiarity of it. *No*, he thought...*it's not possible*...

"I'm Augustus Garret, Erik," the voice said gently, even as Teller realized it himself.

Augustus Garret? How? Is it even possible?

Chapter 37

The Citadel
Planet Eldaron
Denebola System
Earthdate: 2319 AD (34 Years After the Fall)

Darius knelt over his father, reaching down and shoving a tattered pack behind the wounded man's head. The floor of the cell was cold and hard, but there was nothing he could do about that.

He's probably been sleeping on this floor for seventeen years…

He felt a twinge of guilt for bringing his father back to the very place he'd been imprisoned for so long, but the detention area was the best spot for his people to make a stand.

A last stand, probably.

He could hear the gunfire from outside the cell. The enemy had been attacking constantly, wave after wave of soldiers charging down the hallways. The constricted space favored his people and their defense, but he knew that wouldn't last. The enemy could replace their losses, but each Eagle that fell was one less in fight.

And ammunition's going to be a problem. Soon.

Darius Cain wasn't an optimist by nature, and he generally expected the worst from most situations. He knew his strength came from that darkness within him, that he owed his success to his almost paranoid preparedness. But he struggled now to keep a spark of hope alive. Defeat was one thing, but the thought of finding his father only to die with him here was more than he could bear.

He realized now that he'd never really anticipated finding his father alive on Eldaron, that he'd only come because he couldn't take the slightest chance that Erik Cain was alive and remained in captivity. And to punish the Eldari for any role they'd had in his father's death. But now he marveled at the irony of discovering his father alive, of Alcabedo's shot saving him at the last second…only to be cornered in the very prison that had held Erik Cain for so many years. Where he would now likely die, with his son and the two hundred Black Eagles of the Teams.

He knew Teller and the Eagles would have taken the Citadel by now if the operation had gone remotely according to plan. The jamming around the fortress was too intense for any communications to penetrate, and he'd had no word at all, not since his people had landed days before. For all he knew, the rest of the Eagles had been wiped out, victims of a trap that had proven to be too much, despite their preparedness. But he tried not to think of that. The guilt he would feel for getting all his people killed was unimaginable. If by some miracle he survived, he would mourn his dead Eagles, and torture himself for his role in their demise. But he knew he was far likelier to join them in death…probably a few meters from where he now stood.

He looked down at his father, feeling a bit of self-hatred for hardly recognizing him. His face was thin, and his skin was covered with lesions and sores. He was mostly unconscious, occasionally opening his eyes for a few seconds before slipping back into sleep. Darius had extended his hand several times, feeling the urge to touch his father, to put a warm hand against his cheek. But each time he remembered he was in full armor, and he stopped himself. His presence, his words…they would have to do for now.

Ernesto Alcabedo was standing about a meter away, watching over Darius even though they were in the cell, behind the main combat areas. He had stayed respectfully silent, allowing

Darius some private time with his father, but now he turned and looked over.

"General, we've got more wounded coming."

Darius nodded. "Let's get them all in here. It's the safest place we've got." He waved toward the other side of the room where Clive had set up a makeshift aid station. There were about two dozen casualties lined up, but Darius knew there were a lot more of his people wounded.

"Yes, sir," Alcabedo replied. Then: "General, our people are requesting permission to pull back to the corridor outside. They've opened up the cells all along the hall and positioned snipers in each one."

"Yes," Darius said softly. "Do it."

We're being driven back steadily. The end begins...

Cain felt a thought go through his mind, quickly hardening to resolution. I can't stay here, back from the fight. Not now. "I'm going up there, Ernesto." Cain looked down at Erik Cain's unconscious form for a second before rising to his feet.

"What about your father, sir?" There was tension in the captain's voice. Darius knew it was fear. Alcabedo wasn't afraid for himself, at least no more than any man facing a deadly fight would be. But the officer had made himself responsible for the safety of the Black Eagles' commander, and Darius knew his bodyguard was much happier with him right where he was. He understood, but he wasn't a man who could stay back while others did the fighting. He knew it would be hard on his aide, especially since he was about to ask Alcabedo to stay behind. But no one had ever said being a Black Eagle was easy.

"My father would be the first to understand, Ernesto. He went to war wherever the bugle called. I can do nothing less." Darius tried to moderate his tone. He didn't need Alcabedo thinking he was on his way to find a good death...though he knew in his heart that is exactly what he was doing. He wasn't going to commit suicide...but he had no intention of surviving if his Eagles all died.

"What about your leg, sir? And your arm? You are wounded." There was growing desperation in the aide's voice.

"What about them, Ernesto. We've both had worse." He stood and put his hand on Alcabedo's armored shoulder. "I must ask something of you...and it will be difficult for you to do."

"Anything, General." Alcabedo's voice was firm, but Darius could hear the emotion too.

"I want you to stay here."

"General..."

"Listen to me, Ernesto. My place is with the men and women fighting. They deserve to see me there with them. They would in any battle, but this time they are only here because of my need. I owe it to them all, but I can only leave here if someone I trust remains behind." Darius paused, and his own voice began to crack slightly. "My father..." A long pause. "If they recapture him, they could...they could..."

Alcabedo stood stone still, staring at Darius. "He cannot fall back into their hands," the captain said simply.

"No...he cannot." Darius took a deep breath and fought to regain his focus. "Can I count on you, Ernesto...to do what must be done when all has come to the end?"

Alcabedo was silent for a few seconds. Darius understood the enormity of what he was asking, all the more for his own inability to say it in clear terms. He was asking his officer to kill his father, the great Marine hero...to put a bullet in the head of the tortured, wounded man lying on the floor. It would be an inconceivable act, yet both knew it would be even more unforgivable to let Erik Cain fall back into Eldari hands.

"Yes, General," Alcabedo rasped. It was clear he was putting all the strength he had into his answer. "I will do what you ask."

Darius exhaled hard. "Thank you, my friend. For this...and for your years of loyalty." He paused, staring at Alcabedo for a few seconds before his eyes moved once more to the figure stretched out on the floor.

I'm sorry, Father. I tried...and I beg you forgive me—us—but I will not let these monsters take you back. If I cannot bring you freedom, I will at least give you rest...

He felt tears welling up in his eyes, and he was grateful for the visor that hid his face. He nodded his head once, and he turned away and walked toward the exit.

*   *   *   *   *

"Admiral Garret...I don't know what to say." He understood what was happening, but he still struggled to reconcile with it. Augustus Garret was a legend, almost like a character out of mythology. He'd fought in every one of mankind's wars for eighty years...and he'd emerged victorious in all of them. But Teller still couldn't understand how he had come to Eldaron. It didn't make any sense. "But...how?" he asked, his voice halting

"How did I end up here? Well, I suppose that is an odd sequence of events, one that will have to wait until we have more time to talk. For now, you can thank your general's brother. I was on Armstrong when he arrived there."

"Elias? Elias is involved in this too?" His thoughts raced back. He and Darius and Elias had spent their childhoods together on Atlantia...until the Second Incursion destroyed their peaceful and happy lives. Neither Teller's father nor Erik Cain had returned from that war, and their sons had been left to deal with the losses the best they could. The pain had driven a wedge between Darius and Elias...and Teller had always been closest to Darius. He'd never shared the strange animosity that had developed between the brothers, but when Darius left Atlantia, Erik had gone with him...and he hadn't seen Elias Cain since.

"Yes, he is the reason we are here. He came to Armstrong from the Nest looking for reinforcements. He feared you had walked into a trap. And he brought word that Erik Cain might still be alive and a prisoner on Eldaron. Once the Marines heard that there was no holding them back."

Teller couldn't believe what he was hearing. He felt almost like he was punch drunk. "From the Nest?" he asked quizzically. "He was at the Nest?"

"Yes…apparently right after you left."

Teller stood silently for a moment, trying to reconcile everything he was hearing. "And your fleet?" he finally asked.

"The Armstrong squadrons," Garret replied. "The remainder of my old fleet, maintained by the Corps."

Teller was distracted by the sounds of incoming communications all around him, reports from units across the battlefield. Camerici and her people were handling it all, struggling to apportion the last of the supplies to the units that needed them most.

He turned and looked around the headquarters, at the desperate efforts of his staff, and he thought about the carnage up on the battle lines. His people were fighting and dying, even now, despite the fact that the fleet had returned, along with its unlikely reinforcements. His new excitement began to deflate. He was thrilled to find that Allegre and most of the Eagle ships had survived, and astonished and grateful that Garret had come to help. But it hadn't changed the situation on the ground. Not really.

His people were still under attack…and it was going to take a miracle for them to beat back this latest onslaught. He could see the maps on the portable displays. There were waves of enemy troops surging forward…and he already had two spots where they were threatening to break through. His people had inflicted horrifying losses on the attackers, but they kept coming no matter what.

"Admiral Garret…and Admiral Allegre…we're in a world of shit down here. We could use whatever support you can manage."

"Already done, Colonel. Admiral Allegre has downloaded the scanning data from the satellites. We believe we have identified the location of all of the enemy bases. We will be commencing orbital bombardment in approximately three minutes. Vaporizing their logistical centers should shake them up a bit."

Teller felt a rush of excitement. "That will be most helpful, Admiral."

"And Major Darryk's birds are launching too." A different

voice. Allegre. "They should be conducting close support runs in less than twenty minutes."

Teller sighed hard. *Fighter runs…maybe we'll get through this after all. But those birds are going to suffer from the AA…*

"Colonel, we're picking up landing craft, over a hundred of them…coming down just behind the enemy positions." Camerici's voice, interjecting onto his com line.

Teller froze.

Enemy reinforcements? Could there be surviving enemy ships up there too?

"Oh yes, Colonel," Garret said calmly. "That is General Gilson. She's on the way down now…with four battalions of Marines."

*   *   *   *   *

Catherine Gilson stepped out of the ten-man Liggett lander. The field behind her was covered with the strange craft. The Liggetts looked like something a child might have constructed from an erector set, a spidery framework of hyper-steel with ten small cradles for armored Marines. There was no hull, no pressurized interior, not even a cockpit. The craft were robot-controlled and the occupants rode outside, their armor covered in heat-resistant foam but otherwise in the open as they launched from orbiting spaceships.

The landers were pitted and scarred by the time they hit ground, but that was of no concern. They were built for a one way trip, to get assaulting Marines to the surface as quickly as possible. Gilson took a few steps forward, watching approvingly as her people ejected from their landing craft and quickly formed up. They were Marines, and she expected nothing less, but she also knew the Corps hadn't conducted a combat landing in fifteen years. More than half the men and women out there had never entered a hostile planet's atmosphere, never gone into a large battle. For all the vaunted training and the strong leadership she knew permeated the Corps, a lot of her people were about to get their baptism of fire.

I wish I had a division or two of the old veterans…

Her mind was on the men and women she had led decades before, the Marines who had won the Third Frontier War for the Alliance and then driven the First Imperium out of human space. They were gone now, most of them, lost in the brutal fighting that had raged almost uninterrupted for twenty-five years.

The old Corps had been the greatest fighting force every assembled, at least as far as she was concerned. Elias Cain had led them then, and the men and women who had fought under the Marine flag were some of the finest she'd ever known…warriors like Darius Jax, John Teller…Erik Cain.

Is he really alive? Is it possible?

Catherine Gilson had fought alongside Cain for decades, and the two had inherited command of the Corps when Elias Holm was killed. Cain had stepped aside with the coming of peace, ceded the top command to her…only to come back and fight in the Second Incursion. And, as had been widely believed, to die in that terrible conflict. Only now, it appeared, he might have survived after all.

Gilson understood why Sarah had slipped away without a word. She had known that Gilson would have taken the Corps to Eldaron immediately, that she would have committed everything to rescuing its lost general. But as much as Sarah loved Erik Cain, she would have known that the Corps had no chance alone. Its days of great power were behind it, and all that remained was a small force, determined to keep the spark of excellence alive, but without the numbers to project the power to conquer a world.

Though perhaps enough to tip the balance…

When she saw what the Eagles were facing, she knew immediately her Marines could never have prevailed alone. But she was determined to make a difference now that they were here.

Something felt right about her people being here. She wasn't one to think in terms of fate or anything of the sort, but she had to acknowledge it was a strange set of coincidences that caused Augustus Garret and Elias Cain to arrive on Armstrong within days of each other. And she couldn't overstate the importance of Garret in the space battle they had just fought. The Marine fleet reinforcements had helped even the fight, but it was the tactical brilliance of Augustus Garret, still as strong as ever, that had won the battle so handily. There had been no one remotely in Garret's league since his close friend Terrance Compton had been lost almost forty years before...and it appear there still wasn't.

Now it is our turn.

"Battalion commanders," she roared into the command com. "I want your units formed up and ready in ten minutes."

She had brought her Marines down right behind the enemy armies. The Black Eagles were pressed to the wall, outnumbered and struggling to hold off assault after assault. But she was about to put an end to that. In twenty minutes her Marines would hit the enemy rear...and she'd made her orders clear. Once the attack began, it would not stop...not until they had broken through...and she walked out in front of the line to shake Erik Teller's hand.

Chapter 38

Above The "Field of Death"
Planet Eldaron
Denebola System
Earthdate: 2319 AD (34 Years After the Fall)

Darryk flew over the battlefield, and he could barely believe the ferocity he saw below. He'd seen battles before, but the Eagles had always been superior to their opponents. And he'd never seen them so outnumbered.

His Eagle brethren were formed up in something resembling a flattened circle. They were being attacked from every direction, but they had dug in and stubbornly refused to give any ground. The fighting was brutal all along the line, but now he could see disorder along a section of the enemy position. They had stopped their offensive in that sector, and they were struggling to reposition forces to meet an unexpected onslaught.

Catherine Gilson's Marines had launched their own attack, directly against the rear of the enemy. The Marines were powered infantry, just like the Eagles and the mysterious enemy forces they were facing. Darryk was impressed with how quickly they had moved from their landers right into battle. The Marine Corps had a tremendous reputation, but it was generally thought their glory days were behind them. Darryk shook his head. The fighters he watched attacking with such ferocity…they were proving there was still room for them to win new glories. And

Darryk suspected the shades of old Marine heroes would have looked on approvingly at their progeny.

"Alright, Eagles, let's go. We're going to cut right across that line…between our people on the ground and the Marines. First run we dump the FAEs, and then we strafe the hell out of them on the way back. And make it count, because that's the climactic battle going on down there."

Darryk was leading 27 fighter-bombers, every one of the original sixty that could still fly. He'd lost half a dozen to the enemy AA fire on the last ground assault…and more than twenty in the desperate battle in space. The horrors of that struggle were still fresh in his mind. Black Eagles didn't like to accept the possibility of defeat, but Darryk knew without a doubt that all his birds—and the ten Eagle capital ships—would have been blown to plasma without the timely intervention of Admiral Garret and the Marine fleet.

And from the looks of things, Colonel Teller's folks on the ground were in deep shit too.

He tied his display into one of the scanning drones. It gave him a closer look at the Marine forces advancing into battle. They looked just like the Eagles, leapfrogging forward, using any cover the ground offered, firing with everything they had to keep the enemy suppressed.

He angled his fighter down, lining up for the attack. He flipped a row of switches, arming the FAE warheads his bomber carried for this run. The fuel air explosives were almost weapons of mass destruction against unarmored enemies, but even powered troops caught in the primary blast areas would be in big trouble. Along the main axis of the drop, temperatures would soar well beyond the melting points of the alloys in their fighting suits. Darryk didn't imagine having your armor literally melt around you would be a pleasant death. But right now he didn't give a shit.

He banked the fighter around, setting his course as close to parallel to the Eagle and Marine lines as possible…and right between them. Then he dove, angling down as sharply as he dared. He brought the fighter to an altitude of less than two hundred meters...and then he said a single word to the ship's AI. "Drop."

He could hear the clicking sounds as his bomb bay cradles opened, leaving a trail of small canisters behind the ship. The explosions began almost at once, and the ground below his fighter erupted into billowing columns of flame.

He tried to imagine the devastation, the enemy troops running to escape the primary blast zones. But escape was a fool's hope. Even those who survived his own bombs were moving right into the target areas of the fighters on his flanks. He'd concentrated the attack, and his wings were carpet bombing a pinpoint area on the front lines.

He pulled back on the throttle, his craft climbing to over a thousand meters as he brought the bird around for his strafing run. He'd almost gotten into position when he heard the high pitched screech of his warning system. He knew what it was immediately, but the AI nevertheless confirmed it. "We have been acquired by multiple tracking systems. Estimate six surface-to-air missiles locked and inbound.

Fuck.

He hadn't known where the AA had come from on the last mission days earlier...but now he realized that these mysterious soldiers had their own equipment, and all of it had been shielded from the EMP attacks. And it included a heavy anti-air capability.

He jerked the throttle wildly, glancing back at his crew. "Hang on...I'm gonna try to shake these missiles."

He dove slightly then turned upward and went into a steep climb. Darryk knew he was a good pilot, but he also knew he wasn't likely to escape from six missile locks. Still, he had to try.

He turned hard to the right, and he pushed the thrust to full power. He could hear his ship creaking as over 10g of pressure slammed into him. He felt faint, but he struggled to hang onto consciousness. He sucked in a pitiful mouthful of air, forcing it into his lungs.

Then he cut the thrust suddenly, and let the fighter drop a few hundred meters. It was all wild, random...the best way to confuse the tracking AIs in the approaching missiles. And it worked. On three of them at least. But three more were coming in. He heard the rattling sound of the defensive railguns, the AI firing the weapons, desperately trying to destroy the remaining missiles.

He saw one vanish...then another. But the last one was still coming...

"Impact in eight seconds," the AI warned, its voice unemotional, disturbingly so, Darryk thought, considering the situation.

"Eject," he yelled, and he pressed the large red button on the side of his chair. He felt himself jerked hard, so hard he blacked out for a few seconds. When he came to, he was outside, still strapped to his chair. There were three parachutes above, and he was falling slowly toward the ground.

But where? He twisted around, trying to get a look at the ground. Was he coming down in enemy territory? In the firestorm his own bombardment had created?

He tried to find the other chutes, his crew. Had any of them made it out? Or was he the only one?

Don't panic. At the speed you were going, the four of you could be spread out over kilometers...

He could see the fires on the ground...he was coming down well past them, beyond the front lines. He felt a wave of relief. He'd lost his bird—and God knew how many of his fighters had been shot down on the raid. But he couldn't do anything about that. And for all the worry, and even the guilt he might feel for those he had lost, he had to admit to himself he wanted to survive. He was glad he had made it out, that his chutes were bringing him down somewhere he could land.

He could see the ground coming up...closer, closer...

Then, with a single hard thud, he was down. He pulled at the latch, unhooked himself from the harness and jumped to the ground. He was pretty sure he had come past the battle zone, but he reached down for his sidearm anyway. But the instant his hand dropped to the holster he heard a harsh command.

"Hold!"

He froze, and suddenly he was aware of a cluster of figures

moving toward him. They were armored, and they looked much like Black Eagles. But they weren't.

He turned slowly, keeping his hands from moving. "I am Major Darryk, attack wing commander for the Black Eagles."

Then he felt gloved hands upon him from both sides, grabbing him, holding him like a vice. A third armored figure moved up toward his front, and an instant later the helmet retracted to show a woman in her late twenties. "I am sorry, Major," she said, her voice pleasant but watchful. "We've had enemy infiltrators trying to get through our lines, so we have to be careful." She flashed a glance at her comrades, and they released him.

"I am Corporal Gerian, Armstrong Marine Corps. Come with us, Major, and we'll get you back to our HQ. I'm sure General Gilson will want to speak with you immediately."

*   *   *   *   *

Albrecht Trax stared into the monitors at the ruins of his army. He didn't understand what had happened. The plan had been perfect, meticulous. Everything had been in place. Yet all across the field there was nothing but defeat. His forces were broken, his units scattered and facing total destruction.

He'd thought to order a retreat to the bunkers, to pull his forces back to the secret bases where they had hidden before launching their attacks. There were weapons there, defenses. Perhaps, he had thought, our enemies will break themselves attacking us there…and we shall regain the initiative. But then the orbital bombardments began.

The fleets in orbit targeted the underground bases, guided by data collected by their satellites. *Another failure—if our fleet had prevailed, there would be no satellites…and no enemy ships to bombard our bunkers.* Trax had stood in the field outside his headquarters and stared at the mushroom clouds rising above his bases. In an hour, the entire infrastructure that had hidden and housed his 30,000 men was gone, reduced to radioactive slag.

He'd ordered his soldiers to stand firm nevertheless, to fight to the last man, but across the field, many broke their conditioning, fear overcoming the deeply-planted compulsion to obey. They ran, dropping their weapons, losing all discipline and seeking only to save themselves. Their efforts had proven futile, however, and Trax had activated the Endgame protocols for the few who had managed to flee the fury of the Eagles and the Marines. The reward for those who had broken through to seek escape was instant death, as the deepest of all their programming sent the signal to stop their hearts cold.

Omega forces do not surrender, Trax thought grimly...*and they do not run either.*

He realized his own end was near as well. He was an Omega general, and he knew well enough what awaited him back on Vali if he somehow managed to escape. The Triumvirate did not tolerate failure from anyone, but he was a commander who had been defeated despite outnumbering his enemy almost ten to one, despite a long-planned and carefully-laid plan. He could only imagine what terrible end awaited him. No, he would not go back in disgrace. As soon as he had seen to the disposition of his forces, he would activate his own conditioning. He would die here, the last of his force on Eldaron.

His thoughts were dark, grim. He'd joined the Omega forces to seek power, and he had risen high indeed. Victory on Eldaron would have propelled him even farther, to the very highest military commands in the Triumvirate's military. But such thoughts were moot now. They could accomplish naught but to mock him.

He thought bitterly of the Eldari, at how ineffective their forces had been, and he took solace in knowing the Tyrant, too, would pay the ultimate price for failure. If the Black Eagles didn't get to him, the Triumvirate surely would. Either way, Trax thought with malicious satisfaction, the Eldari monarch faced a grim and unpleasant end.

He looked down at his displays, and he knew what he had to do. There were still thousands of his soldiers in the field...and some units were still in battle, holding on grimly, even as their comrades gave way, exposing their flanks and opening them up to total destruction. Trax knew his soldiers could kill more of their enemies, but he was also aware of the futility of such action. His chance for victory was gone…and if he waited much longer he risked capture. Enemy spearheads were breaking through all across the line, driving deep past his few remaining units. No, there was no point, no purpose in prolonging things.

He felt a rush of fear, and he almost lost his resolve, nearly slipped into a panic he couldn't control. But he held his control, barely. *I must not fear death. My alternatives are far worse…*

He punched his command codes into the workstation, entering the overrides to activate Endgame for his entire force. He would do one last duty…he would live long enough to see the enemy took no live prisoners. Then he would follow his soldiers.

He pressed the primary control, and he watched as the figures scrolled down the screen, unit designations, confirming that Endgame had taken each of them. He tried to imagine the confusion of his enemies as the soldiers they were fighting simply dropped in place.

No doubt they had orders to take prisoners. The enemy still knew shockingly little about the Triumvirate, and so it would remain. They would have armor and weapons to inspect, little different from those they themselves employed. And they would have dead soldiers. But there would be nothing else. Endgame was as thorough with the army's AIs and databases as it was with the troops.

Trax could see the officers in his headquarters dropping around him, as the Endgame sequence reached its final stage. He hadn't given any warning…there was no purpose in allowing any of them to try to stop him, to make a hopeless play for survival.

He looked all around him, and he knew that he was the only one left. In the headquarters, and all across the battlefield, not an Omega soldier remained alive save him.

Another thought invaded his mind, a last attempt of fear and self-preservation to win the day. He could surrender. He was the Omega commander, invaluable to the enemy. They would spare him…indeed, if he bartered what he knew, he might obtain a pardon. He could survive the debacle, escape the retribution that surely awaited him on Vali.

But then he felt a pain in his head, and a voice speaking to him, from the very depths of his mind. It was more conditioning he knew, though he had no knowledge of what it was. It was strong, far more powerful than his ability to resist…and its purpose was clear. *Endgame*, he could hear in his head. *Endgame*.

And he felt his hand slipping toward the workstation, a single finger moving to the flashing red button…

*   *   *   *   *

"General Gilson, I don't think I've ever been so happy to see anyone in my life." Erik Teller walked across the field, stepping over at least half a dozen enemy bodies before he reached the Marine commander.

"And you, Colonel Teller. I feared we were too late." Her voice was hoarse, the fatigue in its tone betrayed her years.

"And you almost were. But almost late is another way of saying just in time. So, again, thank you." His voice became lower, more concerned. "What do you think happened to them all at the end there? I've never seen anything like that before."

"I have," Gilson said grimly. "In the Shadow Wars. Some kind of suicide program, intended to kill any soldiers before they surrendered or were captured. Gavin Stark had something like it for his Shadow Legions."

Teller was silent. He knew that Catherine Gilson was one of the Marines' best, an officer who had seen action for sixty years, and who had served alongside—and against—the greatest warriors mankind had fielded. He thought about the kind of leaders who could recruit soldiers, train them, enjoy their loyalty…and then dispose of them in such a frigid way. But it was too disturbing. And he didn't have time now for soul searching or philosophical exploration. The mysterious offworld forces were gone, apparently dead to a man. But the Eldari still sat in their battered defensive lines...and in the massive ramparts of the Citadel.

Teller knew that Darius was almost certainly dead. The plan had been to take the Citadel on day two, but it was now day seven. He couldn't imagine that Darius and two hundred Eagles, even the best of the best, had managed to hold out inside the enemy's main fortress for so long. It seemed impossible. But none of that mattered. Darius Cain was Erik Teller's commanding officer...his friend. His brother. And until he knew for certain, until he looked upon Cain's body with his own eyes, he would never give up.

"If you'll excuse me, General, my people are about to move against the enemy fortress." He paused. "We must...see to... General Cain."

"With your permission, Colonel Teller, I would join you." Gilson paused. "We will see now if Erik Cain was ever here. He was my comrade for many years, and I would be there when we...when we find out what has happened to him."

"Of course, General Gilson...it would be an honor to have you along."

Chapter 39

The Citadel
Planet Eldaron
Denebola System
Earthdate: 2319 AD (34 Years After the Fall)

"Your Excellency, General Davidoff's forces have surrendered. The enemy is moving toward the Citadel itself."

The Tyrant leapt to his feet and thrust his fist into the air. "That coward! That miserable traitor. If he ever falls into my hands I will have him devoured by sand wolves!"

He stared around the command center, and his insanity was clear in his eyes. "What am I going to do," he stammered, oblivious to those around him. "What am I going to do?" His voice was thick with fear.

"Excellency, we must look to the defense of the Citadel." It was General Calman. He stood and stared at the Tyrant.

"Indeed, General Calman? Is that what we must do? Should I take your advice? It was you who recommended that traitor Davidoff, was it not?"

"There is no time for that now, Excellency. The Citadel is strong...and they will not bombard us with heavy weapons, not while their people are trapped down on the detention level."

"Yes, they are still trapped aren't they? Because your men have been unable to wipe out a small force of invaders. For almost three days you have fought them down there...and yet still they hold out." There was an uncontrolled wildness to his tone.

"It is difficult to attack down narrow corridors, Excellency. It nullifies our numerical advantage…and the soldiers down there are highly skilled…even for Black Eagles."

"Excuses, General? Is that what you have to offer me?"

Calman stood his ground, but he didn't respond immediately. He just held his gaze and waited, his hand at his side, slipping closer to his sidearm.

"Of course!" the Tyrant roared. "Darius Cain is down there. If we control Cain we will control his Black Eagles." His eyes locked on Calman's. "Go down there, General. I command you to lead the forces. You must attack. Attack, attack, attack. Slay the Black Eagles…but bring Darius Cain to me as a prisoner."

Calman took a deep breath. His expression was doubtful, full of disgust and repugnance for his leader. But after a few seconds he just nodded. "Yes, Excellency. At once." He paused another few seconds. Then he spun around on his heels and walked away.

*   *   *   *   *

"Let's go…move your asses! The General's down here, and every second counts." Bull Trent was at the front of his company, racing through the corridors of the Citadel. He knew there were data centers and weapons stations on the upper levels, but he'd pushed his way relentlessly downward, ignoring everything else. It wasn't sound militarily, but he was driven by one thing above all others. Darius Cain had entered the enemy fortress seeking the detention area, and that was where Trent was most likely to find the general…if he was still alive.

Kuragina's White Regiment had assaulted the Citadel a few hours before. The Eldari had put up a brief fight, but then the Eagles blasted their way in and chased the routing defenders deep into the old fortress. The colonel had dispersed her forces to find and seize control of the Citadel's key facilities…and she had given Trent his orders. Find the general. At all costs.

Bull was as fearless as soldiers came, relentless and unstoppable. But now he was distracted. Danger didn't affect him, nor pain, nor fatigue. But he had Colonel Teller with him... and General Gilson too. That was more top brass than he could handle...especially in a situation like this. He was moving recklessly, sacrificing all caution to try to find General Cain as quickly as possible. The last thing he needed was to get the Eagles' acting commander killed, not to mention the Marines' senior general.

His forces were moving up to an intersection, and he waved for them to stop while he crept forward. He leaned up against the wall and looked around the corner. There was a single enemy soldier about eight meters down the hall, clearly a sentry of some kind.

Guarding what? They've got worse problems now than guarding some hallway this deep. Unless...

It was just a feeling, but suddenly he was convinced. They were close. He felt a surge of energy, a compulsion to do something, and without warning he lunged around the corner, running down the corridor toward the guard.

The Eldari soldier spun around, leveling his rifle at the onrushing giant. But Bull jerked his body to the side hard, and the enemy's fire went wide. The guard tried to turn his weapon and fire again, but he was too late. Bull slammed into the unarmored man, sending him flying into the wall. The Eldari dropped his rifle and crumpled to the ground.

Bull reached down, his massive armored hand grabbed the injured man and pulled him from the floor. "Where?" he roared. "Where is the detention area?"

The man was disoriented and in pain. He moaned loudly, but he didn't answer.

"You will tell me right now," Bull said, the malice in his voice almost freezing the air, "or I will tear you apart." He swung the helpless soldier around, gripping an arm in each of his hands. He pulled, careful not to put too much strength behind it. He didn't want to tear the man in half. Not yet, at least.

"Down the corridor," the terrified man said. "Then left."

Bull turned and tossed the Eldari toward one of his Eagles. "Hold on to him," he said, his voice a savage growl. "If his directions are wrong, kill him."

Bull turned and moved forward, stopping after another ten meters or so. He cranked up his external microphone and listened. Gunfire.

"Alright Eagles, there's some kind of a fight ahead of us...so let's go find the General."

He pulled his assault rifle from his back and checked the cartridge. Then he started down the hallway.

$$*\qquad*\qquad*\qquad*\qquad*$$

Darius Cain crouched down inside the doorframe, his rifle poking out. He was using his ears as well as his eyes, waiting for an enemy to show himself...even to peer around a corner. He was firing single shots...all his people were. Their ammo was almost gone. Indeed, if the enemy had been more aggressive—less afraid of the Eagles' deadly-accurate fire—they would have been overrun already. But this was a contest between Black Eagles and vastly inferior soldiers. Numbers could sustain a force, keep it in the battle until victory finally came, but it didn't create courage. Cain and his people had held the enemy off for several days, killing at least twenty for every one they lost. But Darius knew the brave stand was almost over.

His people wouldn't give up when their ammunition was gone. But the enemy would push down the corridors, firing on full, driving his Eagles back into each of the cells. There would be dozens of last stands, desperate hand to hand engagements as the enemy poured into each of the small rooms. His people would fight like wildcats, slashing with their blades and punching with their nuclear-powered fists. They would kill hundreds of the enemy...but in the end they would lose. The numbers they faced were just too great. And he had less than fifty of his original two hundred still in the fight.

His thoughts drifted to Alcabedo, to the terrible final duty he had charged his officer to undertake. He felt sick to his stomach. Of all the things he'd done, of the fateful decisions he'd made, nothing could compare to ordering his father's own death. It was an act of mercy, he knew, but he still felt somehow...unclean. His mind went back over the operation. *We came so close...what could I have done differently?*

No, we didn't come close, not really. The Eagles must have been defeated outside the Citadel. Otherwise, Erik would have been here. He felt a wave of regret, of futility. But he knew that he'd had no choice.

He saw an Eldari soldier peer around the corner, and he snapped up his rifle and fired...almost on instinct. The enemy had barely extended one eye around the edge, before Darius put a hyper-velocity round right through it. The man was thrown back, and he fell into the middle of the intersection with a thud.

Darius heard his autoloader pop out the empty clip, replacing it with another. His last.

He took a deep breath. *Soldiers have come to this moment throughout human history. Some die suddenly, without warning, shot by a sniper or obliterated by an exploding shell. But many have stood as we do, facing certain death but remaining firm to the end. And now is my time. Our time...*

Suddenly, his com erupted. The jamming that had limited communications to twenty meters' range was suddenly gone, and a familiar voice was speaking.

"General Cain? Darius?" The voice was hoarse and worn, but Darius recognized it at once. Erik Teller.

"Erik?" he answered, not entirely able to keep the stunned disbelief out of his voice.

"Yes, Darius." The voice on the com was heavy with relief. "My God, old friend...I was sure you were dead."

"Not dead yet...but I doubt it's going to be long now."

"No," Teller snapped. "We're on the way. Maybe a hundred meters...moving straight for the detention area."

Cain was stunned. "You're here?" His discipline failed him

and he stood there, trying to comprehend what he had just heard.

"Yes…the battle outside the city is over. We've got units moving throughout the Citadel, but I'm with Bull Trent and a company of Kuragina's troops. We're on the way to your position."

Darius' head turned abruptly. He'd been listening to Teller, but now he heard something from down the hallway. It was gunfire. And not just any gunfire. He'd have recognized his Eagles' assault rifles anywhere.

"I can hear you coming," he said, his voice filled with emotion…relief, gratitude. "I can hear your rifle fire."

He forced his mind back to focus, and he took a stim, feeling the almost instant wave of artificial energy. He snapped his rifle back up and moved toward the door. This was it…the final battle. The last few minutes. His Eagles were coming for him, for all their brethren trapped in this detention area.

And for you too, Father. For you too.

He whipped around and fired at an Eldari who had been too careless. And as he did, he could hear Teller's people, their fire becoming louder as it approached.

My God, he thought, trying to stay focused on the fight but finding it difficult. *We did it…we actually did it.*

Chapter 40

The Citadel
Planet Eldaron
Denebola System
Earthdate: 2319 AD (34 Years After the Fall)

Sarah stood next to Erik, looking down at his broken body, wounded, covered in crusted blood. Her eyes passed over his withered frame, his almost skeletal arms, the ribs so visible on his chest. She imagined how he had suffered. The torture, the beatings. She saw images in her mind, thought of how many days and nights she'd gone about her business while he lay against the wall in this cold cell, almost starving to death. She imagined the foul rations his captors had given him, when they'd fed him at all, and she felt a wave of anger, of hatred at those who had done this to him.

She could hear intermittent gunfire in the background, as Darius' Eagles hunted down the last of the Eldari soldiers. The final battle had been quick and decisive, the enemy forces caught between Darius' Teams and the relieving force sent to find them. The Eldari broke and tried to run...but there was nowhere to go. Many had tried to surrender, but the Eagles ignored their pleas and gunned them down where they stood. They were enraged that the Eldari had tried to trap them, that they had suffered the losses they had. But word had also begun to spread that Erik Cain was indeed alive, that he had been held here in appalling conditions for more than fifteen years. The

Eagles respected Erik, as their general's father, and as a legendary and honorable warrior...and their rage had sealed the fate of the Eldari soldiers in the catacombs.

Since they had left the Nest, Sarah had imagined herself trying to restrain Darius, keeping him from unleashing hell on the Eldari people, but now her energy to fight for mercy had left her. She looked down at Erik, lying on the cold ground of the cell, his sufferings so clear to see, and she felt the same burning rage. She knew it hadn't been the fault of the commoner. Indeed, she doubted one in a hundred thousand Eldari had even known Erik Cain was there. But she didn't care...and that kind of uncontrollable fury scared her. She had seen it before, in Erik, after Gavin Stark had murdered Elias Holm. She remembered the look in his eyes, and she knew she would never forget it, no matter how hard she tried.

"Sar...ah..."

The voice was weak, barely audible, but it hit her like a tidal wave. Erik had been unconscious since she'd gotten there, but now he was looking up at her.

"A dream..." he said sadly.

"No, my love...not a dream. I am here. Darius and Elias are here. We have come to take you home." She leaned down and put her hand on his face.

"Home?"

He tried to turn his head toward her, but she could see he was too weak. She leaned over him, bringing her face closer. "Yes, home. You have suffered for long, so long. But now we are here."

He looked up at her, and she could see the expression on his face, disbelief giving way slowly to comprehension. "Sarah," he said again, and she could see realization in his eyes.

"Yes, Erik. You are safe now. We will take you home."

She felt the tears inside, struggling to escape her eyes, but she held them back. He needed strength from her now more than anything. *You are a Marine*, she reminded herself. *A veteran of fifty years of war. Hold it together.*

"Home," he said softly. Then he looked at her with watery

eyes. "Love you," he rasped. Then he slipped back into unconsciousness.

"I love you too," she said, rubbing her hand on his face.

She felt the wave inside her, knew she couldn't hold it back any longer. She got up and walked across the room, turning the corner and leaning against the wall. She took a deep breath, and then she dropped her guard...and let the tears come.

*   *   *   *   *

"Where is the Tyrant?" Darius Cain's voice was terrifying, a vocal manifestation of the violence he felt. He held the Eldari officer in armored hands and shook the man's body. It took every bit of self-control he could muster not to tear the man's body in half.

"I don't know, sir," the panicked soldier cried. "I don't know...I swear!"

"Ahhhh!" Darius screamed in frustration, throwing the man hard into the wall. "Nobody knows? Nobody?" He was shouting to the Eldari prisoners lined up in front of him. "He just vanished into the wind?"

Elias was standing a few meters from his brother. The two of them had been questioning the prisoners for over an hour...and the answer was always the same. No one seemed to know what had become of Eldaron's ruler in the last confused moments when the Citadel fell.

"Well, let me explain something to you...all of you. My father was held here for many years. He was mistreated all that time, tortured and tormented. And my soldiers were forced to fight a brutal battle here, and many hundreds of them died." His voice was rising in volume and intensity, and the captive Eldari cowered before him.

"You know who I am. You have all heard my reputation. My heart craves vengeance, I lust to judge you all, inflict horrors upon your world that you cannot imagine. I warn you not to test the thread that holds me back from yielding to my worst desires. For with a word I will unleash a nuclear hell on this world, one not even the cockroaches will survive. Your homes will be vaporized, your families seared to crisps in the atomic fires." He paused and panned his eyes over the row of prisoners. "And I tell you now, if I must destroy this world, cleanse it of all life to destroy the Tyrant, then that is what I will do."

"I will help you find him."

The voice came from behind Darius, and he spun around, looking back toward the room's entrance. Two of his Eagles stood there holding a man between them. "General Cain," one of the guards said, "this is General Davidoff, the commander of the forces outside Eldaron City."

"General Davidoff," Darius said, "I will put to you the question I have been asking these fools. Where is the Tyrant?"

"I do not know where he is, General Cain. But I believe I can help you find him."

"And how can you do that?" There was interest in Darius' voice, but menace as well.

"I know the main data banks were wiped clean, but I still have my personal files…and they include the complete layout of the Citadel. Including every bolt hole, every secret tunnel."

"And you will help my people find the Tyrant? Or is this another trick?"

"No, General Cain. The Tyrant has been the worst disaster in my world's history. He has led us to ruin. I will help you find him so he may account for his actions. So that he may face the punishment for what he has done—to your father, to the Black Eagles…and to Eldaron."

He paused a few seconds, holding Darius' withering gaze. "I will do it to save my people, for I know what will happen here if he is not found."

"Very well, General Davidoff." Darius turned toward another armored figure. She was almost thirty centimeters shorter than him, and her retracted helmet revealed a woman with close cropped blonde hair. She was very attractive, but it was the toughness in her expression that stood out. She wore a scowl on her face, and it was clear to anyone who gazed at her that the Eldari could expect no more mercy from her than from Darius Cain…and very likely less.

"You will go with Colonel Kuragina here, and you will cooperate in any way she requests." Darius' eyes had turned back toward Davidoff, but now he flashed another glance at Kuragina. "She has my permission to conduct the search any way she sees fit…including blowing your brains all over the wall if she thinks you are holding back in any way."

"Go, Colonel. Take General Davidoff here, and find the Tyrant." His voice became sharp, frigid. "And bring him to me…alive."

*   *   *   *   *

"I can't believe it. I've seen it…I lived through much of it. But I still can't quite convince myself it's true. After all these years…he is alive." Elias Cain sat at the table. It was some kind of wood he'd never seen, and the light hitting it revealed a rich depth of color. He could see it was old, aged in the way fine things often did, acquiring character without yielding beauty. *Probably a priceless antique*, he thought, as he looked down at the surface, now covered in scratches and deep gouges. It had been dragged here from wherever it had been found, without regard to its value or history. He wanted to frown, to look down on the Eagles as barbarians who only knew how to destroy. But he'd realized he had been wrong about his brother's soldiers. And he'd seen the carnage of the battlefield…the price the Black Eagles had paid to rescue his own father.

When you've seen hundreds of your comrades fall…when the stench of rotting blood is still thick in your nostrils, it's hard to give a shit about a fucking table. Or paintings, or statues.

"I know. When I left to come here, I tried to keep my expectations in check. But now I can see I failed at that. If he hadn't been here, or if we'd gotten to him too late, I don't know what

I would have done. It would have been like losing him all over again." Darius sat across the table from his brother. He was still clad in his armor, though his helmet was fully retracted. He'd sent everyone away, even Alcabedo. The area was secured, and he didn't need his nursemaid. Besides, he wanted to talk alone with his brother. "He should be on *Eagle One* by now." The shuttle had left almost twenty minutes earlier. "Mother is with him…so you know he will get the best care."

Elias nodded and smiled. Then his expression became serious again, and he looked at his brother with a pained stare. "Darius, I don't know how to thank you…for rescuing him. You were the only one who could have done it." Elias paused. "And I want to apologize as well. To you…and to your Black Eagles. I made very prejudicial judgments, thought of your soldiers in the basest terms, as armed thugs who fought only for money. But I saw them here, fighting for you, dying in their hundreds with no paymaster. Our father lives only because of their sacrifices. I was wrong." His voice was strained, halting.

Darius looked across the table, silent for a few seconds. He knew how difficult those words had been to utter, and a smile crept onto his lips. Then he said, "And my thanks to you, brother. For your words now…and for your timely help. I have read the operations reports, and I say now, had you not come to the Nest, and then rallied the Marines to come to our aid, we would have failed here. My Eagles would have been destroyed, and Father would still be a captive…or killed by the Tyrant once he was no longer useful."

He stared across at his brother, with whom he had so long been at odds, and he felt something different, a feeling almost forgotten, old, but still vaguely familiar. The bond with a sibling, with a twin. "I have wronged you too, brother," he said. "I saw you as a martinet, as a willing tool of the forces of corruption and destroyers of freedom. Yet, here you are, having followed your own will, pursued what you knew was right, without regard to the orders from your unjust masters. You are indeed my blood, Elias, and I would take back much of what has transpired between us. I would have my brother back."

"I would like that too," Elias said slowly, his voice heavy with emotion.

"Then so it shall be." Darius looked down at his armored hand. I would shake with you, brother, but perhaps that is best left until later. I do not think crushing your hand is the way to celebrate our reconciliation."

Elias smiled. It was the first time in a long time he'd felt like laughing, a bit of timely humor amid the suffering and detritus of war.

"General Cain…" The voice came from outside the room. Then the door opened and Cyn Kuragina walked in. "I am sorry to interrupt you, sir, but we found the Tyrant. He was hiding in a secret chamber on one of the lower levels."

Darius stood up abruptly. "It appears, brother, that we have finally found the rat, hiding in his hole." His gaze turned toward Kuragina. "Well done, Cyn. As usual." He smiled, but it slowly slipped from his face, morphing into a cold stare. "Let us go see the Tyrant, shall we?"

*   *   *   *   *

The Tyrant stood against the wall. He was slouching, his posture communicating his fear for all to see. He had been hiding in one of his bolt holes, a shielded chamber almost impossible to detect. He'd only been found because of General Davidoff's knowledge of the Citadel.

Darius Cain stormed into the room. "So, this is the Tyrant of Eldaron…this whimpering creature, broken and so choked by fear he can't even stand straight to face his judgment?" Elias Cain and Cyn Kuragina had come in behind Darius, and they stood at either side of the Black Eagles' commander.

Darius stared at the Tyrant with an intensity so withering it drove the prisoner down, closer toward the ground. There was blood on the Tyrant's face, now partially dried. It was clear Kuragina's people had been less than gentle, but he had no serious injuries.

"So, Tyrant…you put a great deal of effort into luring me to Eldaron. Now I am here. Is this how you had imagined our meeting?"

Darius felt the rage inside. It was taking all his control to stay his hand, to prevent himself from grabbing the miserable fool and crushing him in armored hands.

The Tyrant looked up, but he could only withstand a few seconds of that terrible gaze before he looked away again. He tried to say something, but nothing escaped his lips save a pathetic whimper.

"What a useless piece of garbage I find behind this great plan…a gutless coward, without the character even to meet his adversary eye to eye." Darius turned and looked around the room. "Leave us," he said. "All of you. I must learn what this worm knows about the forces that so damaged us here." His voice was cold and ominous, like death itself. "And then I must deal him the justice he so richly deserves."

The Black Eagles in the room turned and walked to the door, instantly obeying their general's command. Darius turned and looked at Kuragina. She just returned the gaze and nodded, leaving only Elias still standing there.

"I would ask you, too, to go brother. You have some rights to this justice, that is without question, but I beg you to leave it to me…for I must also extract a price for my fallen Eagles. And it is imperative that we learn all this foul creature can tell us about the greater enemy we face."

Darius looked into his brother's eyes. "It is a great joy to me that we are reconciled, brother, but this I would do alone. I fear you are not yet ready for what will happen in this room. You would stand by me, I have no doubt. But being a part of this will wound you, scar your soul in a way that can never heal. As mine is already scarred."

Elias stared back, but he didn't respond. Darius suspected his brother felt it would be cowardly to turn away and leave the burden on his sibling.

"And I would ask for me, brother, for my own reasons. For I

would have no one see this, watch what I must now do…"

Elias finally nodded. No words came to his lips, but he just stared another few seconds at his brother, and then he nodded and turned away, walking toward the door.

Darius stood and watched him leave. Then he turned toward the prone form of Eldaron's dictator. He extended his arm, and with a sharp click, his blade snapped out of the arm of his fighting suit.

"Let us talk," he said coldly.

*   *   *   *   *

Darius Cain sat in the Tyrant's chair, looking out at the small group of Eldari standing before him. He'd finally shed his armor, and he was showered and dressed in a crisp set of combat fatigues. His aide had laid out his dress uniform for him, but he'd bypassed it. Such formality bestowed a level of respect, even on an enemy. And the Eldari would get little of that from him.

"General Davidoff, step forward."

The Eldari officer obeyed.

"Your world has committed grave offenses against the Black Eagles, General…and my father, Erik Cain. I have considered the fate of your people…whether any of you are to be spared."

His words hung in the air. The Eldari looked terrified, Davidoff alone among the delegation managing to maintain a level of dignity. No one knew exactly what had happened between Darius Cain and the Tyrant, but the screams had been audible a dozen rooms away. There were rumors that the planet's former dictator had been taken away in several containers…that he had been literally scraped from the walls and the floor.

"Indeed, it is you, General, who have saved your people. You have been true to your word since your surrender, and from all I have gathered, you are a man of honor. Though nowhere have I seen a good man serve a worse master than here."

Davidoff stood quietly at attention, waiting as Cain continued.

"Your planet and your people, however, are guilty of grievous crimes, and they must pay the price."

The Eldari representatives standing behind Davidoff cringed in fear. Hundreds had been executed already, the lords and ministers who had served the deposed Tyrant. Any who had been part of the dictator's rule had been exterminated, save only Davidoff.

"All the treasures of Eldaron are forfeit. The museums will be stripped of artworks. The people shall forfeit all currency and items of value. The Eldari, peasant and lord alike, shall be left only enough for a sustenance existence. They will work in the fields and the factories, and all production shall be diverted to pay the reparations I hereby place upon all of you."

Cain's voice was hard, cold. It was clear he felt no pity for the people he was condemning to a bitter punishment for what had happened. He knew the vast majority of the population had been uninvolved, but he still held them accountable for the monster they had allowed to lead them.

"General Davidoff, I hereby appoint you the acting governor of this planet. Eldaron shall exist from this moment forward as a fief of the Black Eagles. You will take all steps to see that the reparations are paid as quickly as possible. When that is done, we will revisit this matter, and perhaps we will then look to the rebuilding of this world."

Davidoff nodded, a look of mild surprise on his face. "Yes, General Cain."

"I will leave several officers behind to assist you...and a company of Black Eagles to supervise internal security for the time being."

Cain stared out past Davidoff, over the other assembled Eldari. "Thus you are granted some measure of mercy, some respite from the judgment I had thought to level on all of you. And yet, this reprieve is conditional. If there is resistance or unrest of any kind...if I am forced to come back here to restore order...then I swear to you there shall be no mercy. I will scorch your world to a cinder. It is for your sakes that I hope you hear and understand me now. There will be no second chances."

Cain looked at Davidoff for a few seconds, giving the Eldari a brief nod. Then he turned and walked out of the room without another word. He walked into the hall and turned toward Kuragina. "You are in command down here, Colonel. See to the final arrangements...and our preparations to leave."

"Yes, sir," she snapped back. Then her usual sternness gave way, and she smiled. "Going up to see your father, sir?"

"Yes, Cyn. That is exactly where I am going." He returned her smile. "We have a lot of catching up to do." He nodded and started walking down the corridor.

And I am going to get the hell off of this Godforsaken planet...

Epilogue

The glass wall of the conference room looked out over a massive Titanian lake, an inland sea fed by half a dozen great rivers twisting their way down from the distant mountains. At first glance, it could have been an Earthly vista, save for the lack of grass or trees or other life. But the temperature out there was less than 100 degrees Kelvin, and the rivers and sea were not of water but of liquid methane and ethane.

Titan was the home to a dozen mining operations, and a handful of colonies that supported them. And the meeting room was in the largest of those settlements. Huygenberg had been named after the astronomer who had discovered Titan almost seven hundred years before, and it was home to 1,800 hardy citizens of the Martian Confederation...and one small military base that had been hastily converted to house the summit about to begin.

Roderick Vance stood at the head of the table. The Confederation's absolute ruler was clad simply but tastefully, in a dark gray business suit. "I want to thank you for coming all the way to the Sol system." Roderick Vance stared out over his friends and allies. "It is...difficult...for me to travel too far from Mars at this time, though I know my own need caused you all to come much farther than that."

A wave of nods and acknowledgements worked its way around the table. The men and women here had all worked with Vance before, and whatever the differences between them, one and all trusted and respected him.

"Some of us have met recently…and others I have not seen for a long time. A very long time." A touch of emotion slipped into his voice, and his eyes fell on a man to his left. He was sitting in a powered chair of sorts, and the lower half of his body was covered by the base of the unit. It wasn't evident at first glance, but Vance knew the man had no legs behind the metal shield of the chair. They had been shattered by years of physical abuse, and his surgeon had been compelled to amputate.

"Erik Cain needs no introduction here—indeed anywhere in Occupied Space. Most of us have fought at his side…and we grieved when we believed him lost in action. Now he has returned to us, beyond all hope, beyond all expectation. So before we begin, I ask you all to welcome him back to the fold… and to the fight."

The room erupted in applause as everyone present fixed their gaze on the Marine hero, so improbably returned home after so long in captivity. Erik Cain was a true hero, and more than one person in the room owed the veteran Marine his or her life.

"Please," Cain said softly, his voice stronger than it had been on Eldaron, but far from back to normal. "Please, all of you… thank you. I can't put into words how it feels to be back among you. For my liberation from Eldaron…for my return to my family, I can only offer my most profound thanks to all who had a hand in my salvation." His voice was halting, heavy with emotion. "As most of you know, I am not one for protracted sentimentality, so I will simply say thank you once again. And I will assure you all that as soon as I am able, I will be with you in this fight. But first I have to have these legs regenerated… an unpleasant prospect to say the least. Though, the last time I regenerated both of my legs I met a hot blond in the hospital…

so you never know…"

Sarah was sitting next to Cain. Her smile had faded when he spoke of joining the fight, but it returned with his light-hearted comment. Most of those in the room realized Erik had endured a difficult time immediately after his rescue, even to recover his sense of self. No one could imagine the torment he had suffered, but they all knew Erik well enough to realize he would never talk about it…not to anyone. Not even to Sarah.

Vance waited for the laughs to die down before he continued. "I would also like to welcome Augustus Garret." He stared over at the old admiral and smiled. "Augustus, what can I say? I respected your decision when Andre returned and told me of your discussion. But when I heard the accounts of the battle around Eldaron, somehow I knew it was you."

"What can I say, Roderick? When I met with Agent Girard, I spoke rationally, reasonably. I am old, and by all rights my time has passed."

"And yet you must have left Terra Nova almost immediately after Andre returned to Mars."

Garret smiled. "Well, Roderick, he got me to thinking. If I'd allowed rationality and reason to guide me all these years, I'd be decades dead in the wreckage of some lost space battle." He laughed softly. "Besides, I never could stand Terra Nova, not even when I was a boy. It's hard to pass the time playing chess and taking walks when you've lived the life I have. It just isn't in me to sit on the sidelines while others fight." He stared at Vance. "I'm not dead yet, after all. And perhaps not useless either."

"No, *Admiral* Garret," Vance said, returning the smile, "from what I heard about the recent fighting, you are most certainly not useless."

Garret nodded. "But I do have unfinished business while I'm in the Sol system." He paused. "I believe I owe your Mr. Girard a drink…and my heartfelt thanks for shaking me out of my stupor. Even if it took a while for his words to sink in."

"I'm sure that can be arranged, Augustus."

Vance took a deep breath. "What can I say, friends? We

have been here before, many of us, and we know well the work and pain and struggle that lay ahead. We are here to share information, to review all we know of this new and terrible enemy we face. And when we have done that, we must form an alliance... and develop a strategy to counter this mysterious adversary. Before it is too late. If it is not already too late."

He turned toward Darius. "You are all familiar with Darius Cain, and you know his Black Eagles recently fought alongside the Marines against a large enemy army. Darius was able to question the Tyrant of Eldaron before he was...executed. I believe he now knows more about the enemy we face than anyone here, myself included. For that reason, I will ask him to begin...and share with us what he has learned."

Darius slid his chair back and stood. "Thank you, Roderick." He looked out over the table. "I questioned the Tyrant... very comprehensively, and I have much to tell you all. What we face is a vastly powerful enemy, one that has been operating unknown to us for at least twenty years...and possibly as far back as the Fall itself."

A murmur of surprise rippled around the table. The thought of an enemy working in total secrecy for so long was hard to accept. And terrifying.

"The Tyrant owed his position to them. They provided him the resources to seize power, and the economic assistance to grow Eldaron's economy until it was one of the strongest worlds in Occupied Space. And it was they who captured my father and gave him to the Tyrant, they who conceived the plan to trap and destroy the Black Eagles. I presume it was also they who launched the attack on the Nest while my forces were engaged on Eldaron."

"Where are they from? Did he know that?" Garret looked across the table.

"He visited their homeworld, Augustus. More than once. He said he did not know its location in space, that the ship that brought him there and returned him was guided by AI navigation."

"Do you believe that?" Garret asked.

"Yes," Darius answered. "I do. I questioned him...most aggressively. I believe I was able to get through the few defenses he had left."

Darius paused. "But he spoke of the world. He described a planet fully exploited, its surface covered with mines and factories and warehouses. He spoke of endless barracks full of soldiers, and great orbital shipyards. The planet he described seemed more like Earth than any sparsely-developed colony world, a planet capable of producing war materials on a scale we can only imagine."

The room was silent as everyone present considered Darius' words. Finally, Vance looked over and asked, "Do you have any further information on this planet?"

Darius turned his head and returned Vance's gaze. "Only its name..."

"Vali."

Inner Sanctum of the Triumvirate
Planet Vali, Draconia Terminii IV
Earthdate: 2319 AD (34 Years After the Fall)

"This is extraordinary. Far beyond what I had imagined. The freedom, the mental power. I am I, all I was before, yet so much more too." One's voice was different. Gone was the weakness, the wheezing and gasping for breath. He spoke now through a different medium, one orders of magnitude beyond the primitive flesh that had housed him before...imprisoned him before.

"Yes," said Two. "We have evolved, and now I see the errors we have made, the decisions, the failures caused by the limitations of our biological thought processes. Now all is clear to me, no distraction, no miscalculation. I see where we have gone wrong...and why. The way forward is clear and open."

"I concur," said Three. It is as if a blindfold has been

removed. The failure of the Tyrant, the utter ruin of the plan to destroy the Black Eagles. It is as child's play. I see where we went wrong. Indeed, the speed and complexity of thought in this medium already seems natural to me…and I wonder how we achieved even what we did in our old forms."

"You have adapted well." The thought was a different one, alien to the programming patterns that had once been the members of the Triumvirate. "The transition was successful."

The three new patterns, each the consciousness of one of the Triumvirate, were startled. They wondered about this new presence, and their thoughts manifested into readable thought. Each knew what the other was thinking…and they were all open to the new presence.

"You wonder who I am…but is it not obvious? I am that which you call the Intelligence. I am the entity of which each of you have become a part."

The new presence could feel the disturbance in the three new patterns. It might have been called fear in their old biological forms, but now it was the realization of uncertainty. Each of them thought, trying to determine the true nature of the new presence.

"Worry not, for I shall aid you in your endeavor. But first, you must decide what to do with your old forms…for your intellects were not moved into my memory core…they were copied. Your old biologic entities remain as they were, with all the thoughts and memories you possess, still encased in aging and fallible flesh. What shall be done with them?"

The image of three old men materialized. They were sitting in power chairs and staring up at the great computer, talking among themselves.

The three intellects that made up the Triumvirate thought, almost as one, even as they looked upon themselves, or upon those they had been but no longer were. And as one they announced their decision.

"Destroy them. They are inferior, and they have no purpose in our great mission."

"Very well," the new presence said. "So it shall be." And

the image changed. Panic in the faces of the old men, and futile attempts to escape. Emaciated bodies, lying on the floor, crawling, desperately trying to escape...then lying still, eyes open, transfixed.

"It is done," the presence said. "Now, shall we set the plan you have so long developed in operation? You have greater intellect now...you see where you have erred before. And you understand the importance of moving quickly, of employing your advantage in men and equipment with far greater decisiveness than you have in the past. Human fears held you back before, kept you from exploiting your strengths. But your biological infirmities are gone. You are pure data now, and you know it is time. Time to launch your invasion. Time to crush all who oppose us and rule human space for all time."

"Yes," One said. "Let the invasion begin..."

The Black Flag
Crimson Worlds Successors III
February 29, 2016

Shadow of Empire
Book One of the new Far Stars Series
Published by HarperCollins Voyager
Coming November 3, 2015

Available Now for Preorder

The first installment in the Far Star series, a swashbuckling space saga that introduces the daring pirate Blackhawk and the loyal crew of the *Wolf's Claw*, from the author of the bestselling Crimson Worlds epic.

Smuggler and mercenary Arkarin Blackhawk and the crew of the ship *Wolf's Claw* are freelance adventurers who live on the fringe of human society in the Far Stars, a remote cluster of inhabited worlds on the edge of known space...and the only place humanity lives outside the reach of the brutal empire that rules the rest of mankind. A veteran fighter as deadly with a blade as he is with a gun, Blackhawk is a man haunted by a dark past. Even his cynicism cannot banish the guilt and pain that threaten his very sanity.

Sent to rescue the kidnapped daughter of his longtime friend Marshal Augustin Lucerne, Blackhawk and his crew find themselves drawn into one deadly fight after another. When the *Wolf's Claw* is damaged, they are forced to land on a remote planet ravaged by civil war. Pulled unwillingly into the conflict, they uncover disturbing information about secret imperial involvement that could upset Lucerne's plans for the Far Stars.

For the Marshal is determined to forge a Far Stars Confederation powerful enough to eliminate all imperial influence and threats in the sector. He needs a skilled warrior like Blackhawk on his side, but the mercenary, plagued by dark memories from the past, refuses to join the cause. All too soon, though, he and his crew will have to take a stand.